THREATS
AT THREE

THREATS
AT THREE

ANN PURSER

BERKLEY PRIME CRIME, NEW YORK

THE BERKLEY PUBLISHING GROUP
Published by the Penguin Group
Penguin Group (USA) Inc.
375 Hudson Street, New York, New York 10014, USA
Penguin Group (Canada), 90 Eglinton Avenue East, Suite 700, Toronto, Ontario M4P 2Y3, Canada
(a division of Pearson Penguin Canada Inc.)
Penguin Books Ltd., 80 Strand, London WC2R 0RL, England
Penguin Group Ireland, 25 St. Stephen's Green, Dublin 2, Ireland (a division of Penguin Books Ltd.)
Penguin Group (Australia), 250 Camberwell Road, Camberwell, Victoria 3124, Australia
(a division of Pearson Australia Group Pty. Ltd.)
Penguin Books India Pvt. Ltd., 11 Community Center, Panchsheel Park, New Delhi—110 017, India
Penguin Group (NZ), 67 Apollo Drive, Rosedale, North Shore 0632, New Zealand
(a division of Pearson New Zealand Ltd.)
Penguin Books (South Africa) (Pty.) Ltd., 24 Sturdee Avenue, Rosebank, Johannesburg 2196,
South Africa

Penguin Books Ltd., Registered Offices: 80 Strand, London WC2R 0RL, England

This book is an original publication of The Berkley Publishing Group.

FIRST EDITION: December 2010

Library of Congress Cataloging-in-Publication Data

Purser, Ann.
    Threats at three / Ann Purser.—1st ed.
        p.   cm.
    ISBN 978-0-425-23705-2
    1. Meade, Lois (Fictitious character)—Fiction.   2. Murder—Investigation—Fiction.
3. England—Fiction.   I. Title.
PR6066.U758T46   2010
823'.914—dc22   2010035454

PRINTED IN THE UNITED STATES OF AMERICA

10   9   8   7   6   5   4   3   2   1

THREATS
AT THREE

One

⌘

"We shall need a subcommittee, of course," said Mrs. Tollervey-Jones.

Derek groaned inwardly. He waited for the chair's eagle eye to fall on him. Sure enough, she said that the one person who knew all about organising was Derek Meade. He ran a successful one-man electrical business in Long Farnden, a small village in the heart of England, and was, so said Mrs. T-J, just the man to mastermind the centenary celebration event.

This would celebrate the hundredth birthday of the village hall, a wooden structure that had miraculously survived rising damp, woodworm and rot. But without serious attention, its days were now numbered. Estimates for repair and renovation had been sought, and the most conservative of those submitted was still a very large sum of money. This would need to be raised. In the present climate of financial belt-tightening they could not rely on grants.

"So the event has to be really spectacular, Derek," said Mrs. T-J. She added that she was sure the subcommittee would come up with something remarkable, which they would submit to the parish council at the next meeting in a month's time.

The subject was then thrown open for discussion, and, as expected by most of the eight members of the council, was at once hectic to the point of violent disagreement. In other words, Mrs. T-J was faced with a punch-up. In her best justice of the peace voice, she quelled the riot. "Now settle down, all of you," she said severely. "I am well aware we have two factions in this matter."

"Three," said Derek glumly. "There's us, and them, and then the others."

"Very clear," said the vicar, Father Rodney. "Perhaps you could elucidate, Mrs. Tollervey-Jones?"

"Not in here, I hope," whispered young farmer John Thornbull to Derek, who managed to turn a guffaw into a sneeze.

"Bless you," said Floss Cullen, the newest co-opted member of the council.

"Youth," Mrs. T-J had said, "we need a young person, preferably a woman, to represent young people in the village." Derek and John had sighed. Their chair, as she liked to be called, was known for getting sudden bees in her bonnet. These would be pursued enthusiastically, and when achieved, she would be on to the next innovation. Old Tony Dibson, the oldest and longest serving councillor muttered on each occasion that he didn't think there was anything wrong with the council as it was, and if it weren't broken, why fix it?

Floss had been co-opted, and had indeed brought a breath of fresh air to the council proceedings. She could persuade even diehards like Tony Dibson to her point of view. She worked for Derek's wife, Lois Meade, who ran New Brooms, a cleaning service based in the village, and with an office in Tresham, the nearest large town. Now married to Ben Cullen, Floss continued her cleaning work because she enjoyed it, though she had done well at school and had been expected by her parents to do something better than scrubbing other people's floors.

Now the three factions had settled back into their seats, and Father Rodney asked again if he could be told exactly what the proposals were.

Derek looked at his watch. "I can tell you, Vicar," he said. Mrs. T-J nodded her approval, and he said, "Repair the village hall. Knock it down and build a new one. Adapt the old cat-gut factory to be the village hall. That's the three, and I suggest we have a vote right now on which one we're going for."

"Just to recap on these," Mrs. T-J said, taking charge, "the first, to repair the hall, is a straightforward job. Expensive, but straightforward, and well in line with a celebration of one hundred years serving the village. The second would be hugely expensive, and the third is impractical, the catgut factory being outside the village and the other side of the railway line."

"Which may one day be reopened," said the vicar. "And anyway, that factory is an eyesore and a danger to the children who play there."

"We always played there," said Tony Dibson. "Never came to any harm, not none of us."

Mrs. T-J said that was irrelevant, and could they please get on. She took a vote, and the first of the proposals won. "So there we are, Derek," she said. "Repair and renovate, and in due course a celebratory opening. Perhaps I can persuade my son, who is, as you all know, a well-known barrister, to perform the ceremony."

"Hold yer water, missus," Tony Dibson said. "Let's get the money first, do the work, an' then it'll be time to think about openin' ceremonies. As fer who should open it, I reckon we should be thinkin' of somebody off the telly. One of them celebrities," he added.

The rest of the agenda was swiftly dealt with, and Mrs. T-J

closed the meeting, saying she would leave it to Derek to get a representative subcommittee together and report to the next council meeting.

THE PUB WAS ALREADY BUSY, AND DEREK AND JOHN THORNBULL pushed their way to the bar. "Usuals?" said the barman. They nodded, and took their pints to a table in the corner just vacated by a couple from Waltonby. "Evenin'," Derek said. "Bit chilly out there. Winter's comin' on." He and John settled down, took long drafts of ale, and were silent for a few minutes.

"Who shall we ask, then?" Derek said finally.

"And how many?"

"Oh, I should think five of us would do it. Don't want too many, else you get nuthin' done. So there's us two, old Tony, for what he can remember about the village in the past, and who else?"

John frowned. "We need somebody with a bit of experience of fund-raising," he said. "After all, we're aiming for a really big lump sum. Don't want a load of footling little craft fairs, book sales and all that. Hard work for everybody and tuppence-ha'penny profit at the end of it."

"What about the vicar?" Derek said. Father Rodney was new and untried. He had replaced a nice, gentle man, who had been popular with the older ladies, but ineffective in raising the church's profile and certainly not a great money-spinner.

"What do we know about him, apart from the fact that he's a widower?" John said. "I suppose one of our churchgoers would know a bit of his background. After all, vicars get interviewed, like anybody applying for a job. He's youngish and seems keen."

"I'll ask Lois," Derek said. "She and the girls clean for him once a week. She'll have all the info we need. You know my Lois!"

New Brooms was not exactly a cover for Lois's work with

the Tresham police, but ever since the business was set up she had investigated cases locally on an independent basis, using her cleaners to gather information. Snooping, she admitted. "Ferretin', gel. That's what I'd call it. Sticking your nose into dark corners and gettin' all of us into trouble," Derek said.

She worked for no pay on cases that interested her, or when on one or two occasions, her own family had been involved. And her connection with the police was restricted to one ramrod straight and serious policeman, Chief Detective Inspector Hunter Cowgill. A reserved and highly efficient professional, he said frequently that he valued her input. He also loved her dearly, which he didn't say, at least, not very often. His nephew Matthew, also a policeman in the Tresham station, fancied Lois's daughter, but that was Josie's affair.

"Good idea," said John. His own wife, Hazel, ran the New Brooms' Tresham office, and would certainly be able to help. He had a sudden thought. "Shall I ask Hazel to do the secretarial work for the subcommittee?" he asked, and Derek approved the idea with alacrity.

"One more, then," he said. "What about Gavin Adstone?"

"The lone parishioner attending our meeting, and unsquashable? Are you serious?" John said. Gavin Adstone was one of the bright young incomers, disliked by most people for his instantly given opinions on every subject raised, and obvious contempt for the old tried and tested village ways. But Derek thought he could see good in the man. All that brash exterior covered a willing spirit, and he could see that they would sorely need such a one on the village hall project.

"Better to have him working with us than against us," was all he said, and John reluctantly agreed. "You ask him then," he said. "And on your own head be it."

WHEN A SUITABLY MELLOW DEREK ARRIVED HOME, LOIS WAS waiting for him in the warm kitchen. Gran, Lois's mother, had gone to bed with a book, and the kitchen was quiet and peaceful.

"Good meeting?" Lois said.

"Not bad," Derek said, wondering how to break the news to her that he was now chairing the village hall project sub-committee. He need not have worried.

"So did you get the job?" she asked. When he did not answer straightaway, she added that the parish council meeting agenda was fixed to the notice board, so she knew about the project and had guessed the rest. "I thought it would be dumped in your lap," she said. "Can't say no, that's your trouble."

Derek put his arms around her shoulders and kissed the back of her neck. "Luckily for you," he muttered into her silky hair. "When you proposed to me, I mean," he added, and retreated quickly as she rounded on him, as expected.

Two

❧

GAVIN ADSTONE HAD ARRIVED IN THE VILLAGE WITH HIS wife and toddler daughter a year and a half ago, and had immediately thrown himself into village activities without realising that a more considered approach would have made him more acceptable to the small community. He had joined the playing fields committee, the darts team at the pub, offered to play cricket for Long Farnden, even considered the reading group but decided it was a lot of old fogies reading romantic novels and not for him. He worked for an IT company in Tresham, and had yet to discover that Lois Meade's son Douglas had a senior position in the same company. He was thirty-two years old, and had the confidence and cheek of the devil. In other words, as Derek had guessed, he was perfect for the task of raising a large sum of money for the village hall.

"How was it tonight?" asked his wife, as he came into their small cottage with a blast of cold air. Gavin had gone along to the meeting out of curiosity, rather fancying the idea that at some point he wouldn't mind being a parish councillor himself. He was told that he could not speak unless prearranged with the secretary, but this had not bothered him unduly, nor stopped his interjections, and he was not overawed by Mrs. Tollervey-Jones.

"Much as usual," he said. "I reckon nothing's changed for the last fifty years. Some posh old dame is in the chair. The one who lives at Farnden Hall, I think. Talk about feudalism! You should have heard her keeping the unruly peasants in order!"

"So what did they talk about? Strip farming? Poaching in the squire's woods?"

Kate Adstone was a small, dark-haired thirty-year-old, very dry and sharp. Their daughter Cecilia took all her time at the moment, but she intended to return to her job as a family mediator in due course.

"No, it was mostly about the proposed centenary celebrations for the crumbling village hall. We've talked about it in the pub, as you know, and I am all for bulldozing the old shed down and bringing the village up into the twenty-first century."

"So what happened?"

"They had a vote. Restoring the old shed won by one vote. So that's what they're going to do. Big effort planned to fundraise enough money to do the job. What a waste! The whole place will fall down in another ten years anyway."

Kate laughed. "They need you, Gavin," she said, and added to herself that Gavin needed them, too. Since they had moved here—a mistake, in her opinion—he had been like a caged tiger. He had boundless energy, was good at getting things done, and could strong-arm his way into and out of any situation. Perhaps she should have a word with somebody. Put his name forwards?

A preliminary little cry from upstairs brought them both to their feet. Cecilia was their first child, and neither had any previous experience of handling toddlers. So they crept upstairs to see if she was even a little bit unhappy. They peered into her cot, and she opened her eyes, saw their anxious faces, and opened her tiny mouth to give a surprisingly loud bellow.

TONY DIBSON HAD ENJOYED HIS PINT OF BEST IN THE CORNER OF the bar beside a roaring log fire. The ritual of the council meeting, followed by a pint in the pub and a game of dominoes with his good friend Fred Smith, had played its part in his village routine for years. At each council election, he allowed his name to be put forwards, and he always commanded a sizable vote. This year, however, he had only just scraped in by a few votes. Time to go, he told himself. Too many new people in the village, and he was too old to fight for what he believed was good for the community. Not that he had ever thought about it in those terms. Being on the parish council was something he'd always done, and his father before him, and he had known instinctively what most of the villagers would want. Not anymore though, he thought, as he put his last tile triumphantly on the table.

Then Derek Meade and John Thornbull had come over, and asked him to be on the subcommittee to organise fundraising for repairing the old village hall. It wouldn't be the first time it had been repaired. He remembered over the last forty odd years many occasions when the roof had leaked, the plumbing seized up, when windows had been broken by vandals, and the kitchen tap had been left running and flooded the whole place. Money had been found to cope with these, and there was always a generous donation from her up at the hall.

Now they were planning a big renovation, Derek Meade had said, to celebrate the old building's hundredth birthday. Well, good on them, he thought. That hall had been part of village life for generations. Wedding receptions, christening parties, WI meetings, concerts of local talent, and a hundred other uses marking high points in the lives of village families.

In due course, Tony walked slowly down the street to his home in the row of cottages on the corner where the High Street met Church Lane. He could have found his way with his eyes shut, without slipping or tripping.

He had told Derek he would think about it. As he unlocked and opened his front door, his wife sat as always in her chair by the window, although it was dark and she couldn't have seen anything outside, even supposing she still had her sight. She turned her head towards him with her usual sweet smile. Now disabled by arthritis and various ailments the social worker called "age related," she relied on Tony for almost everything. He didn't mind. He would do anything to keep her from going into one of those places where he knew the heart would go out of his beloved Irene.

"Any news?" she asked. It was always her first question, even if he had only been to the shop and had a chat with shopkeeper Josie Meade, daughter of Derek and Lois.

He took off his coat and told her about the village hall. "And Derek Meade wants me to help fund-raise," he added. "Be on some committee or other. They need my experience of village needs, but I reckon I don't have time for all that rubbish."

"So you said no?" said Irene, frowning. He said that he had told Derek he would think about it, but he had made up his mind on the way home. He would refuse. "Too old and too busy," he said, and turned off the boiling kettle to fill their hot-water bottles.

"Tony Dibson!" his wife said. "You'll do no such thing. People rely on you to represent the real village people, like you and me. Families who've been here for years. Not the newcomers who buy up houses for weekending, nor them that say they love the village and then try to change it."

"So you think I should do it?" She nodded, and after a

couple of seconds added that if she could she would love to do more to help. Smitten by the suggestion he had been criticising her, he kissed her fondly on the top of her head. Flattening out the hot water bottles to release hot air, he screwed them up and trudged upstairs to warm up their bed. Then he returned to his wife and began the long and arduous business of getting her undressed, and carrying her upstairs.

"Good thing I've always been a little 'un," she said.

"Light as a feather," he said, as he always said every night, and picked her up in his arms, trying not to notice the stab of pain in his back.

JOHN THORNBULL GOT OUT OF HIS CAR IN THE YARD AT THE BACK of the farmhouse, and thought he should check that his wife Hazel's bantams were shut up. If she had forgotten, as she often did, the stupid things flew up into a tall silver birch tree and roosted in the high branches. Sometimes he took the clothes line prop from the garden and tried bashing them down to go into their perfectly comfortable house. But they squawked like banshees and flew up even higher.

Tonight she had remembered, and he went into the farmhouse calling for her as he went.

"Here!" she said, and when he went into the sitting room where she was watching television with the sound turned down low, she put her finger to her lips. "Sssh! Lizzie is restless tonight," she whispered. "Hope she's not sickening for something."

She did not ask him how the meeting went, knowing that he would tell her, all in good time. First things first, he would have said, as he poured himself a good-night snifter from the whisky bottle. Now he settled down beside her and watched the end of the news bulletin.

"Same old stories of death and disaster," he said. "I don't know why we bother to watch."

"There was a nice one before you came in," she said. "A jockey who'd entered every Gold Cup race since he was a lad, actually won for the first time today. You should've seen his face, John!"

"Hope for me yet, then," he said, though he had never entered a race more important than the local hunt point-to-point every year.

There was a companionable silence, and then he said, "Meeting got a bit warm tonight. All about the village hall, believe it or not."

"Tell all," Hazel said, and switched off the television.

He gave her a colorful account, and said that he and Derek were setting up a committee to raise funds for renovating the old hall. Would she be willing to take care of the secretarial side of it? Write letters, put up posters, all that kind of thing?

Hazel groaned. "Blimey, John," she said. "As if I haven't got enough to do!"

"So you'll do it, then?"

"On one condition," she said. "I get a laptop for my birthday."

John thought for a moment. "Reconditioned one?" he asked.

Hazel took his hand. "Done," she answered. "But I'm not sure who's got the best of the bargain."

Three

❧

THE VILLAGE HALL RENOVATION FUND-RAISING SUBCOMMITtee had been derided by Lois. "What a ridiculous name!" she had said to Derek. "Let's call it the No Chance Committee."

"Well, thanks for your support!" Derek had replied. "Anyway, it wasn't my idea. Mrs. T-J coined it. I suppose she thought the longer the name the more authority it had, or summat."

"Well, if you don't like No Chance, why don't you call the campaign Save Our Shed? It's always been known as the Shed, ever since I can remember."

"Quite right," said Gran. "All the women at WI call it the Shed. Good idea, Lois."

The three were sitting round the big kitchen table in the Meade's solid Victorian house in the main street of Long Farnden. The Rayburn in the kitchen ticked over day and night, providing not only cooking, hot water and central heating, but also a warm heart for the family.

The Meades had not always lived in a big house. When the three children were small, Lois and Derek, with Douglas,

Josie and Jamie, had squashed into a small council house on the Churchill Estate in Tresham, and Gran, a widow, had lived in a bungalow not far away.

When all the children had started school, and with Gran's help taking and fetching them, Lois had fancied the idea of becoming a special constable in the police. The job involved working as a volunteer for the force, but not fully one of them. She had gone for an interview and been turned down because, they said, she seemed to have more than enough to occupy her time already, much to her disgust. After that, she had continued cleaning other people's houses, and then set up the New Brooms business.

On the side, by way of revenge, she became a snoop for Inspector Cowgill, but on her terms. No pay, only cases that appealed to her, nobody locally to know what she did. No pressure. She had grown to love the snooping, discovering that she had a flair for deduction. It was like a hobby, but, as Derek frequently said, a dangerous one.

The move to Long Farnden had been a stroke of luck, in a way. The local doctor, one of Lois's clients, had been involved in a murder and the scandal had caused him to move away. Because of the grim association, the house had not sold and the price continued to drop until Derek and Lois could just about afford it. Gran had moved in with them as volunteer housekeeper and dispenser of advice. For most of the time, it was an excellent solution, especially since Derek had won the lottery jackpot, when the family financial situation eased considerably.

The big kitchen in the house had become their favourite room, and now Derek had to agree that Lois's suggestion was a good one. "SOS, Save Our Shed. Yeah, that's good," he said. "I'll put it to the others at the first meeting tonight."

"So are they definitely coming here?" said Gran. She was looking forwards to serving coffee to the five, and planned to make a batch of shortbread to go with it. She loved the idea of being at the centre of the new campaign, and if they wouldn't include her in their meetings, she would hover and leave the door ajar and generally gather what was going on.

Lois had refused point blank to be co-opted to the committee, saying she had quite enough to do with New Brooms and a family to run. But seeing Derek's face fall, she had hastily added that she would always help whenever help was wanted.

AT HALF PAST SEVEN THAT EVENING, THE FIVE WERE ASSEMBLED. Kate Adstone had spoken with Josie in the shop, and also talked to Derek about Gavin not agreeing with the proposal, but probably willing to change his mind if given a job to do. So Derek had put the request tactfully, stressing to Gavin the importance of his talents and potential contribution, and received an enthusiastic response.

"Evening all," Gran said, coming into the sitting room with a laden tray. "What an exciting idea for the village! We shall all have lots of ideas, I'm sure. I know the WI will want to help, and you can always call on me. . . ."

"Mum!" called Lois from her office on the opposite side of the passage. "Mum! Come in here—got something to show you!"

Gran reluctantly shut the door on the committee and joined Lois. "What is it?" she said impatiently.

"Photos from Jamie!" Lois said, and showed her a series of photographs of her younger son larking about with a tasty-looking blonde on a sunlit beach in Australia.

Gran melted. "Ah, look at him," she said. "Doesn't he look wonderful, all brown and bonny! And who's that girl, I wonder?"

Jamie Meade had become a rising star as a concert pianist, traveling the world for concerts and always keeping in touch with his parents at home. From childhood he had had a special musical talent, and with hard work and all the support his family could give him, he had prospered. Now his email with attachments had provided a useful way of enticing Gran away from the first meeting of Derek's committee.

In the comfortable sitting room, Hazel took out her notebook and pen and looked at Derek.

"First meeting," she said, "so no minutes. Do we have any apologies?"

"What for?" said Tony Dibson.

"For not being able to attend," said Hazel, smiling at him. Dear old chap. It must seem a load of rubbish to him, but this committee was to be conducted properly, with minutes of meetings kept and circulated to the full parish council.

"No, we're all here," Derek said. "Welcome, everyone. And thanks, Gavin, for deciding to come and help us. A newcomer's view will be really useful."

So that's put me firmly in my place, thought Gavin. This electrician Derek was not such a thicko as he had expected. "Thanks. Glad to be here," he said.

"Now," continued Derek, "the first thing on the agenda is to decide what our main fund-raising event will be. The sooner that's settled the better. Then we can get on with planning the campaign."

Hazel cleared her throat. "Um, can I suggest something, Derek?"

He nodded. "O' course, Hazel. Fire away."

"Well, I know we must have a big project to raise a respectably large sum, but to involve all the village—which I think is necessary—we should ask all the various groups, like WI and Guides and Scouts an' that, to have their own money-raising events as well. It's surprising how it all adds up, and it would keep people interested."

"Hear, hear," John Thornbull said, looking proudly at his wife. "Great suggestion, Hazel."

Gavin thought to himself that this was a very secondary matter, and said, "So shall we get back to the big project?"

"Do you have a suggestion, Gavin?" Derek said. "We shall need three or four ideas before we decide."

"Yep. This is a winner," Gavin said. "We did this where we lived before. We'll have a really big summer show. The Long Farnden Festival. Exhibitions, sporting fixtures, concerts, you name it, we'll have it. I've got lots of contacts."

Silence followed this, as the others reeled.

Derek was first to speak. "Wonderful idea," he said, swallowing hard. "Any other suggestions?" he added, praying that someone would speak up.

John raised his hand. "I got one," he said. "I was watching telly last night, and they had a bit on the news about a soap box race up in Derbyshire. All kinds of soap boxes, homemade. Amazing, some of 'em. And quite a crowd watching. We could do that, couldn't we? Have our own grand prix?"

Tony Dibson's face lit up and he leaned forwards. "My God, boy," he said. "You got it! We used to have soap boxes when I was a kid. High Street's on a slope, and we'd start one end with a good shove from behind, and pick up speed as we went. Leg power, it was. I were nearly always the winner. That gets my vote," he said cheerfully, and subsided in his chair.

"And where would our big profit come from?" Gavin said scathingly. "A quid's entrance money from half a dozen competitors, and rattle a tin round the spectators?"

"Good point," said Derek, but John's idea had caught his imagination and he could see the others were looking keen. "Any other suggestions?" he said, but they shook their heads.

Hazel stopped writing, and glanced around the silent room. She looked at Derek, and decided to rescue him.

"Couldn't we combine the two ideas?" she said. "We could have the soap box grand prix down the High Street, and then around the village we could have some of the other things Gavin has suggested for his festival. What d'you think?"

They all nodded except Gavin, who said that wasn't quite what he had in mind. How about a vote? Festival or grand prix with side shows?

Derek obediently took a vote. It was as he had hoped. "Soap box has it, then," he said, "and with Gavin's expertise, I know the sideshows will be real money-spinners."

The discussion then continued until late in the evening, and when the meeting was finally closed, Derek walked into the kitchen where Gran and Lois were waiting.

"Phew!" he said, and gave them a brief summary. "The thing is," he said, "all I can think of right now is how I'm going to steer the awkward brigade to achieve what we set out to do."

"You'll do it," said Gran, "with Lois and me helping."

Four

❧

"Mum? Douglas here."

"Hi, son. What can I do for you?" Lois smiled broadly. If she allowed herself to have a favourite offspring, it would be Douglas. Her firstborn, he had been easy from the start. Even tempered and cheerful, he had lulled her into a sense of false security on the child upbringing front. When Josie came along, she was fretful, needing constant attention and yelling if she didn't get it. Derek had said that girls were always more difficult, and what did she expect? Three stroppy generations of women, in his view. Gran, Lois and Josie. All dedicated to making his life difficult.

"It's what we can do for you, for once," Douglas said now. "Me and Susie and young Harry are going to the National Space Centre at Leicester on Sunday, and wondered if you and Dad would like to come along?"

"Isn't Harry a bit young for the space centre?" Lois asked. She knew that Derek would jump at the idea, but you could hardly expect a one-year-old to take much interest in the wonders of rocket science.

"There's something for all ages, it says in the leaflet. A mate of mine has been with his kids, and says its wonderful. D'you want to see what Dad says? You can ring me back. Got to go now. Big meeting."

Lois put down the phone and shook her head with a smile. You don't fool me, Douglas Meade, she said to herself. It's like that supersize train set Harry had for his half birthday. Doug plays with it all the time, and it'll be Doug who wants a simulated ride in a space capsule. Ah, well, why not? A family outing would be a nice distraction for Derek, already frowning with worry about how to raise at least twenty thousand pounds in a frighteningly short period.

At around this time, Josie Meade, shopkeeper and occasional helpmeet in her mother's detecting activities, was thinking about babies. Here she was, living alone after her longtime partner had been killed, now more or less restored with the help of Mum's cop's nephew Matthew, but with a blank future in front of her. When she saw Matthew pulling up outside in the police car, she wondered if this was an omen. Would he make a good father? This was such a ridiculous thought that she laughed out loud, lifting Matthew's spirits as he came into the shop.

Matthew Vickers had settled well into Tresham police force, and despite the fact that the chief detective inspector was his uncle, he had finally been absorbed and accepted by his colleagues. He had fallen in love with Josie Meade long before her partner died, and had tried a few forays to see how secure that relationship was. Then the disaster had happened and he had concentrated on being a solid comforting presence for her, nothing more. Her smiling face was a really good sign.

"What's the joke, Josie?" he said, and blew her a kiss across the counter.

"Can't tell you," she said. "Except that I was wondering whether to give up the shop and go back to education as a mature student. I'm done with grieving, and have to think about the future."

"You can't!" he said. "What will Long Farnden do without you? The whole place would fall apart if you gave up the shop."

"I could sell it. It's doing really well now, and they say you should sell when a business is doing well, not when it's on the slide."

"Are you serious, Josie?"

"No. I love my shop and my village." And maybe you, Matthew, just a little bit, she added to herself. "Now, are you investigating a crime? Or just calling for a packet of Polo mints?"

"Both," he said. "But seriously, we've had an anonymous call, probably from the usual nutcase, suggesting there is a local conspiracy to burn down your village hall. The caller said he had seen a prowler with a can of petrol, and whoever it was ran off when he saw he was observed. Have you heard anything?"

"Good heavens, no! Sounds like someone with a fertile imagination. Seeing conspirators where there are only shadows! It *is* very dark around the village hall. We've got a big plan to renovate the old place and proper lighting is on the list."

Matthew sighed. "I'm sure you're right," he said, "but we have to look into all these things. Wasting our time, usually. How are you doing? Want to come to the pictures tomorrow?"

"Since you ask me so politely, I accept with thanks," she said. "What's the film, anyway?"

"It's a French film at the art cinema. Called *I've Loved You for So Long.*"

She stared at him. "Are you joking?" she said.

"Nope. Look in the local paper if you don't believe me. I'll pick you up about six?"

He turned and strode importantly from the shop to continue his quest for the phantom arsonist.

Two minutes after he had gone, the telephone rang. It was Josie's brother, Douglas. "Hi," he said. "Busy?"

"Not at this moment, but any minute now an evil character will come in and demand protection money, so make it snappy."

"Ho, ho," said Douglas. "The thing is, I'm ringing to invite you to come along with us to the space centre on Saturday. Susie and Harry and me are spending the day there, and wondered if you would like to come along. Mum and Dad are coming, I hope."

Josie frowned. There must be some hidden motive. A day at the space centre with screaming kids and frazzled parents was not her idea of fun, and surely Douglas would know that?

"Who else is coming?" she said, on a sudden inspiration.

"Well, actually, I ran into Matthew Vickers and happened to mention it, and he said he had always wanted to go, but would feel a bit of a nerd going on his own. Jumped at the chance of coming with us. So how do you feel?"

"Douglas, you are about as subtle as a steamroller," Josie said. "But yes, I'd love to come, if only to see little Harry's face when he sees his father blasted off into space."

"Good. Be ready about ten o'clock, then. Gran said she'd be happy to fill in at the shop."

"Wow! A family conspiracy!" Josie marvelled at Doug's deviousness, and was not sure whether to be pleased or not. She knew they all thought she should clinch things with Matthew. He was clearly keen to settle down. He had a newly renovated cottage originally bought as a holiday place, but now he had announced his intention of staying in the area for as long as possible. He had made many friends, and being tall, dark and fairly handsome, had not been short of girlfriends. But he had made it quite clear in a man-to-man chat with Douglas that Josie was his first choice.

But was she ready for the big commitment, as emphasized in all the advice columns in the women's magazines she sold in the shop? Before Rob had been killed, he had wanted her to marry him, and she had consistently refused, not being at all sure he was the one with whom she wanted to spend the rest of her life. Ah, well, she would go along with the family plot and see what happened. After all, there was something very reassuring about being wooed by a policeman.

"Morning, Josie," said Lois, breezing in with a couple of politically correct hessian bags over her arm. "We've run out of everything." She handed Josie a list, and perched herself on the stool in front of the counter. As Josie moved round the shop, collecting up her mother's favourite items, Lois said casually, "Have you heard about some idiot trying to set fire to the village hall? Are people talking about it?"

"By 'people' I suppose you mean my customers? As you know, I make it a rule not to gossip, and in any case I only just heard from Matthew that there had been a rumour from someone who thought they'd seen a sinister intruder with a barrel of gunpowder and a long fuse."

"You may joke, miss," Lois said seriously. "But it is apparently true. Someone else has come forwards now. Tony Dibson, who keeps the grass and paths around the village hall tidy. Says he found traces of petrol in several places around the edge of the hall. O' course, if it *was* fired it'd go up like a tinderbox."

"But why should anyone want to set fire to it? I thought we'd just decided to spend loads o' money restoring it to its former glory?"

"Exactly," Lois said. "As you know, Dad is heading the

fund-raising committee, and he says that by no means does all the village agree with the project. Money could be spent more wisely, they say. Some want a new-built hall, regardless of cost."

"Pie in the sky," said Josie. "They'd never get the money. Especially now, when people are losing their jobs and money's tight. Even charities are in the mire."

"Yes, well, that may be so. But you must know by now, there's some pretty rum customers in Farnden. I can think of one or two who could well take matters into their own hands."

"Who?" said Josie. She knew her mother's tendency to overdramatise, but at the same time she was often right, seeming to know things before anyone else did. "Who've you been talking to?" she added. "Has Hunter Cowgill been in touch again?"

He had, of course. But knowing Josie's burgeoning relationship with Cowgill's nephew, Lois decided to deny it. "Not yet," she said. "But if there really is something in the rumour, no doubt he will be. So keep your ears open. Now, how much do I owe you?"

Josie took the money, thanked her mother, and held the door open for her as she left with two heavy bags. If only everyone was as loyal a shopper as Mum!

"See you Saturday, if not before!" she yelled, as Lois marched off up the road. "I've always wanted to go into space. . . ."

FIVE

Lois got up early on Saturday morning, and seeing a cheerful blue sky and jolly clouds scudding across in the fresh wind, decided to take Jeems, her little white terrier, for a walk before breakfast. Gran would be up betimes, and with luck, would have bacon sizzling in the pan before she returned. Derek could be relied upon to be ready for the expedition well in time, as always.

One of Jeems's favourite walks was down the lane to the village hall, with attendant good sniffs, and round the playing field, out beyond the football pitch and through a field to the Waltonby road, then back home through the High Street. Passing the shop, there was always a chance that Josie would see them and come out with a dog treat.

As they approached the village hall, Lois saw that she was not the only one up with the lark. Tony Dibson was there, his back bent over the grass, scratching away with a small garden fork. He straightened up when he saw her and said, "Morning, missus. Lovely morning. Best time of the day, this is. Not many people realise that these days. When I was a lad—"

Usually Lois loved to listen to his tales of the past, but this morning she had to keep going, and interrupted him with a question. "What on earth are you doing there?" she asked.

"Cleaning up, as usual," he said, his voice muffled as he returned to his scratching.

"What is there to clean up? I can't see anything," Lois said, frowning. Tony looked for all the world as if he was hiding something.

He straightened up, and held out his hand, palm up. Lois peered more closely, and saw two matches, unspent. "So?" she said. "Kids smoking substances again?" The rear of the village hall was a well-known haunt for a group of youths and girls to gather. The police periodically raided the spot, but the kids were a dab hand at melting into the night. So far, no serious damage had been done, except, of course, to themselves.

"'ere, missus, smell this," Tony said, extending his dirt-covered hand further towards her. She blenched, but leaned forwards and sniffed. "Petrol," she said. They stared at each other in silence. Then Tony said, "So they was right, the ones who said there was a plot to burn down the village hall."

"Oh, my God," Lois said, feeling sick. "So why didn't it work?"

"Damp matches," Tony said flatly. "Otherwise the whole lot would have gone up. And with that wooden fence along the back of all them houses, God knows where it would have stopped."

"The police, then," Lois said. "I'll ring them straightaway. Can you keep those matches safe?"

Tony nodded, and said that as far as the petrol was concerned, the ground was soaked in it, so that wouldn't go away. "You do it, missus. You can phone your inspector and get some action."

Lois was so used to people knowing about her association with Inspector Cowgill that she did not even notice his sly grin.

"LOIS? TO WHAT DO I OWE THIS EARLY MORNING TREAT?" Cowgill beamed. He had woken feeling the old depression weighing him down. It had returned on and off ever since his wife died some years ago, and he knew the only remedy was to get out of bed, put on some old clothes and go for a run around the park. He had drawn back his bedroom curtains and was about to set off when his telephone rang. The moment he heard Lois's voice he knew there would be no need for a run.

"Early morning?" snapped Lois. "I don't call this early morning. Now listen, Hunter. I've just come back from walking Jeems, and met old Tony Dibson . . . What? . . . Well, give me a chance and I'll tell you who he is. He's the old caretaker for the hall, has a blind wife and looks after her, has lived here for centuries and knows everybody and everything. What? Yes, a great source of information. Now, listen! I'm going out for the day and haven't got much time."

When she mentioned the arson rumour, she could tell he immediately snapped into professional mode and was quiet. "So I smelled the petrol for myself," she continued, "and saw the matches. Tony says the ground was dry as a bone, so they must have been damp in the box."

"Going out for the day, did you say, Lois? What time are you going?"

"We're all leaving about ten o'clock." She looked at her watch. "In about an hour's time."

"I'm on my way," he said briskly. "Can you meet me at the hall in twenty minutes? Good girl," he added, and ended the call before she could reply.

Derek was not pleased when Lois explained that because of what she had seen she had to be at the hall to meet the police. "By 'the police' I suppose you mean Hunter sodding Cowgill? Honestly, Lois, haven't we had enough of all this? Why don't you leave them to deal with some nutter who likes the idea of a good blaze? He's obviously no real arsonist if he can't even keep his matches dry!"

Gran, putting hot toast on the table, nodded. "Quite right, Derek," she said. "This is a special day out for all of you. Don't spoil it, Lois."

Lois suppressed a strong desire to tell her mother to mind her own business, and said only that she would be back well in time for Douglas to collect them. "Are you sure you'll be all right in the shop, Mum?" she added, in an endeavor to change the subject.

Gran bridled. "No, of course not," she said tartly. "I shall give out wrong change, make a mess of cutting the ham, annoy the customers and in general ruin the shop's reputation."

"Okay, okay," said Derek. "Let's just concentrate on the day, shall we? Just be back here by ten, Lois. Otherwise," he said seriously, "I shall have to come and find you and give Cowgill a piece of my mind."

"No need for that," Lois said. "And anyway, with your new SOS responsibility, you'll need all the mind you can muster, without giving away any pieces of it."

Escaping from the decidedly chilly atmosphere of home, she returned to the village hall to find Cowgill already there. How does he do it? she wondered. Half an hour ago he had clearly just got up, and now here he was, immaculate as always. And with no woman to look after him . . .

Tony Dibson was also there, still clutching the matches, and he had already told Cowgill all that he knew. "Not usually a matter for the chief inspector, sir?" he said, with a meaning look at Lois.

"Arson is a very serious matter, Mr. Dibson," Cowgill said smoothly. "And we try to have as little rigid hierarchy as possible at the station, you know," he added.

What was the bugger talking about? Tony looked at Lois enquiringly, and said could he go home now, as his wife would be needing him.

After he had gone, Cowgill walked round the hall and along the fence, prodding and sniffing, and then asked Lois if she would sit in his car with him for a couple of minutes while he made some notes. She said fine, so long as he didn't have any etchings to show her, and ten minutes later she was on her way back to the house.

"Where've you been, Mum?" Doug said, as he and his family cruised past her a yard or two before Meade House. The name had been suggested by Josie, who said that's what everybody called it anyway, so why not regularize it?

"Nowhere," replied Lois, waving to little Harry. "We're all ready, so I'll just call Dad. Isn't that Josie on her way? Good. That means we won't have to stop again."

"Hi!" Josie called as she approached. "We're off to see the wizard! The wonderful wizard of space!"

Harry chortled and waved his hands about. He had no idea what his aunt was on about, but he loved her dearly. She slid across the seat to sit next to him, gave him a smacking kiss and said he was her favourite nephew. Doug did not fail with the ritual reply that he was her *only* nephew, so far.

"Plenty of room," Doug said, as Lois and Derek climbed into the seven-seater, and with cries of delight for Harry's benefit, they got under way.

Six

❧

THE MORNING HAD NOT STARTED SO WELL IN WHAT WAS STILL known as Pickerings' house, though the Pickerings had sold to a mysterious single man who had turned out to be a sinister people trafficker. Needless to say, he had been sent to jail for a long stretch, and the house had been put on the market again. A spry village character had bought it in order to rent it out. He had a deal with the local Social Services Department who needed accommodation for the deserving homeless. One such family were the Hicksons, and they had moved in under the watchful eyes of the villagers.

The house was one of the many old ironstone buildings in the village, and in bright sunshine it glowed a warm dark gold. The end wall had been built with bands of limestone alternating with ironstone, and on an otherwise perfectly plain family house, the pattern of stripes was a glimpse of a long-gone village builder's unexpected flight of fancy.

Inside the thick walls, it was warm and welcoming, and when Paula Hickson had first seen it, she couldn't believe her luck. Her husband, Jack, had walked out after the fourth boy had been born, saying he couldn't stand the racket, and she had no idea where he had gone. In a way, she knew they were better off without him, as any money coming in had, since Jack lost his job, gone out again rapidly to be spent on booze, and when he boozed he was violent.

The house had four bedrooms and a decent bathroom, and downstairs a couple of big rooms and a largish kitchen. Paula was able to furnish the sitting room with stuff provided by Social Services, which was adequate, though she sometimes thought it looked a bit like a junk shop. Still, she told herself, beggars can't be choosers. She would not forget in a hurry the bailiff's visit to their old home.

She decided the other main room, a dining room in the old days probably, would make a good playroom for the boys. A playroom! It was like a dream to a woman who had been living in two small rooms, one of which was a curtained-off bedroom for herself and the boys. Jack Jr. was now thirteen and at Tresham comprehensive. He needed private space for homework, if and when he got round to it, and now he could have one big bedroom to himself. The other two spares, much smaller, were for eight-year-old twins Jim and David, in the hope that separating them for sleep would give them all a bit of peace. Nine-month-old Frankie still slept in a cot alongside his mother.

The morning had started badly because on going to wake Jack, Paula found he was not in his bedroom and had clearly not slept in his bed. This was the second time he had stayed out somewhere all night, and Paula groaned. He had promised that if she had gone to bed, he would let himself in, and it would not be too late. The previous time this had happened he had said airily that he'd slept over with his mate in Tresham. "Missed the last bus," he had said, and added that if they had to live in a godforsaken village in the middle of nowhere with only two buses a week, what was he to do?

"You could let me know! That's what you could do!" Paula had shouted at him. "Ever heard of the phone?" she had added, and then regretted it, because she could not possibly afford for him to have his own mobile.

Now she gave the others their breakfasts, and prepared to send the twins off to a school friend's house for the morning with stern warnings that they were to go straight there and not dillydally on the way. Thank God they had taken to the village school like a pair of ducklings to water. No complaints from them. In a small class with a cheerful young woman teacher, they had blossomed from their first day. They were identical twins, and Rebecca Stockbridge confessed they were a challenge in her class, but one she intended to enjoy.

Paula sighed. She hoped that Jack Jr. had slept sensibly in his friend's house in Tresham, and she would see him arrive home on the afternoon bus. She had little confidence in this scenario, and thought it much more likely that her firstborn would be wandering round the streets of Tresham, hood concealing his face, until he managed to thumb a lift back to the village.

She stood at the gate, waiting until the twins were safely on their way, and her eye was caught by the sight of Douglas's vehicle moving slowly down the village street. As it passed her, she could see it was full of happy smiling faces, and one or two waved to her. She recognized Josie Meade from the shop, who had been really helpful to her since she arrived. Must be her family, Paula supposed, and felt a stab of envy at their obvious togetherness. Then she shifted the baby to be more comfortable on her hip, and turned to go indoors. "No good feeling sorry for yourself, Paula Hickson," she said aloud, and the baby smiled at her. Things could be a lot worse.

BY THE TIME DOUGLAS HAD TAKEN A COUPLE OF WRONG TURNS in the outskirts of Leicester, and had shut his ears to all the varying instructions from his passengers, little Harry was asleep and Derek was desperate for a pee. Finally they pulled into the big car park, and as they looked out of the windows an awed silence fell. A bulging silver balloonlike structure stretched up into the sky, dwarfing the crowds of families making for the entrance.

"Look at that!" Douglas said. "Hey, Susie, wake up Harry so's he can see it."

"Not a good idea," Lois said quickly. "You know how fractious he is when he's woken up. Let's all get out first, and then we can unload him straight into his pushchair and get going. That'll take his attention and we won't get the usual screams."

Susie frowned. Sometimes she wished her mother-in-law wasn't quite so ready with the voice of experience. Harry was hers and Douglas's, and they were best at managing him. But she bit back a sharp rejoinder and heaved the pushchair out of the boot space. She saw Matthew Vickers approaching, and said, "Nice to see you. Always useful to have a policeman in the party."

"Off duty, I'm afraid," he said, and grinned at Josie. They all set off across the almost full car park towards the main entrance, and as they got closer, Lois began to feel oddly apprehensive. Inside the reception area children and parents and grannies and granddads milled about. She stood still to get her bearings and saw a snack café off to the side. Suggesting that they have a snack lunch before everyone else converged there, she led the way.

With only one cashier, it took a while to get settled, and Lois had a chance to look around. The low lighting in the wide reception area heightened the feeling she already had on glimpsing vast models of distant planets of being in an alien environment, and she was glad when they sat down with their trays in the sunlit café, though another near-panic hit her when she caught sight of what looked like large upturned buckets hanging down from high above the chattering families.

"Derek! Isn't that where the great fire that launches the rockets comes from?" she said nervously. She realised they were now inside the silver balloon, and she could see that this housed two huge rockets stretching up above them. A sudden memory of the Challenger that crashed back to earth killing all inside, including a lovely young woman, jolted her.

"Yep, that's what gets 'em up into space. Want me to put a match to them?" He laughed at her, and patted her shoulder. "We're quite safe, gel," he said.

Meanwhile Matthew and Josie seemed oblivious to anything but themselves, seated as they were at a cozy table for two. The others had grouped together, with a high chair for young Harry, and then made short work of sandwiches and coffee, anxious to get going.

As they filed through the paying booths, Lois suddenly saw ahead of them a man going through the turnstiles and was sure he was familiar. When he turned to talk to a woman she recognized as Kate Adstone, she was sure it was Gavin. Following them, and clearly part of their party, came a tall, portly man with thinning ginger hair and a boozer's nose, bright red to match the rest of his complexion. Lois and the others were still waiting in the queue for tickets when the Adstones and friend disappeared from sight.

"Did you see him?" she said to Derek.

"Who?"

"Gavin Adstone. You know, from Farnden. On your SOS committee."

Derek shook his head. "Nope. Still, it could've been him. We might bump into him as we go round. His toddler's a bit young for this, I'd have thought."

"Older than our Harry," Lois replied.

"Get on, then," Derek said. "You're holding up the queue."

"No point in our trying to stay together," Douglas decided, as Susie said Harry needed a nappy change, and Matthew and Josie elected to start with the lift to the top of the rocket tower. "Let's say we'll all meet in the shop when we've seen everything. O' course, I expect we'll bump into each other going round," he added, and Lois whispered to Derek that they might well get another look at Gavin Adstone and his funny-looking friend.

"Lois!" Derek said sternly. "Forget it! Why shouldn't the man be here with a friend? Nothing suspicious, no ferretin' needed! For God's sake, woman, forget all that rubbish and enjoy a family day out." He marched off towards the planets and disappeared from sight into space. She hurried after him, and found him staring incredulously at a row of Heinz baked bean tins.

A couple of schoolboys were also intrigued by this unexpected earthbound display of tins, and began to lift them up, one by one. Derek was now reading the text above, and turned to Lois. "Gravity, Lois," he said authoritatively. "Shows you the different pulls of gravity on different planets. Have a go."

"Try the sun," the biggest boy said, grinning at the other.

Lois shrugged. Blimey, anybody could lift a baked bean tin. But when she tried, she couldn't move it, and the boys chortled. Then she moved on to others, and felt distinctly different pulls, as if invisible hands of varying strengths were holding on, determined not to let her run away with the valuable exhibits.

"Does that mean if we landed on one of them with not much gravity we'd fall off into nowhere?" she asked the boys. She trusted them rather than Derek to know the answer. But they had turned away and were heading for the weather forecast.

"Oh, look, Derek," Lois said. "Over there, where the boys have gone. That sort of cabin thing. Something to do with the weather satellite. See, there's a television screen inside. Let's go and look."

A small group of people had gathered, and Lois saw with interest that Gavin's party were amongst them. The two boys had gone into the booth, and were staring at the screen and giggling. Lois edged her way forwards so that she could see what was going on, and saw the bigger of the two boys pressing a button and a weather map coming up. Then text appeared on the screen and the boy began to read, looking alarmed but ploughing on, using his hand as a pointer to indicate locations on screen.

"He's pretty good at it, Mrs. Meade," said a voice behind her, and she turned to see Gavin Adstone looking down at her.

"Fancy seeing you here," she said, including Kate and Cecilia in a warm smile. "We Meades are here in strength," she added, as if Gavin had threatened her with abduction. Why did she feel so uneasy? "And is this another member of your family?" she asked him, seeing that he showed no signs of making an introduction to the ginger-haired man.

"Good God, no," the man said. "No relation. Just good friends," he added and laughed.

"This is Tim Froot," Gavin said shortly. "A Tresham business associate."

Froot obviously thought that sounded a little abrupt, and added that his building company head office was in Holland. "But I spend most of my time in Tresham," he explained. "My Amsterdam office runs itself, and as there is much work to be done in the UK, I prefer to be here. Now, we had better be getting on," he added to Gavin. "No peace for the wicked!" This last was directed at Lois, along with a knowing smile.

"Speaks very good English, for a Dutchman," said Derek, and then in spite of Lois's mocking laugh, he stepped inside the now vacant cabin and began pressing buttons.

MATTHEW AND JOSIE HAD FIRST GONE UP A FLIGHT OF STAIRS and on to a gallery, which led to the rocket lift. Halfway along, they stopped to stare at what they read to be an actual Soyuz spacecraft, found in a Russian car park. It looked used, secondhand, and Josie said she felt a bit sorry for it. "Looks a bit like it was made of Meccano," she said sadly. "Got left behind."

He took her hand and squeezed it. "Cheer up," he said. "Come on, let's go. Space awaits us!" He was feeling a little light-headed, something to do with a combination of Josie's hand in his, and the undeniable atmosphere of excitement that pervaded the whole place.

Fathers and sons were playing games based on magnetic attraction, and Josie said, "Why does that dad always win? He could lose for once. Give the boy a chance."

Matthew looked at her seriously. "Any son of mine would probably win anyway," he said. She was about to answer that it would depend on whose genes the child inherited, when her eye was caught by a familiar figure. "Hey, that's that new bloke from Farnden," she said. "Comes in the shop occasionally, and has his groceries delivered from Tesco."

"Where? Who is it?"

"Him, over there. Adstone, that's his name. Gavin Adstone, with his wife, Kate. She's all right, but he's a real know-all. Treats us all like country bumpkins. He's on Dad's SOS committee, unluckily for Dad."

"Not taken to him, then, Josie? I expect he's harmless enough," he said, and began explaining the function of a hoodlike piece of equipment apparently lined with gigantic shirt buttons.

SEVEN

As THEY ALL MADE THEIR WAY TO THE CAR PARK, JOSIE
announced that she would go back to Farnden with
Matthew. They were both effusive in thanking Douglas for
organising the outing, and Josie said she intended to give the
centre some publicity by pinning details to the shop notice
board.

"That'll certainly up the attendance figures," said Douglas with a straight face. "Mind how you go, Matt," he added.
"Won't do for a policeman to be caught speeding!"

Matthew Vickers sighed. How many times had this been
said to him? But he was a good-humored soul, and smiled
dutifully. "Precious cargo," he said. "I shall be extra careful."

"Blimey, our Josie's a precious cargo, is she?" muttered
Derek to Lois. "Getting serious, d'you reckon?"

"Hope so," said Lois. "Time Josie got wed."

"Mum! I heard that," Douglas said, as he started the
engine. "Don't push. Best way to put them off, that is."

They turned out of the car park, and this time they took

no wrong turnings but drove steadily down a mercifully quiet M1 motorway. Conversation consisted entirely of an exchange of views about the centre, what they had liked best, what they'd missed. The general consensus was that it was a great day out, and they'd certainly go again soon.

Harry's head soon drooped, and he was asleep.

"Look, Doug," Susie said, turning round from the front seat. "He's smiling, bless him."

"Probably dreaming of walking in space," Douglas said.

They were silent for a while, and then Lois said, "Hey, Derek, isn't that Gavin Adstone and family?"

A large black car with darkened windows sped past them. "Idiot driver going too fast to be sure. Must be doing at least a hundred," said Derek.

"And with a child aboard! And if you don't mind my mentioning it, Doug, you're doing eighty yourself," said Susie.

"Could you see *two* men?" persisted Lois.

"Give it a rest, Sherlock," said Derek, and settling himself comfortably, he closed his eyes.

EIGHT

ॐ

MONDAY MORNING, AND JOSIE STOOD AT THE SHOP WINDOW, looking up and down the street, wondering if any customers were likely to appear. She opened up every morning at eight o'clock, though she had to be on duty much earlier to take in and sort the post. This morning, apart from one or two early birds who came in for a newspaper, she had sold nothing.

It was half term, of course, and there wouldn't be the usual kids who came in for unhealthy snacks before the school bus came along. In spite of their daily fix of chocolate bars and cans of sweet drinks, they all looked rosy-cheeked and healthy to her. The only one who was pale-faced and had a persistent cough was a girl from Blackberry Gardens whose parents were strict vegetarians. Josie hoped she was able to stuff herself with sausages at school dinners.

A woman came hurrying out of the house opposite. Josie retreated behind the counter, and saw it was Paula Hickson from across the road. "Morning!" she said. "Children all at home this week, I suppose?" She thought the woman looked even more harassed than usual, poor thing.

"Well, the twins and little Frankie are at home," Paula said. "Only one missing is Jack Jr. Staying over with a friend in Tresham. Rang me this morning."

"That's nice," Josie said. "He's quite a big lad, your Jack. I expect he misses living in town with all his friends."

Paula nodded. "I worry about him, though," she said. "I've got no idea who his friends are, or where they live. If anything happened . . ." She trailed off, and took a packet of biscuits off the shelf. "Better get back," she said. "I left the twins minding Frankie. Not legal, I know, but I can see the house from here."

Josie handed over her change and frowned. "You can always give me a ring and I'll pop over with whatever you need," she said.

"Thanks," Paula said. She started towards the door, then stopped and turned back. "You don't know anybody wanting cleaning done, do you? I've got to get some extra money, what with Jack Sr. not contributing. He's disappeared off the face of the earth."

"Oh, my goodness," Josie said. "But how would you manage with the baby still so young?"

"I was told the local nursery would take him two days a week. I'd get help from Social Services for that. Then with the twins staying for dinner at school, I could do quite a few hours. Anyway, if you hear of anybody . . ." She looked anxiously at her house over the road and began to open the door.

"Just a minute," Josie said quickly. "My mum might be able to help. She runs New Brooms, the cleaning business. Shall I ask her?"

Paula's face cleared. "Could you? It'd be ever so good of you. I'm a good worker, you can tell her. Got references, an' all. Paula Hickson's the name. Better get back, an' thanks." She ran across the road and into her house. As she opened the door, Josie could hear screams, and hoped the twins hadn't thumped the baby.

Were children really such a good idea? Josie was well aware she had a pleasant, well-organised life, devoted to her shop and able to manage her own time as she liked. Matthew was certainly more attentive than ever, and she had the feeling that any minute now the question might be popped. Well, perhaps it would be best to give Mum a ring about a job for Paula and let true love take its bumpy course.

LOIS WAS IN HER OFFICE WHEN JOSIE PHONED. GRAN HAD JUST brought her a cup of coffee, and she had settled down with her computer. New Brooms team would be meeting here at noon, and she had a morning's work to do organising schedules and other admin that had piled up during the week.

"Hello, love. All well?"

"O' course. Nothing earthshaking has happened since I saw you twelve hours ago. No, this is a business call. You know that woman who's moved into Pickerings' house? Mother with four children. Tearaway teenager, lively twins, newish baby. Needs money."

"Yep," said Lois, checking her emails while she listened. She knew what was coming, anyway. "So have I got a job for her?" she said.

"Exactly. So *have* you?"

"I'll certainly have a talk to her. She seems a nice woman, with a lot on her plate. I'll call and see her. I presume she's worked out some free hours?"

"When can you go?"

"Tomorrow afternoon? Say about two o'clock. Will that suit?"

"Yep. I'll slip across and tell her. It's half term, so all the kids will be there. Still, could be a good thing. You'll see the real Paula!"

Lois smiled as she went back to her computer. Soft-hearted Josie! Who would've thought when she was a troublesome teenager that she would turn out to be a good businesswoman with a heart of gold. She was a captive audience for villagers who wanted a listening ear, and always had some words of advice or comfort, even when she was dog tired. Still, Lois thought as she returned to the week's cleaning schedules, it was good business sense to be a cheerful, sympathetic village shopkeeper. Few people had the nerve to come in just for a chat. They almost always bought something, and although most of the village did their big weekly shop in Tresham supermarkets, if Josie had a welcoming smile and the right kind of stock, she could just about survive.

On the dot of twelve, a knock at the door heralded Hazel Thornbull, office manager of New Brooms in Sebastapol Street, Tresham. "How's the family?" Lois asked. Hazel had been with her a long time, and would be difficult to replace. Only one child so far, and no talk of another.

"Fine," Hazel said. "Has Derek told you I've been co-opted on to his village hall committee? I must be mad. A poisoned chalice if ever there was one."

"What d'you mean?" said Lois.

"Well, you know these village committees. Most of the time spent arguing and not much achieved. There's already a split in the ranks, with that Gavin chap trying to take over. Still, your Derek is a match for him. I've always thought Derek was a mild man, but apparently not!"

"Tell me more about Gavin Adstone," Lois said, but there was another knock, and then all the others came at once and settled down for the meeting.

After the usual business had been dealt with, and before they got up to leave, Lois said she had something else to discuss with them. "There's this single mum in the village," she said, and explained about Paula Hickson. "Anybody know anything about her?"

They shook their heads and Sheila Stratford, one of the original members of the team, asked where she came from. When Lois told her, she said she supposed she'd be one of those girls who get themselves pregnant to avoid having to work for a living. Lois explained that Paula Hickson had had a husband who had done a bunk, and that with four children she was still keen to earn some money for herself and not rely wholly on the state.

"Anyway," Lois added, "I'm going to see her this afternoon, but I'd be glad if you would ask around and see if there's anything I should know. Thanks a lot. I'll keep in touch, as usual."

They left chattering to each other, but Floss lagged behind. "Mrs. M," she said. "Have you got a minute?"

Lois pointed to a chair, and said she always had time for the team.

"I don't know if I should say this," Floss began, "but I was talking to Kate Adstone. You know she's got that little toddler, and seems a bit lonely. I asked her round for coffee, just to be friendly, and she was pathetically grateful!"

"Very neighbourly of you," Lois said, looking at her watch, "but what has this got to do with New Brooms?"

"Nothing," Floss said. "But it has got something to do with Derek's SOS committee. The subject came up, and I don't think she connected me with you or Derek. She was saying that Gavin had come home laughing his head off at the committee. A load of no-hopers, was what he had said, apparently. Kate said he had big plans for the village hall, but they certainly weren't those of Derek Meade's committee. Then she looked a bit guilty, as if she shouldn't have told me." She looked anxiously at Lois. "I just thought you should know. Maybe tell Derek, so's he can be prepared?"

Lois nodded wearily. "You did the right thing," she said. "I reckon Save Our Shed is going to Blight Our Lives for a good while. Thanks, Floss. Anything else you hear, report back to me."

NINE

ᔧ

NEXT MORNING DOUGLAS AND SUSIE WERE SITTING AT THE breakfast table, encouraging a reluctant Harry to eat his porridge. "What time did you say you were going?" Susie said, looking at the clock that had been presented to her old granddad when he retired from the railway station in Tresham. He'd been so proud of it, and of his medal pinned on him by the great cigar-smoking leader when he came by train to visit the town. Both house and medal were now Susie's, left to her in old Clem's will, and she and Douglas had "knocked through" to the house owned by Lois next door, making a good-sized home in Gordon Street for the newlyweds and their firstborn.

"Ten o'clockish," Douglas said. "Check-in time is eleven, and the plane leaves about one. Should be there soon after three. I'll ring you from the hotel." He worked at an American company's office in Tresham, and was off to Italy for a jolly bonding meeting in Venice. It was a bit of a waste of time, in his opinion, but he meant to enjoy himself and make the most of it.

"Think of me," said Susie, "talking to this small person here and only ever getting a beaming smile and a load of rubbish in reply!"

"Mum said she'd call in later, to make sure you're all right," Douglas said, and Susie bridled. "Of course I'll be all right," she said. "What on earth could go wrong? And there's always my mum and dad up on the estate."

Susie's dysfunctional parents lived on a run-down estate in the suburbs of Tresham, and were not much good in the way of support for their daughter. Still, she had managed to maintain reasonable relations with them, and they would be better than nothing in an emergency, she hoped.

What emergency, though? She dismissed the thought. "You'll be back on Friday, won't you?"

"Friday evening," Douglas said. He was writing now on the back of an envelope.

"What's that?" Susie asked.

"Just working something out. Nearly finished." He wrote down a number with a flourish, and handed the envelope to her.

"So?" she said. "Maths for idiots? I can't make any sense of it."

"It's just to show you I learned something from our visit to the National Space Centre," he said with mock superiority. "You know it's Mum's birthday next week? Well, if she lived on Pluto, where a year is 246 earth years, she would be around two months old, and so not due for a Pluto first birthday for another ten months."

"Wow! That's worth knowing! Come in very handy, that will." She made a face at him and said she was giving up on Harry's porridge. "Time we got going," she said.

IN THE BIG GENERAL OFFICE OF WORLDWIDE SOLUTIONS, GAVIN Adstone headed for the gents, or comfort station as some of his colleagues called it. As he stood washing his hands, a pimply youth came in. "Hi," he said. "Settling in?"

Gavin recognized a very junior employee, and considered his question as overfamiliar. The lad seemed to think long service with Worldwide Solutions—a whole year—entitled him to take a definitely patronising air.

"Of course," Gavin replied. "Nothing difficult about this job."

"Worked in this kind of business before, then?"

"Yes. Back to work then," he snapped, and headed for the door.

"Just wondered if you'd met Doug Meade," the youth said, looking sly. "Higher up the ladder than us, o' course, but a nice chap. No side, if you know what I mean."

"No, why should I have met him?" Gavin was furious at being bracketed with this spotty youth in front of him. But he hesitated. Meade? That was a familiar name, certainly.

"His mum lives in Long Farnden. Your village, ain't it?"

Ah, of course, Gavin said to himself. Derek Meade, chair of SOS. So his son was Douglas Meade, fast-tracked up the ladder at Worldwide, and highly regarded. A useful bit of information from the spotty youth. He forced a smile, and said he'd look out for Douglas and introduce himself. The smile vanished quickly, and he barked out that he had work to do and left.

When lunchtime came round, he approached his manager and said he needed urgently to collect a parcel from the depot on the other side of town. "Nobody at home to receive it when the courier called. The usual thing. One knock, and if the door isn't opened in seconds, they clear off and leave a card through the letter box. Shouldn't be too long, but if I'm a few minutes late back, is that okay?"

That was the trouble with these out of town business parks, he reckoned, as he set off in his car. Miles from bloody anywhere. Still, he put his foot down and sped out of town, but nowhere near the direction of the courier depot.

The Silent Man, a pub in the village of Broughton, had been rechristened with its ridiculous new name after it had been bought by a chain and redesigned in a way to attract thrusting young business people from the new park. It was formerly the Greyhound, a sleepy farmers' inn, which had been there on the drovers' route to the market town of Tresham for hundreds of years, and had a Scots pine tree in the garden to prove it. It was Gavin's destination, and he parked the car round the back of the pub, out of sight, and went in quickly through the rear door.

Inside it was fashionably murky. Small lamps shed pools of light at each shiny new table, and Gavin stood still, looking round. His eye was caught by a figure waving a hand at him from the darkest corner, and he headed over and sat down.

"Morning, young man," said the heavily built man, smiling at him from the shadows.

"Mr. Froot," said Gavin, with a knowing grin, "a very good morning to you, too."

AT TWO O'CLOCK EXACTLY, LOIS WALKED DOWN THE PATH TO Paula Hickson's front door and rang the bell. She had a slight shiver of unpleasant memory as she heard footsteps approaching from inside. It was not so long ago that she had been dragged into this house and held captive in order to deliver a baby from an illegal immigrant woman who'd worked for the evil trafficker in human lives.

The door opened, and Lois caught sight of little Frankie crawling towards her with a broad smile that warmed her heart. Paula asked her to come in, and Lois instinctively bent down and picked up the warm little body, kissing him on his cherry red cheek. He smelled of Johnson's baby shampoo and freshly washed clothes. A good start, Lois thought, and handed him over to a nervous-looking Paula.

"Come in here, Mrs. Meade," she said, leading the way into the sitting room. Clean and tidy, Lois noted, and a bunch of daisies on a table by the window. A toy box in the corner occupied Frankie, and, refusing tea or coffee, Lois began the interview.

She asked Paula about her life in Tresham when she still had a husband living with her, and heard a tale of sadness and brutality. "Mind you," Paula said with a half smile, "as you can see from my four boys, we got on really well for thirteen years. Unlucky thirteen, it turned out to be. Jack lost his job, and that's when the trouble started.

It was a familiar story of the sort Lois read every week in the *Tresham Advertiser*. Man out of work, spends his dole money on booze and gambling, goes home full of guilt and beats up his wife. Paula was anxious to stress that he had never touched the children. Just her, she said, and bared her arm. A scar about four inches long ran down to her wrist.

"Looks like you were lucky, after all, not to get that cut across the vein," Lois said coolly. "I can see why you had to leave. Anyway," she continued, "that's enough of all that. It's your private business, and I shall see that nobody else discusses it on the team. Now, what hours can you work? Didn't you say the playgroup in the village hall could take Frankie? Would that be on a regular basis?"

Paula said that two whole days had been agreed, and they had been very accommodating about payment. "I *am* very reliable, Mrs. Meade," she said. "Except, of course, if any of the children got sick, and I suppose that's bound to happen sooner or later." Her face fell as she realised this was a problem she had not really thought through.

"Could happen to any of my cleaners who have children," Lois said. "We are well organised to cope. Mostly with me filling in!" she said, and smiled reassuringly.

In fact, she liked to relieve the girls occasionally, keeping her hand in and giving her a chance to check on clients firsthand. And in certain cases, this had given her useful opportunites for what Derek insisted on calling ferretin'.

It was amazing how careless people were with their cleaners. Like servants in the old days, the daily help was in some
ways invisible. Private papers were left out on tables, telephone conversations held at tops of voices, and rows between
husbands and wives carried on, all without a thought for an
observant member of New Brooms' team.

There was an unspoken agreement, never spelled out, that
Lois's team would keep its eyes and ears open if given a hint
from the boss that this might be useful.

After a general chat, Lois had summed up Paula and her
household, and decided she would give the woman a trial
period of four weeks, if only to please Josie. She asked Paula to
provide a couple of references and said she could come along
to next week's team meeting. "Monday, at twelve noon," she
said. "That should be all right with the playgroup?"

Paula's face was scarlet with relief, and she nodded. "Mon-
days and Wednesdays, they said. I hope that will fit in."

"By the way," Lois added, as they went to the door, "where
have you worked before?"

"Oh, I was in a builders' office. Part-time general dogs-
body, on a minimum wage." Paula grinned. "They were quite
big developers in Tresham, with offices in London and several
other cities. Covered the whole country and some abroad."

"Are they still there?" asked Lois.

"Oh, yeah. Head office is in Amsterdam, I think. It'll be
nice to work for a small business like yours. You can rely on
me, Mrs. Meade," she repeated, cuddling Frankie close.

"Mrs. M," Lois said, smiling kindly. "That's what the others call me. Mrs. M."

Ten

WHAT TIME IS YOUR MEETING, DEREK?" GRAN WAS READ-
ing an old recipe book that had been her mother's,
planning what to cook for their evening meal. There was no
longer a butcher in Long Farnden, but Josie at the shop had
lately done a deal with John Thornbull to supply her with
his farm-reared meat, already vacuum packed, and in man-
ageable sizes for elderly people who could not get into town
and were reluctant to have food delivered from supermarkets.
"Don't trust 'em, myself," Gran had said. "I like to see what
I'm buying."

Now Josie had chicken breasts, packets of beef and lamb
mince, sausages of several kinds, all labeled as local produce.
They sold well, and Gran was searching for a recipe she knew
her mother had cooked, using slices of chicken, shallots and
herbs.

"It's seven thirty," Derek replied. "I fixed for it to be in the
Reading Room. I can see we'll probably be having more than

one meeting a week as things go on, and Lois ain't too keen on missing her telly programs."

Gran's face fell. "That's a shame," she said. "I was goin' to make some shortbread for you lot to have with your coffee."

"You can still make it," Derek said, knowing perfectly well that a vanished opportunity for eavesdropping was the real reason for her disappointment. "I'll take it with me when I go."

"Can't think why we need all this fuss about restoring the village hall," Gran said sulkily. "The Reading Room is fine, just the right size for meetings."

"All right for small meetings, but not for putting on concerts and plays, and playing badminton and havin' cookery demonstrations an' that. Anyway, Gran, I must be off now. I should be finished that job over at Fletching today, and then I can start on Sam Stratford's rewiring job."

Gran found the recipe, and decided to walk down to the shop to buy chicken and other ingredients. They needed several other things, and she unhooked her shopping bag.

It was a lovely morning, and Gran thought proudly that the village was good enough to be in a film, with its gold-stone houses and trim gardens and hedges. Hey! That was an idea for raising money! She must remember to tell Derek. If they could persuade filmmakers to use Farnden as a location, that would surely bring in big money, wouldn't it? Her friend Joan, who lived in Blackberry Gardens, had been to the Island of Mull where the popular children's TV program *Balamory* was filmed and crowds of tourists came specially to the island to see the place and the actors in the flesh.

"Morning, Gran," Josie said. "You're down here early. Everybody gone off to work?"

"Yep, leaving me to do the chores and provide hearty meals and comfort and advice," Gran said, hands on hips.

"Oh, go on with you," Josie replied. "You know you love it. What would you do with yourself if you were still in that poky little bungalow on the Churchill?"

"Well, you might be right. But enough o' that. I need some chicken breasts."

"Making chicken Kiev?"

"Certainly not," Gran answered, "whatever that is. No, I found a recipe of your great grandmother's, and thought I'd try it for supper."

"Dad's got a meeting, hasn't he?"

"Yep, but it'll all be ready when they get in. For some stupid reason, they're meeting in the Reading Room in future."

Josie smiled. "Ah, never mind," she said. "You could always drop in on them, bearing cream cakes and tea bags."

Gran huffed and puffed around the shop, gathering what she needed. Then she perched on the old person's stool by the counter, and asked Josie what was new in the village. Half the fun for customers of the village shop was to exchange gossip, and although Josie tried to smile and say nothing, if there was some piece of news that was already common knowledge, then she happily passed it on to Lois or Gran.

"Seems the idea of a soap box grand prix has sparked some interest," Josie said. "O' course, the whole thing about fundraising for the village hall is the hot topic at the moment. Blimey, I've never heard so many heated discussions here in the shop! The village is split, I reckon. Some want a festival—mostly the incomers—and the rest, the old guard, are really looking forwards to the soap box racing. Seems there used to be something of the sort in the past."

"How about that Gavin Adstone?" Gran said. "The festival was his idea, apparently. Big idea, say some. I don't suppose he comes in the shop much?"

"Not him. But his wife does, with the toddler, and she's really nice. I feel a bit sorry for her. She hasn't made many friends yet. Because of him, I should think. He's too clever by half. Thinks the rest of us are bumpkins!"

"He'll learn," said Gran enigmatically. She had seen it all before. "Young couples buying houses in the village. 'It's so quaint!' they say. And then, before you can say knife, they start wanting to change it."

The shop door opened, and a couple of teenagers came in. One of them Gran recognized as the eldest son of that woman over in Pickerings' house, and a right scruff he was, too. She stood up, grasped the hairy handles of her planet-friendly bag, and left the shop.

The boys did not come straight to the counter, but lingered over a display of newspapers and magazines by the door. Josie kept an eye them, knowing from experience that even the best brought up kids can be light fingered if the temptation is too great.

She was about to suggest that if they were going to leaf through all the magazines they might buy one and leave the rest clean and tidy for others, when the boy who belonged to Paula Hickson burst into delighted guffaws. His pal peered at a virtually naked girl carrying all before her.

"That's enough, boys," Josie said. "You've had your fun, now please put that magazine back tidily and tell me what you came to buy."

"You ain't got it, missus, so we can't buy it," said the Hickson boy, and they both left the shop, sniggering as they went.

Charming! thought Josie, remembering how pleasant she had found Paula Hickson, and deciding the boy must take after his absent father. It was not until later, when she was checking the newspapers for the next day's order, that she discovered they were one magazine short.

Eleven

THE EVENING WAS MILD, WITH A GENTLE BREEZE STIRRING
the leaves on the giant chestnut that spread its branches
above the small Reading Room, which had been donated to
the village in 1898 by a benevolent squire at the hall. It had
recently been restored, and Derek unlocked the door with a
feeling of pleasure at the success of a campaign that had saved
the little building from being bulldozed, with the ironstone
to be used for repairing a wall around the new vicarage.

He arranged a table and chairs ready for the meeting, and
sorted through some details about soap box racing that Lois
had downloaded for him from her computer. He had been
considerably alarmed at the technical stuff about construct-
ing the soap boxes, and about safety regulations that would
have to be considered. He would ask Tony Dibson what they
had done in the old days. No doubt Adstone would use it as
an excuse to try turning the committee against soap boxes in
any guise.

"Evenin', Derek," said Tony, as he came through the door,

looking smart and neatly dressed for the meeting. Derek marvelled again at how the old boy managed with a disabled wife and all the household chores to do.

"Nice to see you, Tony, and on time as always! Reckon we could show these youngsters a thing or two." The rest came in ones and twos, and Derek was just beginning to wonder if Hazel Thornbull had forgotten, when she and husband John hurried through the door, apologising for having had to stay with a sick cow.

"Not that blue tongue, I 'ope," said Tony, and Gavin made a disgusted face.

"Do you think we could start, Chairman," he said. "I have some business work to catch up on." He hadn't, but he liked to create an image.

"Right, let's get to it," said Derek briskly. "All here?" He looked around, and saw that Father Rodney was missing. Saying a prayer for the soul of the sick cow? Derek asked if anyone had heard anything from him.

"I saw him in the churchyard as I was comin' down," Tony said. "Gazing upwards, he was."

"Lost in wonder, love and praise, probably," said Hazel, who had a passion for hymns and knew all the words.

"No point in waiting for him," said Gavin Adstone. "I can't think he'll have much to contribute, anyway. Away with the fairies most of the time."

"Hardly," said Derek dryly, and added that the vicar was a good and useful man, and he was sure he would not mind if they started without him.

Good old Derek, thought Hazel, as she opened the minutes book ready to read her notes on the last meeting. "That's put smartass Gavin in his place," she muttered under her breath.

The vicar turned up, and after the minutes had been read they got swiftly down to the main item. "The soap box grand prix," said Derek. "First of all, we need to fix a date. Any suggestions as to the best time?"

Various dates were considered, several of them clashing with other village events. The church fete, the WI outing, a couple of weddings arranged needing the church and a free run through the village for the happy couple and their guests. Eventually a date was agreed, and Derek shuffled his papers.

"Lois has found out quite a bit about how the races an' that are organised these days," he said, "and I must say I hadn't reckoned on something so complicated." He saw Gavin draw a breath to speak, and so continued quickly. "Not that we would want to put on such a formal event," he added. "Most of us were thinking of a few likely lads having a go at making some larky soap boxes and putting on a race or two to entertain the crowds."

"What crowds!?" burst out Gavin. "Think big, man, think big! If we do the thing properly, we could get hundreds of spectators, and with the right extra attractions organised by me, we could make a packet."

Derek raised his eyebrows, and passed Lois's papers to Tony Dibson, who was sitting at the end of the row of chairs. "Have a look at these, everybody," Derek said. "Then we shall know what we're talking about. And while we're doing that, perhaps Father Rodney will tell us about his plans for a flower festival in the church on the same day."

By the time Hazel had given her preliminary report on what other groups in the village might contribute, including an art and crafts marquee on the playing fields, the papers had reached John Thornbull, the last to read them, and he handed them back to Derek.

"Thank you, Hazel," Derek said. "Sounds very promising. Now, you've all had a chance to look through those details, so back to the soap box grand prix."

Recognising that his festival was once more receding into the distance, Gavin jumped in with an offer to take the soap box project outside into a wider world, resulting in a bigger potential crowd on the day. "I could take the details on how to make the soap boxes to the local tech college. They have an engineering department, and might be pleased to make it their big practical learning project for the summer term. As far as safety goes, we just have to liaise with our friendly cops and make sure we comply with the necessary regulations."

Talks like a politician, thought Tony Dibson. He whispered into Floss's young and pretty ear that he bet her a shillin' that Adstone would be MP for Tresham before long. Derek frowned at him, and politely thanked Gavin for his suggestion. Then he asked Floss what she thought would appeal to the young folk in the village.

"It's got to be fun," she said straightaway. "We got to get them putting their own ideas into designing the soap boxes, and have as few rules as we can. I don't see why we have to involve anybody outside the village. For Farnden, by Farnden. That's what I reckon, anyway."

There was a small round of applause, with Gavin noticeably failing to join in.

"For Farnden, by Farnden!" echoed Tony Dibson. "That's it, gel. You got it!"

TWELVE

S O HOW DID IT GO?" LOIS SAID. SHE SOMEHOW MANAGED TO concentrate on her favourite quiz show and listen to Derek at the same time. At least, he hoped she was listening, as he gave her an edited version of the meeting's reasonably pleasant beginning, and far from pleasant end.

"So anyway," he said, "we all more or less agreed on Floss asking if she could go down there next week and talk to the kids, fill 'em in on what we're planning, and see what their reaction is."

Lois nodded, not taking her eyes off the screen. "Sounds good," she said. "And you could try one of you going down the Youth Club and asking the kids what they think."

Derek marched across the room to the television set, stood in front of it, and told Lois that she hadn't listened to a word he'd said, and if she wasn't interested, he might as well save his breath.

Gran, who up to that moment had kept silent, roared with laughter. "You tell her, Derek!" she said.

Lois's face was stony. She reached for the remote control, and with great solemnity switched off the set. She turned to Derek. "I do apologise, Mr. Chairman," she said. "I wonder if you'd mind repeating what you just said."

"Bollocks!" said Derek, and asked if anyone wanted a coffee, because he was parched with talking too much. He marched out of the room, and Lois hastily followed. As she went, she winked at Gran. "A little lovin' will put it right," she said, and shut the door behind her.

When they returned with coffee all round, Gran could see equilibrium had been restored. She decided to take up where Derek had left off, and asked why the meeting had ended unpleasantly.

"Yeah." Lois nodded. "Did Father Rodney suggest an evenin' of lap dancing, or what?"

Derek gave her a warning look, and said it happened after the meeting had closed and they were all walking through the village together, having agreed that a pint in the pub would be a good idea. "Then Hazel stopped dead in the middle of the road, and said she could smell smoke."

"What, a chimney on fire?" said Gran.

Derek shook his head. "No. At first none of the rest of us could smell it, but then Floss said she could, and it smelled like petrol or something oily."

Lois sat up straight, all attention. "So what was it? Did you investigate? We haven't heard no fire engines, have we, Gran?"

"Guess," Derek said flatly.

"The village hall," Lois said. "Go on."

"Well, we all rushed round there, and we could see smoke. Not much, but then Gavin found a bit of smoldering wood shoved in under the porch. You know that wooden roof bit, where it shelters the main door. He grabbed it out, and stamped on it. We could all smell the petrol smell then, and went round the whole building to make sure there weren't no more places where it'd been fired."

"So you told the police?" Lois said.

Derek shook his head. "No point in getting them this late," he said. "We agreed I'd phone them in the morning and report it. In fact," he added, with a look at Lois, "I thought our own village sleuth might like to talk to her cop. You can't beat going right to the top, as I told the rest."

There was silence for a minute or two, and then Lois said quietly that she would be pleased to give Inspector Cowgill a ring, especially as she knew the police were aware of the previous attempt on the village hall.

"Did the others have any idea who might have done it?" she asked Derek.

"Well, Gavin Adstone was full of possible suspects, mostly gypsies and passing tramps, but mainly the others seemed to think it was the kids who meet up round the back of the hall. Tony Dibson said he reckoned the new woman in Pickerings' house has a teenage tearaway who's been in trouble before."

"Jack Jr.," said Lois, with a sigh. "Young Jack Hickson. His mum, Paula, is coming to work for me. She's joining the team. And yes, I've heard she's had one or two problems with her son Jack."

Derek groaned, and Gran nodded in sympathy. "So we're right in it, Lois, once more," he said.

"Trust you, Lois," Gran added. "All the nice women there are around needing jobs, and you have to take on a single mother with four sons, living on Social Services, abandoned by a violent no-good husband who could turn up any minute. Great. Well done, Lois."

Lois stood up. "Have you finished, both of you?" she said coldly. "Then I'm off to bed. I'll make the call first thing in the morning, Derek. And for your information, Paula Hickson is a very good, responsible mother, desperate to earn a bit of extra and not be a total drag on the state. *And*, unless I'm a lousy judge, she'll be a reliable, honest member of my team. Don't wake me up when you come to bed," she added, barely suppressing her anger. She left the room, leaving Derek and Gran looking at each other in dismay.

"The end of a perfect day," Derek said gloomily.

"She'll come round. She always does." Gran knew she was on thin ice here. Living with your daughter's family was not always a cushy billet.

Thirteen

❧

"D on't forget," Derek said next morning, as he pulled on his boots ready to go up to the allotment.

"I don't need reminding," Lois said. "I reckon something very nasty is going on, and I don't mean gypsies and passing tramps. You go, and I'll tell you what Cowgill says at lunchtime. He may not be in his office yet, but I can get hold of him anyway. Cheerio, love. See you later." She smiled sweetly at him, and he went off to start his van, pretty sure he was forgiven.

Around nine o'clock, Lois dialled Cowgill's number, and he answered with a brisk, "Good morning, Lois. How are you and the family?"

Must have someone with him, thought Lois. His opening words were usually something silly, like "how's the light of my life." She always snapped at him, but now missed the affection in his voice.

"There's been another go at firing the village hall," she said, and told him what had happened.

"Why weren't we told straightaway?" he said, and then obviously turned away from the phone to say goodbye to someone. After a pause, he said, "But before we start, how's the love of my life?" he added, his voice softened in the daft way that immediately triggered a sharp reply from Lois.

"Why don't we just start again, instead of all that rubbish?" she said. "It was Derek's decision to leave it 'til today, and the others backed him up. They made sure the hall was safe, then went home. Derek said they agreed it should be me phoning you. Can't think why."

"I can," he said. "I am taking this seriously, Lois. Arson is a very nasty thing. It doesn't necessarily stop at destroying a building. People can be involved, too. Remember the fire in the gypsies camp? A miracle nobody was hurt. No, I'll get the best men for the job to look further into it. One attempt may well be a kids' prank, but this second go at it nearly succeeded. If Derek and friends hadn't noticed the smell of smoke, the fire could have taken hold and then God knows where it might have spread. Can you meet me down there at ten o'clock. I'll have Chris with me."

"Chris? Who's he?"

"She," Cowgill said. "Chris Botham is my new assistant. You'll like her. She's not unlike a certain dear girl who runs a cleaning business. Bright and quick. Not bad looking. Doesn't tolerate fools gladly. Sharp tongue at times . . ."

"Ah, you can't mean she's like me, then," said Lois. "I'm known for being a soft touch."

"Ha!"

Lois could hear Cowgill chuckling, and then he said, "See you in a while, then."

THE ANONYMOUS-LOOKING CAR DROVE INTO THE VILLAGE HALL car park, and Lois watched the tall figure of Cowgill get out, then a slim, dark woman wearing a grey jacket and skirt that revealed a pair of well-shaped legs and sensible shoes. The two of them headed across to join Lois in the hall porch, and after the introductions were made, she showed them the charred beam where the smoldering stick had been shoved in behind.

A burst of loud, jolly music came from inside the hall. "Aerobics," said Lois.

"Very good for you," said Chris Bowler.

"Not for me," Lois said. "Tried it once an' it nearly killed me. Anyway, I get exercise enough in my job. Scrubbin' and cleanin' and—"

"—washing and ironing, not to mention gardening and cooking," finished Cowgill, and he put his hand on Lois's shoulder. "She's a wonder," he said, turning to his new assistant. "I couldn't do without her," he added, and to Lois's embarrassment, his voice was husky.

She changed the subject, said they should go inside. She added that Inspector Cowgill might like to see aerobics in action. He'd certainly get an eyeful of the female form, she said innocently.

Once inside, Lois was interested to see Kate Adstone with a sleeping baby in a pushchair. And there was Floss, waving to Lois from behind the rest, a surprised look on her face.

Cowgill walked up to the instructor, a trim-looking woman, blonde hair tied back and not an ounce of fat on her. Lois could see the old charm working its magic on her, and then a break was announced. Cowgill signalled Lois and Chris to go around the edges of the hall with him.

"How's your sense of smell, Lois?" Chris said.

"Good, more's the pity sometimes."

"Great. Any whiffs of smoke or petrol, call me over."

"I'll go into the kitchen," Lois said. "That's where the villain would be most likely to break in, if he wanted. Mind you, I reckon they planned to set the fire going from outside, without bothering to come in. Quick getaway, an' that. After all, this old wooden building would go up like bonfire night, once the fire took hold."

Chris nodded. "Still, worth checking," she said.

Lois stood in the kitchen and sniffed. Instant coffee. Damp. Mice. Drains. Nothing unexpected. She walked into the toilet, which was old but clean. Disinfectant and air freshener. And then, yes, petrol . . .

She looked up and saw that the small window was unlatched. She followed the sniff to the corner of the cubicle behind the lavatory brush, where it became strong. Oh no, was that a small puddle on the floor? Pee? She couldn't smell pee. A small wad of toilet paper was enough to dip into it. Petrol. Through the open door she called out to Cowgill, and he came quickly, with Chris at his side.

"Here! Smell this." She held out the toilet tissue, and he took it gingerly.

"If this is some kind of a joke, Lois, I shall be forced to . . ." He sniffed, then held it out to Chris. She nodded. "So we need to lock up the place and get the chaps down."

The aerobics instructor was not pleased, but dismissed the class and said she sincerely hoped she would see them the same time next week.

By the time Lois reached home, Gran had lunch well on the way and Derek was back from the allotment, his feet up on the kitchen table, reading the local paper.

"D'you mind!" Lois said. "We have to eat off that table, in case you hadn't noticed, Derek Meade."

He grinned at her, and didn't move.

"Any luck with your tame inspector?" he said. He had now come to think that the two attempts to burn down the village hall had been made by the same person, and he was fairly sure he knew which person. A swift and strong warning from the police was all that was needed, he was certain, to

stop the young fool. No doubt he'd find other places to van-
dalise, but as long as it wasn't in Farnden, Derek could put it
out of his mind.

"Three of us met down there. Cowgill, his assistant and
me. And I got the lucky break. I found the toilet had been
broken into, through that dodgy window, and there was a
strong smell of petrol."

"Did you find the can?"

Lois shook her hand. "Just a puddle," she said. "But I
reckon there must've been more than one person. It'd take
a skinny bloke to get through the window, an' he wouldn't
have a hope in hell if he tried carrying a petrol can. Must've
been handed to him once he was inside."

"So why didn't he set fire to it there an' then?" Gran said,
beating eggs as if they had insulted her.

"He'd got to get out first," Derek said. His attention was
now fully on what Lois was saying. "Probably frightened
off—maybe by us—before he could throw a match in. Ye
Gods, Lois," he added. "It don't bear thinkin' about, the damage they could've done. Is Cowgill taking action? You told
him about the Hickson lot, I hope?"

He could've bitten his tongue out. Lois's face darkened,
and she turned on her heel and stalked out of the kitchen.

"Oh, dear," Gran said. "I should lay off that one, Derek, if
I were you. Let's wait an' see what the police find out."

Derek sighed. "I wish we'd never heard of the bloody
police," he said.

"Language," Gran said automatically. "Go on," she added,
"go and make your peace. And don't forget that I'm on your
side, as well as Lois's."

At this piece of lousy logic, Derek burst out laughing and
went off to find Lois.

Fourteen

ᔥ

Father Rodney walked briskly through the old cemetery, across the road and into the churchyard. The clock struck ten o'clock as he quickened his step through the rose bushes and fragrant lavender to greet the bell ringers, who were already waiting to go into the church.

"We've had more turnover than Tesco's," Tony Dibson said, catching sight of the vicar. He was pushing his wheelchair-bound wife up the uneven path, just as he did every Sunday for morning service. She listened while the bell ringers, including Tony, rang out the peals, if a little unevenly, across the surrounding countryside. "Come *to* church, come *to* church," they seemed to call.

The vicar, smoothing his wiry hair in front of the small, cracked mirror in the vestry, wished the call was answered by more people than the elderly faithful few who turned up, rain or shine, to worship their Maker and reserve a place for themselves in the hereafter.

The Dibsons had arrived inside the church, and Irene said, "What did you mean, about Tesco's and turnover?" Tony pushed her to a suitable place where she would not block the exit in case of fire. The thought of fire reminded him of the village hall and he wondered if Lois had found out anything more.

"Tony! What did you mean?" Irene could see his mind was elsewhere, but persisted.

"Vicars," he said. "Turnover in vicars. They never stay long in Farnden. Must be something about this village."

"Nothing wrong with us," Irene said, "except maybe we could do with a few more in church. Go on, then, I'm all right. Off you go. Get ringing, boy."

THE VILLAGE HALL AND THE PLAYING FIELD AT THE REAR WERE approached by a narrow lane, and Gavin Adstone walked along trying to avoid piles of horse dung left by a group of girls on ponies heading for the bridle path that led out of the playing field and over the stream. "More horses than people in this village," he muttered to himself, cursing as a dollop of the sticky stuff stuck to the toe of his shoe. "And the horses would win in an IQ test every time," he added angrily.

He was heading for a meeting with John Thornbull, the only member of the SOS committee who might possibly be persuaded to Gavin's point of view. John was a practical man, a farmer with education and a small daughter a year or two older than Cecelia. He was more likely to be able to see a future for Long Farnden than the rest of the old codgers or dim-witted women Derek Meade had enlisted.

He could hear voices coming through the open door of the hall, but not John Thornbull's. Damn, he couldn't see him anywhere. Still, he could go in and have a look round. He'd never really examined the place properly, and with a few informed criticisms of the structure and its proposed renovations, he might still be able to persuade SOS into seeing the folly of the restoration proposal.

The cricket wives were gathered in the kitchen preparing tea for the afternoon match. Gavin looked in, smiled his most charming, and asked if he might wander round. "I'm a newcomer, as you already know," he said, addressing Floss, who seemed to be in charge. Her Ben was captain of the team, and she presided over sandwiches and cakes and umpteen cups of tea.

Far from being bowled over by Gavin's charm, Floss stared at him. "What do want to look round for?" she said sharply. "There's nothing going on here today, except cricket."

Gavin bridled. "In case you've forgotten," he said, "I am a SOS committee member and have every right to come and inspect the 'shed' we're intending to pour money into for its restoration. And in any case, I have a meeting scheduled with John Thornbull—"

"I suppose you can, then," said Floss. "It's just that we've been told to be very careful since the arson attempts. That's all. Look round all you want, but don't get in our way. Look, there's John now, just parking his quad bike."

"Morning, Gavin," John said. He led the way into a small room where meetings were held, and asked what exactly he wanted to talk about. He explained that he had several cricket matters to attend to, and hadn't much time to spare.

"Just wanted a few words about SOS," Gavin said. "I felt a bit odd man out at the committee meeting, and had a sort of feeling you might be more in tune with me than the others."

John frowned. He was a Farnden man, born and bred, and he had no wish to side with this unpopular incomer. It was true, however, that he privately thought the others had grouped themselves unfairly against Gavin's ideas, and though they were much too ambitious as they stood, a lot of them could be adapted to widen the scope of the soap box grand prix. After all, the man was young and keen, and that was not easy to find in Long Farnden.

They talked for a while, and when Gavin left the hall and walked back up the muddy lane, he realised that he had gained nothing. John had been very polite, sympathetic, but in the end committed himself to nothing. Waste of time, then, Gavin decided. He could have been at home, playing with Cecilia.

"Morning, young man," said a voice behind him. It was Tony Dibson with his wife, Irene. Gavin could see that pushing Irene's wheelchair through the muck on the lane was heavy going.

"Here, let me have a push," he said. "Been to church?"

Tony said they were on their way home, and had stupidly decided to come along the footpath and home by the longer route.

"The Thelwell girls have been along here," Gavin said. "D'you remember those cartoons, Tony?"

"O' course I do," the old man said firmly. "Long before you were born. Wicked little girls on small fat ponies. D'you want me to take over?"

Gavin said he was fine, and added that his mother had loved the Thelwell brats on ponies and had kept books of them.

Glad to talk about something other than SOS, Gavin chatted to Irene, asking her questions about her disability without reserve or false sympathy. Tony could tell she was warming to another side of Gavin Adstone. When they reached the Dibson's gate, Gavin insisted on pushing the chair right into the house, and accepted an offer of coffee with what seemed to be genuine pleasure.

But what is he up to? thought Tony suspiciously. Wouldn't trust the bugger as far as I could throw him.

"What a nice young man," Irene said, after they had drunk coffee, chatted of this and that, and Gavin had left, promising to bring Cecilia and Kate to meet Irene.

"GUESS WHO WAS IN CHURCH THIS MORNING," GRAN SAID, TAKing off her summer hat and donning her apron in the kitchen.

"President Obama?" said Derek.

"How did you guess?" said Gran. "We had a lovely chat, but he had to get back to saving the world."

"And apart from him?" Lois said, laughing at the pair of them.

"The Hickson woman. Paula, did you say, Lois? There she was, her tribe all washed and brushed and fidgeting in the pew at the back."

"Including Jack Jr.?" Lois said.

"If you mean that unprepossessing teenager with a hood permanently over his spotty face, yes, he was there, too. Sat staring at his feet most of the time."

"How could you see them, Mum?" Lois said. "If they were at the back, and you were in usual place up front, you must've been screwing your head round most of the service." And I bet you weren't the only one, she added to herself.

Gran ignored the question, and went on to say how Father Rodney was all over them in the church porch. "Poor woman looked really uncomfortable. That's the trouble with modern vicars. They try too hard. Puts people off, you know. Now, Lois, get me the milk from the fridge. Time I made the Yorkshire batter. Josie's coming up for dinner, isn't she?"

"Yep," Lois said. "And she's bringing a policeman with her." Derek said, tongue in cheek, that the police had heard that a certain Mrs. Weedon had been seen with petrol can and matches having a go at the village hall, and were wanting to talk to her.

Gran, who was also Mrs. Weedon, menaced him with a

dripping spoon. "That's enough of that, Derek Meade," she said. "Quite enough. I know perfectly well that Josie's policeman is Matthew Vickers, an' he'll be off duty, bless him. We must make him really welcome," she added, and then, remembering her strictures about vicars trying too hard, she resolved not to do the same with a possible grandson-in-law.

FIFTEEN

❧

THE SCHOOL BUS STOPPED OUTSIDE THE SHOP, AND JOSIE watched as the little crowd of variously clad pupils climbed aboard. Jack Hickson was still hovering over the magazines, and Josie walked over to him.

"The bus won't wait, Jack," she said. "Go on, run for it."

He stared at her, and the lack of expression in his almost black eyes made her feel uncomfortable. "Mind yer own business," he said insolently. She opened her mouth to tell him he would not be welcome in the shop anymore. She had had enough of his cheek. But he was out of the door and into the bus like a scared rabbit. Except that he was not scared.

Josie turned back to the counter. Should she report him to his mother? But the poor woman had enough to worry about, and in any case, knew all about her firstborn. No doubt child experts would say he was a casualty of a violent father and a broken home. But the other children were perfectly polite, and certainly Mum seemed to think Paula was making a good job of bringing up a family on her own.

Jack Jr. made his way to the rear of the bus, where his second-best mate, Jonathan, greeted him with a friendly shove. "Did you get it?" he said, and Jack shook his head. "Silly cow was watching too close," he said. "I'll have another go this afternoon, when we get off the bus. Works best if you wait till the shop's full of kids, then she don't know which way to look."

He pulled a dog-eared magazine out of his school bag and they both huddled over it, chortling at the lovely busty girls. "Why don't *she* get tits like these?" Jack said, nodding his head towards a hollow-cheeked fourteen-year-old girl half-way down the bus. He hadn't admitted it to his sophisticated friend, but he felt drawn to the girl, perhaps because she looked so unhappy.

"Andorexia," Jonathan said knowledgeably. "Don't eat much. Can't expect big tits without a few cream buns!" And they were off again into husky sniggers.

As they stopped outside the school gates, Jack stuffed the magazine back into his bag and left the bus. A man stood by the gate, and Jack stopped abruptly, causing Jonathan to crash into him with loud expletives.

"Hi, boy," said the man. "Wanna come for a walk?"

Jack shook his head, his face deathly white. "Sod off," he said. "I'm goin' to school."

"Never used to be s"keen on school," the man said. "Got some sweets here. Cheer you up, they will. Sure you don't wanna come?"

Jack hesitated, and Jonathan gave him a push from behind. "Get into the playground," he hissed. "He won't dare follow. He's big trouble. You oughta know that. Go on, for God's sake."

Another push got Jack Jr. through the gates. He ran into school without a backwards glance. The man shrugged, put the packet back into his pocket and walked away. "Always another day," he muttered to himself.

*   *   *

Lois came into the shop smiling broadly. "Morning, love," she said. "Lovely weather for ducks."

Josie looked out at the sheeting rain, and agreed. "And that young Jack Hickson didn't have a coat nor nothing," she said.

"Jack?" Lois said. "Why did you say that? Didn't know you were concerned about the Hickson family." Then she remembered that it had been Josie who suggested Paula for a job with New Brooms. "Well, I don't really mean you," she added. "It's your father and Gran who ain't got no time for them. Give a dog a bad name, I reckon."

"Not much wrong with that family, except for Jack Jr.," Josie said sadly. "I nearly banned him from the shop this morning. Very lippy he was. It's almost like he wants trouble."

"He's going the right way to get it," Lois replied. "Anyway, don't let's bother about him now. He's neither one thing nor the other at the moment, not a real teenager nor a child. His voice isn't properly broken, even. I shall see Paula at the meeting later on. D'you want me to mention it? Or shall we just see how he goes?"

Josie smiled. "Good old Mum," she said. "Feet on the ground. No wonder Matt's uncle is so smitten."

"Josie!"

"Sorry, sorry! Just that Matt says the lads at the station know that Cowgill's always in a better mood when he's made a call to Long Farnden."

"Change the subject," Lois said firmly. "Did he have any news about the village hall? Any ideas about who might be having a go at burning it down to the ground?"

Josie shook her head. "If he did know anything, he wasn't telling me," she said. "He's very strict about that. Off duty means just that. And police business is confidential."

"Doesn't stop him having a normal conversation about village matters, does it?"

"We got better things to talk about, Mum," Josie said, and that was that.

PAULA WAS ENJOYING HERSELF. LOIS HAD SENT HER UP TO FARN-den Hall, where Mrs. Tollervey-Jones had sighed with relief on seeing her. "Mrs. Meade telephoned earlier about Floss being unwell," she said, ushering Paula through the kitchen door. Tradesmen's entrance, thought Paula, and then reminded herself that Mrs. T-J was a JP on the magistrate's bench in Tresham and might well have come across Jack Sr. in her work in the family court. She had had to go to the doctor with her wrist when Jack had slashed her. She was pretty sure that he hadn't meant to do it, but he was blind drunk at the time and his hand had slipped. That's what he had said, anyway, and this is what she had told the doc as he treated her. She could see he didn't believe her, but there was nothing more she could say.

In a way, it had been a relief when Jack Sr. had left. Being on her own was hard, but at least she could concentrate on the kids and not worry about keeping them out of Jack's way when he was in the drink.

Now she picked up a tiny porcelain foxhound, one of a group surrounding a finely modelled horse and rider. As instructed, she took great care and replaced them all exactly as she found them. Mrs. T-J had gone into the village, and Paula wanted everything to be perfect for when she returned. This job with New Brooms was heaven sent, and she intended no fault would be found with her work.

"Don't open the door to anyone," Mrs. T-J had cautioned her. "Not even a policeman." The ghost of a smile crossed her face. "When you've been a magistrate for as long as I have," she added, "you are bound to have made an enemy or two."

It was so peaceful and quiet, Paula thought, and perched on the edge of a spindly legged chair for a moment. What must it be like to be the old girl, living in luxury, not a care in the world and never a worry about where the next penny was coming from?

A sudden snort from an armchair at the other side of the room startled her, and she jumped to her feet in alarm. Then she saw it was a fat old spaniel, white and liver colored, lumbering across the room towards her, wagging its tail. She bent down and fondled its velvety ears. "You made me jump," she said. "Must get on," she continued, and picked up the wax polish and duster and headed for the door.

As she crossed the hall with its chessboard black and white tiles, her eye was caught by a figure walking up the gravelled drive. As he approached she watched him with growing apprehension.

"Oh, God!" As he came closer, she recognized him. "No, no, no!" she yelled, and ran out of the hall, down the passage and into the kitchen. She checked the door was locked, and then shot the bolt in the scullery. Then she heard the front doorbell. He was keeping his finger on it without pausing, and Paula stuck her fingers in her ears. She cowered behind the larder door and prayed that he would go away.

Then she heard the blessed sound of Mrs. T-J's car sweeping into the stable yard. She ran quickly to the long windows and saw the figure retreating rapidly across the park and disappear into a thicket bordering the road. Her heart was thudding, and she made a desperate attempt to pull herself together.

"Paula? Are you there? All well?" Mrs. T-J was in a good mood. She had put a card in the shop window advertising for an under-gardener to help out Bob, who was certainly in need of assistance. With the present job situation, someone was bound to apply, and all she had to do now was find a way of explaining the need for an assistant to the old man who had been tending the gardens at the hall for what must be more than fifty years.

"Ah, there you are. Are you all right? You look a bit surprised. Surely I told you I would be back? Only been to the village, you know."

"I'm fine, thank you, Mrs. Tollervey-Jones. Just this dear old dog." She bent down and patted the spaniel. "Gave me quite a start. She was asleep in the big chair, and I hadn't noticed her until she snorted!"

"Dog lover, are you?" Mrs. Tollervey-Jones smiled. Splendid, she thought. Must tell Mrs. Meade that she can send Paula Hickson anytime she liked. Hickson? A familiar name, surely? She shook her head, and called the spaniel to offer a biscuit treat from the shop.

Sixteen

ॐ

LOIS HEARD THE DOORBELL, AND WAS NOT SURPRISED TO SEE Paula Hickson on the front step.

"Hope I'm not too early?"

Lois smiled, and said she was on the dot of noon, and to come in. "The others will be here shortly," she said. "They come in dribs and drabs, according to what time they finish work. Sometimes clients want a bit of extra done. The customer is always right!" she added. Then she took a good look at Paula. She was neatly dressed, but pale, and when she fumbled in her bag to find a notebook and pen, Lois noted that her hand was trembling.

"Are you all right, Paula?" she said. Perhaps it was nervousness at her first day in a new job.

"Oh, yes, I'm fine," Paula insisted, though she still felt considerably shaken by her husband's sudden appearance at the hall. She was dreading what he might do next, but was making a huge effort to concentrate on Mrs. Meade and the prospect of meeting the others on the team.

"Morning, Mrs. M!" Three more were standing on the step, and Lois brought them in to her office. "This is Paula Hickson, new member of the team," she said. "Sheila Stratford, Hazel Thornbull from our office in Tresham, and Bridie Reading, Hazel's mum." They all smiled and said welcoming things to Paula.

Last to arrive was Andrew Young, a cleaner on the team but also an interior designer who combined the two. The arrangement was a comparatively new development for Lois and had proved very successful. She was beginning to wonder if Andrew might one day soon give up cleaning and concentrate on what was, some would say, though probably not Gran, a more manly profession. So far, Andrew had insisted that he loved cleaning, was not gay, and found the two jobs complementary. He could drop in a commercial for his design business whilst polishing the silver, he joked.

One by one, the girls gave their reports. The previous week had been uneventful, until Bridie's report caused Lois some concern.

"All was going well, Mrs. M," Bridie said, "until I went to the pub in Waltonby on Friday. The new landlady there, Mrs. Coppice, is really nice, and we were having a quick cup of coffee halfway through the morning when the bell on the bar counter rang. Almost nobody comes in the pub on a Friday morning before midday, and Mrs. Coppice asked me to go through, saying it was probably a salesman on his rounds, and to get rid of him. I was to say she had popped out to a neighbour.

Lois happened to glance at Paula, and was alarmed to see her sway on her chair. "So what happened, Bridie? Was it a talent scout, wanting you to star in the next Bond movie?" Lois tried to keep her voice light. Bridie was known for her love of telling a good story.

"He weren't a salesman, for sure," Bridie said. "Big bloke, looked as he'd bin living rough. Filthy jacket, black hair needed cutting, black eyes that didn't look straight at you. Real shifty, he was. He asked if the missus had any jobs needed doin', and I said straightaway that we was fine and taken care of. Told him to try up the road at the farm, just to get rid of him, though I knew they'd not touch him with a barge pole. Gave me quite a turn though, and Mrs. Coppice insisted I took a very small brandy. Just tellin' you this, Mrs. M, in case somebody smelled alcohol on my breath in the afternoon and got the wrong idea."

The others listened spellbound. Wherever else Bridie was at fault, it was certainly not in the spinning of a good yarn. Lois turned to Paula, who had been staring at Bridie with a horrified expression.

"You did well, Bridie," she said, "and I reckon I would've needed a brandy in your place. Thanks for keeping us informed. It might be useful if he turns up anywhere else on our patch."

As the others drifted off after the meeting, Lois said quietly to Paula that she would like her to stay behind for a few minutes. When they were alone, she motioned her to a chair, and Paula sat down.

"You know who he was, don't you, Paula," Lois said. Best not to beat about the bush.

"It was him, my Jack," Paula said, her lip quivering. Her knuckles were white with the strain of keeping her hands steady. "He turned up at the hall this morning, when Mrs. Tollervey-Jones was out down the village. Luckily she came back before he could get at me. But he saw me, and he'll try again."

Then the strain was too much, and she covered her face with her hands. In a muffled voice she said that she would be going home now, and was really sorry that it had all come to an end before she'd had a chance to show what she could do.

"What d'you mean, come to an end?" Lois said. "Do you think I'd give you your cards just because of that? Blimey,

what kind of a person d'you think I am? No, you just sit here
and I'll get Gran to make us a cuppa. Take it easy, Paula.
You're a New Brooms team member now, and we'll stick by
you."

Reflecting that she sounded like a character from a bad
movie, Lois went off to the kitchen to persuade Gran.

"ALL WELL?" SAID DEREK WHEN HE CAME IN FOR LUNCH. HE
sniffed good smells and said he was starving. "Running up
and down stairs on the new rewiring job has given me an
appetite," he said, patting Gran on her shoulder. She smiled,
and said a bit of running up and down stairs would not do
Lois any harm.

"She's been sitting at her desk all morning," she said.

"How did the meeting go, me duck?" Derek gave Lois a
peck on the cheek, just to even things up.

"No so bad," Lois said. "Bit hairy at the end, when the
new woman—"

"Oh, yes," interrupted Derek, "the new woman. Paula
Hickson? Not trouble already?"

"No, not her," Lois said hastily, remembering that Paula
was a big mistake as far as Gran and Derek were concerned.
"I meant Bridie. She's back at work after her operation. Sort
of a new start."

"Nice try," said Derek. "Anyway, what happened?"

Lois gave them the gist of Bridie's story, and said that the
others had looked a bit alarmed. "Not Andrew, of course, but
the girls said they often have to answer the door, when clients
are out, an' that."

Gran shrugged. "There's always been tramps trudging
round the villages," she said. "I remember when I was a kid,
one bright moonlight night I heard this terrible singing.
More yelling than singing, it was. I got out of bed to look
out the window, and there was this man, drunk as a lord,

stumbling by in the middle of the road, and I was scared
stiff! I shot back into bed and pulled the covers over my head.
O' course, it was just some poor old sod on his way to the
workhouse."

Derek chuckled. "You and Bridie Reading," he said, "should
set up as a double act as storytellers. You could have a tent on
the playing fields for Soap Box Day."

"If you want your dinner," Gran replied huffily, "you'd
better sit down and be grateful, in case I decide to give it to
Jeems here. At least dogs don't answer back."

IN A DESERTED BRICK BARN ON A FIELD OUTSIDE WALTONBY, JACK
Hickson Sr. snored on a heap of dirty straw in a dark corner.
He had managed to coax a sandwich out of a scared housewife
up the road, and while she'd gone to make it he'd snitched a
couple of bottles of Old Best from the outside toilet. Funny
place to keep supplies, he'd thought, but very handy. Now he
whiled away the warm afternoon in an alcoholic doze. The
problem of where he would be next day had been postponed.
All he knew was that he had to keep moving, but never too
far away from Paula and the kids. Especially his namesake,
Jack Jr.

SEVENTEEN

᠎

AFTER THE MEETING ANDREW YOUNG HAD SET OFF ON FOOT to find Gavin Adstone's wife, Kate. There was nobody at home, and as he had not made an appointment he decided to wander about for a while. She couldn't have gone far, as a car was parked in the open garage.

Andrew had met Gavin in the pub a couple of evenings ago, and in the course of conversation had mentioned his interior décor business. Gavin had said that his wife had been talking about giving the cottage a makeover. It was very dingy, he said, but as they'd been so busy with bringing up baby since they moved to the village, they hadn't had time to think about what they would want to do about decorating.

Now he walked briskly around the village, turning back into Church Street, and if she had returned, he intended to say he had just been at a meeting in the village and thought he would look in as he was passing. There had obviously been some kind of family service in the church, and knots of young mothers with pushchairs and small hangers-on were grouped on the pavement. Andrew had no idea what Kate Adstone looked like, so kept going until he reached the cottage. He knocked at the door, and heard a shout from behind him. An attractive, dark-haired girl was running towards him, the pushchair bumping over the uneven pavement.

"Looking for me?" she gasped, out of breath as she approached.

"Are you Kate?" Andrew asked.

He didn't look like a salesman, Kate thought. He was dressed casually, had curly dark hair, and an open smile. "Yes, I am. Can I help you?" she said.

Andrew explained that he had met Gavin in the pub, and that as well as cleaning for New Brooms he ran an interior décor business, and wondered if she would like to have a chat. Gavin had said they might be interested in brightening up their cottage.

"We had talked about it," she said. "He mentioned meeting you in the pub. But I think it would be best if you came when he was at home. He hates being left out! How about this evening? He usually gets back around half six. Would that be any good?"

"Fine," replied Andrew, abandoning his plan for an evening with a takeaway and a film. "I'll come around seven, shall I? Or half-past, maybe? We men always think better on a full stomach."

As he made his way back to his car, still parked outside Meade House, Andrew remembered Bridie Reading's dramatic story, and wondered who the poor sod was who'd been looking for work. It was a downwards spiral, being homeless, as he knew from his work in the Tresham shelter just up the road from his flat. No permanent address, so no job. Stealing money to buy alcohol and drugs was all part of the sad decline.

Andrew had been through bad times himself after his parents were killed in a car crash, and remembered only too

well the awful lethargy that overtook him when he should
have been out looking for a job, starting a new life. At least
he had had money to tide him over.

"COME IN, ANDREW." GAVIN ADSTONE SAID HEARTILY. HE STOOD
at the door of his cottage, authoritative and welcoming.

Aha, thought Andrew, he's been on a self-assertion course.
First rule: establish who is boss straightaway, especially when
someone is trying to sell you something.

"Hello," said Andrew. "Lovely evening. Nice of you to give
up some time to see me. I am sure we shall have an enjoyable
discussion, and if nothing comes of it, no matter. I shall have
gained a couple of friends, I hope!"

Kate appeared with small Cecilia in her arms. Andrew
made a clown face at the little one and raised a laugh. "Three
new friends, I should say," he said. He had been on a course
or two himself.

Eighteen

❧

"I saw Andrew Young in the pub," Derek said. He opened yet another junk mail envelope and added it to an untidy heap on the floor. "Talking to Gavin Adstone like they was old mates."

"Perhaps they are," Gran said. "And don't expect me to pick up them leaflets."

"Oops! Who's upset you this morning?"

"My darling daughter, if you must know."

"Lois? What's she done now?"

"Only offended my best friend, that's what. Told Joan Pickering that she hoped she'd give that Hickson woman a warmer welcome than the last new member of WI got."

"Paula Hickson? Is she joining the WI? Where's she going to find time, *and* the money to pay a babysitter?"

"No doubt New Brooms will subsidise her," Gran said bitterly. "Lois always did like a lame duck or two."

Derek looked at his watch. "Is Lois still upstairs? Time I went."

He walked out of the kitchen and called up the stairs. Lois's voice answered him from her office, and he stamped along the hallway to find her. "What the hell d'you think you're doin'?" he said. "You've had no breakfast, haven't said a word to me, and now it's time I went. And," he added angrily, "your mother is sulking in the kitchen. Seems you've upset her friend Joan."

"Not a bad morning's work so far, then," said Lois, with a smile. "Sorry, love. We'll talk at lunchtime. Something urgent I just had to see to. 'New Brooms Sweeps Cleaner,' as you know."

Derek sighed. "Just as well I love you, Lois Meade," he said, and disappeared off to work in his van, while Lois went to placate Gran in the kitchen.

"Mum," she began, "would you do something for me?"

"I don't feel much like it," Gran said without looking at her.

"Yeah, well, it's important," Lois said. "And confidential."

This did the trick, and Gran said she supposed she would help if she could.

"I need to find out where that rough bloke is. The one who frightened Bridie."

"So?"

"So you've got friends in the village, and a sharp eye. Can you ask around?"

"Why d'you need to know? Is it him has been trying to burn down the village hall? Maybe breaking in to find shelter at night? Lighting a fire, like they do, and it getting out of hand?"

"Possibly," said Lois. Maybe Gran was on to something here. The last case she worked on with Cowgill involved gypsies. Now tramps? She shook herself, as if to get rid of unwholesome thoughts, and changed the subject.

"Derek's SOS meeting is tonight, so we'd better have supper early," she said.

"I'd already thought of that," Gran said. "And you'll be

pleased to know that Joan Pickering plans to sling a banner across the hall for WI tomorrow. 'Welcome Paula Hickson,' it says."

Lois hooted with laughter. "All right, you win," she said.

"I ain't yer mother for nuthin," Gran said. "Now leave me to get on. An' pick up those leaflets off the floor. I'm too old to be bending down clearing up after your husband."

THE SAVE OUR SHED COMMITTEE SAT IN A HALF CIRCLE IN THE Reading Room. Derek had drawn the blinds against a fierce low sun, and there was a feeling amongst them that some good progress had been made. Floss had been down to the Youth Club and talked to the kids. All had been strongly enthusiastic about the soap box racing, and had started thinking about what they would build.

"The rest of it, they said," Floss reported, "could be left to the oldies. 'Let them have their cake stalls and craft bits and pieces, and knittin' an' that.' Those were their very words," she added, with a sideways look at Gavin Adstone.

To the surprise of the rest of the committee, Gavin commented pleasantly that he was really pleased about that. It was so important to involve the young people in a village, otherwise it became a community of pensioners.

"And what's wrong with pensioners?" grunted Tony Dibson.

"Nothing at all," Gavin said hastily. He had worked out— and was keeping to himself for the moment—a major strategy for the SOS fund-raising day, and he needed to keep all persons on the committee on his side.

"How would we feel about a subcommittee dealing with the soap box side of it?" he said to Floss. "I would be very happy to organise that, with you, perhaps, Floss?" He smiled at her and saw from her expression that he still had some way to go before she joined the Gavin Adstone fan club.

Derek thought for a moment. He was well aware that

Gavin was up to something, and he had to be quick-witted to forestall him.

"Thanks for offering," he said, "but I reckon committees are bad enough, and subcommittees worse. We're all involved here, and all of us want a hand in the way the whole day is organised. After all, some of us remember the Farnden soap box racing from years ago. What say we try our best to stage the same again? There'd be more point to it then." There were enthusiastic nods of agreement.

Gavin frowned and said, "But we have to abide by Health and Safety. That'll make a big difference."

"It can be absorbed," said Derek confidently. "Now, shall we take a vote on a subcommittee as proposed by Gavin? Those in favour?" Only Gavin raised his hand. "And those against? Right, that's that, then. Shall we move forwards? Item three: entry forms."

Gavin opened his mouth to speak. Entry forms were part of his strategy. But he was interrupted by the vicar. "I'll take care of that, if you tell me what's required," said Father Rodney. "I've got the copier in the vicarage, so I can print as many as you like."

Tony raised his hand. "Mr. Chairman," he said, "I could get together with the reverend on that. I've still got a form from those old days somewhere. Kept it as a souvenir, after *Blunderbuss II* won the last grand prix." He turned to Floss. "That were my old gal. Me and my dad put her together out of this and that. Went like the wind, she did."

"Your 'old gal' was not, presumably, your wife?" Gavin looked round for a laugh, but none came. People in the village didn't make jokes about Tony's wife in a wheelchair.

DEREK WALKED BACK TOWARDS THE PUB WITH JOHN THORNBULL, and they agreed that the meeting had gone well. "Feels like we're on a roll now," John said. "If we can keep that Gavin chap under control. You know what, Derek?" he added. "I reckon we ought to give him a job, something that'll sound important but not interfere with our idea of re-creating the old soap box grand prix. What d'you think?"

"Good idea," said Derek. "But what job?"

"Dunno," said John. They turned into the pub doorway, and John added that ideas always seemed to come more easily after a pint. "Let's see what we can come up with," he said, and walked up to order the beer.

JOSIE SAW THEM GO BY AS SHE WORKED IN THE SHOP STACKING shelves. It had been a busy day, and several items needed replenishing. She had the local radio station on as she worked, and paused to listen to the news. The first item was an unpleasant one: "Police are searching for witnesses who can help them with the identity of the body of a man found in the canal behind the Tresham Industrial Estate. They have released the following details: The man is in his late thirties, heavily built, with long hair and clothes in poor condition." Details of the police number and assurances of confidentiality followed, and then the newsreader moved on to the latest case of vandalism at the supermarket.

"Some poor down-and-out," Josie said to her mother, who had just come in through the back door into the stockroom. "Probably drunk out of his mind on meth and missed his footing. Ended up headfirst in the canal. Anybody falling into that sewer wouldn't stand much of a chance."

Her mother's reaction surprised her. "What's the time?" she asked. "There'll be local telly news in a minute. Let's go up to the flat and put it on. Come with me, Josie, I don't want to miss anything."

"Mum! Don't be so ghoulish! One of them no-hopers loses it most weeks. Sad thing is, nobody cares and nobody misses 'em. Sometimes they stay in there for weeks. Nothing for you to get fussed about."

"Don't argue," Lois said sharply. "Just come. Now."

By the time they got the television on, the story was heading the bulletin. "Oh, look!" Josie said. "There's Matthew, giving the report!"

"Sssh!" Lois snapped.

"Ah," Josie continued, "isn't he lovely? Look at those eyes, Mum . . ."

Lois glared at her, and said that if she didn't shut up and listen, she personally would see that Matthew Vickers was transferred to a remote police station in the Highlands of Scotland.

NINETEEN

⨯

So here's a pretty kettle of fish," Cowgill said to Lois. They were sitting in his car in a deserted cul-de-sac on the far side of Tresham. "We have the body of a drowned man, with all the signs of being a homeless drunkard who fell into the canal in the dark. He'd not been there long, but long enough. We've had no calls, not from witnesses or anxious relatives or friends reporting a missing man. The shelter people say they get a lot of such unfortunates who come in once or twice and are never seen again. In short, Lois my dear, we could wrap this up pretty quickly."

"Except for me?" Lois frowned.

"That's right. You say you might know who he is, but are not going to tell me. That right?"

"Not yet," Lois said. "Sorry to spoil your day. But too bad. Of course, one more drowned tramp is neither here nor there to you. I might know who he is, but I need to find out a lot more details before I tell you. And before you say it, I know

I am breaking some law or other. But tough. There are other people involved in this, including children."

Cowgill sighed. "So how long do you want?"

"A few days. Don't really know yet. Listen, Hunter—"

His heart missed a beat. Stupid old fool, he charged himself. What's in a name? Everything to him. In all the time he'd known her he could count on the fingers of one hand the number of times she had used his Christian name.

"I'm listening, Lois dear," he said, with a fatuous grin.

"Oh, for heaven's sake!" Lois said. "I was going to say that surely by now you trust me? Haven't I always come up with the goods when it was the right time? So, give me a few days, and I'll be in touch."

"All I can say is that I won't press you to tell me. Naturally, my team will be carrying on their investigations in the usual way. If we discover something you might need to know, I'll ring you, as always."

"Huh!" Lois was only too well aware that Cowgill, who, after all, was a top cop, told her exactly as much as he thought fit, whilst he expected her to tell him everything. Well, in this case it would be different. If the body was that of Jack Hickson Sr., then she was determined to help Paula and her children as much as possible. That might not amount to much, but at least, with luck, she could give her a warning and perhaps a little time.

"I must go," she said now, opening the car door. "No, I don't want a lift. I got the bus here and I'll get it back into town. My car's in the multistorey. See you."

Cowgill sat in his car for a long while after she had gone. He wondered what he would do if he retired and had little hope of seeing Lois again for any longer than a brief chat on the street on Tresham market day. Then he remembered Matthew, his nephew. If his romance with Josie blossomed into marriage, then he'd have every reason to be in touch as often as he liked!

Greatly cheered, he started the engine and drove back to his office. Never mind about old tramps in the canal, he thought. I'll put my mind to fostering certain nuptials, and if it works I'll retire with good grace.

PAULA HICKSON WAS BACK AT FARNDEN HALL, ON THE LAST stretch of mopping the large expanse of tiled floor at the entrance. She glanced nervously from time to time through the long windows and down the drive. She had seen the news, of course, and had been so shocked that it wasn't until at least an hour later that common sense had returned, and she considered the likelihood of the drowned man being her missing husband. Tresham was a big town, almost a city, she told herself. There must be dozens of such poor souls tramping the streets. She had seen them herself, but mostly the cleaned-up ones who shivered on corners offering the *Big Issue* for sale. Although she had no money to spare and the newspaper was now more than a pound, she always slipped them fifty pence. There, but for the grace of God and Social Services, go I, she thought.

"Ready for coffee, Mrs. Hickson?" Mrs. Tollervey-Jones did not believe in familiarity with servants, and for two pins would leave out the "Mrs." But her grandchildren had told her that this would be unforgivable.

Paula put her mop temporarily into the bucket and headed for the empty kitchen. There were never matey chats with this client! In any case, she had been told by Lois that her cleaners were allowed a ten minute break but were not to be seduced into a gossip. Unless, of course, the talk concerned a matter that Lois had in passing suggested might be of interest to her. . . .

It was quiet in the kitchen, and the old dog snoozed in her basket. Paula wondered if she should open the door into the yard. With the Aga ticking over all winter and summer, it was too hot now, with the sun streaming in through the windows. She finished her coffee quickly, and went down the corridor, through the swinging green baize door and returned to finish the last one or two tiles.

"All well?" said Mrs. Tollervey-Jones, standing at the top of the curving staircase. "I thought you looked a bit peaky last time. Must be difficult for you, coping without a husband and with those boys of yours." Paula was surprised. The old woman had seemed remote, uninterested in her, but here she was, knowing all about Paula and with a sharp eye, missing nothing.

"I'm fine, thank you," Paula said. "I do have a husband, by the way. He's just not with us at the moment."

"Upside down in the canal, possibly," said Mrs. Tollervey-Jones bluntly, and swept down the stairs and into the drawing room, from whence came sounds of a piano being played with what Paula reckoned was a pretty nifty pair of hands.

Why did she say that? Surely she wouldn't be so cruel deliberately? Paula wondered whether she could ask Mrs. M to transfer her to another client, but immediately rejected the thought. Difficult as it might prove to be, the hall was a magic place to work. Then, for the first time it occurred to Paula that if the dead body *was* Jack, then she need never look anxiously down the drive again. She stood stock-still, leaning on the mop, overcome with the desire to weep.

"Why don't you pack up, now, Mrs. Hickson. Get along home." Mrs. Tollervey-Jones had not meant her tactless remark to be taken to heart, and hearing muffled sounds, had returned and tried to make amends. She was careful not to look at Paula, but asked her if next time she came, would she like to have a try at flower arranging? "Heaps of them in the kitchen garden, just for picking," she said. "Whenever I do them, they end up looking like a bunch of carrots."

Paula finished everything she had been told to do, and asked if there was anything else. Reassured that her work had been excellently done, she went out to her car and chugged off down the drive. Her mobile rang and she stopped to answer it.

"Paula? Mrs. M here. Could you spare me a few minutes before you go home? Good. See you then."

TWENTY

❧

"SIT DOWN, PAULA," LOIS SAID. "YOU ALL RIGHT?"

Paula nodded. She wasn't all right at all, but was desperate to keep in control in front of her new boss. "Yes, thanks," she said. "I had a good morning at the hall. Mrs. Tollervey-Jones has asked me to do the flowers next time I go. Is it allowed?"

"Sure. If you can make a good job of them. Thank goodness she's never asked me!"

"I went to classes several years ago. Before I was married."

"Ah," said Lois. "Now, that's why I asked you to drop in. I expect you saw the news? About the man in the canal?"

Paula nodded. "It's not him, o' course. Not my Jack." She felt her heart begin to race and couldn't catch her breath. "You've not heard nothing?"

"No, not much more than you already know," Lois said. "But if you could tell me about your Jack, I can probably do some checking."

"What d'you want to know?"

"Everything," Lois said. "Where you met, married, lived.

But first, what does he look like? Tall, short, dark, fair, bald . . . ?" She was careful to put him in the present tense, to consider him alive rather than dead. Paula's "my Jack" was a giveaway that she still felt something for him, surely.

"He's a good-looking bloke, or was, before he went on the drink and began to neglect himself. Tall, big built, dark hair cut short. Or should be. It was his eyes that I first noticed. Not often you see such black eyes. Well, I know they can't be really black, but they're quite scary sometimes."

"What was his work?"

"He was a gardener, worked for the borough in the parks an' that. Loved it. But they started laying men off, last in first out, and he'd not been there long. We came from Bedford, where he'd had the same kind of job."

"Why did you move to Tresham?"

"His old mum. She was very poorly, an' he wanted to be near to help. Only child, was—is—Jack. She died soon after we'd moved here, so it was a bad decision as it turned out. He tried to get back to the Bedford job, but they'd filled his position, so we just stayed on in Tresham."

"Bad luck," said Lois. "Had he ever had any trouble at work? You know, quarrels with workmates, an' so on?"

Paula shook her head. "He was popular. Good at making friends. He really liked the job after being there a good while. Then he was made redundant, and his friends tried to get him taken back but no luck. Then he began to change. You know the rest."

"Last question, then we'll have a coffee. Has he got any marks on him, you know, birthmarks or scars or moles? Sorry, Paula, but it's important."

Paula looked at her suspiciously. "Why d'you need to know that? Who are you goin' to talk to?"

Lois sighed. "A friend in the police," she said, and Paula's face took on a stubborn look.

"Oh, no. Not the police, Mrs. M. I don't want no truck with them."

"You might have to," Lois said. "You'd rather tell me than some young cop, wouldn't you?"

Paula was silent for a few minutes, and Lois walked over to the window, deliberately looking away.

"He's got an appendix scar." Paula's voice was very quiet. "Had it out when he was a kid. Scar's still there, though."

Lois turned around. "Thanks," she said. "Come on, let's go and find Gran. She'll fill you in on the excitements of the WI tonight."

"WE STILL SING 'JERUSALEM,'" SAID GRAN, MAKING AN EFFORT. She was still convinced that Lois was making a big mistake employing this woman, but was not able to be rude to her face. "Not very well, o' course. And the piano in the village hall is terrible. Sometimes only about half the notes work. Mostly we sing without."

"I like singing," Paula said.

"Yes, well, then we have the business of the meeting. That takes some time, with Mrs. T-J liking the sound of her own voice. Then we have a speaker or someone demonstrating cookery or needlework, or some such."

"What is it tonight, Mum?" Lois said.

"We got a police dog handler coming. It was Sheila Stratford's idea. Says they got good stories to tell, about dogs catching villains an' holding on to 'em with their teeth. I reckon it sounds a bit bloodthirsty, but still . . ."

Paula gulped down hot coffee and said she really must be going. She had shopping to do, and then it would be time to fetch Frankie.

Lois saw her out, and then returned to the kitchen. "Well done, Mum," she said. "That sent her packing."

Gran sniffed and said, "I don't know what you mean, Lois. But then," she added, "I seldom do."

KATE ADSTONE SHUT THE FRONT DOOR AND LOCKED IT, THEN maneuvered the pushchair down the narrow path and set out for the shop. Cecilia was fast asleep, and Kate, seeing that the shop door was wedged open, parked the pushchair outside and went in.

"Hi, Kate," Josie said cheerfully.

"Is it all right to leave Cecilia out there? You hear such terrible stories of babies being stolen."

"Bring her in if you're worried," Josie said. "I very much doubt if there's any baby snatchers in Farnden this afternoon, but most mums bring the babies in."

Kate returned to Cecilia and met Paula Hickson coming across to the shop.

"Can I give you a hand?" Paula said, and together they lifted the pushchair into safety.

"Just being silly," Kate said apologetically.

"Better safe than sorry," Paula said. "You first, Mrs. Adstone. You were here first."

Kate looked at her closely. "Haven't we met somewhere before?" she said. "Excuse me if I'm being cheeky, but I'm sure we've met."

"Probably seen me around the village," Paula said. "I'm working for New Brooms now."

Kate frowned. "No, it wasn't in the village. Did you work in Tresham at all?" She paused, then said quickly, "Ah, I've got it. Do you remember fishing a small child out of the lily pond in the park? I went to pull him out. You were talking to one of the gardeners and then you dashed to help me. Surely you remember?"

Paula smiled broadly. "Yep, I remember. It wasn't that deep, was it? But the child and its mum had a nasty fright.

'Course I remember now. Nice to see you again, Mrs. Adstone. Sorry I didn't recognize you. And this is your little girl?"

Kate nodded. "So you're living in the village? Children?"

Paula said yes, four boys, and they chatted on.

Looking round the two mums, Josie saw a strange man get out of a car and stare up at the shop. She interrupted the conversation and said could she help anybody? Had Kate seen these new children's biscuits? "No additives," she said encouragingly. Early on in her shopkeeping career, she had discovered that nothing was more off-putting to new customers than having to fight their way through gossiping villagers.

He was a bulky, formally dressed man, and he marched straight up to the counter. "Do you have a local paper?" he said.

Josie handed him the *Tresham Advertiser* and put the money in the till. "Are you new around here?" she said with her best welcoming smile.

"No," the man said. "Thank you," he added, and walked out of the shop, got back into his car and drove off.

"Talkative chap," said Kate, handing the biscuits to Josie. "Sounded foreign, didn't he?"

"Dutch," said Paula, and then asked if Josie had any more of those eggs from the farm up the road.

TWENTY-ONE

❧

THE EVENING WAS COOL AS GRAN WALKED SLOWLY DOWN TO the village hall for the WI meeting, and she was glad of her woolly cardigan.

"Elsie! Wait for me!"

Gran turned around and saw her friend Joan Pickering, hurrying along to catch up with her. "Lovely evening, Joan," she said with a smile. "Them stocks in your old garden are wonderful. Can you smell 'em?"

"I miss them," Joan said. "Still, that new woman was out there earlier, weeding and watering. She seems a nice sort. The children were playing happily and the baby crawled about the lawn."

"What about the biggest boy?" said Gran. "I bet he wasn't playing happily, or even there at all."

Joan laughed. "'Always look on the bright side of life,'" she hummed. "You know, Elsie, he could've been doing his homework."

"More likely wandering around Tresham with his no-good

friends," muttered Gran. "Anyway, she's coming to the meeting tonight. If she turns up. Apparently my granddaughter is babysitting for her. For free, if I know Josie."

"Perhaps we should call for her?"

"No," said Gran quickly. "She'll be there already, I expect. Come on, else we'll be too late for 'Jerusalem.'" The two of them laughed, and quickened their pace until they reached the hall.

Mrs. Tollervey-Jones sat at a table covered with a green cloth decorated with the WI badge, rapped with her pen, and called the meeting to order. "Good evening, ladies," she said benevolently.

"Good evening, Mrs. Tollervey-Jones," chorused the women, for all the world like a bunch of infants in reception class.

"First of all," Mrs. T-J continued, "I would like to welcome a new member, Mrs. Paula Hickson. Welcome, Paula. So glad you have decided to join us. Anything you would like to know about the WI, don't hesitate to ask. And our treasurer will be after you later for your subscription!"

A flutter of laughter came from the semicircle of women. Their treasurer was known to be a terror for collecting the subs, and then was very loath to spend them.

The business of the meeting was then conducted, with only one or two interruptions. Paula got the impression that Mrs. T-J ran the whole thing, and did not welcome suggestions or objections. She glanced to her left, where her colleague Sheila Stratford, also on New Brooms' team, sat comfortably looking out of the window, obviously listening to none of it.

Eventually, when a scratch rounders team had been raised, representatives for the County Scrabble Competition appointed, and a decision on who should go to the AGM at the Albert Hall in London once more postponed, Mrs. T-J got to her feet. She looked down at the patient policeman in uniform sitting next to her, his German Shepherd dog perfectly well behaved at his side, and said that she had great pleasure in introducing James Smith. "Dog handler extraordinary," she added with a deep chuckle.

"I'LL SAY THIS FOR 'IM," GRAN SAID, SIPPING HER WI TEA AND nibbling a slightly soft digestive biscuit, "he knew his stuff. I reckon everyone was riveted, didn't you, Joan?"

"Well, I was," Joan Pickering answered, but her attention was elsewhere. "Come on, Elsie," she said. "That new woman's all on her own, nobody talking to her. Come *on*," she repeated. "You know what your Lois said."

Paula smiled as they approached. "That was interesting," she said, though Gran noticed her hands were tightly clenched.

"You haven't got any tea," Joan said. "I'll get you a cup."

"No thanks," Paula said. "I don't drink tea. Doesn't suit me. Thanks, anyway."

"Did you like the video?" Gran said slyly. "Specially that bit where the dog caught the tramp stealing food from a garden bird-table! That *was* exciting, wasn't it! What a nerve! Deserves all he got."

"What would he've got, Mrs. Weedon?" Paula said. "Maybe a night banged up in a cell would have been better than sleeping in a smelly doorway?" Her voice was shaky, and Joan Pickering intervened.

"Tell us about your boys, Paula," she said. "That little tot is a real charmer! I help out some mornings at the playgroup, and he's bright as a button."

And so Gran's unpleasant remarks passed, and Paula relaxed. As she walked home afterwards with the two of them—Joan Pickering had insisted—she wondered if Mrs. Weedon knew about Jack Sr. Would Mrs. M have told her? She doubted it, but this nasty old woman would be quite capable of picking up bits of info from here and there. She was always hanging about outside Mrs. M's office door when Paula had been in there.

"How was it for you?" Josie said with a grin, as Paula arrived home.

"Not bad," Paula said. "Thanks a lot for looking after the boys. No trouble, I hope?"

"Little lambs," Josie said. "Makes me think children are not such a bad idea after all."

Paula laughed. "Maybe you should try it," she said. "Now, how much do I owe you?"

"Don't be daft," said Josie. "Just keep shopping at my shop," she said. "That'll do well."

"Any messages?" Paula said, trying to sound casual.

"Oh, yes—I almost forgot. The phone went, and I answered it. It was for Jack Jr. A man's voice. I called Jack, but he yelled down from his room that he was too busy with his homework. He'd ring back later."

"Did the man leave a name?" Paula said, anxious now.

Josie shook her head. "Nope. Just put down the phone when I gave him Jack's message. I hope I did right?"

"Oh, yeah. It'd be one of his teachers, I expect. Probably wanting to know where he is most of the time when he should be in school. He's a problem, Josie. But still," she added, doing her best to smile, "I don't want to put you off kids! And thanks again. I'll do the same for you, one day."

AFTER JACK HAD REFUSED TO SPEAK TO HIM, THE MAN SWORE AT the waste of money hard come by, and went out of the phone box into the street. He looked up and down the empty street and decided to take the Tresham road out of the village. No rain tonight, he judged, and set off for last year's straw stack in a field bordering the road. He had noticed a reasonably clean spring that bubbled up there and fed a running stream that led to the river. In his rucksack he had a couple of stale bread rolls retrieved from a wheelie bin at the back of the shop, and with what was left of a hunk of cheese from the night shelter, he reckoned he would be fine until tomorrow, when he intended to put Plan B into action.

PAULA CLIMBED THE STAIRS WEARILY, HOPING THAT TONIGHT SHE would drop off to sleep straightaway, before the onslaught of old worries crowded in the moment she shut her eyes.

"Mum!" It was Jack Jr., still fully dressed, standing in his doorway, pale and tired looking.

"Time you were in bed," she said sternly. "You're not even undressed. Get into your 'jamas straightaway. Then if you ever reach school tomorrow, at least you'll have had some sleep."

"Mum!" He put out his hand towards her and burst into tears.

"Jack! For heaven's sake, what's the matter? Here, come into my room. You'll wake the others. Come on, get moving."

It was some while before he stopped the wrenching sobs that shook his thin body, and Paula's anxiety mounted. Finally he stopped, shrugged himself free of her comforting hug, and sat on the edge of the bed. There were dark shadows beneath his red-rimmed eyes, and her heart bled for him.

"It was a bloke who gets kids to buy things," he said in a croaky voice. "On the phone. I didn't speak to him. That shop lady told him I was doing my homework."

"What things?"

"He hangs around outside the school. Offers kids what he says are sweets. They're not, o' course. Uppers, downers, you name it. Some kids sell 'em on."

"Are you sure it was him?"

Jack frowned. "Who else?" he said.

"Could have been your father," she said reluctantly.

Jack shook his head. "Why should he ring me?" he asked bitterly. "No, it was either this drug dealer bloke or the school police. I'm not scared of them, Mum, but I am of him. Can't you get him to leave me alone? He was outside the school gates the other day, waiting for me."

"When? Which day?" said Paula urgently.

Jack shook his head. "Can't remember," he said. "Anyway, I ran into school. Jonathan was with me, and we scarpered. Jonathan's never had no truck with him, and I guess he just buggered off."

Paula sat down beside him and took his hand in both of hers. "Jack, try and remember which day."

"Does it matter?"

"Yes. It could matter a lot," she said.

TWENTY-TWO

࿅

A MESSAGE FROM LOIS AWAITED COWGILL WHEN HE REACHED his office next morning. He had been out of town, visiting his sister Eva, who was in hospital after what her daily help described as "having it all out, dear." He felt somewhat bruised after a day of tea and sympathy.

Eva had once more given him a dozen sensible suggestions why the two of them should set up house together, and he had given her his usual evasive answer. The idea appalled him. When his wife had been alive, she wasn't a very warm companion, but it had taken him quite a while to get used to being alone. Now he had achieved a more or less satisfactory solitary life, making decisions that affected him only. His work occupied most of his time, and he had taken up golf which, although he was a late comer to the game, worked its addictive magic on him. He played most weekends, and told himself he was improving.

Now he dialled Lois's number and waited. He saw that her message was timed at three thirty yesterday, and swore. He hoped it was not too late, knowing that she would never call him unless it was something important.

"You took your time," Lois said, without introductory pleasantries.

He explained that he had been away on a mercy errand, and had just arrived back in his office. "How can I help you, Lois?" he said. Apart from inviting you to rush down here straight into my waiting arms, he added to himself.

"More like me helping you. It's a vital piece of information. I don't want questions, Cowgill. Just listen to this: an appendix scar from childhood, but still clear to see."

"Got it," he said firmly.

"I don't suppose you're any further forwards on the identity of the body in the canal?"

"No time to check yet," he said. "But I'll be in touch immediately I know more."

He was about to thank her warmly, when she snapped, "Do that," and rang off.

She turned off her computer, tidied her desk, and went through to the kitchen to tell Gran she was off to the shop. She knew Josie had been babysitting for Paula, and wanted to check that all had gone well. Gran had come home last evening from WI full of the dog-handler policeman. "He'd got this video, Lois," she had said. "Great bits of film chases with the dog catching the villain. Better than the telly! Specially the one with the vagrant. The dog made a great rip in his trousers when he tried to run away! Still, the trousers was in rags anyway, and it served him right."

Lois had lost her temper then, and had called her mother a narrow-minded old bag and other names, and the two of them had yelled at each other with Derek vainly trying to keep the peace. Now they were scarcely speaking, both being reluctant to back down.

"Going down the shop," Lois said. "Anything we need?"

"No," said Gran. "I'm well organised."

Lois was just leaving the house when the phone rang again. It was Mrs. Tollervey-Jones, and Lois's heart sank. It was going to be that kind of day. It couldn't be Paula again, because it was Floss's day at the hall.

"Mrs. Meade? Bit of a drama here. Your Floss has fallen off a stepladder. Turning out the kitchen cupboards, as arranged. Yes, she's hurt her ankle. Says she can't drive home. Be here within the next half hour, please. I have to go to a meeting in Tresham. Goodbye."

THE ACCIDENT & EMERGENCY UNIT AT TRESHAM HOSPITAL WAS crowded. It was always crowded, and as Lois looked around for a seat for Floss, she realised they were in for a long wait. There were no spare seats, but a man got up and offered his to hobbling Floss. He was holding a hand over one eye, and nodded to them. "Nothing much wrong with me," he said. "Just a wretched mote in my eye."

"Thanks. But what did you say?" asked Floss, sinking gratefully into his chair. She winced as she caught her foot in the chair leg, and Lois patted her on the shoulder.

"It's in the Bible," she said, noticing the man's dog collar. "Don't worry, Floss. Think of beautiful things."

"Like what?" said Floss.

"Hot coffee and chocolate cake," Lois answered, and the reverend said no sooner said than done.

"Though chocolate cake is not a comforter mentioned in the Bible, so far as I am aware," he said bravely, and set off towards the refreshment counter. There was a queue, and Lois saw that he couldn't possibly carry a full tray with one hand. She told Floss to stay put, and followed him.

Floss tried hard to ignore the pain shooting up her leg, and looked around the room. There were two lads joshing each other, apparently fit and well, an old lady sobbing quietly into her handkerchief, a small, pale child held tight in her mother's arms. And a tramp, bowed over in his chair, one hand held out, slowly dripping blood into a small puddle on the floor.

"Nurse!" said Floss, as a harassed girl passed by.

She stopped and looked at Floss. "We'll get to you sooner or later," she said.

"No, not me," Floss replied quickly before the nurse could move on. "It's that man over there." She pointed to the tramp. "He needs help."

"Everybody here needs help," the nurse snapped. "He'll wait his turn. He's a regular, that one."

"You could at least mop up the blood," Floss said crossly. "And give him some tissues. You got tissues in this hospital?"

The nurse didn't reply, but walked over to the tramp, said something, and disappeared.

"Here we are then," said the reverend, appearing with Lois, who carried a tray of mugs and chocolate muffins. "This should put new heart into us."

"Sorry about that Bible thing," Floss said. "New one on me. 'Mote,' did you say? Must be very painful. Do you want a turn at sitting down?" The reverend protested that he was really a fraud and her need was greater than his.

As Floss took her coffee from Lois, she balanced it with the muffin and looked up to thank her, but Lois was staring across the room at the tramp. Floss was about to tell her about her conversation with the nurse, when Lois began to walk towards him. At that moment, a different nurse appeared and took the tramp by the arm. He struggled to his feet, and they vanished into the depths of the hospital.

JACK JR., LURKING OUT OF SIGHT OF THE BUS SHELTER, HAD SEEN Lois drive her van off towards the hall and shrugged in a resigned way far beyond his years. He'd missed the bus again, deliberately this time. He dreaded that he would be met at the other end with more appeals to take sweets, gum, cigarettes, other stuff. He hoped to get a lift and by not arriving on the bus he would be able to slip into school without being noticed.

Now, nearly into Tresham, dawdling along with his head down, he heard a vehicle coming. No good. It was going the wrong way, and he recognized the New Brooms van. He ducked into a gateway and hid behind the hedge, but too late. The van stopped and he heard Mrs. Meade's voice calling his name. He didn't move, hoping she would go away.

"Ah, there you are." She was standing by the open gate, staring at him. "Just what do you think you're doing?"

"Walkin' to school," he grunted. "None o' your business."

"Don't you speak to me like that!" Lois said, advancing on him. She took him by the arm and marched him to the van. Thrusting him into the backseat, she climbed in and began to reverse into the gateway.

"What're you doing, Mrs. M?" Floss said. "He lives in Farnden, opposite the shop."

"I know that," Lois said. "And he knows I know that." She maneuvered the van, put on the brake and turned off the engine. "Now," she said, "first you apologise, then you tell us exactly why you're causing your mother so much worry and trouble."

Silence from the backseat. Then, to Floss's horror, she heard a very loud, rasping fart. To her amazement, Lois burst out laughing. "Good God, boy," she said, "you don't think that's goin' to shock me, do you? I ain't brought up two good lads for nothing!" She turned round in her seat and looked at the sullen face. "How old are you, Jack?" she asked.

The boy was discomforted. He'd hope to be turned out and left to his fate, but this hadn't happened. "Thirteen," he said. "Nearly fourteen."

"Can I open the window?" Floss said. She had no idea what Mrs. M had in mind, but wished she would get on with it. The painkillers were beginning to wear off, and she wanted to be home with her leg up. And the smell was awful.

Lois opened the windows, allowing a welcome rush of

fresh air. "Nearly fourteen, eh," she said. "And the eldest? The man of the family?"

"I'm not! My dad is the man of the family," Jack said, his face bright red. "Or should be, if he hadn't taken off and left us in the shit."

"Maybe he'll be back?" Lois silently put her finger to her lips, asking Floss to be silent.

"Not my dad! Mum wouldn't have him." Jack thought for a moment, and decided a little honesty would go down well. "An' yes, I am scared of going to school. There's this man who lies in wait for me."

"Who d'you mean? Where does he lie in wait?"

"Dunno who he is. He's every bloody where. Mostly outside school. Meets the bus. Us kids are too scared to tell the school. Let me go now, missus. I'm gonna be hours late as it is. I'm in for more lectures on truancy, more extra homework . . ."

"Mrs. M," Floss said quietly. She could hear tears in the boy's voice. "Couldn't we run him into Tresham, back to school? Poor kid's had enough, I reckon."

"What d'you think, Jack? Shall we let you walk the rest, or drop you outside school?"

"Take me to school," the boy said quickly, "an' wait 'til I'm inside."

Lois started the van, and they cruised along the Tresham road in silence. As they neared the school, she said, "I'm going to have to tell your mother, Jack. This can't go on, y'know. He can be stopped."

"Mum knows. And we don't want the police! He's got friends, and they'd kill me."

Lois stopped outside the school gate and reached behind her seat. She took hold of his hand. It was cold and the nails were bitten down to the quick. Nearly fourteen, she reminded herself. A child still.

"Get going, then," she said, and then, as an afterthought, shouted after him, "You know where I live."

On the way back, they said nothing for a while, and then Floss cleared her throat. "It isn't right, is it, Mrs. M? It isn't fair."

"No, it isn't," said Lois. "D'you think I should mind my own business, Floss?"

"Are you serious?" said Floss. "That kid needs help. His mum works with us now, and everybody knows you're well in with the cops. You're probably his best hope. Couldn't we all help?" she added.

Lois frowned. "Against the rules, Floss," she said. "My own rules. Family first, then New Brooms, and a poor third comes my work with Inspector Cowgill. I don't think your Ben would think much of me if I involved you in a nasty court case. It could come to that, with witnesses an' that. No, you're a good soul, but all I ask is that you keep your eyes open for that boy's father. There may be no need for that now, but it's not certain yet. Now, here we are, gel, let's get you out and into the house. Then I'll phone your mum."

Joan Pickering was round at her daughter's house minutes after Lois's call, full of concern and plans for looking after Floss. "Just you be more careful in future," Joan said, and with a sideways glance at Lois added that she didn't think turning out cupboards was part of the job description anyway.

"Don't fuss, Mum," Floss said. "There's worse things to worry about than a sprained ankle."

Twenty-Three

ॐ

THE REST OF THE WEEK HAD PASSED WITHOUT ANY UNDUE events. Lois and Gran had made friends, and had now decided that instead of going to Sunday church, Gran's preference, or weeding the flower beds, Lois's choice, they would do neither, but would take the little terrier Jeems out for a walk in the woods.

Lois had heard nothing from Cowgill, nor had she mentioned her encounter with Jack Jr. to his mother. If, as was possible, the drowned tramp had been Jack Sr., it was going to be tragic and difficult for the Hickson family, but no longer a dangerous threat. She had cautioned Floss to keep the whole thing to herself, promising to let her know if any solution suggested itself.

It was a beautiful morning, and the two set out with Jeems tugging eagerly at her lead. "Walk properly!" said Gran. She shortened the lead and the terrier immediately obeyed. "Pity some kids are not so easy as this little dog," she said reflectively.

"Meaning?" said Lois.

"That eldest Hickson boy," Gran said. "He was at the cricket match on the rec yesterday, fooling about with another boy—not from the village—and disturbing people who were trying to have a picnic and watch the match."

"What were they doing?"

"They'd got their bikes, and had made a track of hollows and bumps down by the hedge at the bottom of the field. Then they were riding as fast as possible, shrieking and yelling until they fell off. Wheelies, do they call it?" Gran could see from Lois's face that she did not think this a great crime, and decided to change the subject. She had no wish to start another quarrel with her daughter.

"How's Floss's ankle coming along?" she asked, as they climbed the stile and took the footpath into the wood.

"She says its much better," Lois said. "Mrs. Tollervey-Jones sent her a bunch of flowers! How's that for a changed character? Mind you, she's always been fond of Floss. I don't like the girls to get too close to the client, as you know. That's why I send Paula there alternately with Floss."

Gran thought of saying that she would bet a pound that Mrs. T-J wasn't as devoted to Paula Hickson as she was to Floss. But she bent down and released Jeems, who headed at once towards a rabbit hole.

"Damn!" she said. "Will she come out?"

"Don't worry. We can grab her tail," and saying this, Lois took hold of Jeems's rapidly waving tail and pulled her out backwards.

They strolled on, enjoying the dappled sunlight through the trees, until Gran stopped suddenly. "Who's that?" she whispered. She pointed to a figure seated on a stool with an easel in front of her, painting away, totally absorbed and unaware of their approach.

"It's that new woman," Lois whispered back. "They've bought one of Thornbull's old farm cottages for weekends.

She's in the wood most weeks. All weathers, apparently. Painting the trees. Doesn't like anybody talking to her. Lovely paintings, people say."

"No accounting for folk," said Gran, "though she looks friendly enough."

They walked on, talking idly about Jamie and his concert tour, and Douglas and Susie, and young Harry. They agreed they would do certain things differently in his upbringing, but also agreed that it was best not to interfere.

"I suppose you know the way? We're not lost are we?" Gran said, as Lois stopped and gazed around her.

"No. It's just there's something different about the bushes over there. Looks like somebody's made a hide of some sort."

"Bird-watchers," said Gran. "They're everywhere these days. You'd think birds couldn't exist unless someone watched them. Barmy lot, if you ask me. They should let the little dears get on with it, without bein' watched all the time. Enough to make them emigrate, I say."

"Just wait a minute. I'll go and look," Lois said, and pushed through the bracken. It was a rough hide, but not for bird-watchers. Ashes from a fire had been spread out neatly to make sure there were no smoldering cinders. A small wooden box turned upside down proved to be a mini-larder. In it, Lois found a plastic bottle of milk, half-full, and the remains of a loaf of white bread, both covered in protective wrap. Insulation, Lois supposed. She rewrapped them carefully and replaced the box.

"What was it?" Gran said, as Lois returned.

"Just a shelter for bird-watchers, like you said. Come on, let's see if we can find wild strawberries. There used to be some on the Waltonby side of the wood. Are you up to a bit of a trek?"

Gran bridled. "O' course I am! I'm used to plenty of exercise from being on me feet all day round the house, down to the shop, round to WI, over to Blackberry Gardens for coffee with Joan. It all adds up, you know. Not an ounce of spare fat on me. You must've noticed."

Lois had to admit that this was true. "But then, I *sit* at my computer, sit in my van, sit in the Tresham office, sit interviewing clients, and I weigh exactly the same as I did when I was twenty. How come, d'you reckon?"

"Nervous energy," Gran said confidently. "You worry it all away. Anyway, are you still sure we're on the right path? I can see a man over there, looks like he's got a gun."

"Morning, Mrs. Weedon, Mrs. Meade!" It was John Thornbull, and he explained swiftly that he was out shooting rabbits. "Pesky things!" he said. "Hazel is mad because they ate all the new lettuces before we'd had a single one. Funny thing, though, they took the whole plant out of the ground. One by one, they went. Never seen that before."

"Perhaps them rabbits had an order from Tesco's—lettuces on the vine, an' that," Lois said lightly, but in her mind she was beginning to see a pattern forming. Self-sufficiency, she thought. Whoever was the culprit, he was clever. Never in the same place two nights running, on the move. Locals might say it was the Green Man. She knew there were legends about this wood, with many sightings of a tall ghostly character with leaves for hair and a face carved out of wood. But she'd never heard tell of a Green Man living on half-liter plastic bottles of milk and sliced white bread.

"What's funny?" said Gran.

"Nothing much," Lois said, and then pointed excitedly at a green patch ahead. "Look! Strawberries. Come on, Mum. We can get cream from Josie on the way back and have them for pud."

JOSIE WAS ABOUT TO LOCK THE SHOP DOOR AS THEY APPROACHED. Sunday mornings she opened up, mainly for newspapers and sweets for the children, and now she looked forwards to an afternoon with Matthew Vickers. He was taking her over to his cottage to see his latest acquisition, a king-sized double bed. "One careful owner, good as new," he had said persuasively.

"We need cream, Josie. Look, we picked these in the wood. Just enough for lunch. Enough for you too, if you want to come up to the house?"

Josie explained about Matthew. "By the way," she said, "I've been meaning to tell you about my babysitting evening at Paula's."

"Troublesome children?" said Gran hopefully.

"No. It was this phone call, Mum. A man wanting young Jack. The lad wouldn't speak to him, and he rang off before I could ask who he was. Bit odd, I thought. I meant to tell you earlier."

"What was his voice like?" Lois said urgently. "Can you remember? Did it sound like he was disguising it?"

"Here we go!" said Gran. "You read too many crime books, me duck. She sees villains round every corner," she added to Josie. "Now, have you got any double cream left? We must let you get on."

Lois glared at her, but Josie produced the cream and saw them out of the shop. As they were setting off up the street, she called out, "Mum! Here a minute!"

Lois came back a few steps, and Josie said quietly, "He wasn't from round here. Up North, I would say. Any use?"

TWENTY-FOUR

◈

THE TINY WILD STRAWBERRIES VANISHED IN SECONDS, AND Derek ran his finger round the pudding plate appreciatively. "Nothing like these wild ones," he said. "The big buggers are all right, but nothing to compare with these."

"You can grow the little ones in the garden," Gran said.

"Wouldn't taste the same," Lois said. "Something to do with the soil, I suppose. It's all leaf mould in the wood. An' worms and grubs an that, keeping it fresh."

"Well, thanks," said Gran, making a face. "Glad I've finished mine!" She turned to Derek, and said that they'd met John Thornbull shooting rabbits. "And we found a bird-watching hide in the middle of the thicket," she added. "Lois tore her jeans goin' to investigate."

"Where was that, then?" Derek said.

"Over towards the Waltonby side," Lois said. "Just a bit of a shelter. Not doing any harm. I left it as I found it. They might've been watching badgers at night. There is a sett close by there."

"Better not tell John," Derek said. "He hates badgers more

than he hates rabbits! You'll not find a farmer say a good word about either of them."

"He knows," Gran said. "There's not an inch of that wood that John Thornbull don't know."

Lois wondered if this was true. If John knew about a man using that makeshift shelter as a hiding place, he might know more about him. She made a note to mention it to Hazel at the meeting tomorrow. By then, she should have heard from Cowgill about the body from the canal. He should have had a chance to check whether it had an appendix scar. If he did not ring her, she would ring him.

"What are you up to this afternoon?" Derek had planned an afternoon up at the allotment, but knew he should check with Lois, in case she had other ideas that would involve him.

"Nothing," she said. "Just pottering around. Might go down to the hall. They've got an exhibition of old photographs of the village, put on by the WI. Mum's on duty, aren't you?"

Gran nodded. "Three 'til four," she said. "Me and Joan an' that nice Doris Ashbourne from Round Ringford. They say she's lost without Ivy Beasley."

"Has she died?" Lois knew the old thing's reputation for a sharp tongue and a warm heart. She'd certainly been at the receiving end of the former, but never seen any evidence of a warm heart.

"Gone into an old folks' home," Gran said. "Miles away, in Suffolk. She's got a cousin living nearby, apparently, who organised it all. They say Doris gets letters from Ivy, not a bit unhappy and busy making changes to the place."

"Sounds about right," said Lois. "Perhaps Doris will go and live with her."

"Can't afford it, otherwise she would. So they say."

THE VILLAGE HALL WAS PLEASANTLY FULL OF PEOPLE, PEERING AT the photographs and exchanging memories. Gran and Joan

Pickering sat at a trestle table, taking entrance money and directing questions to Doris, who had lived in Ringford and around, including a few years in Farnden, and had known many of the people who smiled at the camera years ago.

Lois stood in front of a picture of her own house, taken when it was owned by Dr. Rix. She remembered when she was still living in Tresham and coming out to clean houses in Farnden village. Dr. Rix and his wife, Mary, had been her clients, and she had been involved in the tragedy that struck them.

"Penny for 'em," said a familiar voice. She turned around to see Hunter Cowgill, smartly dressed and smiling widely. "I love old photographs," he said, "so thought I'd come over and take a look."

Lois, for once, was speechless. She was quite sure he did not love old photographs. The only photographs he was interested in were mug shots of criminals. She found her voice and said exactly that. Cowgill laughed delightedly. "Chris! Come over here," he said, turning to beckon to his assistant. "You've met Lois, of course. She has a story to tell about this house." He pointed to the photograph.

"Isn't that where you live?" Chris said.

Lois nodded. "It's a long story," she said, "so some other time. Why don't you go and find the tea and coffee hatch? Then you could wander round and take your time."

Chris left them, aware that she had been got rid of, and made for the hatch, where Kate Adstone and Paula Hickson had taken over from Gran and were doing a roaring trade with refreshments.

"So?" hissed Lois. "Was it him?"

Cowgill nodded. "At least, the body has an appendix scar," he said quietly. "Can't say more here, except that without more description and perhaps a hint of who you think it might be, we haven't got a lot further forwards."

Lois managed a wintry smile. "Patience," she said. "An' if

you want to talk to me, you'd better think of somewhere better than a crowded village hall on a Sunday afternoon. Unless you got another reason for being here?"

He had, of course. He explained that he and Chris were observing, following up the arson attempt. It was one thing seeing the hall empty and quiet, but much more useful to watch how it operated when something was on. How people came and went, what check was kept on visitors, if any.

"And eavesdropping?" Lois said. "Always useful, listening in to other people's conversations. I've been known to stoop to that myself, but not lately. Now, I have to go. You've paid, I hope? All in aid of restoring the village hall, so extra donations welcome. I'll be in touch."

"Before you go, Lois, just remember that many people have appendix scars. I need more."

"Bye," Lois said, and disappeared off towards the kitchen, where Kate and Paula were surprised to hear her offer of help, but accepted gratefully.

"You go and have a look round, Paula," she said. "By the way, where are the children?"

"Down by the swings. Jack Jr.'s looking after them. He's good at that. I've told him to send one of the twins if he can't manage. It's only a hundred yards away, so I reckon they're quite safe."

"Better go and check," Lois said. "They get some rough characters on those swings."

"Don't alarm the poor woman," said Kate confidently. "A country village is not the same as the backstreets of Tresham. You used to live in Tresham, didn't you, Mrs. Meade?"

Lois did not deign to reply. She knew a snide remark when she heard one, and decided Mrs. Kate Adstone was not quite the anxious-to-please person she had thought her to be.

"Um, Mrs. M," Paula said. "I suppose you wouldn't just take a look, would you? Jack is more likely to take notice of you, if he isn't keeping a proper watch. The baby should be asleep in his pushchair, but . . ." She trailed off, and Lois said of course she'd go. She was used to teenage boys, she said, and walked quickly out of the hall.

As she set off towards the play area, she could see that there were no other children there, nor any watchful parents. Just the Hicksons. She began to quicken her step. She ended up half running, and saw with alarm a figure emerge from the hedge bordering the play area. It was a man, and he approached the tallest child, who was, of course, Jack Jr. Lois shouted out to him that she was coming, and ran full pelt towards the motionless, staring group of children.

The man heard her, and with an amazing turn of speed, retreated the way he had come.

"Jack!" A quick look showed her that all was well with the other children. The twins were still sitting goggle-eyed in their swings, and Frankie smiled sweetly in his sleep.

"I was watching over them, missus!" Jack said. "He weren't nothing to do with me!"

"But was it him, your father?"

"My father? O' course not. I told you. He buggered off."

"But—" Lois stopped and took a big breath. "So who was at the school gates? The one you were frightened of?"

"God knows," Jack said. "Some pervert or other, I s'pose. Anyway," he added, "is Mum coming soon? I got things to do."

"I'll send her over," Lois said, staring at him, trying to decide whether he was telling the truth. And then once more she was angry that a child of thirteen should be required to be devious and unpleasant, through no fault of his own. She noticed the tender way he straightened the baby in his pushchair, picking up and dusting off the toy dog that had fallen to the ground.

"Second thoughts, Jack," she said. "You run over and tell Mum she can finish now doing the refreshments. I'll take her place. Tell her I'll walk back slowly with the others. I'll meet you coming back."

"Afraid of nasty men, are you?" said Jack with a sneer. "Whatever," he added, and began to slope off towards the hall.

When Paula arrived to take charge, Lois told her that a man had approached the children but had been scared off, and left it at that. She did not have to say more, and could see the alarm in Paula's eyes. "Best to keep a close eye on them. Thanks, Mrs. M," she said, and Lois hurried back towards the hall.

Cowgill's car was still in the car park, and he and Chris were standing outside, deep in conversation. Lois couldn't avoid them, so smiled at Chris and asked if they had picked up anything useful in their hunt for the arsonist.

"This and that," Chris said.

"Must be catching, this way of saying nuthin'," Lois said. "He's the champ," she added, looking at Cowgill. "Anyway, it's a good exhibition, isn't it?"

"Very good indeed," Cowgill said. "I specially liked a photo Gran had contributed. A small girl with long dark hair flying in the breeze, swinging much too high."

"Couldn't have been me, if that's what you think," said Lois, her eyes softening. "We lived in Tresham."

"According to your mother, the three of you had come out from town to Farnden for a picnic. You were six, she said. And lovely, as always," he added quietly, as they walked to the car, so that only she could hear.

"We left a donation," Chris said, smiling. "And not from police funds, either. Mr. Cowgill has another side to him, you know."

Cowgill got into the car and lowered the window. "Seriously, Lois," he said, "I need to know what line you're following. It could be a matter of life and death, and I'm not saying that lightly. Bye now, take care."

TWENTY-FIVE

❧

T HE WEATHER HAD CHANGED. HEAVY RAIN POUNDED DOWN
outside Lois's office window, and not a soul was to be seen
in the village High Street. The usual muddy pond, formed
by torrents of water overflowing from fields and ditches, had
formed on the corner by the turn to the playing field.

"Drain's blocked again," Gran said, "and Derek said him
and Tony Dibson were off to clean some of the mud away so's
it can flow away."

"If only others on the parish council were as good as
Derek," Lois said. "It's always him unblocking drains or fixing broken hedges. Chasing escaped sheep. Him and John."

"And Tony Dibson," said Gran. "You could hardly expect
Mrs. T-J to come out with buckets and boots, could you?"

"Don't see why not," Lois said grumpily. "Anyway, I have
to go out this morning. Possible new client. I'll be back in
time for the meeting."

Gran retired to the kitchen. Her daughter was obviously
in a bad mood, but she had no idea why. But then, she had

always been a moody girl. Took after her grandmother, so her father always said. Best to leave her to get over it, he used to advise and was usually right.

A nagging worry had haunted Lois on and off all night, and she was tired from lack of proper sleep. She could not decide what to do about Paula and her missing husband. Would it be better to tell her that the body in the canal had an appendix scar, and leave it to the machinery of the law to involve her in endless questions and identification of the corpse, and all that entailed? Or should she persist on her own, following up the sightings of a tramp who could be Jack Sr., still alive, and do what she could to help Jack Jr. sort himself out? She could see no need to pile more worries on to Paula unless and until it became really necessary.

The possible new client lived in Waltonby, on a new development on a parcel of land sold off by Mrs. T-J. The poor old thing must be feeling the pinch, thought Lois, slumming along on a frequent cleaner, a full-time gardener, and Floss, who loved all things equine, to help with the horse.

The front door opened as soon as Lois pulled up outside. Mrs. Belvoir, an elderly woman supporting herself on a stick, had a welcoming smile. "Come along in, Mrs. Meade," she said, and led the way into the house.

Lois hung back, wiping her wet, muddy shoes on the door mat, and noticed a portrait hanging in a prominent place in the hallway. A distinguished military man, with neat mustache and plenty of gold braid, looked out at her sternly.

"My late husband," said Mrs. Belvoir. "He wasn't really as fierce as he looks! It was having to sit for hours being painted. Very difficult to keep up a smile, he said."

"Very handsome, though," said Lois pleasantly, and followed Mrs. Belvoir into an inoffensively bland sitting room.

Lois went through the motions of explaining New Brooms to a new client, taking notes, promising excellent service, and all the while her mind was on a thirteen-year-old boy walking away from her with a defiant shrug and misery in his dark eyes.

"Mrs. Meade?"

Lois realised that she had not heard Mrs. Belvoir offering her coffee, and apologised. "Just sorting out my best girl for you," she lied. "Mind you, they're all good," she added hastily. "All my girls are excellent, and I'm sure you'll have no problems. If you do have any queries, here is my card and I'm available day and night."

She refused coffee, saying that she had to get on to her next appointment, and left Mrs. Belvoir standing on the step waving a friendly hand. What a nice woman! Probably Dot Nimmo would be the best to look after her. Dot was a character and tended to act independently of Lois's rules, but she had a heart of gold and a nice way with old ladies. Yes, Dot would be the one for Mrs. Belvoir.

Halfway back to Farnden, she saw a large obstacle in the road and braked to avoid it, but too late. There was a nasty crunching sound from under the van, and she stopped immediately.

"Sod it!" she muttered, as she saw the exhaust pipe hanging loose. The offending obstacle proved to be a jagged piece of masonry which had tumbled from a heap at the side of the road.

She looked at her watch. Half past eleven, rain pelting down, and the team would be arriving at noon. This small back road, a short cut to Farnden, was little used, and there was not much hope of being rescued. Nothing for it, then, but to walk. She had her mobile, but was reluctant to ring Derek. He had a complicated rewiring job to finish, and wouldn't be too pleased to be asked to collect her. She slung her bag over her shoulder, collected the briefcase, and locked the van. With a backwards glance to make sure she had pulled off the road as far as she could, she set off at a smart pace towards home.

A couple of miles from the village, she passed a ruined

cottage with gaping windows and a splintered door bang-
ing in the wind. The rain had soaked her to the skin, and
seemed to be increasing. Maybe she should shelter for a few
minutes while she tried to find the number of her garage on
her mobile.

She stepped across the dripping, soggy grass and walked
gingerly over a broken paving stone leading into the house.
A startled mouse looked at her and then scuttled away. Mice
I can take, Lois said to herself. But not rats. Oh God, I hope
there's not rats! Apart from the swinging door, it was completely quiet, a threatening, heavy quiet that made Lois
shiver. She found her mobile and switched it on. Nothing,
except the signal for low battery showing. She groaned. Why
now? This was the worst morning of her life, she decided, and
was later to regret tempting fate.

A creaking sound broke the silence, and she turned round
in alarm, looking into the shadowy depths of the cottage. A
shadow moved. "Who's that!" she said loudly.

There was no reply, and she turned to run, when a man's
voice said, "Stay where you are. Don't move, else you'll be
sorry."

"Come on in," Gran said, looking worried. "I don't know
what's happened to Lois. She said she'd be back well in time
for the meeting."

Hazel Thornbull, Sheila Stratford and Dot Nimmo looked
at each other in dismay. In the entire time they'd been working for New Brooms, Mrs. M had never been late. In fact, she
was such a stickler for punctuality that the team had learned
to be on time or suffer a sharp reprimand.

Half an hour ticked by, and the team ran out of things
to say. Andrew voiced all their thoughts by saying that he
thought they should get hold of Derek. He must have a
mobile, and might know where she was. Gran was called

in, gave them Derek's number, and said she was thinking of ringing the police. One particular policeman, she said, who would certainly be worried if Lois went missing.

"Let's ring Derek first," Dot Nimmo said. She had a natural reluctance to ring the police at any time, being the widow of a successful boss of Tresham's dodgy underworld. "I'll speak to him," she added.

"Perhaps it would be better if Andrew . . . ?" Sheila came from a generation who thought important jobs should be handled by a man, but Dot said no, she was most likely to have an idea what to do, where to look. She dialled the number and waited.

"Who are you?" Lois said, keeping as cool as she could manage. She could hardly see the owner of the voice, but thought she caught a northern accent. Geordie? That was it. "And how dare you threaten me!"

"You'd be surprised what you'd dare when you're desperate," he said.

"For God's sake come out where I can see you," said Lois, beginning to lose her cool.

The man stepped forwards, and she could see that he had all the sad signs of being down and out. Straggly, unkempt hair, rough red complexion and rheumy eyes. His clothes were layers of rags, and he had a filthy rucksack over his shoulder.

"I see," she said. "So what do you want from me, and what will you do if I don't give it to you?"

"Answer to the first question, money. If you don't hand over what you got in that bag, I'll take it by force. Christ knows I've never hurt nobody, but I'm frozen and hungry and tired of tramping about. Hand it over, then I'll let you go."

Lois peered more closely at him. His eyes were bloodshot, but without question a deep, unfathomable black. "Who are you?" she repeated. "Answer me a couple of questions, and I'll give what money I've got in my purse. Bargain?"

"How will you know I'm telling the truth?" he said, and in that instant he could have been young Jack. Intelligent, cunning and wary.

"Oh, I shall know, Mr. Hickson," she said, and immediately knew she had gone too far. He moved towards her, and she ran, out of the cottage, across the wet grass, almost blinded by the heavy rain. But she was well nourished and sheltered, and he was weak and hungry. She outstripped him easily, and finally turned and looked back. She could see him stumbling back towards the cottage, and then he disappeared.

A familiar van came slowly towards her, and she knew it was Derek. The girls and Gran must have told him. He stopped, opened the door and walked towards her, holding out his arms.

"IT WAS LIKE ONE OF THEM FILMS, WHERE THE MAN AND WOMAN run towards each on a sunset beach, into a passionate embrace. Me and your dad," Lois said to Josie later that afternoon.

"And what romantic thing did Dad say?"

" 'You got wet feet, me duck.' That's what he said, bless 'im. We managed to have the meeting, anyway, and I didn't say anything to Paula. But I'm sure it was him, Josie. Same eyes, same way of speaking as young Jack."

"You've got a lot of thinking to do now, then, Mum. Shall we just tell Matthew and Cowgill and let them find Hickson? It might be for the best."

Lois shook her head. "He may be desperate, but he's also clever. He's been keeping out of sight for a long time now. Probably got regular hidey-holes where he can lie low for as long as it's safe. Then, when it isn't, move on. And anyway, Josie," she said, "s'far as we know, he ain't committed a crime.

Leaving his wife and kids is not a police matter. And I'm not at all sure yet that Paula wants him back. She's making a new life for herself in Farnden."

"What about the boy?"

"Ah, young Jack. Yes, well, he is a problem, and probably needs a father. But maybe not that father! But you're right there. Something has to be done."

She slipped off the stool by the shop counter and picked up her shopping. "Better get back and do some serious thinking. I don't have to ask you—"

"—to keep it to myself," finished Josie. "Of course I'll not say a word. But I do think you're taking a bit too much on yourself."

"Don't I always?" said Lois, and set off for home. She had decided to take Josie into her confidence for two reasons. First, she knew her daughter was a good source of village gossip from her listening post in the shop. And second, her encounter with Hickson had shaken her up, and Josie was the obvious person to confide in.

TWENTY-SIX

ॐ

THE RAIN HAD CLEARED AWAY IN THE NIGHT, AND A BRIGHT sparkling countryside failed to grab Gavin's attention as he drove much too fast along the narrow tree-lined lanes to work. He was late, having been drawn into an anxious discussion with Kate about three spots on Celia's chubby cheek. Was it measles? No, she'd had the jab. Chicken pox? Not the right kind of spots. Ringworm, then, caught from other children at the Mums and Tots group? Finally they had agreed that Kate should take her to the surgery and check with the doctor. Couldn't be too careful, Gavin had said.

Now he arrived in the office car park, locked his car and ran towards the front entrance.

"Gavin!" A tall, heavily built man with sandy hair carefully combed over a pinkish scalp, emerged from behind a car parked to one side and blocked his way.

Damn! Gavin said to himself. What the hell did Tim Froot want with him now? And surely he had more sense than to come here to find him?

"In a hurry!" he gasped, hesitating for a moment. "Can I catch up with you later?"

"Now," said Froot flatly. "In my car. Get in."

The darkened windows shielded them from onlookers, and Gavin said again that he was late for work and in a hurry.

"I need some action, Gavin," Tim Froot said. "Time for you to come up with something positive. Do we have a development site or not? I can't waste any more time on it. Either you produce something definite, and earn your commission, or I lose interest and take my money elsewhere. It's not exactly the biggest deal, is it? But I like you, and I like Kate, and I'll put this thing your way if you play your part. Do I make myself clear?"

Gavin nodded. "Very clear," he said. "Give me a couple of weeks, and I'll come up with what you want. Now I have to go, else I'll have no job to go to."

The office was quiet as he slipped into his place, hoping not to be noticed. But as he bent over his computer as if he'd been there since dawn, he felt a presence stop beside him.

"Gavin Adstone?" He looked up, and saw a broad-shouldered young man smiling at him.

"That's me. Something amiss?"

"Douglas Meade. And no, there's nothing wrong! Just thought I'd introduce myself. You're newly moved in to Long Farnden, my grandmother tells me. She's Mrs. Weedon, and my mum's Lois Meade. Runs New Brooms cleaning service. Gran monitors everything and everybody in Farnden!"

Gavin stood up and stretched out his hand. "Glad to know you," he said. "Actually, I'd heard about you, too." He didn't mention the post boy. "Yes, we're incomers in the village, but I hope we'll be accepted in ten years' time!"

"Make it twenty-five," said Douglas. "Anyway, must get on," he added, looking at his watch. "Hope you'll be happy there. Nice village, if handled tactfully . . ."

Gavin watched him walk away briskly. Friendly chap, he thought. But no fool. Have to watch your step there, Gavin boy.

TIM FROOT COASTED SLOWLY INTO FARNDEN, AND HIS SATNAV told him to turn right. "Destination on the left," said Prudence, the name he had given the calm, patient voice. She never blamed him for taking a wrong turn, never sulked when his own route was more sensible than hers.

He pulled up, and looked across at the village hall, at its outdated wooden structure and grubby paintwork. The roof was sorely in need of repair, and the window frames were clearly rotten.

"Ripe for it," he said aloud. If Gavin Adstone didn't get on with it, he would have to look around for someone else. It was a tiny project compared with his usual plans, but he had taken a fancy to Kate Adstone, and wouldn't say no to meeting her on a regular basis for a while.

"SUPPER'S EARLY TONIGHT," GRAN SAID. "DEREK'S GOT HIS MEETing, and I'm going round to Joan's to talk about what the WI plans to do for the soap box grand prix."

"What, just the two of you, single-handed?"

"How can two people be single-handed, Lois? No, of course not! It's a WI committee meeting at Joan's house. Derek's lot have got the village hall, so we can't go there."

"Sounds like we need a bigger village hall, with meeting rooms an that," said Lois.

"I shall ignore that," Gran said. "Sometimes, Lois, you can be very irritating. Oh, and by the way, that policeman of yours rang. I told him to try your mobile, and he said he had, but it wasn't switched on. Now, haven't you got some work to do, and let me get on with supper?"

Lois dialled Cowgill's number and waited. "Ah, there you are," she said, as he finally answered. "You wanted me?"

All the time, Cowgill said to himself, but aloud thanked her for ringing back. "It's just that we've had a complaint from a woman living in Fletching. She says her garden shed was raided."

"Ah, serious crime," said Lois.

Cowgill proceeded smoothly, "And the reason I'm telling you this, is that it is the third complaint we've had where theft has occurred locally in unlocked outhouses and sheds, and on each occasion it is food stolen. Apples stored on racks, sacks of potatoes broken into, strings of onions. And where freezers were kept, two or three ready-meals missing. Never any great quantity, but a pattern is emerging."

"I see it already," Lois said caustically. "Hungry bear on the rampage. Large brown bears with claws and fangs dripping with massacred cat's blood."

There was a few seconds' silence, and Lois began to think he had finally lost patience with her. But no, now he was laughing. Real, throaty laughter.

"You sound a bit rusty," she said. "Not laughed much lately?"

"Not for years," Cowgill said. "A policeman's lot is not a happy one."

"Anyway, seriously, you think this might be a tramp, a real desperate one, and on our patch?"

"Seems likely. Worth following up. Chris is having a look round, visiting the complainants. Just thought you might like to know, and maybe keep your eyes open even more than usual. Also," he added, risking it, "it is an excuse to talk to the only girl who can make me laugh."

"Forget it," Lois said. "But before I go through the emails from my other fans, have you heard any more about the identity of the canal tramp?"

Cowgill's voice became instantly cool. "Not so far, I'm afraid. We are still making enquiries."

"Great," said Lois. "And so am I. Bye."

DEREK HAD COLLECTED LOIS'S CAR AND FIXED THE EXHAUST PIPE. She had not told him or Gran about the tramp, unwilling to provoke another burst of disapproval. But now she settled down in her office and tried to face the Hickson problem. The police knew less than she did, she guessed. And in any case, to them the whole thing was small beer. A friendless no-hoper, probably a drunk, who fell into the canal. Case quietly closed. Then there were a few unconnected petty thefts of food in the Farnden area. Nothing that would keep Cowgill awake at night.

So what did she know that was more disturbing? First, Paula Hickson, now one of her team, had been deserted by a violent husband and was making a new life in Farnden. Second, although all seemed to be going well for Paula, there was her firstborn son, Jack Jr., who was far from doing well. He was being approached by a stranger—or maybe his father?—outside the school and in other places, and she did not know whether he had told his mother. The boy was disturbed, unhappy and possibly in danger.

This last thought was the crux of the matter. She should tell Cowgill or Paula, or both, what she feared, and enlist their support. But she knew in her heart that if she alerted Cowgill, the might of the welfare state would be put on the case and young Jack would probably do something drastically awful. When Josie had been a teenager, she had gone off the rails and had run away with an older mixed-up lad. It had been a desperate time for them all, and needed very delicate handling by her and Derek. And yes, the police had been brought in, but only because the lad had committed a crime.

That was it. In what seemed to be his present frame of mind, Jack Jr. was quite likely to flout the law, if it was only to draw attention to himself. The classic cry for help.

"Coffee," said Gran, coming in with a steaming mug. "You going to be much longer?"

"Why?"

"The sun's shining, there's people going up and down the village street, the garden needs weeding and you've got a grandson in Tresham who'd probably like to see his grannie more than once a month."

"Oh! Right! Thanks for the lecture, Mum! I'll certainly bear in mind your helpful suggestions."

"Huh!" said Gran, and banged the door behind her.

Lois sighed, stood up and looked out of the window. Gran was right, as usual. She opened the window, letting in fresh air and sunlight. This afternoon she would go into Tresham and see Susie and little Harry, maybe stay until bath time. She could also call in at the office first and see if Hazel had any news about the local thefts.

But for now, she would ring Paula and ask her to call in on her way back from the hall, just to have a chat.

MRS. T-J WAS IN THE ROOM SHE CALLED THE DEN. THE BELL ON the board in the kitchen, no longer in use, was labeled "The Den," and she perpetuated the name in an attempt to preserve something of the old atmosphere at the hall, when her father had sat at his big desk working on the affairs of his estate, collecting rents, hiring and firing workers, dealing with his bank manager.

As she now settled down in the big leather chair, more like a throne than a chair, she was reminded of hiring and firing as she checked her diary. A hopeful applicant for the gardener job was due at eleven o'clock for interview. His letter was in good English, clear and comprehensive, listing the jobs he had done. He had worked in municipal parks, as well as in smaller private gardens, and was looking for work only because he had been made redundant in the present climate of financial squeeze.

It was a shame, she thought, as she put down the application on her desk, that there were earthy smudges on the paper. Still, perhaps that was a good sign! At least he could have no qualms about getting his hands dirty, unlike one young man who'd expected to be supplied with gardening gloves at her expense.

Paula, busy cleaning silver in the kitchen, looked at the clock. A quarter past ten. She just had time to finish her favourite job before making coffee. Mrs. T-J had said she was expecting a possible new gardener, and would have her coffee early. "I don't wish to offer him refreshment," she had said firmly. "You never know with these out of work people. They'll trump up any kind of a story to get a job."

Paula thought to herself that if Mrs. T-J was desperate for money and work, she too might tell a few white lies. But she just nodded, and said she would bring in coffee at half past ten.

At eleven o'clock exactly, there was a knock at the kitchen door. "Damn!" Paula said. She supposed it was the gardener man, and she was on the point of collecting Mrs. T-J's coffee cup. Still, at least he had not rapped loudly on the front door, opened it and yelled, "Anyone there?" which had scuppered another applicant's chances.

She walked over to the door and opened it. A man stood there, and he was very familiar. She saw first that he was very thin, with dark hollows beneath his eyes. For a gardener out in the open air, he looked very unhealthy. Then he smiled and spoke to her.

"Morning, Paula," said her husband. "I have an appointment to see Mrs. Tollervey-Jones."

*   *   *

AN HOUR LATER, GRAN USHERED A WHITE-FACED PAULA HICK-
son into Lois's office. Lois could almost see a "Told you so"
think bubble form above Gran's head, and said at once that
they'd be really grateful for a couple of cups of strong coffee.
Gran shrugged, and left the room.

"Sit down, Paula," Lois said, "before you fall down. You
look terrible."

"I feel terrible," Paula said in a small voice.

Lois could see she was fighting to keep control. "No hurry.
Take some deep breaths, and then we'll have a coffee before
you tell me what has happened. I'll just finish these schedules, so you can sit quietly."

After hot strong coffee and encouraging smiles from Lois,
Paula began to speak. She described the shock of seeing her
husband at the back door, and the superhuman effort needed
to take him through to the den and announce him to Mrs.
T-J. As they had walked through the long corridor, Jack had
whispered to her that there was no need to say who he really
was. His name was Jack Stevens now. He relied on her to
keep her mouth shut, he said, and there was menace in his
voice.

"He was so changed, Mrs. M!" Paula said. "Thin as a rake,
but cleaned up." Her lip wobbled. "He used to be such a
tough chap, big and strong," she said.

Lois came straight to the point. "Did he get the job?" she
said.

Paula nodded. "He was always a good talker," she said.
"Could charm the angel Gabriel if it were necessary."

Lois raised her eyebrows. "Mrs. T-J is far from that," she
said. "Now, we have to make a plan, Paula. The first thing is
to decide how you're going to tell Jack Jr."

"Oh, I can't tell him yet!" Paula said. "He's so difficult
to handle at the moment. This'll tip him over the edge, I

reckon. The headmaster wants to see me next week, to have a serious talk about Jack Jr., he said."

"So are you going to the police? Tell them that your husband has been violent towards you, and has now come to work just up the road? Are you going to say you're scared stiff of what he might do, and ask them to take action? Because," Lois added, before Paula could answer, "if you do, they're certain to take up the matter. Domestic violence is common enough, but they still have to take action if a case is reported to them."

Paula frowned. "I don't know. I don't know what to do, Mrs. M, and that's the truth," she said sadly. "I thought it would be all right now, living in Farnden with the children, and working for you. I was just beginning to feel safe, and now this happens."

"Does there have to be secrecy?" Lois said. "Why can't he use his real name, let Mrs. T-J know he's your husband, but tell her you're separated, and intend to live apart?"

"I expect that's what he'd like to do, but he's got these charges hanging over him."

"What charges?" Lois said. "What else has he done, apart from beating up his wife?"

"It was at his job. There was a man there who'd come to work there long after Jack started, but he was kept on and Jack got sacked. He was a nasty piece of work, but had a friend in the management. He crowed over Jack in front of his mates. Jack went for him. Knocked him to the ground and left him with a broken tooth. Jack's mates stood up for him, told the bosses it was all the other bloke's fault for taunting Jack, and Jack was warned. O' course, they'd already given him his notice, so they couldn't use dismissal as a punishment. Anyway, up to then Jack had always been a good worker, so they decided not to take it any further. But if the police do get a whiff of what happened, Jack will be in for it."

Lois was quiet for a minute or two, debating whether to tell Paula about her encounter with the man in the ruined cottage. She didn't know for certain that he was Jack Sr. All she had was a suspicion based on a likeness to young Jack and his reaction when she used his name. No, for the moment she would keep quiet. This new crisis was more important.

"So what would you advise, Mrs. M?" Paula said.

Lois realised that Paula had nobody else to ask. She had been an only child, and apparently her parents were killed in a motorway pileup. She appeared to have no friends left from her working days at the building company in Tresham, and had not been in Farnden long enough to find a best friend. Reluctantly, Lois said that bearing in mind all the circumstances, Paula should break it to Jack Jr. that his father was working at the hall. It was bound to upset him, but it was entirely possible that the boy might meet him accidentally and that would be much worse.

"Has he been approached by his father, since you split?" Lois said.

Paula shook her head. "Not that I know," she said. "Jackie hardly says a word to me from one week's end to another. It's not good for him, I know, but I'm so busy with the others I just hope it's a phase and will pass."

Stalemate, thought Lois. She tried to imagine what Cowgill's reaction would be if she told him. After all, what was there to worry about? The Hickson family's problems were their own, nothing to do with anybody else. The father needed a job desperately, that was clear. He had wanted Paula to keep quiet, and if he meant to stay clear of her and his family, then it was up to him and Paula to work it out, wasn't it?

But there was Jack Jr., a young kid already seriously disturbed.

Paula's next request was what Lois had been anticipating. "Mrs. M," she said slowly, "I don't suppose you could be around when I tell Jackie? You're right. He must be told. But if it's just me, he'll be out of the door and gone before I get started. Please?"

TWENTY-SEVEN

ONY DIBSON HAD COOKED TEA FOR HIMSELF AND HIS WIFE, Irene, and now quietly whistled to himself in the kitchen as he washed up their crocks.

"You sound happy!" Irene shouted to him from the living room. "I thought you said these meetings—SOS did you call it?—were a waste of time, and you'd thought of not going tonight?"

Tony dried his hands, took his jacket off a hook in the hall, and came into the room to say goodbye. "And so I did," he said, bending to kiss the top of her head. He winced, finding it increasingly difficult to bend down to be on a level with her, face-to-face. "So I did," he repeated, "but now things seem to be moving. I met Derek in the street, and he said there'd been a good few entries for the soap box race, and Floss has got them going at the Youth Club with all kinds of extra plans for raising money. Should be an interesting meeting tonight."

"How about that new chap, Gavin Whatsit?"

"Haven't heard any more from him," Tony said. "Maybe he's one of those blow hot and cold types. Didn't get his own way at first, so lost interest. I don't know, Irene, but I'll tell you more when I get back. Must go, love, else I'll be late."

As it happened, Tony caught up with Gavin Adstone halfway along the High Street. "Evenin' squire," Tony said. "Lovely evening. How's the family?" In spite of his doubts about Gavin's use to the committee, he was beginning to like the chap and there was room for a sleeper, so long as he woke up before the event.

"All well, thanks," Gavin replied with a smile. "Bit of an emergency this morning, when Kate had to take Cecilia to the doc. But it was nothing much, thank goodness. This parent lark is quite a worry, isn't it! Do you have children, Tony?"

"No, sadly," Tony said, and changed the subject. It had been Irene's greatest wish to have a family, and none had come along.

"Here we are then. Look, there's Chairman Derek, looking out for us. Let's hope we can make some sensible decisions tonight," Gavin said, and stood back to allow Tony to go in first. It was polite things like that, thought Tony, that made you think maybe Gavin's heart was in the right place.

Hazel was the last to arrive, and she stood for a moment, looking across the playing field, with its fenced-off swings and slides for the younger children. There were enough teenagers to make a football game tonight, and a group of giggling girls watched them from the sidelines. It was warm, the trees moved gently in the evening breeze, and a benevolent sun still lingered. She looked up at the village hall and thought of all it had seen in its long life. It was part of the village scene, and as she went through the door to join the others she felt a renewed determination to keep it going. How awful to see it razed to the ground and a ghastly new brick-built monstrosity in its place!

"Right," said Derek. "We're all here, so let's make a start. Any apologies, Hazel?"

"Not if we're all here," muttered Gavin under his breath.

"No? Then let's have the minutes of the last meeting."

Hazel read them smoothly, aware that she had done a good job. Not too verbose, just the facts.

"Matters arising," said Derek, looking around.

"I think the rest will come under that heading," Hazel said. "Shall we have a progress report from each member?"

"Good idea," said Derek. "We know about the Youth Club keen to enter a soap box, and getting help with its design an' that. Now the others. Would you like to start, Floss?"

"Yep, thanks, Derek. Well, I braved the group of kids who lurk behind the village hall, and asked them if they had any ideas for the soap box day. Much to my surprise two or three were really keen, and after a bit of persuasion, the others began to join in. One of them had seen a bucking bronco at the church fete in Waltonby. People pay to have a ride, and if they can stay on the horse longer than three minutes they get a pound back. It's not a real horse, of course, but it bucks mechanically and it's difficult to stay put. Apparently it's very popular with the pony girls in the village, as well as almost everybody else! They made a mint over at Waltonby. One of the kids knows where to hire the horse."

"Well done, Floss," Derek said.

"There's more," she said proudly. "Once they'd started thinking, they got fired up, and said they could recruit other friends and there'd be twenty or so. So I've divided up the kids into the various projects they've come up with, and there's five teams, four or five in each, and I've said the most profitable team gets a day out at Alton Towers. My dad says he'll sponsor that."

"Brilliant, Floss! Thank him very kindly from us," Derek said. "So what are the other projects, and how much space do they want in the playing field?"

"Well, as well as the bucking bronco, there's the tug-of-war, always popular with Young Farmers, and then 'pelt the vicar' with a wet sponge." Here she looked tentatively at Father Rodney, who gulped bravely and said it was fine by him.

"I'm not so sure about that," Derek said. "Don't want him getting pneumonia."

"Oh, I've done it before, in my last parish," the vicar said. "You have a big board in front of you, with a funny figure painted on it, and a hole for you to put your face through, then you shut your eyes and pray. Ritual mortification of the flesh, I suppose you'd call it!"

Gavin laughed in spite of himself. It was a simple idea, but he looked at the vicar and saw the potential.

"Right, thanks, Vicar," Derek said. "So what else, Floss?"

"Those were mostly the lads' ideas. The girls suggested 'dance 'til you drop,' a sort of marathon, where each person is timed, and, a bit like the bronco, if you go on more than twenty minutes, you get a pound back. They'd need a reasonable space, and one of the girls said her dad could get hold of a wooden dance floor they could put down. They'd have more than one dancer at a time o' course. Probably quite a few. Could be quite an entertainment to watch, as well as raising money."

"Bags me first go," said Hazel. "I love it, Floss!"

"There was one I had some doubts about," continued Floss, "but I said I'd ask the committee. They suggested a 'bonny baby show.' Certificates for all, and each one having a studio type photo taken. Entry money reasonably high, and a parade of bonny babies at the end of the afternoon. They said it would be best if they didn't do it themselves, but it would be one for responsible adults to organise." She did not report their comments about responsible adults, most of which were decidedly uncomplimentary.

"Sounds good," Hazel said. "Why the doubts, Floss?"

"I know why," said Tony Dibson, smiling. "We used to have one of those bonniest baby competitions at the church fete, but it nearly caused a punch-up one year. This beefy mother from Fletching claimed the judge picked a Farnden baby that was not nearly as bonny as hers. Then the winning mother started arguing, and it took Mrs. T-J to sort them out. Which she did, o' course, with no trouble at all!"

"Ah, yes, Tony," Derek said. "But this one wouldn't be competitive, would it, Floss? They'd all get certificates and a photo. Could be a real attraction, an' there's plenty of girls with babies in the villages combined. I reckon we should go for that one. For all of 'em, Floss. You've done really well."

"Not me," said Floss modestly. "It was the kids. They're not a bad lot, whatever people say."

Gavin cleared his throat, and Hazel was sure he blushed. "Um, I'd like to enter Cecilia straightaway for the 'bonny babies.' She could be an example to the others," he added proudly.

"Good lad," Tony said.

"Shouldn't we have a vote on all the projects?" Hazel said, remembering her duty as secretary.

"So we should," Derek said. "Right, then. Any objections to any of the ideas? Or shall we take a block vote?" There was a general nodding of heads, and the vote was unanimously in favour.

"What's next, then, Hazel?" Derek said.

"The soap box race itself," Hazel said. "John has been collecting up entries already, and Gavin has kindly offered to help. So over to you, John."

"We've got eighteen entries so far, so it looks like we're going to be a real success," John said. "Me and Gavin have been getting together over some of the arrangements to be made. My jobs are lining the track with straw bales for safety, and fixing up a starting ramp. This'll give them a good start, enough to get them down to the finish."

"Which is where?" Derek said, adding that nobody needed three guesses.

"Right first time," Gavin said. "The pub is the obvious

choice. Should be good for business, and a great place to celebrate a good run, or drown sorrows on a bad one. Okay, everyone?"

Then he and John took turns to list other important matters, like public toilets, mobile phone communication between start and finish, dividing entries into classes, like Sports Clubs, Local Hunt, Youth Club, rerouting through traffic, and so on.

"Don't forget the Women's Institute," Hazel said with a straight face.

"You're joking!" Gavin said.

"Oh, no I'm not," Hazel said sharply. "A resolution's been passed, and they are entering. I reckon they'll show you lads a thing or two!"

"I hope so," said Tony Dibson, sotto voce.

"Press and TV publicity," Father Rodney said. "That's important. I could volunteer for that, if it would help?"

"Thank you, Vicar," Derek said, and added that a vicar in the village stocks was sure to be good for a picture of two. "Not sure about too much publicity, though," he added. "We don't want the police coming in with all kinds of regulations and safety measures that'll take half our profits. Keep it low-key, Vicar. Just a small village event. Everybody agree?"

There was general approval, although Gavin Adstone appeared to be about to say something, then didn't.

"And they'll take you seriously, you being a man o' the cloth," Tony said. "Worth a picture or two in the local paper." The vicar agreed glumly, but told himself that being humbled in the stocks was all part of his calling.

After more useful discussion about the length of the course, maybe a commentator with loudspeaker system, first-aid team, and so on, Derek said it was time to fix a date for the next meeting and adjourn to the pub.

"Oh, hang on a minute," Hazel said, stacking her papers. "Shouldn't we decide on a celebrity opener and presenter for the winners' prizes? People get really booked up."

There was a pause, and then Floss said, "Can I suggest something?"

"Good gel," Tony said, looking at his watch.

"Why don't we have a soap box queen for the day? Maybe one of the older girls from the school? Like a May queen . . ."

"Excellent!" said Father Rodney. "A good old tradition revived! I shall speak to our headmistress. If the committee would like me to," he added hastily. He knew only too well how a bossy vicar could end up thoroughly disliked.

And so they all strolled down to the pub, with Derek delighted at the way things were going and Gavin Adstone somewhat discomforted, aware that his part in the whole thing seemed to be going in a completely different direction from the one he had intended.

TWENTY-EIGHT

❧

"I SUPPOSE WE MUST GIVE THE NEW GARDENER A CUP OF TEA," Mrs. T-J said to Paula. "He's starting this morning, and it is expected. None of the old red spotted handkerchief with bread and cheese, and a flask of whatever it was they drank. Those days are gone, sadly." She was quiet for a few moments, and then said sharply, "You'll find a box of those cheap tea bags in the cupboard. Please use those. Now, I have to go out this morning. Meeting at the town hall. You will probably be gone by the time I get back, so please lock up very carefully. You cannot be too cautious with new staff."

I suppose that goes for me, too, Paula thought. If she knew the new gardener was my estranged husband, it would look like a conspiracy. We'd both be out on our ears.

Paula had thought long and hard about what she would do when faced with Jack Sr. She had no idea where he was living, or what he intended. He had looked quite presentable, though thin and pale, and it might be that he had been try-ing lots of other job applications, and this one had come up.

The big question was, did she want him back? She had her new life, and would be able to sustain it, as long as New Brooms still employed her. If only young Jack wasn't so unhappy and confused, obviously needing a father . . .

She saw him arrive, and vanish into the kitchen garden. This was an old-fashioned survivor from grander days, and still surrounded by high walls to protect the vegetables and fruit from wind and weather. An ideal place to hide from view. She looked at her watch a dozen times, checking as coffee-break time loomed. The house was empty, except for herself, and frighteningly quiet. Perhaps Mrs. T-J wouldn't mind if she put on the radio. It was permanently on classical music, but she could always put it back to the right station. But no. The old girl was telepathic. She'd probably stop in the middle of her meeting of justices of the peace at the court, and say that she had to leave early. "My char has switched stations on the radio, and must be severely reprimanded. Meeting adjourned." Paula could almost hear her. . . .

Her daydream was interrupted by a sudden loud knock. Oh God! It must be him. She opened the kitchen door a crack, and peered out. "Morning Paula," he said. "Aren't you going to let me in? The gardener always comes into the kitchen for his mug of tea. The old girl's out, isn't she? I saw the car going like a bat out of hell down the drive. God help anyone who gets in her way." He spoke as if nothing had happened, as though the family was still together.

"I'm not allowed to let anyone in," Paula said firmly. "I'll leave it out on that old bench by the stable." And before he could get his foot in the door, she shut it with a bang. With shaking hands she put on the kettle and found a big mug. When she had filled it with strong, sour-smelling tea from the cheap tea bag, she looked out of the window. He had not returned to the kitchen garden, but was sitting idly on the bench where she had planned to put his mug.

She opened the door, put the tea down on the white step

that she scrubbed every week, and yelled that he could come and get it. Then she skipped back into the kitchen and locked the door, shooting the bolt for good measure. Mrs. T-J had a bunch of keys the size of a prison warder's, so she was certain to have a front door key among them.

She stood in a corner where Jack couldn't see her, and watched him walk past the window to the step, pick up his mug and drink greedily. Suddenly she felt hot tears pouring down her cheeks unbidden, and fled out of the kitchen into the cloakroom, where she sat on the edge of the lavatory and sobbed for all that had gone wrong with a marriage that had once seemed so good.

After occupying herself upstairs with bedrooms and bathrooms, she finally went back to the kitchen. He was nowhere to be seen, and the kitchen garden gate was shut. She could hear the Rotavator working the potato patch, and knew that he was still there. Slowly she unbolted and unlocked the door and opened it. The empty mug was on the step, and next to it a bunch of white daisies, tied neatly with binder twine. He had remembered. She took them in, found a suitable vase and arranged them carefully. Then she carried them through to the hall and put them on the table under the long mirror, so that there were now two vases of daisies, one a reflection of the other.

GRAN WAS INSTALLED IN AN ARMCHAIR IN JOAN PICKERING'S front room, along with four other worthies from the Women's Institute. It was seven thirty, and they were waiting for Mrs. T-J to arrive. This was a meeting of the WI soap box subcommittee, chaired by the president. As the little carriage clock on Joan's mantelshelf tinkled the half hour, a firm knock at the door signalled Mrs. T-J's arrival.

"Evening, ladies," she said, and looked pointedly at Gran, who, well aware she was in the best chair, stayed put and looked the other way. Mrs. T-J perched crossly on the edge of an upright, uncomfortable chair and opened a brand new notebook.

"Now, we are here to talk about our entry for the race," she said. "Other matters to do with refreshments, cake stall, et cetera, can be dealt with without me, but the soap box is a different matter. Does anybody have any idea how we make one, for a start?"

The ladies looked at each other, and four shook their heads. Then Gran spoke up. "A long time ago," she said, "my father made a soap box for the boy next door. My dad was handy with his hands, and I remember it well. I don't suppose any of you remember what a soap box actually was? No? Well, it was a sturdy wooden box for holding soap."

"Never!" said Joan Pickering, in mock surprise.

"And so," continued Gran, undeterred, "it was strong enough to stand on, and politicians an' people not quite right in the head, wanting to sound off about something, used to stand on them to make speeches to anybody willing to listen."

"Thank you, Mrs. Weedon," said Mrs. T-J. "Very interesting."

"I haven't finished," Gran said. "And so kids used to get old pram wheels and fix them on the soap box, make a steering bar with a bit o' wood and string, and away they'd go. No brakes, no aerodywhatsits, no Health and Safety to bother 'em. So what say we go for one of those?"

There was a stunned silence, as each of them envisaged sitting on a small wooden box, overflowing it, some of them, trying to steer with a piece of string and only their feet for brakes. Then Mrs. T-J once more thanked Gran for her contribution, and, to give her her due, performed a clever U-turn and said that with a few adaptations, the basic construction was just what was needed. "In other words," whispered Sheila Stratford to her neighbour, "a wheeled vehicle you can steer, and preferably with brakes."

"What was that?" Mrs. T-J said sharply. "If you have a

useful contribution to make, do let us all hear it, Mrs. Stratford."

Sheila said quickly that if her Sam could tell them what to do, and she was sure he could, she reckoned Mrs. Weedon's daughter Lois could knock one up. So long as they didn't actually get the men to build it, she was sure they could do the job.

"And we could decorate it to look like something WI-ish," Gran said, quite carried away with enthusiasm.

"A jar of jam," said Joan Pickering, meaning this as a joke.

"Perfect!" said Miss Wendover. "And we could all sing 'Jerusalem' as the jar of jam was first past the post!"

Mrs. T-J looked around the circle of faces. Were they serious? Good heavens, they really were. Well, she herself was renowned for solving problems. She squared her shoulders and said, "Well done, ladies! Now, there's one more thing. Who is going to be the driver of the WI soap box?"

There was a pause, and then they all answered as with one voice: "You, Mrs. Tollervey-Jones!"

"YOU'RE JOKING!" DEREK SAID WHEN GRAN ARRIVED BACK HOME. "Lois to make a soap box and Mrs. T-J to drive it? In your dreams, Gran."

"I don't see why not," Gran replied huffily. "You can get us the raw materials, Lois and me can knock in a few nails and stick it together."

"Don't drag me into it!" Lois said. "You'll be the laughing stock of the village."

Douglas, who had called in to bring some new photos of little Harry, said he was on Gran's side. "And I can help, can't I? I don't live in Farnden and am certainly not part of any other team, so I can help the girls, can't I, Mum?"

"If by 'girls' you mean members of the WI, I suppose it would be okay. What do you say, Derek? You're the chairman of SOS. Have you got any rules?"

Derek shook his head. "Not really," he said. "Anything goes, more or less. We wanted to keep it simple. So yes, I suppose it would be all right for Doug to help the WI. I know the pub team are recruiting a chap from Plaistow's Engineering. And he don't even drink in the pub. So good luck, Gran."

When the news about the WI entry broke in the pub later that evening, relayed by Derek and Doug who called in for a nightcap, there was disbelief and delight in equal parts. Tony Dibson, who had been playing darts on the winning side, chortled and said he hoped it was a windy day. He'd give a lot to see Mrs. T-J with the wind in her knickers, he vowed.

It was a clear night, and in the small den he had made himself in the corner of a disused barn on Thornbull land, Jack Sr. drank a flask of tea made from stream water and the tea bag Paula had, in her panic, left in his mug that morning. The tomato soup, heated up in the tin snitched from a storeroom he'd found in the stable block, tasted good, and with a stale half loaf of bread from a refuse bin in the yard, his hunger was assuaged for the moment.

He raked out the smoldering embers, damped them down with an old wet sack, and curled up in the sleeping bag he'd been given at the night shelter. It was not new, but still clean and warm, and after reviewing what had been a satisfactory first day in his new job, he told himself Paula would soon come round to getting back together. In no time at all, he was fast asleep.

TWENTY-NINE

꒭

OUTSIDE THE SCHOOL GATES, JACK JR. GLANCED NERVOUSLY from right to left, then walked along towards the town centre. He had stayed after school to hunt for a lost football shoe, but he'd not found it and missed the bus home. Now he had to decide whether to phone his mother, who would be furious on both counts. She would insist on coming to collect him, with the kids packed into her old car, whatever he said about getting a lift. Or he could try finding his friend Lenny's house and fix up a bed for the night, then ring her and lie, saying he'd been invited. He found lying easy now, since his father had gone. So many times there had been muddles and misunderstandings between him and his mother, and he had finally decided that he'd tell her just what she wanted to hear, and leave it at that.

He trudged along, head down, and did not see the man approach, waiting for him on the corner.

"Where are you off to, then, young Jack?"

Jack stopped abruptly, staring at the man. He had not heard

or seen him for several days and had been relieved, thinking he had finally given up. "Mind your own business," he said.

"Now, now, no need to be rude," the man said. "Specially as I've brought you some nice sweeties. Your favourites. Velly cheap, velly nice, as the Chinaman said. How many would you like?"

"Go away!" Jack said, his voice rising in fear. "If you don't leave me alone, I shall get Mum to go to the police. Go away!" He was now close to screaming, and the man glared at him. "Shut yer face, kid," he said. "Your ma would never go to the police, not after what your precious father done!"

Jack dodged around him and ran full pelt along a side street, not stopping until he thought the man was no longer following him. But when he stopped for breath, he looked back and saw him rounding the corner and waving his hand. Jack looked desperately along the street and saw a signboard saying "New Brooms—We Sweep Cleaner." He opened the door and dashed in, saying, "Can I use your toilet? Got took short."

Hazel Thornbull looked at him in surprise. "Yes, you can," she said. "And don't nick anything." This last was an afterthought. Sebastopol Street was in a poorer part of Tresham, and they'd already been broken into once. A computer stolen, and the place trashed. But this was a lad on his own, and he seemed genuine enough. In fact, he looked familiar, but she couldn't place him. She decided to have a talk with him before he left.

Just then the door opened again, and a man came in, smiling broadly. "Afternoon, miss," he said. "I suppose you haven't seen a boy running by? I thought I saw him dodge in here, actually. My son, the little devil, knows he's in for a good talking-to for not doing his homework. I've just been seeing his teacher."

Hazel thought rapidly before she shook her head. There was something unpleasant about the man. Too smooth, too ready with a plausible explanation. "No, nobody's been in here since lunchtime. Sorry. Good afternoon."

At this moment, she saw a reflection in the window of Jack Jr. coming out of the toilet in the back office. She stood up quickly and placed herself in the doorway, so that he could not be seen. Then she said loudly so that Jack would hear, that she hadn't had any boys in her office, and she was about to lock up, so would he please leave.

When he had gone, she drew the blind and locked the door. Then she turned to Jack Jr. and asked him what on earth he was playing at. "You live in Farnden, don't you?"

"Yeah," Jack said. "My mum works for New Brooms, an' I thought you wouldn't mind if I used your toilet."

"You're lying, aren't you, Jack," Hazel said. "That man was after you. What had you done?"

"Nothing. I done nothing," he said. "He's been following me, trying to sell me drugs. I was scared. I am still scared."

Hazel frowned and looked closely at his face. Was he still lying? He had a real shifty look about him. She knew his father had deserted the family. Mrs. M had given the bare facts to the team before Paula joined, so that they wouldn't ask tactless questions. A kid his age needs a father, she thought.

"So why aren't you on the bus on the way home?"

Jack hesitated. He knew this woman was a farmer's wife, and seemed straight enough. He decided to treat her like his mum, and tell her what he thought she'd like to hear. Then he could ask for a lift home. It would be the answer to his problem.

"You ought to tell your mother about that dealer," she said. "The police could stop him with no trouble. They're usually pretty hot about men who loiter round school gates. Why don't you tell her?"

"I have. She said she'd do something about it, but so far she's been too busy. Scrubbing other people's floors."

Hazel ignored this. For one thing, she knew Paula scrubbed the step at the hall, but this was her own idea, because she liked doing it. But she supposed it would count in Jack's eyes.

On the way back to Farnden, Jack answered Hazel's questions in monosyllables and grunts. It was all round the village that the boy was difficult and in trouble at school, and she was curious to know if he had anything to say in his own defence. After all, she had her lovely daughter who was no trouble at all, but expected things to change when the teenage blues hit them all.

"Do you see your father at all?" she said cheerfully.

Jack rounded on her. "Mind your own business!" he said. "I'm sick of people asking about my rotten father. He left Mum in the lurch, and I say good riddance to bad rubbish! We don't want him back. We can get on all right by ourselves. I help Mum all I can, and the others do, too, except for the little one. I just wish people would leave us alone. Fathers are not that great, anyway. . . ." He trailed off.

"Oh, I dunno," said Hazel. "Mine certainly wasn't, but some people are lucky. Look at Mrs. M's husband, Derek. He's a lovely man, and his kids can't speak too highly of him. Have you met him?"

Jack shook his head. "Wouldn't know him if I saw him," he said. "But your Mrs. M seems all right. I suppose if you got a nice husband it makes a difference all round."

Hazel glanced sideways at him. He sounded near to tears, and she was glad they were approaching the village. Paula might not be too pleased if she delivered her son back home looking as if she'd beaten him up.

"Here we are, then," she said. "Might see you around. Do you go to Youth Club in the village hall? Meets every week, and they do some interesting things. I'll give your mum the details. It's tonight. They're building a soap box and need as many willing hands as possible."

He scuffed his way down the garden path, and as he

turned to go round to the back of the house, he looked back
and raised two fingers to her. This gave her a jolt, and she
reflected that it was a salutary lesson. It was going to take
more than a sympathetic ride home to sort out Jack Jr.'s
problems.

FLOSS WAS WALKING HOME FROM THE SHOP, AND SAW HAZEL'S
car stop outside the Hickson house. She watched Jack Jr. get
out and disappear, and then she crossed the road to have a
word with Hazel. The two were good friends, though Floss
was younger, and they were both loyal members of the New
Brooms team. Hazel had not expected Floss to last long, but
she repeatedly said she loved the work and refused to move,
in spite of pressure put on her by her parents. But they'd
given up now that she was married, and dropped hints about
the patter of tiny feet instead.

She greeted Hazel and asked if her John would be at Youth
Club tonight, adding that the lads needed a strong leader like
John Thornbull to keep them in order.

"Yes, he'll be there," Hazel said. "If you're going, can you
remind him to look out for young Jack Hickson? I gave him
a lift home, and he showed no interest at all when I told
him about building the soap box. I thought he might make
a friend or two. He seems such a lonely, mixed-up kid. But
sometimes his sort do the opposite of what you expect. He'll
need some encouragement if he does turn up. I'll tell John
myself, of course, but by the time he gets to the village hall,
he'll have forgotten!"

"ANYTHING HAPPEN TODAY?" JOHN SAID TO HAZEL AS THEY WERE
having their tea. Lizzie had finished hers, and was tormenting
the cat, trying to dress it up in doll's clothes.

"What d'you mean?" Hazel said. "A lot happened. I got

breakfast, took Lizzie to school, went into work at New Brooms, signed on new clients, reported back to Mrs. M, tidied up and did the filing—"

"Okay, okay! Just an idle question."

"But not an idle day," Hazel said huffily. "Oh, and yes, there was a small drama, when young Jack Hickson—you know, our new cleaner's eldest—suddenly appeared in the shop looking hunted, asked to go to the loo, and disappeared into the back room. A minute later, a breathless man came in and asked if I'd seen a boy running past."

"So what did you say?" said John, his attention caught.

"For some reason, I said no, I hadn't seen anyone. Then I stood so he couldn't see into the back room. I more or less had to shove him out, and then lock up. I gave young Jack a lift home. He gave me a cock-and-bull story about missing the bus."

She got up to rescue the cat, and John said, "Who was the man? Did Jack Jr. talk about him on the way home?"

"Not at first," Hazel replied. "Not a great talker, our Jack Jr., but when I asked about his father, I certainly hit a raw spot. He was vitriolic about his father and hoped never to see him again. Then he said something really important, if it was true. He told me about a man at the school gates, peddling drugs. Apparently he's been pestering the lad, maybe because Jack had tried something once. Jack won't say anything because of getting his mother involved. He's probably regretting telling me by now."

"You'd better keep it to yourself, then," John said. "We don't want our family having any truck with that world."

"Hey, since when were you a nimby? And you a parish councillor, too. That Hickson woman has got enough to put up with, without her thirteen-year-old son being in that kind of trouble!"

John backtracked, saying he'd make some discreet enquiries.

"And also," said Hazel sternly, "I told Jack about the

Youth Club and building a soap box, hoping it might give him something to do, somewhere to make friends. But he wasn't interested, not on the surface, anyway. It is just possible he might turn up tonight, so could you make an effort with him? I've got this horrible feeling something bad is going to happen if nobody does nothing to help him."

JOHN WAS PLEASED TO COUNT FULL ATTENDANCE AT THE YOUTH Club. The soap box idea had galvanised the usually indolent youths, and they were already in a huddle, discussing design and building plans. Apparently their tech teacher at school had got interested and was helping them.

"Right, girls," Floss was saying, "let's make sure we get in on this. Can't have the boys taking all the credit." As she herded the two groups together, she saw the door open and a face look round. Then the door shut again.

"Jack Hickson," she said quickly to John, and dashed for the door. Jack was disappearing up the lane, and she yelled, "Jack! Come here a minute! Can you spare a minute?" Then John was following her, and the pair of them caught up with Jack, who looked fixedly at the ground and said nothing.

"Come on, boy," John said. "We hoped you'd come. Another pair of hands needed, and I've heard you're a handy lad. Come on, let's go." John's man-to-man approach worked, and Floss was relieved to see the pair walk back to the village hall.

"When we packed up," she said to her husband, Ben, later that evening, "Jack Hickson looked a different chap. Head up, laughing at John's silly jokes. And he'd had some good suggestions for the vehicle, so John said."

"Let's hope it lasts," said Ben, from behind the evening paper. "These things can be a one day wonder. Especially with kids. Any coffee going? I've been waiting 'til you came home to put the kettle on."

THIRTY

❧

"ARE YOU GOING TO BE LATE TONIGHT?" KATE ADSTONE SAID. She had been asked if she would like to join the WI, and although Gavin had laughed scornfully and said he thought young wives would be more in her line, she had said yes, she would go along and see if she wanted to become a member. It had been that pleasant woman, grandmother of nice Josie at the shop, who'd asked her. Mrs. Weedon, her name was, had offered to call for Kate and take her along to the village hall. "It's a special meeting," she had said. "We're entering a soap box, and hope to get most of the members involved. Some of us are a bit creaky, but there'll be jobs for everyone."

Now Gavin grabbed his document case, pecked Kate on the cheek, patted the top of Cecilia's silky head, and said that he'd make sure he was back by six thirty.

After he'd gone, Kate stacked the dishes and tidied up. It was Cecilia's first morning at the nursery on her own, and she wanted to get there a little early, so that she could stay and make sure she was settled. There had been a week when she had stayed with Cecilia for the whole morning, and now the idea of abandoning her was awful, She had been assured that it would be good for the child, and she would learn from the other children around her. Kate did not want her to learn some of the less charming ways of other children she had seen, but gave in, and now this important morning had arrived.

"Good morning, Kate! And here's our Cecilia come to stay with us for a little while. Shall we go and see what Sarah is doing in the playhouse?" She took Cecilia's hand, and the little girl toddled off obediently after the woman in charge. Kate stood watching them, wanting to burst into tears, grab her baby and run away forever. But she saw the woman motioning that she should leave and so she turned and made her way blindly out of the village hall and up the lane.

She occupied herself changing sheets and stuffing the washing machine, and then sat down to glance at the newspaper. Her attention was caught by a story about abduction and rape, when there was a loud knock at the door. She rushed to open it, convinced that something had happened to Cecilia, and found Tim Froot standing there, smiling broadly at her.

"Are you all right, Kate?" he said. "You look a little distraught! Gavin been beating you up again?" He laughed heartily, and said he was just passing and thought he would cadge a cup of coffee from her. He'd been meaning to have a chat about this and that for some time.

AT NURSERY, CECILIA HAD BEEN FINE FOR FIVE MINUTES, THEN looked around for her mother and realised she had gone. She was instantly heartbroken, and wept bitterly until Sarah, the young assistant, sat her on her lap and fed her teddy-bear biscuits. "Against the rules," Martha, the woman in charge, had said crossly, but Sarah knew that it was a tried-and-tested remedy for heartbreak, adopted by all the assistants at the nursery.

"Another thoroughly spoiled toddler," Martha said. "We shall soon lick her into shape." Sarah winked at the woman who came in to prepare the morning snack. They both knew that Martha was as soft as grease with the children, in spite of her prickly exterior. The little ones seemed to know it, too, and always ran to Martha for comfort in times of distress.

"Mrs. Adstone seems a very pleasant mother," Sarah said. "Have you met the father?"

Martha shook her head. "I've seen him outside, waiting for Kate. Works in Tresham, I believe, at the same place as Mrs. Meade's son, Douglas. That's another one who should expand his family as soon as possible! They have a little boy called Harry, I think, and the apple of everyone's eye. Needs a little competition! The trouble is, you know, Sarah, it is too easy to plan the family these days."

Uh-oh! Here we go again, thought Sarah.

"In some ways," said Martha, looking nostalgically out of the high windows in the village hall, "it was better when the only family planning method was abstinence! Then children came along one after the other, and you got it all over when mother and father were still young. And grandparents, too, were still young enough to be a huge help bringing up the grandchildren."

"Yeah, all ten of the little dears," said Sarah, smiling. "Not sure I agree, Martha. Still, you can't put the clock back. Most women wait for a bit, building up a career first."

Cecilia was struggling to get down from Sarah's lap and fixing her eyes on a small girl who was bathing a bedraggled doll; she toddled away to join in.

"NICE LITTLE PLACE YOU HAVE HERE, KATE," SAID TIM FROOT, settling his large frame into the best armchair. "How's Gavin liking his new job?"

Kate handed him his coffee, and perched on the edge of a chair opposite him. She was nervous. She had not liked him from the first time they met, which was when he interviewed her for a job in his company five years ago. She had not cared for the way his hot eyes looked at her, nor for the way he seemed to have a hold over Gavin, who worked in the same company. It was there she and Gavin had met, and subsequently became engaged.

The conversation limped along, and then he said, "Seems a long time ago that you fell for your Gavin. Why him, Kate, when you could have had the pick of my young executives?"

Mind your own business, thought Kate. But she didn't answer his question, and changed the subject. "I don't want to hurry you, Mr. Froot, but I have to pick up Cecilia from the nursery group."

"Not Mr. Froot, please! Surely we know one another well enough for you to call me Tim?" He looked at his watch. "And I'm sure Cecilia will be there until lunchtime? I'd love to see round your little love nest, my dear."

Kate felt panic rising, and stood up. "Oh, it's all too much of a mess for the escorted tour," she said, making a desperate effort to lighten the atmosphere. She edged towards the door, but he took hold of her arm. "Let me go!" she said, trying to shake him off.

"Oh, come on, Kate," he said. "I'm sure Gavin would want you to be nice to me. He's probably not told you, but he owes me a favour. I always collect," he added, and bent down towards her.

"Get away from me!" she yelled, and managed to pull herself free. She dashed for the door and ran out in the garden, down the path and along the road, where she almost crashed into Tony Dibson, who was pushing his wife along in her wheelchair.

"Hey, hey! Look where you're going, young lady!" said Tony. Then he realised who it was. "Are you all right?" he added, and put out his hand, as if to support Kate, who looked decidedly shaky.

"Just wasn't thinking," she gasped. "So sorry. I'll just catch my breath. I'm really sorry, Mrs. Dibson." She looked fearfully behind her, and saw the big car slowly move away and disappear round the corner.

"Who was that?" said Tony. He had no qualms about airing his village curiosity.

"Oh, just a friend of Gavin," Kate said.

"Did he upset you?" Irene asked, leaning forwards and taking Kate's hand. "Would you like to come back with us for a cup of tea? We'll wait while you lock up. Go on, love. We like a bit of company, don't we, Tony?"

Kate was about to refuse politely, but began to feel dizzy again, and said that she would really like that, if they could spare the time. Tony laughed. "That's the one thing we got plenty of," he said.

AS THE CAR CRUISED SLOWLY ALONG, PURRING LIKE A SATISFIED cat, its driver was far from satisfied. Tim Froot did not like being thwarted. He was not used to it, and now he plotted his revenge. Up to now, he had handled Gavin very gently, he considered. He had allowed his former employee to think that this village hall scheme was very small beer to him. But he had bigger plans for Long Farnden. He had achieved a similar project in a number of other villages, and by using a careful building strategy he had made a financial killing without the hicks on their parish councils realising it. " 'Softly, softly, catchee monkee,' " he repeated his mantra to himself now. But not so softly as before, Gavin, my lad. Time to put on the squeeze.

THIRTY-ONE

✦

As Gran walked up the little path to the Adstones' front door, she heard raised voices, mostly a man's voice. She stopped, wondering whether she should perhaps come back a few minutes later. But then the shouting stopped and the front door opened.

"Hi, Mrs. Weedon! Come in for a second. I'm nearly ready."

Gran thought Kate looked flushed, but she was smiling and looked calm enough. "Don't worry, dear," she said. "I'll wait in the garden. You've got some lovely smelly nicotiana over there." Gavin appeared, and said what on earth was nicotiana? Not a member of the marijuana family, he hoped.

"No, no. We always call it the tobacco plant," Gran said. "Go on, have a sniff."

"I'll take your word for it," he said, beckoning her in. "Just come in and say hello to Cecilia. She's all ready for bed and smells of baby powder. I must say I prefer it to anything called nicotiana!"

He seems jolly, Gran thought. Perhaps it was just a moment's spat. But when she took Cecilia in her arms to give her a cuddle, she could see traces of tears on the toddler's cheeks. Had her parents' shouting match made her cry?

"Right, off we go then, Mrs. Weedon," Kate said, and then reminded Gavin to make sure Cecilia had her favourite brown doggie in her cot. "Night-night precious," she added, giving Cecilia a kiss.

The two walked off towards the village hall, and Gran chose her moment. As they passed the Dibson cottage, she said she hoped Irene would be at WI. "Her Tony usually pushes her down early to get her settled," she said. "I saw them this afternoon, going for a stroll down to the shop. They said they'd seen you this morning. I did wonder if you'd make it this evening. They said you'd been a bit dizzy and upset. Nasty turn, was it, dear?" Gran had pretty well decided the girl must be pregnant again, but would not ask outright. There were other ways of finding out.

"Oh, I'm fine," said Kate. "It was just that, well, you know. It was just . . ." Her voice trailed off and Gran glanced across at her. Oh dear, the girl was nearly in tears. Not pregnant, then, unless they hadn't planned it. But no, it must be something else.

"Had a disagreement, you two?" she said, and smiled. "It happens in the best of marriages, you know."

Kate shook her head. "No, it wasn't Gavin. I had an unpleasant caller. That's all. He scared me a bit, and when I told Gavin he was pretty angry."

"You should call the police," Gran said firmly. "Was he trying to sell you something?" They were nearly at the door of the village hall now, and Kate blew her nose and shook her head. "No. I knew him, but hadn't seen him for some time," she said. "It was nothing, Mrs. Weedon. All over now. Come on, we might miss the floor show!"

Gran laughed delightedly, but did not forget what had happened. Something to report to Lois, she thought. Strange men calling on vulnerable young women, petty thieving from people's sheds. What was going on? Sooner it was sorted out the better.

"Good evening, ladies," said Mrs. T-J. "Now, first of all, welcome to Kate Adstone, who's come to take a look at us. This is an extra meeting, of course, to discuss in detail our entry for the soap box grand prix, and Lois Meade is here, too, to direct operations. And for once, we have a man in our midst! Douglas Meade here has kindly agreed to help us, and we've established that this is within the rules. Well, what we have really established is that there are no rules, except that the soap boxes have to have brakes! So shall we get straight down to business?"

"Hi, everybody," said Douglas, standing up and looking a little nervously at the assembled group. "Mum says, that is Lois Meade, as most of you know, she says that you have decided on your soap box being a jar of jam! I like it, but we'll have to do quite a bit of design work. I have given it some thought, and reckon we could take a large barrel as our base. I thought if I did most of the construction, then you talented lot could decorate it, make it look like a jar of jam. By the way, will it be strawberry or raspberry?"

"Does it make a difference?" asked Lois, with a grin. They all laughed. Most of them could remember him as a sandy-haired schoolboy, and a nice one at that.

"Of course," said a straight-faced Douglas. "So where shall we find a barrel? Any ideas?"

"I think I can help there," said Mrs. T-J. "My people are in brewing, and I'm sure my cousin would be delighted to let us have a barrel. We shall probably have to clean it out, of course, but shall I go ahead with that?"

Blimey, the old thing is a mover and shaker. "Thank you, that would be a great start," he said, and then suggested they all move into a circle round the big table so that he could show them some preliminary drawings he had made.

Lois was proud of him. He had a gift for bringing out the best in people, either adopting their suggestions or tactfully sidelining them for the moment. Sheila Stratford said she was sure Sam would be able to find some good wheels on the farm. Although he was now retired, he still spent a lot of time there, helping out. Their long patch of trouble and involvement with the police had come to an end, and Sheila was anxious to rehabilitate Sam into village life.

By half past eight, Mrs. Tollervey-Jones announced that they had made really good progress and it was time to wind up the meeting. "We must meet again, weekly, if that is acceptable," she said. "Not much time, and I shall need some practise if you all insist that I drive a jar of jam! I must confess," she added modestly, "that I discovered one of my grandchildren has a similar vehicle, and I had a couple of practise sessions. Reasonably successfully, too. Quite an exhilarating experience, you know," she said confidingly.

The stunned WI members got to their feet, and Mrs. T-J said she would see them all next Monday evening. "Same time, same place," she said, and went out humming what could have been "Jerusalem" if she had not been totally tone deaf.

GAVIN, WATCHING TELEVISION WITH THE SOUND TURNED DOWN low so as not to wake Cecilia, looked at his watch. Kate should be home soon. He had had an uncomfortable evening, regretting some of the things he had said to her, but mostly worrying about Tim Froot. He had devoutly wished over and over again that he had never allowed himself to become involved with the man. He was not a man, he was a monster, so friendly and helpful at first, convincing Gavin that the investment he was recommending was all legal and aboveboard. He even offered, and persuaded Gavin to accept, a considerable loan to make the investment worthwhile. And now he was calling in the debt, so that there was not just a risk of exposure of fraud, but also a horrible threat of blackmail involving poor Kate.

The thought of the monster with his hands on his beloved wife sent blood rushing to his head and he stood up, his fists clenched. As he heard her footsteps along the garden path he rushed out and hugged her tightly until she gasped for breath.

"I'm so sorry," he kept repeating, and she took his arm and led him into the house, putting her finger to her lips and reminding him that Cecilia was a very light sleeper.

"Now," she said, when they were sitting side by side on the sofa, "what exactly are you so sorry about? Not just a mild quarrel with me, surely? After all, I had every reason to send that Froot man packing. He won't try anything again."

Gavin was quiet for a minute, and then ran his hands through his hair and groaned. "It's a long story," he said, adding to himself that he could not possibly tell her all at the moment. Perhaps an edited version would explain his anger and caution her to be very careful with Tim Froot in the future. So he said that when he left Froot's company, he had had to break a contract in order to take up the new job, which offered really good prospects. Froot had been tough, he said, and made a deal with Gavin involving a loan, which he now wanted repaid.

"But can't we pay him in installments?" Kate said. "I can get a part-time job now Cecilia's at nursery. And I can work at home, too. Lots of people do now, using computers. It's a different world out there!"

Gavin nodded. "That'll help," he said. "Don't worry, love. We'll crack it together."

Later on, aware that Gavin was not asleep, Kate said, "You haven't told me everything, have you, Gav? You haven't said why Froot is always cruising round this village, down to the village hall and around the streets. Not because of my irresistible charms, I'm sure of that."

There was a long silence, and then an unconvincing snore. Kate sighed and turned over to face the wall. She had enjoyed the WI meeting, but it all seemed very unimportant now. It was a long time before she finally fell asleep.

THIRTY-TWO

෴

"So I said to her," Gran insisted, "that she must report him to the police. Mind you, I don't think she will. She said she knew him, so I expect it's more complicated than it looks."

Lois frowned. "It was a bit extreme, wasn't it, suggesting the police? After all, if they knew the man, a stern warning from Gavin should do the trick. Anyway, you did right to comfort the poor woman. But it doesn't sound like it was the same man as the mystery food thief, or Jack Hickson's missing father." Or the man who's persecuting him outside the school gates, she decided. Her mother had taken the whole thing a bit too seriously, she thought privately. Probably just a marital tiff, and Mum walked straight into it.

"Could be an old boyfriend stirring up trouble. But thanks for telling me, anyway," she said. "Nothing like a boost from Gran Weedon! Kate seemed quite restored at the meeting. Now, I must get on," she added, returning to her computer screen. "Floss is coming to see me later on, and yesterday's team meeting threw up a few problems. Thanks for a nice breakfast," she added tactfully, hoping she had not been too hard on her mother.

The telephone rang, and Gran lingered. Lois smiled at her and waved a farewell hand. Gran left the room in a huff. After all, she said to herself, Lois is not the only one with a nose for trouble.

"Hi, Inspector," Lois said. "Busy morning. I'm pushed for time here, so what's up?"

"Good morning, Lois," he said, and his tone was brisk. "Chris and I are on our way over to Farnden to investigate another theft, this time from you-know-who up at the hall. You could say we'd been summoned. I wondered if you'd be around for a quick chat? Chris will be with me, of course."

"I don't need a chaperone," Lois said lightly. "Still, she seems nice enough, and yes, I'll be here. But Floss is coming to see me at twelve thirty, so you'll have to make it snappy."

In ten minutes they were there, knocking at the front door and being admitted by a curious Gran. "Good morning, Inspector," she said. "And you, Miss . . . ?"

"Chris," said the policewoman. "I'm Inspector Cowgill's assistant. You must be Mrs. Meade's mother?"

"Yes, I am," said Gran. "I am her housekeeper, and we—"

"Thanks, Mum!" said Lois, emerging from her office. "Come in, you two. Perhaps my housekeeper would bring us some coffee?"

Cowgill smothered a smile, and Gran stomped off to the kitchen.

"Now," said Lois, "how can I help?"

Cowgill reflected that Lois was much more polite and friendly when he had Chris with him, and realised he preferred her as she was when he was on his own. Her abrupt accusations and downright rudeness seemed to him to be the real Lois, the Lois he loved. He knew from many perilous situations they had been in together that she was feisty, brave and impatient, not this mild person facing him now. Unless it was really necessary, he decided, he would not bring Chris with him in the future. In any case, for all he knew, Lois would not be so forthcoming with a third person present.

He was right. Lois held back when they asked if she had any idea who the thief might be, and had nothing to say on the more serious matter of the drug dealer at the school gates. It seemed that one or two parents at Jack's school had seen the man hanging about, and were worried for their own children. They had reported this to the police, and Cowgill asked if Lois had heard anything from parents in Farnden. She was cagey. Hazel had been in touch with her earlier this morning, filling her in on what happened when she gave Jack a lift, and Lois had promised to ask Paula what she knew. It was, after all, a matter for Paula to deal with, and Lois intended to back her up and support her all she could. But it would be better if she, and not the police, could get to her first.

"It happens every so often in most schools," she said now. "I remember when Josie was a teenager and dabbled briefly with substances, as they call them. It wasn't nice at the time, but it was a phase that passed. You should ask some of the kids, the bigger ones. They probably won't tell you, Inspector, but Chris might have more luck, especially if she's not in uniform."

"And the thefts? Any connection, do you think, Lois?" Cowgill said with a sigh. He knew his Lois, and could see they were getting nothing of interest from her this morning.

Lois shook her head. "A tramp, maybe? We've got no gypsies to blame this time, have we? No, I should think it's a cunning old tramp. That's how they survive, though there's not many around now. Welfare State, an' all that."

Cowgill stood up. "Well, thanks, Lois. Can't say you've been a great help, but thanks anyway. We shall be around the village for a while, calling on parents who have children at the Tresham school. We don't want to spread alarm, but it could be serious. We have a list of these children, but if you think of anything that might help, you know how to find me."

"Before you go, and speaking of being a great help," Lois said acidly, "is there anything new on the corpse in the canal?"

"Oh, yes," said Chris. "He was one of the homeless lot, mostly drunk on anything he could get. Nothing to do with any of our investigations. His brother turned up finally and identified him. At least he'll get a decent burial.

"Well, thanks for letting me know, Inspector," snapped Lois.

Sod it, thought Lois, after they'd gone. Now she had to move quickly, to find Paula before they did. She looked at her watch. Paula would be at the hall now, and there'd be nobody at home in the Hickson house.

"Mum! Something's come up, and I have to go out. Shan't be long. If Floss gets here before I'm back, ask her to wait. Thanks."

Gran tut-tutted. Lois would never change. Good thing she had an iron stomach, always rushing hither and thither, not giving herself time to digest. There'd been a pile of biscuits on the tray of coffee she'd taken in, and now the plate was empty.

"Take care!" she shouted to the retreating New Brooms van, and reflected that she might just as well save her breath.

As she drove into the stable yard, Lois saw a familiar fig-ure disappearing into the kitchen garden. Tall, thin, but a lot smartened up from when she saw him last, holed up in a derelict cottage in a rainstorm. She wondered how Paula was coping with this situation, and was even more determined to soften the impact of the visiting police investigators if she could.

Mrs. T-J was in the kitchen and answered the door. "Mrs. Hickson? Yes, she's here. Working upstairs," she added, with emphasis on "working."

"I wondered if I could have a quick word with her," Lois said firmly. "It is urgent, otherwise I wouldn't bother you." At that moment Paula came into the kitchen, carrying her cleaning things.

"Excuse me," she said. "I'll just get a fresh floor cloth. Sorry to interrupt."

"It's you Mrs. Meade has come to see," Mrs. T-J said crossly. "I'll leave you together, but I'm expecting the police soon. We've had a theft from our storeroom. Perhaps you could tell me when you go, Mrs. Meade."

"Old bag," whispered Paula, then apologised. "Is it about Jack, husband Jack?" she said. "He's here now, in the garden, if you want a word. I don't have anything to do with him, but he tries to sweeten me up. It's probably him what took the food."

Lois shook her head. "No," she said, "it's about Jack Jr."

Paula groaned. "Oh, no, not in trouble again. I tell you honestly, Mrs. M, I don't know what to do with that boy. What's he done this time?"

Lois explained as briefly as she could about the man at the school gates, and said she knew young Jack was scared. She told Paula about Hazel giving him a lift, and then said the police were in the village, following up complaints from other parents, as well as investigating the theft. "They'll have Jack Jr.'s name on a list of children in Farnden who go to that school, so they'll be wanting to talk to you. I hoped to give you time to think before they found you. You may have to tell them about your husband an' that."

"Oh, my God," said Paula. "So there *is* somebody pushing drugs. That's the last thing my son Jack needs. Poor kid. It's all that sodding gardener out there's fault! Maybe I'll put them on to him."

"You'd better get back to work now. But think carefully, Paula. I shouldn't be telling you to keep things from the police, but your first concern is young Jack, isn't it? I'm off now, but keep me posted. Bye."

After she had called to Mrs T-J that she was leaving, she drove off out of the stable yard and saw Jack Hickson standing by the gate, staring at her. It was not a friendly stare.

Lois found Floss waiting for her when she got back. "Sorry I'm late," she said. "Had to have a quick word with Paula."

"That's fine," Floss said. "I've got a couple of hours before I go over to Fletching. Nothing bad happened, I hope? Mrs. Weedon said you'd had to rush out unexpectedly. I saw the police in the High Street, outside the shop. I wondered if anything had happened to Josie."

Lois shook her head. "Probably quizzing her," she said grimly. "Village shopkeeper knows everything. You know the kind of thing. It's about the school in Tresham. There's been a dealer trying to sell to the kids, apparently. Parents have complained, and the police are going around talking to families who have kids at the school."

Floss looked at her sharply. "Hicksons?" she said. "Hazel told me about giving Jack Jr. a lift, and him telling her how he was scared of this man."

"Right," said Lois. "Well, that saves me telling you. Yes, Jack's been approached. But I wasn't sure that his mother knew, and I had to get to her before the police."

Floss nodded sympathetically. "Poor old Paula. She's got more than enough on her plate, without a kid on drugs," she said. "Did you find her?"

"Yes. I only hope she has time to think things out before the police catch up with her."

"Why shouldn't she tell them straight that she knew nothing about it? After all, she's got nothing to hide."

Lois took a deep breath and let it out slowly. Then she brushed a hand over her eyes wearily. "She suspected. But no, that's right," she said, "she's got nothing to hide."

IT WAS AFTER TWO O'CLOCK WHEN COWGILL AND CHRIS FINALLY caught up with Paula Hickson. She had had an hour to herself before collecting little Frankie from nursery, and then the twins from school, and had been frantically turning over in her mind what Mrs. M had told her. She wouldn't admit it to anyone, but she had suspected for a while that Jack Jr. had been experimenting with something. Once or twice he had been very shaky in the mornings and had cried off school, saying he felt sick. His violent mood swings were suspicious, too.

She remembered sadly what a nice little boy he had been before all the trouble with his father. A real charmer, people had said. She had taken him as a baby back to the development company where she'd worked to show him off to her friends, and the Dutch boss had come in and been so nice about him. Quite soppy, he had been. Funny, she thought now, she could have sworn she saw him staring at the village hall from his car the other day. It was probably someone else, but he'd smiled at her in that rather smarmy way the girls had reason to mistrust.

She dragged her thoughts back to Jack Jr. What should she tell the police? She lit a forbidden cigarette and stood out in the garden, staring out at the road as if she could will the police to pass her by.

So who was trying to persuade children to take drugs? And why hadn't the police taken him off the streets? She supposed those kids who knew only too well why he was hanging about were probably hooked already, and would be too scared to tell on him. But now parents had banded together and called in the police.

The chances were they would not ask her about her

husband. Why should they? As far as she knew, Jack Sr. had not been in trouble with the law. There had been that scrap with his workmate. Well, it had been more than a scrap, apparently. She'd been told he had had to go to hospital and they found a broken rib. But again, she had not heard that Jack had been reported.

She saw a car cruising slowly along the street, with a man and woman peering out from side to side. Police, for sure. She stubbed out her cigarette under her shoe and returned rapidly to the house. She knew now what she would say to them. Nothing much. There would be no point. They were sure to find out who the dealer was from one of the other parents, and the police would make sure the man was put away, well away from corrupting innocent children. If she told them of her suspicions about Jack Jr., they would question him, and however gentle they were, and with her alongside, it still might tip the poor kid over the edge. No, she would be vague and willing, but not much help. That would be best. After all, Mrs. M had more or less advised her to do this.

Thirty-Three

～

G AVIN ADSTONE HAD RECEIVED A CALL TO HIS MOBILE AS HE walked to his car. The signal wasn't very good, but Tim Froot's guttural voice was unmistakeable.

"I'll give you until tomorrow to tell me your plan," he said. "No more mucking about, Gavin. I need to have a positive plan of action. You have a meeting tonight. Well, that should concentrate your mind. Either you convince me that your shack will be demolished and a builder—this builder— given a contract to develop, or our deal is off. No more time allowed. Pay me back, or else. I have a couple of ideas how to guarantee you'll find the money. Did Kate tell you I called? Good."

Tim Froot had signed off, giving Gavin no time to reply, no time to prevaricate, no time to tell the monster that if he touched his wife, or even threatened her, he would kill him.

Gavin had had a plan for the village hall, in the beginning. Invited on to the parish council soap box subcommittee, he had seen his chance. He would scupper their feeble efforts at fund-raising, ostensibly helping but actually making sure it would be a dismal failure. As things were going, it would not be difficult. He was pretty sure that if he told the police about the many ways the grand prix would flout regulations, the parish council would be loaded down with so many safety measures that whatever profit there was would be eaten up in putting them into place. A total loss from what was intended to be the big event, the grand fund-raiser, should dishearten the parish council sufficiently for the demolish-and-rebuild lobby to triumph. Grants would be forthcoming, especially if there was emphasis on the hall as a sporting facility. And, of course, Froot was known to be adept at securing contracts from local authorities, promising extra facilities alongside his rows of new houses.

So then Gavin would be in the clear and Kate would be safe. They would pay back the loan in installments, and have nothing to do with the monster in future. This, then, was his original plan. But now things were different, Gavin said to himself as he plodded down the road to the village hall for tonight's meeting. For one thing, he was rapidly coming to the conclusion that he couldn't sabotage the grand prix. How could he face Tony Dibson and his nice, brave wife? And good old Derek, wise and patient. He had been a good choice for chairman, and Gavin was beginning to see his worth, and respect it. Then there were Hazel and Floss, both of whom had been so nice to Kate. John Thornbull, a bluff farmer with his head firmly screwed on, who had clearly not liked the look of Gavin but was giving him a chance. No, he couldn't do it.

"Evenin', Gavin," Tony said, as they met at the door of the hall. "How's your Kate? And that lovely Cecilia? She's made quite a conquest of my Irene. Dear little soul doesn't seem a bit scared of the wheelchair, like some of the bigger kids."

"Ready to start?" Derek called from inside the hall. Gavin

and Tony were the last to arrive, and hurried to their seats. "Shall we have the minutes of the last meeting?" Derek said.

"Apologies first," Hazel said. "Anybody not here?" She looked around. "Father Rodney is missing. Anybody seen him?"

Nobody had, though John Thornbull said the vicar had made his usual lightning visit to the pub last evening. "We tried to get him to play dominoes, but he wouldn't. Looked a bit tempted though, so we shall try again. I'm pretty sure he said he'd be here tonight."

"May have been delayed," Derek said. "We'll make a start, Hazel."

They listened to the minutes, then had a progress report from committee members. There was some hilarity on hearing that Mrs. T-J would be driving a jar of jam. Derek protested that they shouldn't mock too much. "That woman could be a fiend at the wheel," he said. "And if any of you men have seen the WI in action at the Albert Hall for their AGM, well! Remember how they cut the PM down to size? The famous charm failed completely. Never underestimate a group of women, that's what a lifetime married to my Lois and her mother has taught me!"

There was a murmur of agreement from the men, and sympathetic looks for Derek.

"I still say the old trout will end up in the ditch," Tony Dibson said, chuckling. "It'll be a big moment for the whole village."

"So how's the Youth Club entry getting on?" Derek asked Floss.

"John knows more about that than me," Floss said. "He's deeply involved now. Got the kids really going. Including the newcomer, Jack Hickson Jr. He's a bit of loner, and we're really glad he's joined. Clever, too. Apparently his father could turn his hand to anything."

"Is the father dead?" Tony said bluntly.

Floss shook her head. "Left the family. Not been seen

since, so Mrs. Hickson is bringing up the kids on her own. She's working for New Brooms, as Hazel knows."

"I knew a chap called Hickson," Tony said slowly. "Nice bloke. Worked for the Parks and Gardens Department in the town where my brother lives. He was a friend of my nephew. Met him once or twice. I don't suppose it's the same man."

Derek felt they were getting off the main subject, and asked Gavin how he was doing with entries and publicity. "Low-key publicity, Gavin. You've remembered that, I hope," he said.

"I'm thinking in terms of it being a village event," Gavin replied. "Spreading the net no wider than surrounding villages. The way the entries are coming in, we shall have to close the list soon, anyway!"

"How long to go?" said Tony Dibson, counting on his fingers. "There's one, two, three full weeks, then it's the following Saturday. Most of the course is planned anyway."

"I've got the straw bales ready on a trailer," John said. "And the ramp is done. Gavin's getting the races sorted out. Four soap boxes at a time, we reckon, will be safe enough. Then we'll have the final."

"We need somebody to check the vehicles at the start," Derek said. "I can do that, if you like. The main thing is to make sure they've all got brakes, and the wheels are secure. That should cover it."

"There's some real work being done with the entries," Gavin said. "I've seen lights burning late in several garages round the villages! I reckon it's going to be a lot of fun."

"How's the rest of it coming along?" Derek said.

Hazel looked at her notes. "We've got a lot going on in the playing field," she said. "The big marquee is full now. Craft stalls, gardening and plants, homemade cakes and stuff, rugs and harness for ponies, and lots more. The school has got a stall, showing the extension they're planning, and we've got a nice display of work to be done on the Shed, with a mock-up of how it will look when it's finished. Oh yes, and the school is happy to select the soap box queen. Not necessarily the prettiest, said the head, but the one who is all-round hardest worker."

"Sounds good," said Derek. "I can tell you a bit more about *Jam & Jerusalem*. That's what they're calling the WI entry. They're planning to have a player blasting out 'Jerusalem' as Mrs. T-J goes first past the post."

"I hope somebody's filming it," said Gavin. "I could get my mother-in-law to come over and look after Cecilia, then Kate can have our cine-camera and make a film record. What d'you think?"

"Wonderful," said John. "Good lad, Gavin."

The door opened, and Father Rodney rushed in looking flustered. "So sorry, everybody! I was called away to give the last rites. Poor soul in the nursing home over at Waltonby. At least, they all thought she was a poor soul, but when I got there she was sitting up in bed drinking brandy and insulting the nurses. Dear me, I should have been pleased for her, but all I could think was that I was about to call on the Almighty for nothing. Still, I am sure he's all forgiving."

"As we are," said Derek. "Sit down, Vicar. Hazel will fill you in quickly with what's been decided. I'm glad to say everything's going brilliantly, and all we shall need the Almighty for is to send us a fine day."

"I shall do my best to intercede," said Father Rodney, and smiled benignly round the rest.

"That'll be a big help," muttered Tony.

"Ssh!" said Floss, who was sitting next to him. "He's doing his best."

Tony grunted. His Irene was still a devout believer, but sometimes, his heart breaking as he watched her struggling to get into her clothes without bothering him, he had begun to doubt. But then he put it to the back of his mind. No point in wondering why, he had decided that long ago.

"Well, if there's no other business, I shall close the meeting for tonight."

"And reopen it in the pub, shall we?" said Gavin.

"That's my boy," said Tony Dibson.

THIRTY-FOUR

༮

GRAN SAT AT THE KITCHEN TABLE, WATCHING THE GOLD-finches sitting neatly on the feeder in the garden, scarlet, black and white flashing brightly now as they flew away, startled by a large pigeon landing on the grass.

They don't look British, she thought, more like something escaped from an exotic aviary. Now a group of chattering, quarrelling sparrows flew in. That was more like it! A football crowd at a big match. She laughed aloud and got up, taking her empty mug to the sink. Lois and Derek had both gone out, and she had a free morning for once. She looked again out of the window. It was a beautiful morning, and Jeems was standing by the door, looking hopefully at her lead.

"Right, dog," she said. "We'll go for a healthy walk. Up to the hall and back over the meadows. Will that do?" Jeems's tail wagged ferociously, and in a couple of minutes they were off, heading along the road towards the hall.

Only two cars passed her, causing her to jump on to the verge, dragging Jeems up after her. For some reason, the dog hated walking on the verge, preferring the middle of the tarmac road. Lois said it was good for her claws. It saves having them cut at the vets, she'd said. The second car had been Paula Hickson's old banger, and she saw it turn up the long drive to the hall. The woman was a good worker, so Lois reported. But Gran had overheard one or two conversations, and had come to the conclusion that the children were suffering from lack of a father. Certainly the eldest, young Jack, was not right, not right at all. There was trouble there, Gran was certain.

As she approached the big, wrought iron gates, operated automatically, she saw at the far end of the drive a figure on a bicycle. She stopped, pretending to adjust Jeems's lead. It was a man, and he was going at quite a speed. Gran wondered if the gates would open up to a bicycle.

They didn't, and the man dismounted, hauled his bike round the edge of the gates, and came towards her. He was neatly dressed in gardener's overalls, and smiled at her. She thought he had a nice face, but reckoned he was too thin to be doing hard physical work. Didn't look well. His hand, as he bent down to stroke Jeems, was bony and she could see the blue veins standing out.

His voice was cheerful as he wished her a good morning. "Just the morning for a walk," he said. "And a nice little dog to keep you company. I might get myself a dog. What make is she?"

"Cairn crossed with farm terrier," Gran said. "My son-in-law got her for my daughter. She's thoroughly spoiled," she added. "That's what happens when children grow up. The parents get a dog instead. We all need something small to love, don't we?" What am I rattling on about? she thought, and then was horrified to see the man wipe his eyes. For God's sake, what had she said?

"I must get on," the man said. "Just going to the shop to get a sandwich for my break."

"I should've thought your wife would make you a sandwich,"

Gran said sourly. Another of these working wives too busy to look after their husbands properly.

"Ah, if only," said the man, and, mounting his bicycle, he rode off towards the village.

Gran walked on, past the farm where the farmer's wife had started a small herd of llamas. More foreigners, thought Gran. They don't look right in our fields, silly fluffy things. What's wrong with sheep, anyway, if you want good wool for knitting? She'd seen some alpaca wool garments in the new fancy shop over at Waltonby. The farmer there had developed his old barns, now too small for huge modern machinery, into retail units, and one of them had this fine, hairy wool. Gran had looked at the price tickets and nearly exploded in front of a party of visiting tourists.

"Just as well we can still buy proper lamb's wool at a decent price," she said to Jeems, and added that even so, it would probably vanish from the shops soon, since no young folk these days knew how to knit.

She had taken off Jeems's lead, as the road was quiet and the dog would come to heel obediently. At least, she usually did, but when a rabbit shot across the road and through the hedge into a field, Jeems followed. Gran called until she was hoarse, but with no response.

Damn! Just when she was enjoying the morning, this had to happen. Gran walked on until she came to a gate into the field, opened it and looked around. No sign of Jeems. At the far side of the field, the woods began, and if she had followed the rabbit in there, it would be impossible to find her. Lois would never forgive her!

Gran stepped out across the grass, fortunately grazed close by cattle, who were still in the field. Hoping there wasn't a bull amongst them, she took the quickest route and reached a ditch dividing the wood from the field. Finding a rotten-looking plank stretching across the ditch, she stepped gingerly on to it and was quickly inside the trees, thanking her lucky stars she had found the footpath that led back to the village.

"Jeems! Jeems!" she yelled, but her voice had nearly given out, and she hoped to see the little white dog somewhere in the murky darkness of the trees. It was very quiet, until a sudden squawk from a frightened blackbird caused her to stop and look carefully into the undergrowth. There she was! Almost disguised by the surrounding thicket, Jeems's wagging tail showed up clearly. Gran forced her way through, scratching her hands and legs and cursing all dogs, until she could grab the tail and haul Jeems out of the rabbit hole.

"Come here, you little devil!" she said, and stood still to catch her breath. Then she peered more closely across the thicket. What was that over there? "Looks like a poachers' lair," she said to Jeems, and began to work her way towards it.

It had clearly once been a gamekeeper's hut, but long disused. Somebody had patched it up with bits of wood and tarpaulin, and to Gran's disappointment, had padlocked the door. She peered through a crack, but could see only a dead pheasant hanging head down from a crossbeam. The glorious feathers were still quite bright, so Gran knew it hadn't been there long. She turned and made her way back to the footpath, dragging a reluctant Jeems behind her. "Our woods are full of surprises," she said. "A secret world, dog Jeems."

By the time she had followed the footpath round three sides of the wood, and then negotiated another field and into the main road, both she and Jeems were hot and tired. Back home in her kitchen, she filled the dog's water bowl and looked at the clock. It was twelve o'clock, and she saw Lois going by the kitchen window.

"Hi, Mum. What's for lunch? Had a good morning?" Then she looked down at Jeems seemingly drinking an entire bowl of water. "Good heavens! Where've you two been? Gossiping in the sun round at Joan's, I expect. Well, don't look like that, Mum. I was only guessing."

This clinched it. Gran had been going to tell Lois about the hut in the woods, but now decided against it. She could hear Lois's mocking voice, teasing her about being a townie and having no idea about the foolishness of taking a rabbit-hunting terrier off the lead right next to an open field. Anyway, the hut was just another old tumbledown place for poachers or them bird-watchers. She put it firmly from her mind.

Thirty-Five

৵

I wouldn't mind driving it," said Jack Jr., standing amongst the others, looking down at the skeleton of their soap box. "I reckon it's going to be the best."

"How old are you, Jack?" said John Thornbull.

"Fifteen," said Jack.

"No you're not," said one of the other boys. "I know which class you're in at school, an' they're all thirteen or fourteen."

"I'm a slow learner," said Jack, and then burst out laughing. "All right, then, I'm thirteen but nearly fourteen. I know I could drive it. I think we should all have a chance. Maybe a competition to see who's fastest? When it's finished, Mr. Thornbull?"

John had been so charmed by the sight of Jack Jr. laughing that he didn't think for a minute as he answered that that was a good idea. "But wait a minute," he said, "there's probably an age limit."

"I don't see why," Jack said. "There's no engine, an' as long as I can reach the brake, I'm no more of a risk than somebody older."

"I'll look into it," John said, thinking privately that a lad as handy as Jack was probably safer than some of the young farmers who drove like madmen round the village.

Jack had to be content with that, and in due course went back home, his spirits sinking as he reached his front gate. The police had been to see his mother, and she had told them about the dealer who had been pestering him. He was doubly scared now. If they caught him, he'd probably know it was Jack Jr. who had told on him. The dealer had threatened him over and over again with reprisals, not just from himself but from his mates. He'd got a lot of mates, he'd said to Jack, and none of 'em too particular about who they cut up. "Spoil your chances with the women, they will," he'd said with a leer.

He couldn't decide who had told his mother. It could have been Mrs. Meade, or her receptionist at New Brooms, Mr. Thornbull's wife. Hazel Thornbull had been really nice, shielding him, and because he liked her he had blurted it out. Well, it didn't matter now. In some ways he was relieved. Nothing he could do about it now the police were on the case.

The twins were playing on the swing Mum had bought with her New Brooms wages, and little Frankie stood unsteadily with his arms outstretched and a broad smile. Jack Jr. scooped him up and hugged him hard. If only they'd had a different dad, one like all the other kids at Youth Club, then Frankie could have a real father to look up to. Jack hated his own father now, and had stopped looking in the mirror in case he saw a likeness. He just hoped Mum wouldn't be tempted to take him back. They were managing, weren't they?

"Hello, young Jack!" It was Derek Meade, cruising by in his van. He pulled up and got out. "Just the man I wanted to see," he said, crossing the road and smiling kindly at Jack. "How's the soap box going?"

"All right," Jack muttered.

"Good. I've heard you're a handy bloke, and wondered if you'd like to give me a hand? Paid work, o' course. I've got a job to do over at Fletching, and it'll probably be in the school holidays by the time I get round to it. Nothing regular, of course, and not to interfere with schoolwork. But we could see how you get on."

Jack looked away, down the road and into the distance. "No thanks," he said, and walked off with Frankie in his arms, not looking back.

"So much for a good deed in a naughty world," Derek said later, as he sat down to watch the evening news.

"What are you on about?" Gran said. Lois had insisted on washing up this evening, and sent her and Derek out of the kitchen to watch television.

Derek told her what had happened with Jack Jr., and Gran said that she was not surprised. "What do you expect, with a family all at sixes and sevens? I don't care what the modern generation says, a child needs a mother and a father, and a mother staying at home until they're old enough to look after themselves. Some of these kids of seven and eight have a door key slung round their necks to let themselves in when they get home from school! And then they're surprised when their kids go off the rails!"

"Better not say all that when Lois is around," said Derek.

"As if I would!" Gran said, and fidgeted in her chair until she had calmed down.

"I shall tell her about me having a go at child therapy," he said. "I suppose I'll get Brownie points for trying?"

"Doubt it," said Gran. "Anyway, shush, they're talking about that reality show that's gone all wrong."

When Lois joined them, she sat down next to Derek on the sofa and tucked her hand in his. "I know what you did," she said. "Paula rang me and said I was to thank you, and Jack had told her about you offering him work and was saying he wished he'd not turned you down. So it's on, if you still want him."

"There you are, then," said Gran. "Virtue rewarded. Now could you please both be quiet while I watch my favourite program?"

THE LIGHT WAS GOING AS JACK SR. WORKED HIS WAY INTO THE wood, avoiding footpaths and keeping his progress as quiet as the thicket would allow. He had managed to filch a few potatoes out of the store at the hall, and he'd picked some nettle tops on his way home, knowing from his horticulture studies that they were palatable as young shoots. On his way home! That was a joke. Still, this old gamekeeper's hut was better than a hole in the side of a bank, like some bloody badger's sett. He'd stayed in one for a single night in desperation, but then he'd found this place and had made it watertight at least. In fact, it was so comparatively comfortable that he was tempted to work on it and make it more so. But if he faced facts, he knew he should keep on the move, a successful policy so far. He'd given Mrs. T-J a fictitious address, and she had obviously not checked. She was being quite nice to him when she saw his work was good.

It would have been a perfect sanctuary, if only Paula had not been working at the hall. Much as he loved to see her now and then, even if she was as cold as charity towards him, he realised that sooner or later she would split on him. Probably tell her boss at New Brooms. But would it matter? He'd got so used to living rough and keeping out of sight, that he had almost forgotten why he was doing it. At first it had been because he couldn't think of an alternative. Paula had chucked him out with threats of going to the police, so he'd gone. But if she'd not put them on to him by now, she was probably not going to.

There was still that bloke he'd punched. Nasty piece of work, he'd been, and swore to get back at Jack sooner or later. That sort never forget. No, it'd be safer if he kept to his secret life for a while yet. He'd learned so many tricks and dodges now, that he was quite capable of disappearing at a moment's notice, should the need arise.

One thing he had learned and was sure he would never forget. He would never hit anyone, especially Paula, ever again. The thought sickened him now. But what would he do if he found somebody else threatening his kids? They were still his kids, and he was only too well aware of how vulnerable they could be without a father to defend them. Not against violence, perhaps, but bullying and all that stuff that schoolkids had to go through. That would be the test.

He opened the padlock and walked inside. The pheasant seemed to accuse him with its milky eye. "You needn't look at me like that," Jack said. "I'll have your head off and your feathers out in no time, see if I don't."

THIRTY-SIX

ꝏ

FATHER RODNEY WOKE EARLY. HE TURNED IN HIS LARGE BED and looked at the clock. Half past six. Too early to get up, even though Sunday was his busiest working day. His first service was a nine o'clock Communion over at Waltonby. The sun was shining strongly through the flowery curtains his late wife, Anthea, had loved so much, and he wondered whether to get up and get some fresh air before spending most of the day in the cold, stony interiors of his village churches. He had four parishes in his benefice: Long Farnden, where he lived, Waltonby, Fletching and a tiny village, Hallhouse, with only half a dozen cottages and an ancient Saxon church, beautiful in its plainness. He tried to give them all services most Sundays, and today Holy Communion was in Waltonby, followed by Matins in Farnden church, and then home to a cold lunch. Evensong was at Fletching, and the tiny village had no service until next Sunday.

His wife had died unexpectedly, five years ago, when she was only thirty-nine. She had been a successful athlete, particularly good at short-distance sprinting. They had had no children, and she was the centre of his world. When she collapsed one hot afternoon at an athletics meeting, he had prayed as he had never prayed before for her recovery, but in vain. She had died four hours after being taken to hospital, where they discovered she had had an undiagnosed damaged heart.

Now he soldiered on alone. He knew he was regarded as an eligible bachelor by presentable spinsters in his parishes, but he could not imagine sharing his life with anyone but his beloved Anthea.

He put his legs over the side of the bed, thinking that by doing so the rest of his body had no alternative but to follow. This always worked, and once upright, he drew back the curtains and was glad. It was a beautiful morning, and he pulled on some casual clothes and set off up the Waltonby road at a brisk pace. Anthea would not have liked to see him go to seed.

As he passed by the hall he quickened his pace. The last thing he wanted was to be spotted by Mrs. T-J and forced to listen to her version of the Gospel according to St. Mark. She must, as a child, have been made to absorb the entire Old and New Testaments by heart. He had learned very early on never to contradict her on a matter of dogma or Biblical reference. She would have made an excellent bishop!

He had been astonished when he heard she was intending to drive the WI soap box. Was there nothing this woman could not do?

"Father Rodney! Helloeee!"

Dear God, could you not have held her back until I was well out of sight? Father Rodney turned and saw a perfectly turned-out Mrs. T-J striding towards him. He smiled his friendliest smile, just to show he could, and wished her good morning.

"Just the person I wanted to see!" she said. "There's always such a crowd waiting to speak to you after the service, and now here you are and I've got you all to myself!"

Alarm bells rang. Surely she was not about to make him some discreet partnership proposal—or worse, suggest . . . But no, she was years older than him, and could not possibly . . .

"How can I help?" he said coolly. "I am up and about early to make the most of this beautiful morning before the nine o'clock at Waltonby."

She looked at her watch. "You've got another hour yet. May I join you? I am quite a fast walker." And a fast worker, Father Rodney said to himself in dismay.

"I was just thinking of turning back," he explained. "Have to get showered and togged up in ecclesiasticals, you know. My Sunday best, as they say."

"In that case," she said, "we'll walk up the drive to the hall, you shall have a quick glass of water and I'll run you back to the vicarage."

Father Rodney gave up. He fell in with her now much slower pace, and to his relief she announced that she had a problem with her gardener. "He is such a good worker, but I find it difficult to get much out of him about his private life."

"Perhaps he regards that as his private affair," Father Rodney said gently.

Mrs. T-J puffed up like a pigeon. "Oh, no. I think as his employer I have every right to know what kind of man I am allowing free run of my estate, don't you? He gave me his name and address, and that is all. I have checked both, and find them fictitious. No such name at no such address."

"So what have you done about it? That surely is enough to justify asking for an explanation?"

"Of course. But so far I have done nothing. There is something about the man that warns you off. As you know, I am a strong character. Used to be called fearless on the back of a horse! But I feel I must tread warily. For once, Father Rodney,

I am not sure. That's why I wanted your advice. What do you think?"

He reflected that she probably would take no notice of anything he advised, so it didn't much matter what he said. "I think your instincts are probably right," he said. "Go slowly. Perhaps you could ask around and find out if anyone knows anything about him? You must have a friendly policeman you could consult, you being a magistrate and so on?"

"Of course I know the commissioner, but it's rather a small matter. . . ."

"So far it may be," said Father Rodney. "But he must have a reason for giving false details. Obviously he doesn't want his real identity known. Why? That is the question you need answering. Have you thought of asking Mrs. Meade at New Brooms? Her girls go cleaning all round the county. They are sure to know something about him. Doesn't one of them work for you?"

Mrs. T-J nodded. "Mrs. Hickson, yes. But she doesn't seem to want to have anything to do with him. I've watched her, and when he comes towards the house she retreats upstairs."

"There you are, then!" he said triumphantly. "She knows something about him, and maybe something bad, if she seems scared. Ask her, Mrs. T-J, that's my advice."

They had now arrived in the stable yard, where her large limousine was parked. In no time at all, he was more or less ejected outside the vicarage with plenty of time to prepare for the service. So much for his solitary, contemplative morning stroll! Ah, well, no doubt He had a reason that would in due course emerge.

THE VILLAGE CHURCH CHOIR WAS NOW REDUCED TO THREE sopranos, one alto, two tenors and a bass who could not read music and made it up as he went along. Their robes were assorted shades of red, resulting in uncomfortable clashes, and their singing was much along the same lines. The popular singing teacher who had been their director of music had left a year ago, and things had gone downhill ever since.

Father Rodney was tone deaf, fortunately, and so continued to congratulate them on their rendering of four-part discord, and the few who remained were intensely loyal to him and to each other. Every so often, they tried a recruiting campaign, and occasionally a couple of new people would try it out. But they faded away quickly, and the small band of pilgrims remained.

"I wonder if young Jack Hickson would be interested in joining us?" said Tony Dibson, the improvising bass choir member. He had been impressed by efforts made by several villagers to get the lad to join in, and now he thought how good it would be to have a treble voice amongst them.

"No harm in trying, Tony," said Father Rodney, as he prepared the bread and wine. He insisted on having small pieces of real bread and not the usual papery wafers that were impossible to swallow before the wine came along the row of communicants. "Why don't you have a word with his mother?" How extraordinary, he thought, that this new family in the village should have come up twice in one morning! But perhaps not so extraordinary. Life in this small community was often nothing like the tranquil existence some incomers seemed to expect, but when presented with a problem, or somebody genuinely needing help, many of the real villagers rallied round, as it seemed they had done for the Hicksons. Derek Meade, he had heard, was offering young Jack some work in the school holidays, and the church should certainly not be the last to stretch out a welcoming hand.

"So can I leave it to you?" he said, smiling at old Tony. "And how is Irene? I see she is with us as usual, and looking very pretty, if I may say so."

She'd be a lot happier if she could be ugly and on her feet,

Tony said to himself, but nodded and said how much she had enjoyed last week's sermon.

THE CHANCE CAME TO SPEAK TO JACK JR. AS TONY PUSHED IRENE back home after the service. The boy was kicking a football up and down the lane that led to the village hall, and as Tony passed by, the ball came fast directly towards Irene in her chair.

Jack had chased it desperately, but not fast enough, and Tony caught it with a nifty sidestep and grab. He held on to it and frowned sternly as Jack stood looking fixedly at the ground. "So what d'you say?" Tony growled at him.

"Sorry," muttered Jack.

"Look at me when I'm speaking to you, boy!" said an exasperated Tony. "That was a very stupid and dangerous thing to do. The playing field is the place for football. So how's about making amends?"

Jack frowned and looked up at him. "Making what?" he said.

"Amends," repeated Tony. "Showing just how sorry you are. You could have injured my wife, and she's got enough to put up with without that."

"What do you want me to do?" said Jack, now seeing a possible escape from yet another lecture from his mother.

"You can put your back behind pushing this wheelchair to our house," said Tony. "But only if Irene allows it."

Irene was looking distinctly alarmed, but took a deep breath and said that was fine, so long as Jack was really careful and made sure they were at the dropped curb before crossing the road. They set off, and when Tony said that they were safely home, Irene said, "Thanks, lad. D'you fancy a smoothie? Hard work pushing the chair, I know. Come on in, we don't bite."

By the time Jack said it was time he went , he had reluctantly agreed to give the choir a go, but only to see if he liked it, and only if the Dibsons agreed not to tell anybody. "The kids on the bus would give me hell if they knew I was a choirboy," Jack said, and one of his rare grins crossed his face.

"See you next Tuesday, then, for practise in the church, seven o'clock sharp," Tony said, and watched as Jack walked off home. "I doubt he'll be there," he said to Irene, as he set the potatoes on the stove, "but at least we've tried."

Thirty-Seven

WHAT ABOUT TRAFFIC IN AND OUT OF THE VILLAGE?" SAID Gavin. "Shouldn't we be in trouble if we don't tell the police." The subcommittee had met for an extra session as the date was suddenly nearly upon them and there were a number of urgent matters to resolve.

"No need," said Derek. "John, you've thought of a solution. Would you like to explain?"

"Simple really," John Thornbull said. "We have a responsible person each end of the course, in communication by mobile phone, and when there's two or three cars waiting to get through the village either way, we hold up the next race until they're through. After all, there's not a lot of cars using our road since they built the bypass.

"How long on average will it take to run each race?" Gavin asked.

"We need to do a trial run," John said. "I thought you and me could do that," he added, smiling at Gavin. "Relive our boyhood and all that."

"I'm game," said Gavin. "But it'll have to be last minute, maybe the night before, when the ramp's up."

John nodded. "Good thinking. It'll be a chance to try out the soap boxes. But it'll have to be just you and me, otherwise things'll get out of hand."

"So that's you in the Youth Club's *Rebellion*, and which entry for you, Gav?" said Tony.

"I'll ask the pub lot. I'm giving them a hand building it, anyway. So that's fixed then. Trial run on the Friday night. Who shall we ask for the two responsible men at each end on the day?"

"How about Douglas Meade?" said Hazel. "He's giving the WI a lot of help, and he's a big lad. Authoritative, like. Get's it from his mother," she added, with a sly look at Derek.

"Fine," said Derek blandly. "I'll ask Douglas. Who else?"

"I would like to volunteer," said Father Rodney. "I don't mind not being the target for a wet sponge!"

There was a small silence, as a picture formed in their minds of the vicar in his black shirt and dog collar stopping the traffic with one hand, and then waving it on again at the right time, mobile phone glued to his ear.

Douglas cleared his throat. "Excellent," he said. "Can't get more authoratatiwhatsit than the vicar. Double authority, eh?"

Father Rodney got the reference and smiled. "I'm sure He'll be with us on the day," he said quietly.

"Any other points we've missed?" Derek said.

"Yes, there is one question. Is there an age limit on the drivers? Minimum or maximum?" John Thornbull had nearly forgotten Jack Jr.'s ambition to drive *Rebellion*. It could be important, not just for Jack, but for any other minors or old idiots who thought they could do it.

"If you're thinking of me," Tony Dibson said firmly, "I have no intention of driving. It's taking me all my time to stop Irene entering herself and her wheelchair!"

"Had you got anyone in mind, John?" Derek said, though he had a good idea who it might be.

"Well, yes and no. Young Hickson mentioned it, and then some of the other kids wanted to be in on it. We shall have to give 'em all a go down on the playing field, and see who's fastest."

"I votes anyone over fifteen," said Hazel.

Tony Dibson shook his head. "Why don't we leave it open to all, provided they can reach the brake? We could have the starter checking them over before they start. I don't think anybody would be stupid enough to drive without a brake." Tony knew Jack Jr. was thirteen, desperate to drive, and undoubtedly capable of doing so. "After all," he added, "I remember lads of all ages having soap boxes, and none of us ever got hurt."

"Let's have a vote, then," said Derek, looking at his watch. "All those in favour of an age limit?"

Only Hazel raised her hand.

"Right, that's carried. Thanks everybody. Next meeting we're walking the course first, then coming in for business. I shall have a list of points for us to check, including the other entertainments. All going well there, Hazel? Right, I close the meeting for this evening."

GAVIN WENT ALONG WITH THE OTHERS TO THE PUB, CONFIRMED that he could do the trial run in the pub's *Speedy Willie*, and then said he had to go home. "Kate's got a migraine," he said, "so I promised to go straight home to be there if Cecilia wakes."

The others chorused good wishes for Kate's recovery, and got down to the serious business of ordering.

As Gavin walked back along the High Street, he tried to imagine it on race day. Straw bales would line the road, with a gang of the biggest lads from the Youth Club making sure people didn't stray off the pavements. Loudspeakers were to be placed along the course, and Derek had agreed to do the commentary. He'd been practising in the bath, and although Lois said he sounded like a man in severe pain, he had assured a doubtful Gavin he could be mistaken for Murray Walker anytime.

Then the soap boxes, careering down the street, hopefully gathering momentum from the sloping length of it. The ramp would give them a good start, and the better they were built, the faster they would go. At least, he thought that was how it would be. Lightest or heaviest? He had no idea, but some of the technical chaps would know. It would be a day to remember, he said to himself as he turned into his lane.

And saw a white van pull away from the pavement next to his cottage, increase speed and disappear round the corner towards the church.

He broke into a run, but couldn't catch it. He turned into his gate and rushed up the path. The house was in darkness, not even a soft light coming from Cecilia's room. He opened the front door and panicked. There were toys everywhere, and story books had been ripped from their covers. He rushed upstairs and as he reached the landing he stopped. A small cry from Cecilia. "Christ!" he said aloud. "Thank Christ." He sank on to his haunches with his head in his hands. Then he stood up slowly and went in to check his small daughter. She had cried in her sleep, and was lying peacefully on her back, thumb firmly in her mouth.

Kate! He went quickly into their bedroom, as quietly as he could. "Gavin? Is that you? Oh my God, thank heavens you're back." And then there were loud sobs.

He wrapped her in his big dressing gown and helped her down to the sitting room. "You sit there, and I'll get us a cup of tea before I tidy up this lot," he said. "And don't try to tell me what happened until you're ready."

When she had downed the hot, sweet tea, Kate held

Gavin's hand and began. "It was after you'd gone," she said. "Cecilia was asleep, and I was picking up toys and things before going to bed myself. I was feeling sick, like I usually do with a migraine," she said, "and when the doorbell went I just ignored it. I could see a white van parked outside and reckoned it was somebody trying to sell something. I could see out of the window the man at the door. He wouldn't stop ringing the bell. He just kept his finger on it, and I was worried he'd wake Cecilia. So I went and opened it."

"Was it Froot?" said Gavin hoarsely.

"No, thank God. But it was one of his henchmen. He pushed his way in and made me sit down. Then he said he had a message from Mr. Froot for me. I was to meet him in the Café Jaune in Tresham. On my own. On Saturday. I should make up some story to tell you, and be there prompt at one o'clock. Or else. He said that several times . . . or else." She began to cry again, and Gavin hugged her tight.

"What happened to the toys and books?" he said, when she calmed down.

"I said he could tell Tim Froot to go to hell, and he started picking them up, one after another, breaking the legs off the dolls and tearing up the books. I couldn't bear it, Gavin. All Cecilia's precious dolls! So I said if he'd stop I'd make sure I would be there on Saturday. Then he went. Next time, he said as he was leaving, it wouldn't be just the doll's legs that would get broken. As soon as he'd gone out of the door, I put off all the lights and hid under the bedclothes. And then straightaway you were home. Thank goodness, Cecilia slept through the whole thing. Oh, Gavin," she said, weeping again. "What are we going to do?"

"What was he like, this villain?"

"Tall, thin, in his thirties or forties. Shaky hands. Funny look in his eyes. That's about it."

"Don't worry, Katie," Gavin said, quietly. "I'll fix it. I'll fix it for good."

THIRTY-EIGHT

❧

THE CHURCH CHOIR WAS ASSEMBLING IN DRIBS AND DRABS and Father Rodney greeted them at the door. Much to their relief, he had announced early on that he would not be joining them, but would give them every support. "Evening, Tony," he said. "Did you have any luck with young Hickson?"

"Don't know yet, Vicar," he said. "We shall see if he turns up. Irene had a word with his mother, and she was all for it. Promised not to tell anyone. The lad was worried about what the thugs on the bus would do to him if they found out."

"Nothing to be ashamed of," said the vicar vigorously. "But I do understand. Young people today are so obsessed with being cool, and sadly anything to do with church seems to be about as uncool as they could imagine."

"Not all, Father Rodney. A lot depends on the church."

Father Rodney frowned. Was there a criticism there? He would have to give it some thought. Anthea had been the one most in touch with the new, edgy generation, and would gently guide him into the best way to handle them, if he ever got the chance. For the first time, he wondered whether he should perhaps think about another partner to share his thoughts.

"Right," said Tony, "are we all here?"

"No need to keep looking at the door, Tony. All present and correct," said the lead soprano, an upright, chilly figure with a loud voice and deaf ear, so that every hymn or anthem was for her an opportunity for a solo performance.

Tony looked anxiously at his watch. Irene, sitting in her chair at the end of one of the choir stalls, beckoned to him. "He's not coming, I'm afraid," she whispered. "Better get started."

"Right, everybody," Tony said, looking sadly at the assorted group. You couldn't blame the lad. Who'd want to be numbered amongst this little lot? Certainly not a scared boy of thirteen. It was possible he might come along late, but he doubted it.

Choir practise was scheduled to last an hour, and although Tony added another hymn for them to go through, Jack Jr. did not appear. Then only Tony and Irene remained in the church, and he asked her if she minded waiting a short while longer. "These books are in a terrible state," he said. "I could just sort them out, so it'd be easier to find them next time."

Irene said that was fine, and thought to herself that poor old Tony was still hoping the boy might turn up with a good excuse. Finally they locked up the church and started on their way home. Halfway down the street, just as they were about to turn into their lane, Tony saw a figure hurrying towards them. It was not Jack, but his mother, and she hailed them without pleasantries.

"Where's my Jack?" she said baldly.

"We've not seen him, Mrs. Hickson," said Irene.

"He didn't turn up," Tony added.

"What? But he . . . Well, he set off about quarter past seven, saying he was going to church, to choir practise! I was so pleased!"

Irene shook her head sadly. "He must have gone somewhere else," she said gently. "Maybe one of his friends?"

"Oh, God, not again," Paula said. "I thought he'd stopped all that lying and staying out late an' not telling me. I've left the kids, anyway," she said, turning back, "so I'd better get home. Sorry about that, Mr. Dibson. He'll get a good telling off from me when he does appear."

Tony and Irene were silent for a moment, and then Irene said, "What d'you think? He did seem honest enough, that time he pushed me back."

"Don't ask me," he replied. "I sometimes think children are a mixed blessing."

As soon as he'd said it, he knew it was a mistake. "I could do with a blessing, mixed or otherwise," Irene said, and again relapsed into silence.

BY TEN O'CLOCK, PAULA WAS REALLY WORRIED. SHE HAD RUNG Jack's friend, but he was not there and they hadn't heard from him. Then she tried the one teacher at his school who had taken an interest in him, and who lived in Fletching. He had probably broken rules in giving her his phone number for emergency purposes, and she had never rung him before. Now he advised her to ring the police, saying that even if Jack Jr. turned up, they never treated it as a waste of time, not with a thirteen-year-old.

Lastly, Paula rang Lois, the one she trusted most, but had least wanted to disturb at this hour. Her boss's levelheaded dealings with the New Brooms team had given Paula reassurance when she most needed it, and now, when she heard Lois's firm voice, she took a deep breath and explained the situation.

"He's stayed out all night before, hasn't he?" Lois said.

"Yeah, but it's always been after school, an' when I've checked, he really was where he said he was."

"And this time? Had he been home for tea?"

"Yes. He'd even washed his hands after. Unheard of.

I teased him a bit about being clean in church, and he'd laughed. He was in a really good mood, Mrs. M. Not like when he was late after school."

"Give me a few minutes, Paula, and I'll ring you back," Lois said. She had a cold, sinking feeling and wanted to have a word with Derek. Why was she assuming the worst? Because absentee fathers had been known to abduct a child for various reasons, and not just for ransom money.

To her surprise, Derek didn't dismiss it with a view that Jack Jr. would turn up sooner or later. He asked her the same questions she had asked Paula, and then said, "Go on, then. Ring him."

Lois stared at him. "Ring who?" she said.

"You know perfectly well who," Derek said. "But you'll have to tell him everything you know, else it'll not be fair. Go on, do it."

COWGILL HAD HAD A PLEASANT DAY ON THE GOLF COURSE, AND was sipping a small whisky nightcap when the phone rang. Ah, well, he said to himself, it was too good to last. Then when he heard Lois's voice he knew that much as he loved her, it was not good news. She would not ring him at this hour unless something bad had happened.

"Cowgill?"

"Evening, Lois. How are you, my dear?"

"Never mind about that," Lois said. "I'm reporting a missing thirteen-year-old boy. And before you say anything, it's young Jack Hickson. Yes, the Hicksons who live in Farnden. Runaway husband, four young kids, Jack's been in trouble at school."

"Yes, yes," Cowgill said swiftly. "I remember. How long has he been missing? Why is it you ringing me and not his mother?"

"Just be here," Lois said, "in twenty minutes. Come here

first. And," she added, "tread softly. Paula Hickson doesn't know I'm talking to you."

"But, Lois . . ." She had ended the call abruptly, as usual, and he got up from his chair at once. He knew his Lois. If she considered the matter an emergency, he did not doubt her. He took his car key off the hook and went out into his garage. In twenty minutes time, he was drawing up outside Lois's house and saw her waiting on the doorstep for him.

To his amazement, she took his hand, and he could feel her trembling. "Thanks," she said. "Come in. Derek knows all about it, and Gran's babysitting for Paula."

When they entered the sitting room, Cowgill saw Derek standing by the window and a woman he vaguely recognized sitting on the sofa. He realised she was Jack's mother, and when Lois introduced them, he thought he had never seen such an anxious-looking woman, and he'd seen a few in his time.

It was Paula who spoke first. "It wasn't me who phoned you," she blurted out. "It was Mrs. M. I didn't want to waste police time. . . ."

Cowgill said quietly that he knew it was Mrs. Meade who had asked him to come over. "Please be assured that young boys go missing all the time, but *every* time we take it very seriously. It's often part of growing up. Giving their parents a good scare and proving they're not children anymore."

"Parent, Inspector," Derek said. "Mrs. Hickson is a lone parent at the moment."

"And has had trouble with Jack as a result," Lois said, putting her hand on Paula's arm. She had talked firmly to Paula after ringing Cowgill, and persuaded her that now there was no option but to tell the police. She could see the poor woman was torn between finding her son and betraying her husband, if that was necessary, but luckily the maternal instinct won, and Paula had agreed.

When Cowgill had taken down all the details, he said

Paula could go back home. "You're the best person to be there when he comes back or gets in touch," he said.

"I'll see you safely back," Derek said, and insisted on taking Paula the few yards to her house. He then waited with her whilst they gave Gran an edited version of what had happened. Gran was unusually gentle and calm. Instead of stating her sharp opinion on the state of the world in general and young people in particular, she recalled the time when Josie had gone missing, but had been found safe and well.

"Try not to worry too much, dear," she had said. "And if you want to talk to someone while you're stuck here with the babies, just give me a ring and I'll pop over."

After Derek and Paula had gone, Cowgill and Lois sat in silence for a few seconds. Then he reached across and took her hand. "Come on, then, my Lois," he said. "There's more, isn't there?"

Lois did not take her hand away, but nodded miserably. "Why didn't you ask her about her husband?" she said.

"Because I was sure you would know all about him, and were more likely to tell me the truth. So tell me."

She told him about the man losing his job, hitting the bottle and then hitting his wife, being chucked out and disappearing, only to reappear as a gardener at the hall. Now she felt set free and floating with relief at having off-loaded it all on to Cowgill. Gran had warned her, and had been right. But was avoiding all possible involvement in other people's troubles right?

The feeling of relief did not last long. Now a child of thirteen had disappeared. And not just any old child. This was Jack Jr., who sometimes behaved like a monster, scorning help and causing endless worry to his mother. And farting in her van! This was Jack Jr., whose father had run away and deserted him, leaving him to cope alone with bullies and a predatory drug dealer.

Cowgill stood up. "I need to get back straightaway to

the station," he said. "The sooner we get things moving the better. The first forty-eight hours are the most important in cases like this."

Lois took him to the door. He leaned forwards and kissed her lightly on the cheek. "Take care of yourself, Lois. Don't do anything stupid, and keep in touch with me."

He met Derek and Gran coming up the drive to the house, and stopped for a brief word. Then he was gone, and Lois touched her cheek with her fingertips.

"What are you smiling about?" Derek said, as they entered the house. "Has Jack been found?"

"No, and I'm not smiling," Lois replied sharply.

"I see," said Derek grimly. "Just a facial twitch? Anyway, we'd better have a family conference, see what we can do to help."

It was now eleven o'clock, but Lois insisted on ringing Josie and Douglas, and Gran insisted on staying up until they'd all decided what would be best. "I suppose it'll be on the telly news in the morning," she said, "and then the *Advertiser* will be on to it. Let's hope he's found before all that malarkey."

"It's important people start thinking about what they've seen, and keep their eyes open," Lois said. "The first forty-eight hours are critical, Cowgill said."

THIRTY-NINE

⌘

THE HOUSE HAD ONCE BEEN A SOLID, MIDDLE-CLASS Victorian residence, but had gradually fallen into disrepair and then dereliction, as a long-running legal battle was fought and refought by the family who had inherited it. In the end, the inheritors had grown too old to care, and the rest of the family had emigrated to South Africa and were no longer traceable.

So number thirty eight, Barcelona Street, Tresham, had become a squat for any homeless unfortunates and undesirables who needed shelter and a fix. It was no place to take a thirteen-year-old boy, even if he was shut away from scenes of degradation in the only room that still had a lockable door.

Jack Jr. was very frightened. He had been on his way along the deserted High Street to choir practise, humming "All Things Bright and Beautiful," the only hymn he knew, under his breath, and thinking about driving *Rebellion*, when the battered old white van had stopped and his enemy got out. In seconds, he had bundled a fiercely resisting Jack into the back and banged shut the door. Jack had kicked and screamed, but the van chugged off towards Tresham before anyone could have heard him.

Now he sat curled up in the corner on a smelly duvet, desperately wondering what would happen next. Why had his enemy picked him up? What did he want? He was sure his mother would start a hunt as soon as she realised he was missing. But then, he had stayed out all night without telling her before, so it would be his own fault if she waited until the morning before alerting the police.

A key turned in the lock, and the door opened. His enemy came in and locked the door behind him.

"Can't be too careful, can we, Jack Hickson," the man said. His smile was cold, and Jack curled up tighter. "Your dad is a real Houdini, so it seems, so you've probably inherited his skill."

"Who's Houdini?" said Jack.

"Doesn't matter," said the man. "Let's get down to business, then if you tell me what I want to know, I'll get you something to eat. If you don't, then I won't. Simple, isn't it? O' course, after a while, you'll be so hungry you'll tell me anything, so you might as well start straightaway."

"Sod off," said Jack.

"Now, now," cautioned the man. "You know me from old times, Jack. I never forget. What I want to know is how to find your father. And I am quite sure you know where he is. When did you last see him?"

Jack looked mutinously at the face held so close to him. He thought of spitting into it, but decided that might provoke something too bad to bear. So he said, "When he left home. Mum chucked him out in the middle of the night. He was drunk and making a lot of noise. Us kids woke up, and I got out of bed in case she needed help. I saw him tumble down stairs, and then she threw him out. That was the last time I saw him."

The man slapped him, hard. "Try again," he said. "When did he last get in touch with you?"

Jack fought back tears. "I told you," he said. "I ain't seen him since."

The man raised his hand, and Jack flinched. "I'm telling you the truth, honest!" he said.

"You wouldn't know the truth if it was a matter of life and death," the man said, and added, "which it very well might be."

Jack stared at him, willing himself not to blub.

"Has he spoke to you on the phone? You'd know his voice, wouldn't you? I bet he told you where to find him if you needed him. He was always worrying about his kids, especially young Jack, his firstborn. So you know where to find him, don't you?" He gave Jack a sharp kick on the leg. "Just to remind you what I can do if you don't tell me the truth. And make it soon," he added, hearing a screech from the other side of the door. "I can't waste time with you. I'm needed."

Jack thought quickly. He had no idea where his father was, and he didn't care. But he had to get out of all this somehow. "Well," he said, convincingly slowly. "I did hear he had gone to Scotland. My uncle lives in Carmunnock, just outside Glasgow, and we used to spend holidays there. Nice place," he said conversationally. "My uncle and auntie are nice. My dad's the black sheep." He forced a smile. "Is that what you want to know? Can I go home now|?"

The man looked at him suspiciously. "Are you lying, you little devil?" he said.

Jack shook his head. "No. Sometimes I do, but now I'm not. You know the cops will be here soon, so you might as well let me go. I promise not to tell. I can say I was doing a sleepover with a new friend. If you're quick, you could say you hadn't seen me, or do a bunk yourself. They must be looking for you anyway, leading kids astray."

The man loomed over him, his fist raised. "You bastard!" he hissed.

BY MORNING, THE WHOLE VILLAGE KNEW JACK JR. HAD DISAP-peared. The early morning telly news had the story, with film of the village and the Hickson's house. Later bulletins had a terrified Paula appealing for help in finding him. The local newspaper had a front page picture of Jack Jr. and one of his mother and the other kids huddling around her.

Jack Sr. had set out from his hut in the woods to go to work at the hall, and halfway there had stopped suddenly at the edge of a field. Something was wrong. He heard the whine of a police car, then spotted a couple of dark figures crossing the next field. They were too far away to recognize, but with the sixth sense that had got him out of trouble so many times, he knew they were policemen.

He did not hesitate. Turning away he ran like a swift shadow in the opposite direction, avoided all roads and well-used footpaths, and did not stop until he was miles away from Long Farnden. He had money in his pocket, and caught the next train that came in to Eastcote Junction. All he knew was that it was going south.

On the seat opposite, someone had left a folded newspa-per, and Jack Hickson picked it up. On the front page was a large photograph of his eldest son, smiling at him from years ago, when all had been well. Next to this was a small photo-graph of himself with Paula, and, stunned and unbelieving, he read the story of his son's disappearance.

"Are you all right, mate?" A railway employee, going off duty, had seen Jack sway, all color drained from his face.

Jack desperately pulled himself together and turned the newspaper facedown. "Might be getting flu," he answered. "It's all round the village," he added.

"What village is that?" said the railman.

Jack ignored the question, and asked what was the next station and how long before they got there.

"Half an hour, we shall be into Southampstead. Is that where you're going?"

Jack nodded. "Yeah. I might get a few minutes kip. Can you wake me up if I'm still asleep."

The rail man was sympathetic. "I should have a couple of days in bed if I were you," he said. "Flu's a nasty old bug."

Jack closed his eyes. He didn't want any more questions from this man, nice as he was. He had to make a plan. First of all, he would have to find a map, so that he could get back as soon as possible. There would be one on the station somewhere. He would need to disguise himself a bit. Maybe get an old hat from a charity shop and pull it well down over his eyes. Then he had to find out the quickest way to get back to Tresham. He dare not take public transport. Rage was mounting inside him, driving him on, sharpening his brain and fueling his tired body.

When he got to Tresham, he would know exactly where to go, and who he was looking for. And when he found him, he would kill him.

FORTY

THE WI SOAP BOX COMMITTEE HAD GATHERED IN LOIS'S SIT-
ting room for a meeting to discuss the final arrangements. The soap box was secretly concealed at the back of
the Meade's garage, awaiting a final test from Mrs. T-J. She
planned to collect in her horsebox after the meeting, and take
it with top security measures, that is, Douglas and Lois on
guard, to test it out in private at the hall.

Exciting as this was, the primary topic of conversation was
inevitably the disappearance of young Jack. All the women
were desperately concerned, except for Mrs. T-J, who said she
was sure the young tearaway would turn up. "He has a his-
tory of disappearing and not telling his mother where he is,"
she said, and Lois, not for the first time, was surprised at how
well the old lady kept her ear to the ground. "I'm more interested in knowing where my gardener is," Mrs. T-J continued.
"I had a long list of jobs for him this morning, and without a
by your leave he's gone missing."

"Heavens!" Sheila Stratford said. "Do you think there's a connection? Is it him who's taken young Hickson?"

"Um, I'm sorry to change the subject," Lois said, digging Douglas in the ribs, "but could we talk about the soap box? I know Douglas has to be back in good time this evening."

She had not spoken to Paula since this morning, and then the poor woman had been too upset to say very much. The news that Jack had not turned up for work this morning was about as bad as it could be for him. If it wasn't him who'd taken Jack, or if Mrs. T-J was right, then he'd have done better to stay put and answer the police questions honestly. Oh Lord, what a muddle! Although she hadn't so far done so, it was only a matter of time before Gran said "I told you so."

"How did the painting go, Douglas?" Mrs. T-J was anxious to get through the meeting and set off for her trial drive in *Jam & Jerusalem*.

"Ask Mum," Douglas said. "She and Josie spent hours on it. The big question was whether the strawberry should be fully ripe."

There was a general laugh, and the meeting relaxed, relieved to have their minds taken off the worrying problem of Jack Jr.

"So we decided on a really ripe strawberry," Lois said. "A nice bright red. And Josie, who is the artistic one, painted a really good label: 'JAM & JERUSALEM—Organic home-made strawberry jam from Long Farnden WI.' Should make a real impact, trundling down the street."

"It'll do more than trundle, Mrs. Meade, with me at the wheel," said Mrs. T-J. "So I need to dress up as a strawberry?"

There was an awed silence, as they considered this.

"Great!" said Douglas. "I can't wait!"

The rest of the meeting was taken up with the minutiae of timing and priming, and as soon as they were finished, Douglas, Lois and Mrs. T-J set off to collect the oversized jam jar and take it up to the hall.

*   *   *

JACK SR. HAD COVERED ABOUT EIGHT MILES ON FOOT, HE RECK-
oned. He was crossing fields and woods, dashing illegally
over railway lines and cursing as he made a detour in order to
cross a precarious footbridge over a disused canal.

He looked at his map again. If he was lucky, he could be
back in his hut by nightfall. He intended to waste no time,
and during his long trek across country had made a plan.
The most likely time to find his target would be early in the
morning. He knew he was gambling on the likelihood of the
villain doing Jack Jr. no harm until then, but on balance it
was safer than busting in late at night with all guns blazing
and causing a knee-jerk reaction.

The light was going by the time he reached the Farnden
woods, and with his old hat pulled well down over his face
he made his way towards his hut. He did not go straight to
it, but made a wide detour around the parkland to check
there were no police cars waiting for him. He had skirted the
edge of the park and now plunged into the spinney of poplars
planted within sight of the drive up to the hall. Nearly there,
he said to himself. He planned to have a few hours sleep, then
start off towards Tresham at dawn, before the day began.

Suddenly he stopped short, instinctively squatting down
on his haunches. Something was hurtling down the sloping
approach to the house. It was bright red, driven by a hel-
meted figure gripping the steering wheel, and, as he watched,
it crashed with a shout from the driver into a holly bush
planted near the turn into the stable yard.

He stood up and ran like a hare. He pushed his way
through the thicket and at last stood, scratched and breathing heavily, at the door of his hut. Good God, what on earth
was it? Some new toy of the police—heat-seeking night-
vision vehicle? But why bright red? He sat down on the pile
of sacks that did duty as a chair and put his head in his hands.

"Oh, young Jack, what have I done? Dear God, don't let him be hurt before I get there. Please."

"NO HARM DONE," LAUGHED MRS. T-J, AS LOIS AND DOUGLAS came running to where she had landed.

Douglas helped her to her feet, and quickly examined *Jam & Jerusalem*. "Not a scratch," he said.

"Thank goodness for that," Lois said. "Josie would kill us if she had to do it all again."

"But did you see how fast she went?" said Mrs. T-J, taking off her helmet. "My goodness, it was most exhilarating! She must have been doing at least fifty miles an hour, Douglas!"

He grinned indulgently. "More like twenty," he said. "It probably felt like more. Tony Dibson said the secret is in the weight. There's no rules about how heavy it's got to be. So we can put a few lumps of rock in with you on the day."

"Lumps of rock!" Mrs. T-J colored with indignation. "There are a couple of blocks of Carrara marble in the potting shed. Been there since that dreadful woman came to sculpt my dear husband's head. Looked nothing like him. I put him in the cellar, and the blocks of marble—which we purchased at great cost—were left over. Awful mistake. But they'll be just the thing. Rocks, indeed! Nothing but the best for *Jam & Jerusalem*! If my gardener returns, I'll get him to carry them."

When the soap box had been safely stowed away in a stable and covered with an old horse blanket, Lois and Douglas set off to walk back to the village. "Notice she didn't offer us a lift back," said Douglas glumly. "Just as well I don't actually have to be back early. Why did you say that during the meeting, Mum?"

"To change the subject. Stop the gossip about Jack Jr. Mind you, nothing I can say will stop it. But I need to find out a couple of things before I can speak with authority. I am his mother's boss, and people are bound to think I know more than I'm telling."

"And do you?" said Douglas.

Lois did not answer, and they walked on in silence. As they reached the edge of the village, Lois said casually, "By the way, Douglas, you know when our mad woman driver was out of control in a jar of jam? Well, did you notice anything over by the hedge at the side of the park?"

"What do you mean, Mum?"

"I thought I saw a shadowy figure moving along the hedge. It stopped when she crashed, and I looked away. When I looked back again it had gone."

"Could've been a fox," Douglas said, getting into his car. "I thought I heard a vixen barking in the wood when we came away. Anyway, I must be going. Susie will wonder where I've gone. All going well, so I'll see you on the day. Bye, Mum." He pecked her cheek and was gone.

FORTY-ONE

J ACK JR. HAD HARDLY SLEPT. THE GROANS AND YELLS COMING from the rest of the house frightened him so much that he lay curled up in a ball under the smelly duvet with his fingers in his ears. A glimmer of light showed through the filthy windows. There had been curtains once, but they had been reduced to rags hanging in strips. It didn't matter. The dirt was so thick on the windows that nobody could see in or out.

"Wake up, kid!" The man's harsh voice pierced through Jack's defences, and he sat up, shrinking away from the looming figure. "Come on, we're going on a visit. Here, take this. You can eat it on the way."

"Where're we going? I want to go home. If you don't take me soon, they'll be on to you and you'll wish you had."

"Persistent little sod, aren't you?" The man took hold of Jack by his shoulder and pushed him out of the room, down the rotting stairs and out of a door at the back of the house. The early morning was cold and clear, and Jack saw the familiar scruffy van. Once more he was pushed into the back, and in seconds he was on the road, having no idea where he was going. He began to eat the stale sandwich and said to himself that at least he had more chance of escape from this old wreck on the move, than from that locked room. For all the man's bluster, Jack reckoned he was not very bright. "Me against him," he muttered, and swallowed hard. The sandwich was disgusting, but he had to keep up his strength.

Lois stared at the telephone in her office, trying to decide whether or not to ring Cowgill. She knew from Mrs. T-J that Hickson had gone into hiding again, and whether or not he had taken his son with him, the police would need urgently to find him. She had already told Cowgill all she knew about Jack Sr., but she still did not know where he was living. Working, yes, and there had been that shadow lurking round the park. If Cowgill had already been up there to look around for him, he might have spotted him. But had he? It was a question of relying on police efficiency, or ringing Cowgill to make sure. She dialled his number.

Chris answered. "Hello, Lois," she said. "Did you want Mr. Cowgill? Oh, dear, he's gone to the dentist. Said he'd be out all morning. No, they don't allow mobiles in the dentist's. Can I give him a message when he comes back, or can I help? Is it something to do with young Jack Hickson's disappearance?"

"Oh, don't worry, Chris. I'll catch him later. Any news on Jack Jr.?"

"Nothing definite. We've got just about every man in the force on to it, and nationwide as well. It won't be long before we find him. How's his mum holding up?"

"Not too well. I'm going round there now. Bye."

Paula opened the door at once. Lois could see she'd had no sleep and been crying a lot. There were big dark circles under her eyes and her skin was blotchy. She was holding baby

Frankie, and Lois could see the twins in the kitchen, sitting at the table eating cereal and looking solemn.

"Shouldn't they be at school?" Lois said to Paula, as they walked through and the twins said hello.

Paula shook her head. "Not until they've found Jack," she said shakily. "I'm not letting them, any of them, out of my sight. Sorry I can't do the work at the moment, Mrs. M."

"Don't be ridiculous, Paula," Lois said. "Of course you can't. But I'm sure you'll soon have him back and we can all get on with life. Have you had any news, or thought of anything else to tell that might help?"

Paula shook her head. "No, nothing," she said.

Well, now there was something she could tell Paula. "Jack Sr. has gone missing, too," she said. "Mrs. T-J said last night that he didn't turn up for work yesterday morning. You've not seen or heard anything?"

Paula shook her head. "Mind you," she said, "I'm not surprised. With his picture all over the papers, he's not likely to hang around here. He'd be suspect number one, wouldn't he?"

"Do you think he's got Jack?"

Paula shrugged. "In a way," she said, "I hope he has. He'd not harm him. I'm really certain about that. Probably just doing it to scare me. And if he has got him, he's dug himself into an even deeper hole than he was in already. Abducting a child is a real crime, the stupid idiot."

The doorbell rang, and Paula started. "Go on," said Lois, "answer it. I'm here."

"Oh, hello, Paula. I hope I'm not intruding. I just came to say . . . well, you know . . ."

Lois knew the voice. It was Kate Adstone, and Paula returned with her visitor following close behind. "Morning, Mrs. Meade," Kate said. "I just came . . ."

"Quite right, too," Lois said. "The more support Paula gets the better. Is there another coffee in the pot, Paula?"

Their conversation ranged over every subject except that

of missing Jack Jr., and then they fell silent. Lois waited. Surely something useful would come up.

"I was thinking about them early days, when we both worked at Froot's Builders," Paula said finally to Kate. "They were carefree compared to this, weren't they. Always having a laugh with the girls."

"Too right," Kate said with feeling. "Me a personal assistant in the office, and weren't you—?"

"I worked in the canteen," Paula said. "It was a good job. I liked it there, except when the boss came round, feeling up all the girls. Old Greasy, we used to call him. Luckily he didn't appear often. No, it was a good job and some nice people worked there."

"Old Greasy!" Kate said, and laughed nervously. "My God, I remember him. He interviewed me for the job. You were lucky. I saw him most days, and I must say I couldn't get away from there fast enough. Gavin worked there, too. . . ." Her face closed up, and she looked at her watch.

"I must go," Lois said quickly. "I'll leave you girls to have a chat. Cecilia at playgroup? You've got plenty of time, Kate, and I know Paula is glad of the company."

After she left, she crossed the road and went into the shop.

"Hi, Mum," Josie said. "What's new?"

"Nothing much, unfortunately," Lois said. "D'you mind if I lurk for a minute or two? I just want to check on when Kate leaves Paula Hickson."

"For God's sake, why? Aren't you carrying the sleuth bit a trifle too far?"

The door opened and the vicar came in. Lois nodded to him, and then pretended to look at the notice board by the window.

"Dreadful business, Mrs. Meade," Father Rodney said. "I pray to God that the child will be returned safely very soon."

"And so do we all," said Lois sharply.

The vicar shook his head sadly, and muttered something about moving in mysterious ways. Then he collected up a basket of shopping and took it to Josie. "Are we all ready for the big soap box day?" he said.

"Most of us think it should be cancelled," Josie said. "You couldn't put your heart into it, could you?"

"Not long to go," Father Rodney said. "But I'm sure we'll have good news before then."

"Well, that's a relief," Lois said. "So glad you're sure."

After he had gone, Josie turned on her mother. "You were a bit sharp! Poor bloke's only doing his job. And anyway, maybe he's right. I reckon a miracle would be just what we need at the moment."

Lois was suitably chastened, and said that probably the most useful thing was that Kate Adstone was still with Paula Hickson, and in her opinion that was worth more than a fistful of prayers.

THE VAN STOPPED AT LAST, AND JACK JR. BLINKED AT THE LIGHT as the man opened the doors at the back.

"Get out," he said.

"Where are we?"

"Never you mind, just get out!"

"I've got cramp. Can't move."

The man advanced on him. He took him by one ear and dragged him out of the van and on to a rutted track. "Cramp all gone?" he said, and laughed. "You don't fool me, little Jack Horner! Good at deceiving yer teachers and your mum, aren't you? But I know you from way back. Lying little toad then and still are. Now, get going. We've got a long way to go."

KATE ADSTONE FINALLY LEFT PAULA AND HURRIED TO THE PLAY-group to collect Cecilia. Like every other mother in the village, she couldn't feel at ease until her toddler was safely cuddled in her arms. There were still police patrolling, knocking on doors and stopping people in the street. It occurred to Kate that even if the kidnapper had thoughts of returning Jack, he, or she, was unlikely to bring him back with this lot all around. More likely the boy would be dumped. Alive, Kate wished fervently.

She had been surprised by how much Paula Hickson had told her. Probably only too glad to open up to somebody, she thought now, fixing Cecilia firmly into her pushchair. But all that stuff about Tim Froot! So he'd had a pretty grim reputation around the offices! And apparently, so the canteen gossip said, he'd also had fingers in lots of pies, dodgy business ones, with a posse of henchmen protecting him. She supposed the one who'd threatened her was one of them. This reminded her that she had agreed to meet Froot in Tresham the day after tomorrow. Gavin had forbidden it, and she had put off thinking about what would happen if she failed to turn up. It was too horrible to contemplate, and she quickened her pace, wanting to be at home on her own territory. Gavin had told her to lock herself in for the moment, and that is what she intended to do.

So Froot had been after Paula, among others! But unlike herself, the poor woman had had to stay there, needing the money. One of the dodgy businesses had had to do with laundering money, Paula had said. And what else? Froot had come from Holland. Amsterdam . . . drugs?

"Gavin? It's me. Yes, I'm safely home, and yes, I've locked the doors. Listen, I've got something to tell you. You're just off out? Oh, all right then, I'll tell you tonight. Say hello and goodbye to Cecilia . . . come on, sweetie, say hello to Daddy."

FORTY-TWO

༐

J ACK HICKSON'S CAREFULLY THOUGHT-OUT PLAN HAD BEEN scuppered. He had set out from the woods at the crack of dawn, just when the pigeons were starting to greet the light, and all went well until he reached the road. He had relied on getting a lift to Tresham with one of the long-distance lorries that took shortcuts through the villages in the early morning, aiming to miss rush-hour traffic round the big towns and cities.

This morning, unbeknown to Jack, as part of their strategy for protecting the Hickson family, the police had put a block on all heavy goods traffic going through a radius of twenty miles round Farnden. Only domestic vehicles were getting through. Jack waited in vain, knowing that it would be disaster guaranteed if he thumbed a lift from a local driver. He needed a stranger, a foreigner preferably, who would drive straight through the village and on to Tresham, where he could be dropped off and make the rest of his way on foot.

After waiting for an hour, when local traffic was beginning

to appear, he decided he would have to walk, skirting the village through the fields, and then on to Tresham as best he could. When he looked at his watch, his heart sank to his boots. It would be much too late when he got there to carry out his plan of surprising the sleeping kidnapper, dealing out rough justice, and then rescuing his son and taking him back home to his mother. Then he would go to the police and tell all.

None of this was now likely, so he needed plan B. His feet were soaking wet from dew-covered meadows and inadequate boots, and he shivered. He had had nothing to eat since last night, and the early morning chill was not helping. But the thought of Jack in the hands of that corrupt villain drove him on, and in time he was within three miles of Tresham.

"Want a lift, mate?" A large van had stopped and a cheery-looking, totally bald driver leaned out.

Jack thought rapidly, and decided it was worth the risk. The van had come from Birmingham, and the driver was a stranger to him. He got in, glad to rest his legs and feet. The warmth inside the cab made his head swim, and he swayed.

"You all right, mate? You look all done in. Get a bit of shut-eye, if you want. Where're you going? I'll give you a nudge when we get there."

"Only into Tresham," Jack said. "You haven't got anything I could eat, have you? Didn't have time for breakfast this morning."

The driver fished out a bread roll with a thick piece of ham liberally spread with mustard, and held it out. "Thanks a lot," Jack said. "This is the best thing I've eaten for months."

"On the road, are you? You don't look like a vagrant."

"No, I'm a professional gardener. It's just that I lost my job and've been out of work for a good while. I'm going into town to try for another place." He did not mention the hall.

The driver nodded approvingly. "Job situation is really bad at the moment, and I suppose people can do their own gardening if necessary. Mind you, in my case it's a hobby. I love it. Out there, on my allotment, away from the wife! Nothing to beat it."

They talked gardening for the rest of the way into Tresham, and then the driver dropped Jack off at a suitable place on the ring road. He remembered the way, and set off through a network of roads lined with redbrick terraces, all built in the affluent nineteenth century, when the town mushroomed. There it was, Barcelona Street, down-at-heel, with wrecks of old cars and wheelie bins spilling over onto the pavements. Number thirty-eight. Ah, yes, there it was, in all its glory!

Jack wondered briefly why the local authority allowed such a place to exist. Surely the site itself would be worth a fair bit? He crossed the road and stood outside. It would have to be a straight confrontation, and now that he was here, fortified by the ham roll, he felt more confident.

A middle-aged man came down the path and stopped. "You looking for somebody, mate?" he said.

Jack gave him a grateful smile, and answered that he had been searching for his young brother for weeks, but had had no luck. "Our old mum's going crazy," he lied. "Can you help at all?"

"I can, a bit," the man replied. "But you're just too late. Sorry about your brother, but the lot who lived here have all gone. Did a moonlight flit, the lot of 'em, thank God. Let's hope they never come back. The council should've evicted them years ago. Anyway, if I were you, I'd turn back to where you came from. Nothing but tragedy and trouble from that house. Several of us have been in, and we found the body of a young girl, about fourteen, needles everywhere. She was still warm. Makes you sick."

He turned away, rubbing his eyes. Then he looked back at Jack. "We've told the police, an' they'll be here any minute. I suppose you could wait and talk to them. One of the women who lives next door said she'd seen out of her bathroom window a man with a kid going in there yesterday, but they weren't there when we looked."

Jack waited until his informant was out of sight, and then ran fast in the opposite direction.

At the end of the rutted track, Jack Jr. and his minder stopped. Jack had been looking all around him as they walked. It was difficult to see far, as the track was lined with high thorn hedges with only the occasional field gate. All the way, the man had hurried Jack along, shoving him forwards if he lingered by an opening in the hedge. "No dawdling," he had said. "I know your tricks, young Hickson. I'm not taking my eyes off you for a second."

"What's the point of all this?" Jack said finally. "They'll have every road covered. Why don't you bugger off and leave me to find me own way home? I won't say nothing. I'll pretend I was stayin' with a new friend. I'll be really sorry to Mum. I'm good at that. I promise I won't tell."

He looked straight into the man's eyes, and saw him hesitate. Jack knew something had gone wrong in the house this morning, and that's why they were miles from anywhere with not a building in sight. The track had come to a dead end, and only the remains of a big straw stack hinted at a reason for its existence. Why would his captor bring him here? Jack shivered. He'd probably hoped to find a derelict barn where he could dump Jack, duly dealt with, and hop it. There'd be no farm traffic down here until next harvest.

The man shook his head. "You're a lying little toad. I don't believe a word of it. You'd have nothing to lose by telling."

Jack shrugged, the gesture older than his thirteen years. "Please yerself," he said. "But you ain't got no option really. Without me, you stand a chance of disappearing without trace. With me around, you ain't got no chance."

"If you don't shut y' mouth, I'll get rid of you forever! That'll be good enough for me, plenty enough for yer father to remember me by." He stepped towards Jack, his fists clenched.

Jack turned and ran.

FORTY-THREE

❧

Lois sat in her office, staring into space. She had eaten only half the lunch Gran had prepared and, as expected, had listened to a mercifully short lecture on the folly of employing Paula Hickson and thereby becoming involved in this mess.

"What can you expect?" Gran had said, playing her trump card. "Anybody who gives her son the same name as her husband must be not quite right in the head."

"Lots of people do," Lois said wearily. "I think it's nice. Anyway, I've got work to do, so I'll be in my office if you want me."

"What about this pudding?"

"No thanks. I'll have some for supper. Sorry, Mum."

After Lois had shut herself away, Gran cleared up the kitchen and then stood at the sink, looking out of the window. She hadn't been very helpful, she knew. But it angered her to see her daughter so worried about a situation that should not really be her concern. If only she could think of something she could do to help. Practical help, that's what she was good at. As she watched Jeems digging in the flower bed, she knew she should go out and stop her. Lois had just planted out new seedlings. Then the little dog pricked her ears and shot off across the garden. Gran craned her neck to see what had caught her attention. It was a cock pheasant, squawking loudly as it rose slowly into the air and escaped over the fence.

A pheasant! Gran caught her breath. Last seen hanging by the neck in a poacher's bothy in the woods. She rushed out into the garden and saw Jeems coming towards her with a sheepish expression, carrying a long tail feather in her mouth.

"Good dog," she said, holding out her hand. Jeems obediently dropped the feather and Gran picked it up. She rushed back into the house and straight into Lois's office without knocking.

"Look! I should've told you before, but I completely forgot! This brought it all back!"

Lois frowned at her mother, and took the proffered feather. "What are you talking about, Mum? I am rather busy."

Gran sat down heavily and said, "Just listen, and don't interrupt." Then she told Lois about chasing Jeems into the wood and finding the hut with a padlocked door. "There were things inside, including a newly killed pheasant, odd bits that somebody had left there and would be coming back for."

Lois snapped alert. "So that's it," she said. "That's where he was living. Young Jack's father. I wish you'd told me before, Mum. It's very important."

She picked up the phone and dialled Cowgill. Chris answered once more. "Sorry—he's not back yet."

"It is very, very important that I speak to him. You can get in touch and tell him to ring me. Do it now, Chris. Please. Trust me."

"Can't I help?"

"Probably. But I need to speak to Cowgill. Sorry. Just get on to him, now."

Gran stood up. She was near to tears, and Lois held out her hand. "Mum, don't worry. You might still save that kid's life. Go and make us some coffee, can you? I'll tell you what happens."

Cowgill phoned back in minutes. His voice sounded strange, and Lois realised he was still suffering. She told him exactly what Gran had said, and he mumbled that he would get on to it at once. "I'll 'ing 'ou back in 'en minish," he said, and rang off.

It was more than ten minutes, of course, and when he did ring, the news was not good. His men had found the hut, but the padlock had gone and it was empty. No trace of any kind of occupation. Completely cleared out. The only sign that there had been anyone there was a pile of ashes neatly swept into a corner.

"That was him, then!" Lois said. "He'd have camped out there. Boiled a kettle on a little fire, an' that. Oh, sod it," she added tiredly. "Poor old Mum, she'd forgotten all about it, and now she's crucified with guilt."

"Tell her we'll find him, and not to worry. If it's his father who has him, the lad won't come to any harm. According to information we now have about Jack Hickson, he was not a bad sort of bloke until he got made redundant and consoled himself with the drink. Adored his children, apparently. He won't harm his son. Tell Gran that. Must go, Lois. Keep in touch."

As soon as she put down the phone, it rang again. This time it was Hazel from the office in Tresham. "Just had a call from somebody over the other side of Ringford," she said. "It may be too far away for New Brooms, but this woman's desperate. She's had an op and her cleaner's just given in her notice. Can we help?"

Lois gave her head a shake to clear it. "Of course we can. Give me the name and address and I'll go across right now. It'll give me something else to think about."

"How is Paula?" Hazel said.

"As bad as can be expected," Lois replied. "And that goes for most of us here in Farnden. Can you ring this woman and tell her I'm on the way?"

THE HOUSE WAS ON ITS OWN, SMALL AND IN GOOD ORDER, WITH A neat garden and well-trimmed hedge, high enough to shield the house from a busy road. Lois parked the New Brooms van outside on the grass verge, and went in. As the door opened, she could see a small, youngish woman holding a stick and not unhooking the chain until Lois had announced her credentials.

"I'm rather isolated here," the woman said, "so I've promised my husband I would be very careful. But do come in, Mrs. Meade. I'm so glad you're able to help."

As Lois sat listening to yet another sad story of ill health and bad luck, she reflected that a large part of New Brooms' work involved being a sympathetic ear and a comforting presence for a short time whilst involved in clients' lives. In Mrs. Brown's case, her husband had a job which kept him abroad for long periods of time. She herself was sickly, and had had one operation after another. "So you see, I can't possibly join him. And now, in this present financial crisis, he can't give up his good job over there and return to be with me."

"Perhaps things will soon change," said Lois soothingly. She didn't believe it, but needed to get down to business and return to Farnden as soon as possible.

This proved to be more difficult than she had thought. Mrs. Brown had a clinging nature, and had perfected the art of pinning her listener down with a seamless monologue. There was no chance of interrupting, and so Lois switched off and let her run on. After all, there was little she could be doing back at home, and at least this would result in another client for the business. Finally, she realised there was a pause, and Mrs. Brown was looking at her enquiringly.

"Um, oh, yes, of course," Lois said quickly. "Now, when would you like us to start? I could fix you up with a very pleasant person to start next Monday? Morning or afternoon?"

"The afternoon would be best for me. It takes me most of the morning to get going at the moment! Yes, afternoon would be fine. Oh, that will be wonderful! You have no idea how relieved I am."

Oh well, thought Lois, as she accepted the offer of a cup of coffee and insisted on making it for the two of them, at least I am useful to someone. Why oh why hadn't Mum remembered sooner about the hut in the woods? Now it was too late. She appreciated Cowgill's efforts at reassurance, but recalled only too well Paula's accounts of her husband's violence. Admittedly, she had always stressed he'd never touched the children, but a man in his present situation must be under enormous pressure.

She rinsed out the cups, made final arrangements with Mrs. Brown, and extricated herself from another tale of woe. "Must be going," she said. "Nice to have met you. You can rely on New Brooms!" she added reassuringly, and made her way down the garden path.

Inside the van, she switched on the radio and listened to the news. No developments. She switched it off again, and headed for home. As she stopped at traffic lights under a railway bridge, she glanced in her rearview mirror and her heart lurched. There, in the back of the van, she saw something move. She turned around and ignored the cars hooting behind her as the lights turned to green. A dirty, exhausted boy crawled forwards.

"Yeah, it's me," Jack Jr. said shakily. "Can you take me home . . . please?"

FORTY-FOUR

❧

"YOU FORGOT TO LOCK THE VAN," JACK SAID. "LUCKY FOR ME. My legs were giving up."

Lois thoughts were in turmoil. Yes, she had forgotten to lock the van, and no wonder. This young person squatting behind her, having difficulty keeping his eyes open, had half the country worrying about him. Not to mention the taxpayers money spent on police procedures in the hunt to find him. She hadn't thought about much else for the last forty-eight hours.

But what should she do now, and in what order? First, call Cowgill? Second, get Jack home to his mother. No, first, drive home slowly and ask him some questions as they went along? Then call Cowgill. She glanced back and saw that there was no dilemma. Jack Jr. had leaned against the back of her seat and was fast asleep.

He looks about five years old, thought Lois, taking the corners slowly so as not to wake him. He is small for his age, poor kid. Where has he been and what's happened to him? But most of all, who took him?

When she drew up outside the Hickson house, she looked up and down the street. Nobody about. She had been able to cut through a private Tollervey-Jones estate road to avoid the police vigils. It was only a tiny track, with grass growing down the middle, but negotiable. Now she wanted to get Jack, still sleeping, into his house without anyone seeing. After that, she would talk to Paula and see what should be done next. Every maternal instinct in her body told her that the last thing Jack needed was interrogation by anyone. He needed sleep in his own bed, with his mother watching over him. After that, it would have to be the police. But Cowgill would see that this caused as little harm as possible to an already damaged child.

But how to get him out, down the garden path and into his house? He was too big for Lois to carry, and she dare not leave him alone in the van. She looked across at the shop, and saw the vicar, Father Rodney, emerging. He waved a friendly hand, and she made a quick decision. She lowered her window and beckoned. As he came near, she put her finger to her lips, signing him not to say anything. Then she waited until he bent down to the window and she could whisper in his ear, praying that he would do what she hoped.

He did. Without a change of expression, he looked into the back of the van, nodded briefly and disappeared round the back. Lois quietly opened her door and joined him, and together they slowly maneuvered Jack Jr., until Father Rodney had him securely in his arms. Nobody had appeared in the street, and with Lois shielding the still sleeping Jack from watchful eyes, they moved quickly into the garden and round to the back door. There Paula stood holding a basketful of wet washing, pale as a ghost and apparently paralyzed with shock at the sight of a limp Jack held tenderly by the vicar.

Lois took her by the arm, said quietly that they should

take Jack upstairs and try not to wake him. "He's exhausted, Paula," she said. "But alive."

Father Rodney and Lois left Paula with her son, and they returned to the kitchen, where Frankie sat in his high chair, staring at them with a wobbling chin. Lois forestalled a burst of crying, and lifted him out, cuddling him close. "Let's go and find some toys," she said and motioned to the vicar to go with them into the sitting room. He followed quietly and they settled down. Father Rodney proved to be a dab hand at wooden puzzles, and whilst he kept Frankie busy, Lois talked.

"Please don't say anything to anybody," she pleaded, knowing that the apparently sensible thing would be to contact the police at once. To her surprise, Father Rodney agreed without protest. "A couple of hours good sleep is not going to make much difference to anybody except young Jack," he said. "I shall leave it you, Mrs. Meade, to know when to make the next move. The boy obviously trusts you, else he wouldn't have crawled into your van. And Mrs. Hickson works for you? So together you will do the best for Jack. I shall go now. It will not look at all odd for me to be seen leaving, since I was actually on my way to offer what comfort I could to Jack's mother."

Lois picked up Frankie and saw the vicar to the door. "I'll let you know how it goes," she said.

After half an hour or so, Paula came downstairs. She stood looking at Lois and Frankie, and tried to say something, but choked. Then she walked across the room and put her arms around both. They stood unmoving for a few minutes, then Frankie began to struggle.

"He's hungry, I expect," said Lois, sniffing loudly. "Come on, let's go and find him a biscuit."

FORTY-FIVE

~

WHEN LOIS HAD REACHED HOME, SHE PHONED COWGILL, having agreed with Paula that this would be best. She had been so overjoyed on the one hand, and shaken and tearful on the other, that after a while she had begged Lois to be the one to contact the police.

"After all, Mrs. M.," she had said, "you found him. And I'm so scared of the police I'll not be able to stand up to them if they want to question Jack before he's ready."

When Cowgill had answered the phone with profuse apologies for a numbed mouth and not making sense earlier, Lois had said, "Just shut up and listen." She had gone over several times in her mind what she would say to him, but in the end she imagined him sitting in his office, hand to his painful cheek, completely professional and trustworthy, and had given him a factual and straightforward account.

"Leave it to me now, Lois," he had said. "You can trust me to organise everything very carefully. You're sure your vicar will not be tempted to talk? No? Right, then. There will inevitably be a considerable media reaction, but I will see that this is postponed until tomorrow. You did well, my dear," he added, "but don't let this stop you locking up your van in future. I couldn't bear the thought of just any old villain crawling in and cadging a lift—or worse."

Lois had for once been lost for words to reply to this, and left him with a caution that she was relying on him and he'd better not let her down.

When she had finally crawled into bed and Derek had cuddled her to sleep, she had not surfaced again until much later than usual. "You've made up for God knows how much lost sleep lately, gel," he had said. "Me and Gran were really worried about you."

Now, sitting at the breakfast table, she knew that Cowgill had not let her down. There was nothing in the morning paper and nothing on the early news. Derek had gone off to work, sworn to silence on the subject, and Gran had promised not to go anywhere until Lois told her it was all right.

"You know me, Lois," she had said. "One question from Josie in the shop, or from one of my friends in the street, and I shall spill it all out. Can't help it. No, best I should stay at home with you, until there's something on the telly."

In the end, it was the lunchtime radio news that had the story first, and then Lois's phone did not stop ringing. She looked out of the window of her office, and saw along the street a police cordon outside the Hickson house, keeping all vehicles and pedestrians at bay. As she watched, she saw Cowgill with Chris emerge from the house and walk across to the shop. She would hear from Josie later.

In some ways, Lois thought, although the general relief is huge, just sitting here watching it all from a window is a bit of an anticlimax. There was a knock at the door, and Gran ran to answer it as usual. Lois heard Cowgill's voice and she went out to rescue him.

"Can I have a word?" he said, and followed her back into her office.

"Sit down," Lois said. "Thanks for all of it."

"It could have been so much worse, Lois. Mrs. Hickson is so grateful to you."

"No need," said Lois. "How's young Jack?"

"Amazingly resilient," Cowgill said, and Lois saw he had a rueful look.

"Ah. Told all?"

Cowgill shook his head. "Not cooperating, I'm afraid. He claims he spent the night in a house in Tresham, tried to thumb a lift home and got taken miles out of his way. He'd then decided to walk back, and that's when he saw your van. He was anxious to stress he'd not broken into it. The door was open, he said."

"It was. And that's all?" Lois said. "No reason why he didn't contact his mum?"

"He forgot, he said. Just forgot."

"The name of his friend in Tresham—did he tell you that, or where they live?"

"No. Said it was sudden decision, and he was with a group of boys from another class. Didn't know any of them. Went along and stayed playing on the computer until it was too late to get home. Slept on the floor. In the morning, he didn't notice where he was in the town, but just got to the ring road and thumbed a lift."

"Oh, my God, what a pack of lies!" Lois said. "What did you say?"

"It was Chris. She left it there, sensibly, and said she'd go back later. His mother was with him all the time of course. There are rules and regs in these cases. But don't worry, Lois. He's not stupid, and I hope we can make him see the wisdom of telling the truth."

"But in the meantime, surely he's still in danger? Even

more so now, if there's some man somewhere in hiding, expecting him to blow the whistle? Perhaps his father?"

"We've arranged for him to stay at home for a couple of weeks, and there'll be police protection. But not obvious, Lois. We have to find whoever it was. I have never been surer that this boy was abducted, but he's decided to keep quiet. Maybe he's scared, or, if it *was* his father, perhaps he has some mistaken idea about shielding him."

"So there's more work to do," said Lois, cheering up. "You're still looking for his father, and or some other sod who snatched the boy."

Cowgill smiled and got to his feet. "You don't think I'd let you off so lightly, do you, Lois? I'll be in touch. Oh, and by the way, there'll be no objection to your calling to see Paula."

TWO OTHER PEOPLE HAD BEEN SEARCHING ANXIOUSLY FOR NEWS of young Jack Hickson, but with very different motives. His father, once more a hunted man, had found a temporary home in a deserted warehouse in the backstreets of Tresham. People said the best place to hide was in a crowd. Well, he would try out that theory. He had spent the night on a pile of plastic sacks which littered the floors. He was not the first. There were the usual traces of needles and empty bottles, but none looked recent. With luck, he would be the only occupant. He intended to find his quarry, and was convinced he would still be somewhere around in the town. So he would stay hidden in the crowded streets until he found him.

Now, standing in a nearby newsagent's with a baseball cap pulled well down over his eyes, he looked at the headlines again to make sure his son was safe. He bought the paper and walked swiftly to the nearby scrubby park, where he sat down next to an old alky so dozy that he would be no threat.

The story had no details. Young Jack had returned home

and was safely with his mother. Mother and father were separated, and the police were anxious to contact Jack's father. There was a photograph and description, which was handy. He could make sure he looked nothing like the senior Jack Hickson casual shoppers would be looking out for.

The second person who peered anxiously at a newspaper headline had spent the night in a terraced house in the area of Tresham known as Far Bottom. It was down by the canal, once a hive of waterborne industry, but now dank and full of the usual detritus of an uncaring population. This suited the man who had returned to town overnight in his battered white van to ask for sanctuary with his widowed sister. She had the *Sun* delivered every morning, and now her brother sat staring at the front page story, his lips moving as he read.

"What've you done now, then?" his sister asked, as she set a mug of strong tea in front of him. "I don't want no trouble here," she added. "There's enough of it round here as it is. Don't you involve me in any of your goings-on!"

"You've got a nasty suspicious mind," her brother said. "I'm as innocent as the driven snow. Ah, well, perhaps not snow. Bad choice of word! As the day is long, then. Innocent as the day is long."

"I never did know what you were talking about, and nothing's changed. You'd better sort yourself out and find another place to live. God knows what went on in Barcelona Street, but it's crawling with police, so the paperboy said."

"Nothing to do with me," he said. He had convinced himself that the stupid bitch who had overdosed was not his responsibility. "Anyway, I just need a few nights here, and then I'll be off. I'm thinking of moving to the country. Maybe get a job on a farm. I rather fancy the fresh air life."

His sister burst out into raucous laughter. "You? Fresh air? A likely story! The only fresh air you're likely to get is in a high-walled exercise yard. You had a good job gardening in the fresh air, anyway, and you made a mess o' that. Now, what d'you want to eat? I got bacon and eggs. Black pudden? Then I'm off out. It's my morning in the Oxfam shop. Me and Mrs. Wilson do Friday mornings."

She brought in a fragrant plateful, and turned to go. Then she said, "Oh, have they found that missing kid? Here, let's have a look at the paper before I go."

"Yeah, he's back home. No details. I bet he just went absent without leave for fun. Kids these days don't think of nothing but themselves."

After his sister had gone, he looked again to make sure there were no hints of abduction or foul play. The kid was home again, and should be left in peace with his mother in Long Farnden.

So the little sod had said nothing, or made up some story to satisfy the police. Not such a bad kid after all, then. But then, he'd been told what would happen if he blabbed, and even though his father had deserted him, he must have *some* feeling for the man who'd sired him. He wouldn't want him hurt, would he? It was a blinding nuisance that everything had gone wrong, but the outcome could have been worse. All right, so he hadn't been able to find Hickson and demand what he supposed would have been called a ransom. More of a deal, he reckoned. You pay up, and you can have your son back. If not . . . Well, it hadn't worked out. He hadn't reckoned on the kid being such a slippery little bastard. And Hickson would have been witless with worry. That would have to be enough, for the moment.

The fry-up was good, and he licked the plate clean. Nobody would be looking for him, luckily, and he had work to do, people to see, connections to make.

FORTY-SIX

꩜

FARNDEN HAD QUIETENED DOWN, ALTHOUGH THERE WERE still one or two unfamiliar cars parked near the Hickson house. Josie came out of the shop to bring in the buckets of flowers that had not been sold. Only two bunches left. That was good. Maybe Mum would like a bunch, and one for Gran. She had still made a profit.

"Evening, Josie!" A fresh-faced policeman approached, and Josie grinned.

"Hi, Matthew!" she said. "You're still on duty I see. Busy day in Farnden for your lot. Still, it's good news, isn't it. Young Jack home safe again. We'll all sleep easier tonight."

"What are you doing later? I'm finished here now, and just have to go home and change. Fancy a meal at the pub in Waltonby? New management, apparently, and the food is really good. What do you say?"

Josie beamed. "Wonderful idea," she said. "I think we all need a bit of a treat, after the last forty-eight hours. I hope Paula Hickson is able to relax, poor soul."

"Your mother's just gone in to see her. We had instructions from Hunter . . . special permission . . ." His smile was knowing, and Josie looked crossly at him. "That's quite enough of that, PC Vickers," she said. "Go away and forget you're a policeman, and I'll be ready in an hour. Oh, and love you, as the kids say."

LOIS HAD FELT CONSPICUOUS AS SHE MADE HER WAY UP PAULA'S garden path. Those unfamiliar cars were not casual callers. They were on the watch. She supposed Cowgill was expecting Jack's father to show up sooner or later, though she did not agree. Surely he would stay well out of the way? Unless, of course, it had not been him who'd taken Jack.

"Mrs. M! Come on in. Am I glad to see you! It's been such a day, and we're all at sixes and sevens. I apologise for the mess and muddle. . . ."

"Don't be silly, Paula. Here, let me give you a hand. Two New Brooms should make quick work of this lot!"

Frankie was duly tucked up into his cot, and the twins were bathed and sat like angels in their pajamas drinking hot milk. Jack Jr. was nowhere to be seen, and Lois did not ask. She would find out soon enough.

"He's asleep again," Paula said, without being asked. "After talking to that nice policewoman, he was really tired. Not eating anything yet. So I thought the best thing was to let him sleep."

"Quite right," said Lois. "He'll get his appetite back soon enough. Did he talk to you at all, after the policewoman had gone?"

Paula shook her head. "No, not really. But . . ." She hesitated, frowning.

"But what?"

"Well, I'm not sure, Mrs. M, that what he told the policewoman was the truth. I know I shouldn't doubt my own son, but you know what he's like. It all came out smooth and pat, like he'd rehearsed it. I've got to know over the years when he's lying."

"And you think he was lying this time?"

Paula nodded, her lips clamped together. Lois saw that she was again on the verge of tears, and changed the subject.

"Oh, by the way, Gran sends her love," she said. "Wants to know if there's anything she can do. She can be a nice old thing, sympathetic and not too nosy. That is, if she really tries!" She chuckled, and Paula's pale face broke into a smile. "It feels like the first time I've laughed for months," she said. The sound of footsteps coming downstairs caused her expression to change. She turned to the door, where Jack Jr. stood yawning. "Ah, here he is," she said. "I hope we didn't wake you, luvvie. Would you like something to eat now?"

He didn't answer for a few seconds, but stared at Lois. Then he said perhaps he'd try a sandwich.

"Ham?" said Paula. Jack shook his head.

"Chocolate spread?" said Lois, and there was a glimmer of a smile.

"Cor, yeah. We got any, Mum?" he said.

Paula went into the kitchen to prepare the sandwich, and Lois suggested Jack should sit down and chat for a minute or two. He looked at her suspiciously, but perched on the edge of the sofa.

"I got a rocket from Derek," Lois said casually. "For not locking my van. Still, it was a good job I didn't. You were completely knackered."

"I could've managed," he answered. "Plenty of traffic along that road."

"Glad you feel so grateful," said Lois with raised eyebrows. "Come on, Jack, give a little."

The chocolate sandwich arrived, and Jack began to eat, nibbling at first, but then wolfing it down. "Can I have another, Mum," he said.

"Please," said Lois, automatically.

Jack stood up, upsetting his plate. "Shut up!" he shouted. "You're not my mum, nor anything to do with me. You got no right to come in here asking me questions about what happened!"

Lois gazed at him calmly. "I haven't asked you a single question about that," she said. "Anyway, I haven't time to waste. I must be going, Paula. Let me know if you need anything. Shall I tell Gran you'll be in touch?"

Paula frowned. "Sorry about—well—you know . . . Thanks a lot for coming round, and for everything. I'll be back at work very soon, I hope."

On her way home, Lois saw the Adstone car go by at speed, and realised there were meetings happening all round the village, organising last minute details for the soap box grand prix. It was going ahead now, with only one week to go, and there was great relief that it would not be overshadowed by a missing child from the village. Should she be at one of these meetings? Ah, well, if there was a WI one, they could do without her. The soap box was finished, and now parked up at the hall being test driven by Mrs. T-J. She hoped the old girl wouldn't crash too many times. After all, a jar of jam is vulnerable.

"How were they?" Gran said, as she came into the kitchen.

"Much better," Lois said. She had decided to keep to herself Paula's confidences and the possibility that Jack was lying.

"That child needs a father," Gran said. "Where is he? You'd have thought he would come forwards now Jack's back. After all, they'll catch him sooner or later, and if he gives himself up of his own accord, it's bound to go easier for him."

"We don't know why he's disappeared, if Jack's story about a sleepover in Tresham is true."

Gran pounced. "You mean it may not be true? Lois, what do you know?"

"Nothing more than you," Lois said honestly. "It could be that Hickson vanished because he knew he'd be suspected, once the news broke."

"Well, let's hope he comes back. That poor woman needs a man about the place. Maybe they should get some counselling, see if they could get back together."

"Maybe," Lois said. "But shall we talk about something else now? What's new with the soap box arrangements?"

"There's a pub entry meeting tonight. Derek's gone down there."

"I saw Gavin Adstone on his way. He's helping the pub lot, isn't he? Surely they don't need Derek as well. Oh, yes, now I remember," she added, "don't tell me. Our Derek's a roving coordinator. . . ."

Gran smiled. "Yeah, well, I reckon he'd rather be roving down to the pub than to any of the others. I know there's a Youth Club one tonight. I saw Hazel in the shop, and she said John has to decide on who's driving their soap box. It was going to be Jack Jr., apparently, but I doubt if he'll be allowed to now."

"I don't see why not," Lois said. "It'd be good for him. Take his mind off the past couple of days." She looked at the clock. "I might slip round and see Kate Adstone. She was talking about helping Paula by collecting Frankie from nursery with Cecilia, and looking after him for a couple of hours. Paula will be needing as much work as I can give her when all this is over."

It was a lovely calm evening, still warm from the day's unbroken sunshine. If only it could be like this next week, they should have a really profitable day. And a lot of fun, too. The soap box had brought the village together in the best way. Nothing like a bit of good-natured competition. She thought of the unresolved question of what had really happened to Jack Jr., and decided to leave it until tomorrow, when her brain had cleared.

When she reached Kate's house and rang the bell, there was a long silence and she began to think nobody was at home. But surely it would be Cecilia's bedtime? Then she saw the net curtain twitch, followed by the sound of locks and bolts being undone. What on earth was going on?

"Oh, it's you, Mrs. Meade." Kate looked worried. "Do you want to come in?"

Lois nodded and walked into the neat sitting room, all the toys now tidied away into a big red plastic box. "I hope you don't mind my calling," she said. "I saw Gavin on his way to a meeting, and thought it would be a good time to tell you about Paula."

"Of course," Kate said. "Please sit down. Would you like a coffee?"

They talked for a while, and Kate seemed pleased that Paula would entrust her small son with her for a while after nursery. "I did wonder whether she would go off the idea after what happened to Jack. What *did* happen to him, anyway?"

Lois gave her the authorised version, and skipped on to ask about Cecilia. Assured that the little girl had settled very happily now, she prepared to leave. But Kate said quickly, "No, don't go yet. It's so nice to chat to someone when Gavin is out, and I expect your husband is with the lads, too?"

Lois sat down again. "Are you nervous about something, Kate?" she said. "I couldn't help hearing all those unlockings! Not scared of anyone, are you?"

"No, no," Kate said airily. "It's Gavin. He always insists I lock up securely when he goes out in the evenings. Especially since the Hickson business."

The conversation stumbled on. In the end, Lois said she had to go, as Gran would wonder where she was. "Gavin should be home very soon," she said. "And look, it's not really dark yet. Listen to that blackbird! There's a couple of them calling to each other. Come out here and listen."

As they stood in the quiet evening, listening to the liquid

notes of the blackbirds, the sound of a rough engine broke the spell. Kate froze as a shabby white van drew up outside her gate. The window was lowered, and a voice shouted out, "Twelve o'clock sharp tomorrow, Mrs. Adstone! Be there!" And the van moved off, juddering as it gathered speed.

Kate turned and rushed back in, followed by Lois. "Who was that? Did you know him?"

"No, no, of course not. Never seen him before. Must have got the wrong house. Sorry to have kept you, Mrs. Meade. Goodbye now." And Kate more or less shoved Lois out of the house and began to lock and bolt the door once more.

Lois shrugged. If Kate Adstone was having an affair with a man in a scruffy van, it was her business. But it hadn't sounded like that, and Lois was pretty sure it *was* the right house. He'd used Kate's name, hadn't he?

FORTY-SEVEN

ꝅ

THE MAN, WHOSE CURRENT NAME WAS ROSS, RETURNED TO his sister's house and parked his van outside, obscuring any view of the turgid canal water on the other side of the road. The house was in darkness. He supposed she was out at one of her many social engagements. Whist, bingo, a coffee evening with her Oxfam mates somewhere in the town. Well, that was good. He would have the house to himself, and could use her telephone to make some calls.

He drew the curtains, opened a beer and settled down. The first call was the most important. He dialled a familiar number, and waited.

"Hello? It's me. Ross. Yeah, mission accomplished. What? Yes, of course I made sure she heard."

The voice at the other end of the line asked if he was certain she had been alone. Ross thought quickly. A small lie was necessary here. "Oh, yeah," he said. "I went to the pub first, and her bloke was there, buying drinks all round for some reason. Something to do with this soap box grand prix they're putting on in Farnden next Saturday. I think they'd finished their vehicle, or something. You'd've been proud of me. I managed to get in on the round meself!"

"So she was alone, except for the kid?" the voice said.

"Yep. I kept it short. She was scared, o' course."

"And did she say she'd be there?"

Another necessary lie. "Oh, yeah. Said she was looking forwards to it."

"Liar," said the voice. "Anyway, you'll be for it if she doesn't turn up."

The call was cut off abruptly, and Ross saw that his hand was shaking. Sod the bugger! If only he'd never got into his clutches. That's how his sort worked, of course. Caught you when you were down, in his case sacked unjustly, and then made themselves indispensable.

His next call was to the dodgy character who'd been his second-in-command at Barcelona Street. "So what's happened about that girl? Cops took her away, I suppose? Did anybody talk? All got away before they got there? Good. Keep in touch, and don't forget that if you blab it's your life or mine. And I'm keen to hang on to mine."

That should fix him, he thought, and hung up. Now the most difficult one. He had to find out where Hickson was hiding out. The score was still not settled. There was no news on the telly. The story had gone quiet, but the evening paper had a small paragraph saying the police were still looking for the boy's father. He knew Hickson had been popular when he worked with the gardening lot at the parks depot. He had good cause to remember that! He rubbed his ribs where the pain still caught him, especially in wet weather.

Well, he had had one or two mates, too. Not that they had supported him much at the time, but he could give one of them a ring and see if he'd heard from Hickson. He still had his number somewhere. He searched and found it in an old notebook in his pocket, and dialled. His luck was in, and he recognized the voice. "Hi, mate!" he said breezily. "Guess who this is?" The answer was quick and final. A click, and then the dialling tone.

Ross sagged in his chair. He finished his beer and opened another. Friendless, he said to himself. All except for that bugger who had him by the short and curlies. He needed to think, and as always when silence began to close in and threaten panic, he switched on the telly.

"GOOD MEETING?" LOIS SAID, AS DEREK CAME INTO THE SITTING room a little unsteadily.

"More of a celebration, ac—ac—actually," he said. "Soap box *Speedy Willie* is finished, and christened with a bottle of champagne presented by the publican!"

"Shouldn't they wait until they've won the grand prix before cracking open the champagne?" said Lois dryly. She didn't grudge Derek his celebration. He had worked really hard on this whole event, and deserved a break. "I wonder how they got on at the Youth Club? Hazel said John had to choose a driver."

"He came into the pub just before I left," Derek said. "They've decided to let young Hickson drive it, all being well. Unani . . . unanimous decision, apparently."

"Is it safely built?" Lois said, with a sudden shiver of doubt.

"Oh, yes. They've had technical advice from the college. It looks a really streamlined job, too. It'll be great for the kid if he wins. And hey, you know he was supposed to turn up at choir the night he went missing? Well, Tony Dibson was in the pub, and he said the lad had sent a note of apology. He's still going to join, as soon as he's sorted out."

"That's all right, then," Lois said. All seemed to be going to plan. So why did she have this nagging feeling that something was still wrong, dangerously wrong?

FORTY-EIGHT

❧

"I WISH I DIDN'T HAVE TO GO, BUT THE CLIENT SAID THIS WAS HIS only free time. I shall be back about four o'clock," Gavin said. "What are you going to do with yourselves, poppet?"

The question was addressed to Cecilia, but Kate answered. She had had a terrible night, with not a wink of sleep. Over and over in her mind she had considered the best thing to do. Gavin had expressly forbidden her to go anywhere near the Café Jaune in Tresham, today or any other day, without him.

But the man had been so threatening! If only she could sort it out without having to tell Gavin. If she did tell him, she knew he would just storm off and tackle Tim Froot head on, and she feared that hot-tempered Gavin would come off worst. He seemed to have put the whole thing out of his mind at the moment, so in the end she decided to wait until he had gone and then see how she could get into Tresham without the car. There was a bus on Saturday mornings, she knew, but had no idea what time it went. If she turned up with Cecilia, Tim Froot wouldn't be able to do anything bad. And after all, a café was a very public place. Then she could sort him out in no uncertain terms and come straight home again. It was nine o'clock now, and Gavin was on his way out of the door. He need never know.

"We shall be fine," she assured him. "Might do a bit of gardening, and then go round to see how Paula Hickson is getting on. Little Frankie might come for a walk with us. You'd like that, wouldn't you, Cecilia?" she added, cuddling her daughter close.

"Take care, then. Bye, both," he said, and blowing a kiss he was gone.

Ten minutes later, Kate had telephoned Josie at the shop and established that the bus went from there at a quarter past ten. Just time to clear up and get Cecilia ready, and then they could be at the shop in good time. Now she had made the decision, she felt much better, and quite strong enough to deal with half a dozen Tim Froots, so long as they were safely observed by a café full of people.

There was a small queue waiting for the bus, and Kate joined on the end, folding Cecilia's pushchair to be ready to load it. She stood behind Father Rodney, and just to make conversation asked him why he was catching the bus and not taking his car into town? He replied that the parking on Saturdays was impossible, and in any case, the bus gave him a chance to chat to parishioners who were not necessarily churchgoers.

They climbed into the bus, already fairly full, and Father Rodney shepherded Kate and Cecilia into a seat and then sat beside them. "Will you come to me to give Mummy a rest?" he said, smiling at the toddler. To Kate's surprise, Cecilia held out her arms, and went without a murmur to sit on the vicar's lap and look around at the other passengers.

"Going shopping, Kate?" he said, after they'd got going again. "Gavin not with you today?"

"No, he's gone to see a client. Back this afternoon. We're

just going into town for an outing, really. Something to do. We'll have lunch somewhere, and then catch the bus back this afternoon."

"There are two today," Father Rodney said. "One about two thirty, and the other just after four. I hope to get the early one. I'm just going to Waitrose to get my favourite drinking chocolate! Josie doesn't have it in the shop yet."

"It's a long way to go for a jar of chocolate drink," Kate said with a smile. "I think chatting to likely converts is the real reason! Anyway, we're very glad, aren't we, Cecilia, to sit next to someone we know."

And so the conversation proceeded comfortably until they turned into the Tresham bus park, and slowly the bus emptied. The vicar said he would walk with Kate into the middle of town. She looked at her watch, and said she would come into Waitrose with him and buy some of the magic drinking chocolate. It was only eleven o'clock, and when he suggested having a coffee in the supermarket coffee bar, she willingly agreed. He insisted on taking charge of Cecilia in her pushchair, and Kate found herself thinking what it would be like to be a vicar's wife. It was different, she quickly realised. People made way for him, and it was as if an invisible barrier surrounded all three of them. How odd, she thought. Worse than being a doctor! There were three pedestals she wouldn't want to inhabit: the pulpit, the doctor's surgery and the teacher's desk. There was no doubt that people still set these slightly apart from the rest, giving them extra respect and keeping a little distance.

After they had finished their coffee, and cleaned up Cecilia's massacre of a chocolate muffin, Kate said it was time they went off. "See you on the early bus, with a bit of luck," she said. "And thanks for coffee."

Father Rodney said it was he who should thank both of them for their company. In truth, he had enjoyed it so much that when they went off, with Cecilia waving an enthusiastic goodbye, it made his loneliness twice as bad. But he was being stupid, he told himself. He had God's work to do in his parish, and he must concentrate on that, though he couldn't help thinking it would be so much easier if he had a loving companion, and maybe even a small Cecilia. . . .

Kate's heart was thumping as she approached the Café Jaune, and she was relieved to see that it was fairly full of customers already. She maneuverd the pushchair through the door and looked around. For one wonderful moment she thought he was not there. Then a bulky figure stood up from a table in a dark corner. It was Tim Froot, and he was smiling. Like a snake, thought Kate. Smiling like a poisonous snake.

"Well done, Kate!" He came across and helped her move the pushchair between the tables.

"She'll stay in her chair," she said, as he began to undo the straps that held Cecilia in. She had already planned a quick getaway after she had said her piece. She sat down and glared at Froot. Let him make the first move. He offered her the menu, and asked what she fancied to drink.

"Water, thanks. Tap water."

"And Cecilia?"

"I've got her drink in my bag."

"Right, now what will you both have to eat. I've been looking forwards to this meeting for days!"

"I'll have a pizza, and Cecilia can have some of it. She doesn't eat much at lunchtimes, and still has an afternoon sleep." She had worked this out as a useful time limit on their meeting. His next remark, oh so casual, scuppered this.

"I thought we might have a stroll in the park after lunch," he said. "Cecilia will probably drop off as we go. I seem to remember my young ones were always lulled to sleep by movement. Car, pushchair, train. Quite useful, really, when they were bored on journeys."

Anyone overhearing this conversation would think it the most natural thing in the world, thought Kate. A young mother and her child, with maybe an uncle or father, even, meeting for a pleasant lunch. If that was all, fine, but the new suggestion of a walk in the park was not so pleasant. Anything could happen. It was a big park, and there were always deserted paths through tall shrubbery areas.

"Something wrong, Kate? You look a bit alarmed. I'm not planning anything harmful, you know. Nor am going to ravish you behind the bushes! Not this time, anyway, and not in front of an infant. No, I asked you here for a talk, and mostly about your wayward husband."

"What do you mean, 'wayward'? The only other girl he's ever looked at has been Cecilia!"

"Not wayward in that sense. Do relax, Kate. This is a very preliminary talk. Ah, here's our drinks." He downed half his glass of red wine in one gulp, and then said that Gavin had been wayward in not fulfilling a bargain that he had with Froot, and this was not satisfactory.

"Nothing to do with me," said Kate. "And if I had my way, we'd be rid of you for good. I personally would be happy never to set eyes on you again."

Tim Froot put back his large head and hooted with laughter. Two women at the neighbouring table looked across and joined in the laughter, nodding approval. How nice to see the little family enjoying themselves! Even the little girl was chortling with delight.

"That's how I like my women," Froot said. "Good and feisty. A real challenge."

"I'm going," said Kate, putting down her glass of water.

Froot's tone suddenly changed. "No, you're not," he hissed. "Stay exactly where you are, and smile."

Kate subsided back into her chair, but did not smile. Oh my God, she whispered to herself in panic. Why did I come? What is he going to do? Then common sense took over. What could he do, right here in a crowded café? She would have to tell him what she had rehearsed and then leave, regardless of what he might say. He could do nothing.

"Now," he said, "listen to me, Kate Adstone. Your husband is deeply in debt to me. His part of the bargain was to wreck all chances of restoring your pathetic village hall, and instead to persuade the oafs on the parish council to go for the rebuild option. He did not do this. Not only that, but he now appears to be determined to wreck plan B, which was to make sure the soap box grand prix will be a financial disaster. It will be closed down on the night before the event. By the police, of course, who I understand have not been consulted. You can't just organise this kind of thing without consulting them, you know. Gavin is to see that this happens, at the last minute, of course, to cost the organisers the most possible trouble in terms of money and disappointment. You are to see he does that, Kate. Otherwise, I shall take steps to make your marriage unbearable. A total disaster. Oh yes, don't interrupt. I can do it. You can be sure of that."

He sat back in his chair and smiled again. The pizzas arrived, and Kate cut up small pieces to feed to Cecilia. Her head was reeling. Most of what Froot had said was a complete surprise. But one odd thing occurred to her.

"But why do want the village hall rebuilt? Surely not a job for contractors of your size?"

"Not just the village hall, Kate. It would be a package, taking in the playing fields. Lots of lovely executive dwellings for young families with children to play with Cecilia. And before you ask, I shall of course make sure alternative playing fields are provided."

"But even so," she protested, "it could only be a small development compared with your usual projects. There's another reason, isn't there?"

"That's where the bargain comes in," Froot said, leaning forwards confidingly. "When Gavin brings off his part of the assignment, I have promised to waive the debt and make a place for him at the top of my team. He's a clever lad, Kate, as I'm sure you know. I want him back." And his wife, too, if possible, he thought, but kept that to himself.

"You must be mad," Kate said. "Gavin is no performing monkey! He has principles and a mind of his own. We'll pay off your rotten loan, if it takes everything we've got."

"Everything?" said Froot, and now his smile was slimy.

Kate shivered. "Come on, Cecilia," she said, standing up, glaring at him. "We're off home. And don't send your disgusting heavy round to intimidate me again, or I'll be the one going to the police. And not to shop the soap box lot! I'll see you in jail, Tim Froot, if you put one more foot wrong. We'll make regular payments until we're clear of you and everything to do with you."

She turned her back on him and pushed Cecilia out of the café and walked as fast as she could along the crowded pavement, away from the worst half hour of her life.

Over the other side of town, in the small terrace of houses by the canal, Froot's faithful henchman was slumped in front of his sister's television. They were watching her favourite soap, and he was nearly asleep. Then his mobile rang, and when he saw who was calling he ran into the kitchen, slamming the door.

"Hello, boss? How's life?"

"Shut up!" said Tim Froot. "Listen carefully, you idiot. I shall say these instructions only once, so get it right. If anything goes wrong this time, you're a dead man. Perhaps floating gently past your sister's house in the murky canal? No, that's too good for you. So just listen."

FORTY-NINE

ᔓ

FATHER RODNEY HAD DRIFTED AROUND TRESHAM, BUYING things he didn't really need but passing the time until the bus to Farnden returned. He was early back at the bus station, and looked round, vaguely hoping that Kate and Cecilia would also be in time. They were nowhere to be seen, and in due course the bus was almost full. The driver climbed into his seat and started the engine.

"Hey, wait a minute!" a woman called from the rear of the bus. "A woman with a baby is coming! Wait a minute, driver!" she repeated.

Fortunately, the driver was the good-humored one who usually drove this bus on a Saturday. He nodded, and opened the doors again. Father Rodney got up from his seat and rushed to help Kate aboard, taking the pushchair from her and stowing it, and then sitting the two of them down next to him. "You made it, then," he said calmly. He supposed it was the dash for the bus that had caused Kate to look so upset and shaky, and when Cecilia tried to climb on to his lap, he lifted her up gladly.

Kate nodded and tried to thank him, but instead she choked and put her hand up to her mouth.

"My dear, are you all right?" he asked with concern. "Has something happened in town? Anything I can do to help? No, don't try to answer. Take your time."

He was quite sure there must have been some nasty incident, but when Kate had recovered herself she just gave him a crooked smile and said no, she was just out of breath from running.

Father Rodney then made small talk and pointed out a passing fire engine to Cecilia. "Wha-wha! Wha-wha!" she said dutifully.

For Kate, the journey seemed endless. She desperately wanted to be in her small cottage, safely locked in until Gavin came home. She had decided to risk his wrath and tell him what she had done. At least that would put him on his guard in case Froot decided on violent retaliation. She knew now that the man could do it. The expression on his face as she stormed out of the café was scary, and all eyes had been turned on him. She hadn't looked back, but guessed that he would not have followed her. That would have made him too conspicuous, and he was a man who liked to be in the shadows. It would be that villain in the dirty white van. He was the one they should be looking out for.

When they got off the bus, she assured the vicar that she would be fine walking home. She did not explain that there were plenty of people about, and she meant to walk fast. As she passed the Hicksons' house, she heard Paula's voice. For a moment, she wanted to walk on, pretending she had not heard, but in the end slowed up and stopped, looking round.

"Got time for a cuppa?" shouted Paula. "Been shopping in town? Thirsty work," she added hopefully.

Kate sighed. "Oh, well, thanks," she said, turning the

pushchair round. "Kind of you. Can't stay long, but a quick cup would be great. Thanks."

"I've been alone with the kids all day," Paula said, as they went into the house. "You get desperate for a bit of adult conversation, don't you?" she added. "I could almost have my husband back, just for that."

"Are you serious?" Kate asked, suddenly aware of a change in her new friend. So this wasn't just a casual invitation. She took her mug of tea and sat down, watching Cecilia and Frankie sparring over a pile of toy bricks.

"Not really," Paula replied slowly. "But yes, I suppose I am. It's Jack Jr. that I'm thinking of. He needs his father. He's a difficult boy—always was—but I thought I could manage him on my own." She gave a rueful smile, and added, "But it's obvious that I can't. O' course, he's bright. Everybody says so. But if I'm not careful, it's all going the wrong way. He'll use his cleverness in bad ways, and end up one of them dropouts outside the town hall in Tresham.

"You might meet some other guy, who'd be a better influence than Jack Sr.," Kate suggested. She could concentrate with only half her mind, her thoughts still whirling round her encounter with Tim Froot. Supposing he got to Gavin before she did? She drank her tea in big gulps, and shifted in her chair, preparing to leave.

"Better the devil you know," Paula answered, with a half smile. "My old man was a good husband and father until he lost his job, you know. It was the disgrace, really. Where he was brought up, losing your job was your own fault. This time it wasn't. But anyway, it was the stigma what really got him down."

Kate subsided back into her chair. This was costing Paula quite a lot, telling her this stuff about her husband. She wanted to say that if all she had to worry about was a depressed husband, she was lucky. Then she reminded herself that Paula had had a terrible few days, and tried again.

"Well, when they find him, why don't you suggest getting together with one of those marriage adviser people. Maybe you could both try hard and make a go of it again?"

"*If* they find him, Kate. That's the number one problem at the moment. I'm just crossing my fingers that he doesn't do anything stupid. Anyway," she added, making an effort to brighten up, "I mustn't keep you. It was really kind of you to come in for a few minutes. And to offer to meet Frankie and have him for a couple of hours. I'll pay you, of course, the going rate! I shall tell Mrs. M that I can be available extra hours."

"So where's young Jack now?" Kate said, as she and Cecilia walked back down the garden path.

"In his room," Paula said. "He doesn't seem to want to leave it. The social worker said he's probably still a bit shocked."

"Do you think that?"

"No," said Paula. "I think he's plotting something."

GAVIN DROVE BACK IN THE EARLY EVENING THROUGH HIS PEACE-ful village with a feeling of relief. He was tired and looking forwards to seeing Kate and Cecilia. He wouldn't admit to himself that he was anxious for their safety, but all day it had lurked at the back of his mind. Froot was used to getting his own way, and in the past had stopped at nothing to get it. Thank goodness Kate had decided against meeting with him.

He turned the car into their lane, and saw Tony and Irene in her wheelchair outside his gate. Christ! What was happening? He screeched to a halt and leapt out of his car. To his relief, he saw that Tony was smiling. Nothing too bad, then.

He greeted them, and then stood, breathing heavily. Irene stretched out her hand. "Evening, Gavin," she said. "Hasn't it been a beautiful day? We've been having tea in your garden with Kate and Cecilia. Such a treat for we oldies!"

Gavin looked towards his front door, and saw Kate standing there, holding his daughter, both of them waving to him. He said a silent prayer of thanks, and went to meet them. Apparently Tony and Irene had insisted on coming round to keep Kate company, bringing a sponge cake and homemade biscuits, and she hadn't been able to refuse. In fact, they had all enjoyed it, and Cecilia had been thoroughly indulged.

Together, Gavin and Kate put their daughter to bed, and then settled down to a pizza and a bottle of red wine he had bought on the way home.

"Are we celebrating something?" Kate said.

"I suppose we are," he said. "Got a new client, and an offer of a job."

Kate gasped. How had Froot found Gavin already? "Who with?" she stuttered.

"Well, the bloke I went to see, of course. Robin Crossley. He wants me to join his company and take on the side of the business I'm already doing in Tresham. What's the matter, Kate? Are you ill?"

"Not really," she said, "but listen, I've got something important to tell you."

IN HIS MAKESHIFT HOME IN THE WAREHOUSE, JACK HICKSON HAD cleaned a filthy window so that he could see out into the street below. He had spotted the paragraph in the paper saying that the missing boy had been safely at a friend's house all the time. There was some adverse comment about wasting taxpayers' money. Jack could not have explained exactly how, but he knew that his son was lying. The lad had his faults, but he wouldn't have put his mother through all that worry voluntarily. No, he was absolutely certain that he had been abducted, and he knew by whom. No doubt young Jack was too frightened to tell the truth.

He knew there was little likelihood of seeing his quarry

by chance. He would have to carry out his plan to pace the streets patiently, keeping his eyes and ears open, until he picked up a clue. Every so often he would slip into a public toilet or a menswear changing room or some such, and change his appearance. It was easy, really. A woolly hat, or heavy-framed glasses, or the false beard or mustache bought from the joke shop, and there he was, no longer Jack Hickson, but a perfect stranger. Or so, in his inexperience, he thought.

Suddenly his attention was caught by seeing a dirty white van pull up outside the newsagents opposite the warehouse. His heart began to pound. A man got out and scurried into the shop like a frightened rabbit. It was him! Jack could swear that it was the man he was hunting. He turned away from the window and dashed down the stairs, taking them three at a time, but when he emerged onto the street, he saw the van pulling away from the curb. Sod it! He thought of running after it, but that would be stupid, drawing attention to himself. No, it was still close enough for him to read the number plate, and Jack, who had a good memory for such things, stored it in his mind.

But how was he ever going to catch up with it? And what could he do, even if he saw it parked in town? No, he needed wheels. A bike, that's what he needed. An old bike, not easily traceable, and lightweight enough to manhandle up to his warehouse lodging. Should he buy one or appropriate one left carelessly unattended? Not the latter, he told himself. Even the pettiest theft was a bad idea. He decided to go to the town dump. They always had old bikes that nobody wanted. He could slip a pound or two to the dump chap and be away in minutes, no questions asked. Then if he saw the van again, he would follow it. With the many traffic light stops, he would be able to keep up.

He returned to his watching position, feeling a lot more cheerful. Progress had definitely been made. And a bike would be good exercise. You can go anywhere on a bike, he said to himself. Even out into the country. Even to Long Farnden, if necessary.

And the best news of all was that his quarry was still around, still local.

FIFTY

༝

LIKE EVERYONE ELSE, DEREK HAD BEEN RELIEVED WHEN IT became apparent that the only danger threatening Jack Jr. had been catching cold from sleeping in a cold draft on a friend's floor. "No doubt having another try at drawing attention to himself," he had said to Lois, pleased that this time she would have no reason to ferret about trying to find a mythical kidnapper.

To his annoyance, she had raised her eyebrows and said if he believed *that* story he would believe anything. "The poor kid's the best liar in the county," she had said.

Now, as they sat in silence at the breakfast table, Gran attempted to get a conversation going. "Only five more days to go to blast off," she said cheerfully. "How's it going, Derek? All the entries finished and rarin' to go?"

"Sorry?" said Derek, looking up from opening his post.

"You didn't hear a word I said, did you!" said Gran, thumping the table. "Well, if you two want to carry on this silly business, I don't. So you can stack the breakfast things yourselves. I'm off down the shop to have a civilized talk with Josie, who knows how to behave like an adult. Unlike some people I know."

"Hey, Mum, what's all this—?"

But Gran had stormed out, grabbed a coat from the hall, and was on her way before Lois could reach her.

"Oh, dear," said Derek. "Do you think she's possibly offended?" He looked at Lois with a serious expression, and for a moment she glared at him. Then she began to laugh.

"Looks like it," she said. "Silly old bat. But no, she's not silly. We are. Look, Derek, I know you think Jack Jr.'s explanation is the truth, but the person who knows him best, Paula, thinks otherwise. And if she doesn't believe him, then I don't either. I'm getting to know that young man, and I think he's a good liar and a very scared thirteen-year-old child. What's more, his mum thinks he's planning something, and it could be very dangerous. So I'm working on the probability that he was abducted, and the need to find whoever did it as quickly as possible."

"And Cowgill? Does he think this, too?"

Lois nodded. "And before you ask, he was thinking this before I talked to him."

Derek sighed. "So is this going to be general knowledge? Is the soap box grand prix still to have this hanging over it?"

"Bugger the soap box grand prix!" retorted Lois. "That boy's life is more important. And for all we know, the lives of other people. Don't forget his father's not been found yet. He didn't go missing again for nothing. And no, it is not going to be general knowledge, so don't worry, nothing will spoil the soap box day."

"I heard that," said Gran, coming silently back into the kitchen. "And I shouldn't bet on it."

"I thought you were—"

"Shop's not open yet. I didn't look at the time. There's a quarter of an hour to go, and I wouldn't knock and be a nuisance at this hour of the morning."

"How thoughtful," said Lois acidly. "Well, as you have obviously heard, we are now talking to one another. Come on in, Mum," she added, relenting. "Let's make some more coffee. We're sorry, aren't we, Derek?"

"Heartbroken," said Derek. He stood up and gave both of them a peck on the cheek. "Must be off now. Last meeting tonight before the final rehearsal on the playing field on Friday."

After he had gone, Lois said she needed a quiet morning in the office. "Can you keep callers at bay, Mum?" she said. "I want a clear run without interruptions this morning."

Gran beamed. Nothing she liked better than keeping callers at bay, but making sure she found out what they wanted first. "Leave it to me," she said. "The only interruption will be when I bring in your coffee."

Within ten minutes, Lois's phone began to ring. Before she could reach out for the receiver, it stopped. Then she heard Gran's loud voice from the kitchen, saying she was sorry, but Mrs. Meade was unavailable this morning. Lois grinned, and turned on her computer.

Time to take stock, she had thought. Priority number one: find Jack's father, and persuade him to give himself up, for the boy's sake. This was supposing he had been the kidnapper. Even if he wasn't, he was needed by Paula and her family.

Priority number two: if he wasn't guilty, then find out who was and bring him to justice. Again, for Jack Jr.'s sake. If he *was* protecting someone with his lies, then he would never be at peace and stand a chance of being a normal teenager until it was sorted out.

And then she thought of something which was glaringly obvious, but so far she had missed. *Why* would someone not his father want to kidnap the boy? What was to be got out of it? Certainly not money. Paula Hickson hadn't a spare penny, so that couldn't be it.

The telephone rang again, and this time Gran came to the

office door with a resigned expression. "It's him, the inspector," she said. "Won't be put off."

Lois nodded, and lifted up her phone. "Yeah? Lois here."

Cowgill wasted no time. "I think we've got a feud here, Lois," he said. "If Jack Jr.'s father wasn't the one who took him, then the only possible reason for another to have done it is an old score to be settled. What d'you think?"

"Telepathy," said Lois. "I was nearly there. Looks the most likely, I agree. So what next?"

"Find out who has a grudge against Jack Hickson. Speak to Paula, if you can. She respects you, and probably trusts you. She might well have the answer. Can you get down there straightaway?"

"I don't need to," Lois said. "I know who had a grudge. It was at the time Jack was given his cards. Another bloke was taunting him, and Jack fetched him one. It landed in a bad place, and he had to be treated in hospital. Is that grudge enough, d'you reckon?"

There was a silence, and then Cowgill said, "How long have you known this, Lois?"

She didn't give him a straight answer, but muttered something about being sure she had told him at least some of it. Then she said that the urgent thing to do now would be to find out who it was. Paula had not given her the name of Jack Sr.'s tormentor at work. He had apparently refused to tell her, and his other workmates had decided to keep their mouths shut, too, thinking it would all pass over and be forgotten. That would be the best thing for Jack, they had agreed amongst themselves. The injured man had also been sacked when other redundancies had been necessary. Knowing he had been partly guilty for Jack's attack, he too had said nothing more, but it was known that he had apparently blamed Jack for having to take sick leave and then finding himself out of work.

"Did Paula tell you all this?"

"Some of it," Lois said. "The rest has emerged in dribs and drabs. I have not been idle, Cowgill, whatever you may think."

Cowgill left it there. He said he would now contact the Parks and Gardens Department and see what they could tell him. There must be someone willing to talk.

"I'll keep in touch, Lois," he said. "And well done. All I would say, my dear, is that you could be in a dangerous position, knowing what you know. There is a man on the run somewhere, possibly desperate. If you could bring yourself to let me know any more dribs and drabs that might come your way, I would be most grateful."

"Bollocks," said Lois, and ended the call.

"I love you when you're angry, Lois Meade," Cowgill said to the dialling tone.

"What did you say, sir?" said Chris, coming in for her meeting with the boss.

"Never you mind," said Cowgill. "It was a private call."

FIFTY-ONE

≫

IN NO TIME AT ALL, THE PARKS AND GARDENS DEPARTMENT OF the local authority had supplied Cowgill with the names and addresses of all those made redundant after Jack Hickson had left the department. No, they answered when he asked about a punch-up in the department, they had no knowledge of any such disturbance. In fact, they were quite put out by the suggestion. Good staff relations were a priority with the authority, they insisted.

Cowgill had handed the list to Chris, filled her in with details of Jack Sr.'s fight with a fellow gardener and asked her to do some legwork. "Go and see them all," he'd instructed, "and don't let them know you're coming. This one will be a slippery eel, I suspect. Even a hint that we're on to him will send him slithering off to a new hideaway. Meanwhile," he added, as she prepared to leave his office with a bundle of papers, "I shall be out for the rest of the day. I need to have a chat with my most useful contact in all of this."

"Of course. I'll find you somewhere in Long Farnden, then?"

"Get going, Chris," Cowgill said.

NEW BROOMS WEEKLY MEETING BROUGHT TO AN END LOIS'S WORK on setting down information and endeavoring to make sense of it. She felt she had cleared up some of the puzzles, but was not a lot nearer solving either of the priorities. We're going round in circles, she had decided. There must be another way in. Who else might be sitting on useful clues without knowing it? After his second disappearance, Jack Hickson Sr. was obviously keeping his distance and was unlikely to reappear in the village. But she was sure he wouldn't be far away. From what Paula had said lately, it was not impossible that she and Jack could get together again.

As for the other man, Lois was not so optimistic. The only hope of him being still around was that the grudge had not been settled. Or, she thought, as the first of her team rang the door bell, maybe it is not wholly his show. Maybe someone else is pulling the strings, and he's just the puppet? Perhaps they should be looking at the whole thing as a network of connected motives?

"Oh, lor, it get's worse!" she said aloud, as the door opened and Andrew looked in.

"Okay to convene, Mrs. M?" he said.

The rest of the team followed, and Lois welcomed them. "Let's hope this week we can concentrate on our jobs, without the distraction of missing kids and the police crawling all over us," she said. "Now, Hazel, shall we start with the list of new potential clients?"

"Twenty of 'em," Hazel said flatly. The others stared at her. This was at least twice as many as usual for a weekly count. "Seems the village being in the news has brought in an influx of helpless housewives. I reckon, and Mrs. M agrees with me, that they're all nosy blighters who think one of us would be good for a juicy gossip. Anyway, Mrs. M and me have been through the list, and sorted out four clients most likely to stay with us, gossip or no gossip."

"Can we cope with that many extras?" Sheila Stratford said. She was now the acknowledged senior cleaner, having been there longer than anyone else, and she usually spoke for the rest.

"Yes, I think so," said Lois. "I've been through schedules carefully, and with Paula being able to do a couple more hours, and Andrew not having any interior décor projects on at the moment, we can work things out. I may have to look for another member of the team later. We'll see. If any of you would like some extra hours, let me know."

Dot Nimmo's hand went up, like the girl at the back of the class. "Please, Mrs. M," she said, "I would. I've got time on my hands now. My sister Evelyn has moved away, as you know, and to tell the truth, I'm lost for company." Lois smiled. She tried not to have favourites among her staff, but she could not help having a soft spot for Dot.

Dot Nimmo! Of course! Why hadn't she thought of her before? With her past connections with the underworld of criminal gangs in Tresham, she could well be sitting on information that would be vital! She was not even sure the connections were all in the past. After all, Dot's husband and his entire family had carried on businesses which all sailed close to the wind, and involved the odd mysterious drowning or apparent suicide. Then Dot's husband had died, as had his brother and father, and not all of natural causes, but this did not mean that Dot had lost touch with the rest. The reverse was more likely, Lois was sure.

"Good, that will be helpful, Dot," she said. "Can you stay behind for a few minutes, and we'll go through your schedule with Hazel. Now, any other matters?"

Floss had a breakage in a client's house to report, but said that it had been a pottery figure of a clown that the owner had never liked, so there was no problem. Sheila reported that Edwina Smith was happy to give young Hickson some odd jobs around the farm at weekends, if he was interested. Now that she was a widow, she was having a hard time getting through the work, even with help from Sheila's husband, Sam.

Finally all the details were dealt with, and the meeting broke up. Only Dot and Hazel remained, and in a short time Dot's revised schedules were worked out. Then Hazel went, saying she would see everybody at the soap box grand prix on Saturday.

"Next year," said Dot, "can we have a New Brooms soap box, Mrs. M? I know some of my nephews would be really good at getting a speedy one knocked up from odds and ends. Not sure where the odds and ends might come from, but no questions asked!"

This gave Lois the perfect opportunity. "Sit down again, Dot," she said. "I wanted to have a chat about your family."

Dot looked alarmed. New Brooms was her life now, and she dreaded something bad happening inside the Nimmo gang that would cause her to lose her job.

"Don't look like that!" Lois said. "It's nothing alarming. No, I really wanted to pick your brains. In strict confidence between me and you, and I really mean that, Dot, we are still not happy with Jack Jr.'s story about what happened to him. It might be that he's made up all that stuff about being at a friend's house."

"So he could've been taken, after all?" Dot's eyes had brightened with the chance of a good mystery to work on. In the past, she had loved the idea of being Mrs. M's assistant in the ferretin'.

"Look, Dot, your family knows every dodgy character in Tresham, every member of other gangs, and you could find out if any of 'em specialise in abduction."

"Could well be," Dot answered, "but if they were after

money, they'd pick somebody else. They may be villains, but they're not stupid. Why snatch the son of a woman on benefits, with a husband gone missing and living hand to mouth in a council rented house?"

"On the nail, as usual," said Lois. "That's it, Dot. So why?"

"Settling a score, that'd be the most likely reason. You'd be surprised, Mrs. M, how long these grudges last. Some of 'em from generation unto generation."

"Very biblical, Dot," Lois said, and laughed. "But that's where you come in. Can you do a bit of ferretin' for me and find out if there are any really wicked grudges still around in your family's acquaintances. I won't say friends."

"Don't worry about offending me," said Dot. "My eyes were opened when I married my dear departed. Nothing shocks me now. Leave it to me. Say a couple of days, and then I'll report back?"

"Great," Lois said. "Off you go, then. And thanks for offering some more hours. It'll be good to keep the new clients going. Times is hard, as everyone knows, and even New Brooms will need all the work we can get."

As Dot went down the path, she saw a tall figure approaching. She recognized him at once, and hurried past, hiding her face.

"Morning, Mrs. Nimmo!" said Cowgill cheerily. "Family all well?" He carried on, chuckling to himself, and as he approached the front door, it opened. "What do you want?" said Lois.

"Don't pretend you're not delighted to see me, Lois Meade," Cowgill said. "And don't worry, it's business, so can I please come in?"

"There's nothing more I can tell you at the moment," Lois said, half closing the door.

"At the moment?" said Cowgill, sticking his foot in the opening. "Then perhaps you could elaborate on that? I shan't keep you long. I can smell good smells coming from Gran's kitchen, and I must get back to my lonely sandwich in the office. And seriously, Lois, I do have one or two things to ask you. Thanks, love," he added, as she opened the door wide and he stepped inside.

FIFTY-TWO

᪁

I WANT YOU OUT OF HERE BY THE TIME I GET BACK THIS EVE-
ning," Ross's sister said, hands on hips and a threatening
expression on her face.

It was ten o'clock in the morning, and her brother was
reading a newspaper spread over his unwashed breakfast
dishes still on the table. He was unshaven and had wrapped
himself in an old dressing gown which had belonged to her
late husband. This grubby garment had been the last straw.
It reminded her that she had rejoiced at getting rid of one
useless man about the house and now here was another,
apparently staying indefinitely. Well, he could think again.

"And if you're not gone when I come back from the shop,
I'm dropping a helpful hint to the Tresham constabulary."

He looked up at her sharply, hastily covering up the blonde
on page three. "What d'you mean? I'm not wanted for nothing."

"I can think of something," she said caustically. "Always
stayed on the right side of the law, have you? Don't make me
laugh. No, you think about it. And I don't want no forwarding

address. Just be gone when I get home." She turned and went out of the door and he heard her footsteps disappearing along the path outside.

Never mind about brotherly love, he thought, what happened to sisterly loyalty? He sighed. She always meant what she said, so he supposed he'd better be on his way. He got up, stacked the dishes in the sink, and went upstairs to get dressed. He was thinking hard about where he should go. Not to a country retreat yet. He smiled at the idea of himself as a country bumpkin. He still had a job to do for the boss and one of his own, and he had a plan worked out. Anyway, finding a bed for a week or so with one of the shadier contacts he'd made since being out of work shouldn't be too difficult.

Dot Nimmo let herself into her redbrick terraced house in Sebastopol Street in Tresham. It was a long street, built cheaply to house workers in the days of industrial expansion in the town. New Brooms office was at one end of the street, and Dot's house at the other. She almost never called in to see Hazel in the office, not wanting her old friends and associates to connect her too closely with Mrs. M. Lois Meade was now well-known to the gangs in town as Cowgill's favourite grass, and Dot was anxious that her family should not clam up on her.

She sat down with a cup of tea and a sausage roll from the shop on the corner, and began to consider who best to approach. Her sister Evelyn had cut herself off completely from the family, but there were several of the next generation who could be useful, Evelyn's son for one. He had also been included in the persona non grata cutoff by Evelyn, who had been disgusted when he was caught supplying to known dealers. Getting caught was the crime! Dot loathed him, with his flash clothes and smarmy ways, but she was quite capable of pretending family affection if it looked like being productive. She picked up her telephone.

"Hello? It's Auntie Dot. No, I do not want a taxi, Victor! Are you at home this evening? I just need to pick your brains. Ha-ha! Of course you got brains. All the Nimmos got brains." Of a sort, she added to herself, and then said she'd call in around seven o'clock. "That'll still give you plenty of time to get to the pub," she said. "See y' later."

Now, what to do next. Dot had to be at her new lady at two thirty, and it was only just after half past one. Who else in the Nimmo circle could she have a chat to? There was one old friend, but she hadn't been in touch with her for years. She had had a family, all still around Tresham, so it might be worth giving her a bell. What was her name? She'd been at school with Dot, in the same class. Martha? Martha Ross! That was it. And she married a Smith. Oh God, finding her in the telephone directory would take a while, and even then she might not get the right one. More thought needed on that one.

She looked out of her window. Her garden was full of sunlight, and a large grey pigeon was sitting in the birdbath. It looks like a stupid duck, thought Dot, and she began to laugh. She felt ridiculously happy to be ferretin' with Mrs. M again. And knowing the world of the Nimmos, it was more than possible she would uncover a great deal of dirt before they were finished.

VICTOR NIMMO WAS WAITING AT THE DOOR AS DOT DREW UP outside his tall, wrought iron gates. He lived in some style on the edge of town, and his house and large garden were fortified against all intruders. He had enemies, he knew. You couldn't get as rich as he was without making enemies. Now he operated the gates remotely so Dot could drive in.

"Bloomin' 'ell," she said. "You expecting a terrorist attack, or something? Anyway, how are you, Victor? And how's the wife?"

He ushered her into a long room lavishly furnished and decorated in shades of cream and gold. "Pammie's gone to her mother's for a few days," he said.

Dot knew for a fact that she had been gone a few months, probably never to return, but said nothing.

"Now, Auntie," Victor said. "What can I do for you? In a spot of trouble, are you?"

"Of course not," Dot said sharply. "No, it's information I need. I know you still keep the old rackets going, and might know something useful."

"What's it worth?" he said, pretending to be joking.

"Could be your entitlement to all this," she said, waving her hand around. "But we Nimmos must stick together. It's important, Victor, and you know the form. You scratch my back an' I'll scratch yours. Now, what I want to know is to do with missing persons."

In a skillful way, she then described the kind of person she was looking for without alerting him to the actual case of Jack Jr. "The missing person's probably been taken as part of an old grudge," she ended up, "and God knows there's still plenty of grudges in town. My old man may not have made your kind of money, but at least he settled everything before he died. Anyway, what d'you reckon?"

Victor was silent for minute, taking it all in. He might well have had brains, but they needed time. "Can I have a think, Dot, and let you know?"

"It's urgent," she said. "Give me a bell tomorrow. Don't let me down, will you, Victor. But you got more sense than to do that, I know. Now, you'd better let me out of this prison and get yourself down the pub. And, by the way, I don't want this spread around. You know how to do it. I'll hear from you tomorrow."

FIFTY-THREE

❧

IT HAD BEEN A BAD FEW DAYS IN THE ADSTONE HOUSEHOLD. After Kate had told Gavin about her meeting with Tim Froot, he had been stunned and silent. This had not lasted, and ever since then he had burst out into fits of anger, first at her, for taking matters into her own hands, and then at Froot for having the nerve to attempt to blackmail Kate into an intimacy that made him feel sick every time he thought about it.

"And you took Cecilia with you!" he repeated, day after day.

This evening, when he said it once more, Kate began to think this was his most important concern. "He was quite nice to her," she said finally. "She thought he was great."

At this, Gavin covered his eyes and moaned. "Kate, what have you done? Don't you know that Froot never gives up? He has so many poor sods at his beck and call that he always gets his own way, especially when he has his victim over a barrel."

"He doesn't have us over a barrel," she replied. "I told him straight. We would pay back what you owe in installments, and he was to leave us alone. Of course, I didn't know about the bargain you'd made. I'm not sure I can forgive that. If anybody in the village got to know your part in it, we'd be drummed out."

"But I haven't done what he wanted!" Gavin shouted at her. "You know I haven't. And I'm not going to! Christ knows what'll happen, especially since you stuck your oar in, but I've finished with Froot. I just wish you'd let me handle it all myself."

Kate was near to tears, and then she remembered something Froot said. He would make our marriage a disaster! And now it was happening. She began to see what Gavin meant about Froot being all powerful. But he hadn't won yet. She went over to where Gavin sat and crouched down beside him, taking his hands in hers.

"Gavin, we've got to stop!"

"Stop what?"

"Shouting and quarrelling and starting to hate each other. It's just what Froot threatened. He said if you didn't play your part in the bargain and wreck the soap box day, he'd make sure our marriage was destroyed. And here we are, on the way!"

After that, they sat silently hand in hand until it was time to check on Cecilia and then go to bed.

"I love you, Kate," Gavin said, as he moved up close to her warm body.

"I love you, too," she said, and added, "and as I told Tim Froot, we'll see him in jail if he doesn't leave us alone."

Gavin sat up. "Why did you say that?" he said. "How could we possibly—?"

"I was going to tell you. I was chatting to Paula Hickson, and discovered we both worked for Froot at the same time. She was in the canteen, and I don't remember seeing her. But she remembered me, and we compared notes. She had some horrific stories to tell. Girls who'd been virtually raped by Froot and then paid to keep quiet. Men who had been threatened with the sack if they didn't do really dodgy jobs for him. Oafs like that heavy he sent out to threaten me, I suppose. Yeah, Froot is into drugs and God knows what else. Paula didn't say if he'd had a go at her, but she certainly loathed him. I reckon if we needed her, we could get her to be a witness."

"Oh, my God, Kate, you have really got us in deep. But you're right. If we stop trying, we'll be in his clutches forever. Let's get some sleep now, and talk some more tomorrow."

NEXT DAY, PAULA HICKSON WAS DUE TO BE AT THE HALL AS usual, and she had told Lois she thought it would be safe now to get back to the job, as Mrs. Smith at the farm had said she could give Jack Jr. some work that would keep him busy all day. She would give him lunch, she said, and keep an eye on him. The work was all in the garden and the chicken run, all within sight of the farmhouse.

"In any case, Mrs. Hickson," Edwina Smith had said, "he's explained it all now, and we should be showing that we believe him when he says he won't be so thoughtless in future."

"But I don't believe him," Paula said to Lois. "Still, I can't lock him up in a back room and give him bread and water forever. So I'll be okay for the hall, if you want me there."

Lois accepted the suggestion at once. It was not that she had come to believe Jack Jr.'s story any more than his mother did, but the pressure of work made her agree, though with some misgivings.

Now, with the twins at school, Frankie at nursery and Jack Jr. at Smith's Farm, Paula knocked at the hall kitchen door and walked in. Mrs. Tollervey-Jones greeted her kindly, and said she was pleased to have her back.

"Before you start work, Mrs. Hickson," she said, "I have

a treat for you. I want to give you a private preview of the future soap box champion, *Jam & Jerusalem*!" She led the way out to a stable over the yard, and with a dramatic gesture pulled a tarpaulin off the gleaming scarlet soap box. "There!" she said. "Isn't she fine?"

It was all Paula could do to stop Mrs. T-J giving her a demonstration of the vehicle's speed, and they returned to the house. "Right, off you go, then. Your colleague has been very good, but not quite up to your standard." She turned to leave the kitchen, and then stopped. "By the way, do you remember my new gardener who left me in the lurch?"

Paula's heart stopped. She took a deep breath, feeling faint. But after a second or two she rallied, and said as casually as she could manage, "Yes, of course. What about him?"

"I could swear I saw him in Tresham yesterday. I was coming out of my solicitors in the market square, and he passed close by me. I think he had a funny sort of beard, and a strange woolly hat—much too warm for this time of the year—but when I caught his eye I could see it was him. Certain of it. Isn't it odd? He seemed so happy here, and really knew his stuff, and yesterday he looked old and ill. Ah, well, I'll give him a week or two and if he doesn't return, I shall have to advertise again. Must do some work now. I shall be in the den when coffee's ready."

Paula stood quite still, unable to say anything. Mrs. T-J appeared not to notice, and disappeared. At last, Paula moved to the window and looked out. So he was still around, maybe living in Tresham? The beard and the woolly hat sounded like an amateurish attempt at disguise, and this would be just like Jack. He was not a natural deceiver, never had been. And he was ill.

More and more lately, she had thought back to their happy days before he lost his job and everything went wrong. If only they could get together in some kind of normal circumstances, without all this mystery of what happened to Jack

Jr. Then maybe they could have a go at sorting things out calmly. She had begun to think they'd have a reasonable chance. The thought of being a proper family again brought tears to her eyes, and she reminded herself that she had a job to do and had better get on with it before Mrs. T-J's euphoric mood changed.

AFTER PAULA HAD FINISHED HER MORNING'S WORK AND GONE home, Mrs. T-J went to have another look at *Jam & Jerusalem*. What a beauty! she said to herself, and stroked the shiny red bonnet. Maybe she would take her out for a little run, just to make sure the wheels were performing smoothly. She went back into the house and fetched her hard riding hat. She would need to tow it behind the car to the top of the sloping drive, and then coast back, practising her steering and crouching down in her seat as Doug Meade had told her to, in order to lessen the wind resistance, or something like that.

She had parked her Land Rover halfway down the slope on the grass verge and unhooked the soap box when there was a hooting from behind. She looked round and saw to her irritation a dirty white van veering from side to side up the drive. What on earth did it want? She wasn't expecting a delivery, and in any case would never buy from such a scruffy-looking outfit.

"Go away!" she shouted, as it drew up closer. "You've got the wrong road! This is a private drive. Go away at once. And keep off the grass!"

But the van had stopped now, and a man got out, walking towards her. He was grim-looking and scowled unpleasantly at her.

"Keep yer hair on, missus," he said. "How can I go back? Not room to turn round, for a start. And anyway, I've got some business to do with you. So you'd better tow that thing back to the house, and I'll follow."

Mrs. T-J bristled. "Don't you order me about! If you don't go at once, I shall call the police. And yes, I do have a mobile with me, and I am a close friend of the commissioner."

"I don't care if you're a close friend of the Almighty. I ain't doing nothing wrong, so if you won't let me up to the house, we can have a little talk here. It's not a criminal offence to talk, is it?"

"Very well, but be quick about it. My time is precious."

"I doubt it," he muttered, and then added more loudly, "I just wanted to know if you've seen a friend of mine. Used to work here in y' garden. He always kept in touch, but for a couple of weeks I ain't heard nothing."

Mrs. T-J's eyes narrowed. "What's his name?" she asked.

"Hickson. Jack Hickson."

Mrs. T-J shook her head. "Nobody working for me of that name," she said, silently asking God to forgive her lie. Hickson was, of course, her cleaning woman's name, but the gardener had given her another, which for the moment she could not remember. But she knew it wasn't Hickson.

"You sure? I heard he was definitely working here. Used to be a workmate o' mine, but we got made redundant and lost touch."

"I thought you said you heard from him regularly?"

"Don't try and trick me, missus!" he said, and moved towards her, fists clenched.

"Ah, now you'll have to move," Mrs. T-J said calmly. "I see a police car coming up the drive. You'd not want to obstruct their enquiries, I presume?"

He hesitated, sure that she was lying. But as he turned, he saw the familiar striped vehicle, and jumped into his van, revved up the engine and shot off towards the house.

"Any problems here, Mrs. Tollervey-Jones?" the sergeant said, stopping his car and getting out to greet her.

She shook her head. "No, no. Nothing I cannot handle. Just an itinerant salesman. I directed him to the tradesmen's entrance at the back of the hall. He'll find his way back to the main road along the grassy lane. How can I help you?" she added, smiling as she saw him take in the glories of *Jam & Jerusalem*.

FIFTY-FOUR

~

THE VAN ROCKETED DOWN THE NARROW, POTHOLED LANE
until it reached the junction with the main road to Tresham. Ross turned left, having no idea where he would go
next. That had been a near thing. That woman must have
spies everywhere. He'd certainly not go near her again. And
what was that bloody stupid soap box doing? She must be
mental, playing with kids' toys. Ah, well, the rich could
indulge themselves. Not like us ordinary sods, living from
hand to mouth. A small voice in his head reminded him
that if he had not tormented Jack Hickson until there was a
punch-up, he would still be on the payroll of Parks and Gardens in Tresham.

Where to go now? His sister had turned him out, but
he had no intention of leaving the area. He would find Jack
Hickson if it was the last thing he did, and finally settle
the score. The Hickson kid had outwitted him, he had to
admit, but he'd think of something else, once he'd located
his target. He took the next turning to Tresham, intending

to investigate the now run-down factory site by the canal. There would be one or two contacts making use of the empty building down there, in touch with the underworld network of useful information. He accelerated, hooted and shook his fist at an elderly woman travelling at twenty miles an hour in the middle of the road, leaving him no room to pass, and felt better.

IN HER HOUSE IN SEBASTOPOL STREET, DOT NIMMO HEARD THE church clock strike two o'clock and stretched out her hand to the telephone. She had heard nothing from Victor since her visit to him on Monday, and now considered he had had enough time to do what she had asked. She knew these things took time, making contacts with care and tact. Victor was not of the brightest, but he knew the form. He would tread carefully, she was sure of that. But a less than gentle reminder would do no harm. As she lifted the telephone, there was a sharp knock at the door. Damn! She replaced the receiver and went through her narrow hallway to the front of the house. As usual, she did not open the door at once, but went into the sitting room and peered out from behind the curtain. Victor!

She slid out the chain, unbolted and unlocked, and opened the door.

"Good God, Dot," he said, "are you expecting the Mafia?" He had not forgotten her jibe when she came to see him.

"No, only you. And about time, too. Don't just stand there! Come in, do. You'll wear out the pavement."

She settled him in her best armchair, and put a large gin and tonic in front of him.

"Middle of the afternoon, Dot? You got depraved habits since your man died! Still, I reckon I need it after all the work I done for you."

"Get on with it, then. What did you find out?"

"Your man is still around. That's the first thing. The

second is that he's on the move, and for the moment we've lost track of him. He was working at Farnden Hall, we know that."

"So do I!" snapped Dot. "You better tell me something more recent than that."

"Hold your horses," Victor said. "Not s'fast, Dot. We tracked him down after that. You know his kid went missing—"

"—that was all over the papers, for God's sake! Where is he *now*?"

"We thought he scarpered out of the area, but then we picked up the scent on a train. One of ours had a bit o' business in that direction and sat near this bloke. He thought he recognized him from the picture in the paper, though he wasn't sure. Said the man on the train was much older and thinner. Still, he thought there might be a profit to be made in following him. He shadowed him almost back to Tresham, then lost him. But that was not long ago, so we got men out looking right now."

"So what you're tellin' me is that he's probably still around these parts, but you don't know where?"

"Not exactly where, nor are we sure it was him," Victor said, taking a large gulp of his gin.

"Is that it, then?"

"No, there is one more thing. Might be useful. You know old Carl who runs the joke shop in that little alleyway off the marketplace? Still on our list for past misdemeanours?"

Dot nodded, scowling at him in a threatening way.

"Well, he reported a skinny, ill-looking bloke who came into the shop asking for a false beard and mustache. Said he was doing kids' parties, but Carl said no sane person would employ him anywhere near kids."

"And?"

"And he reckoned he was a bit like that father of the kid that went missing. Carl still had the picture in the paper, but there wasn't much of a likeness. Could've been his brother, he said."

"Did he ring the cops?"

"Did he hell! You know better than that, Dot! Nimmo friends don't communicate with the law. They wait for them to approach, then decide whether or not to be helpful."

Dot sighed. Sometimes she wondered how these Nimmo idiots had kept afloat all these years. Still, there was one nugget of information that might help. Jack Hickson could be around town wearing a false beard and mustache. The idea was so ridiculous that she burst out into a raucous cackle.

"What's funny, Dot?" Victor said, getting to his feet. He had decided to go while the going was good. Dot had a reputation, and he would be happier on his way back home in the limo waiting for him outside her door.

"Nothing, nothing at all," she replied, sobering up. "Thanks for not much, Victor. Anyway, if you hear anything more, let me know." She saw him to the door and secured it after him.

Mustache and beard? Where would that be more of an everyday sight than a joke disguise? Where down-and-outs congregate, that's where. She tidied her kitchen, found her handbag, and left the house, walking swiftly down Sebastopol Street and waving to Hazel as she went by the office.

MRS. T-J WAS NOT CONCENTRATING. SHE HAD JOINED HER FELlow magistrates in the anteroom and discussed the cases coming before them this afternoon. They had had a difficult one this morning, but now the list consisted mostly of vagrants picked up off the streets, drunk and disorderly, and one parking offence committed by an eighty-year-old man accused of scraping the wing of a car parked in front of him, then leaving the scene of the crime without reporting to the police or his victim.

Now it was time to convene the afternoon session. She took off her glasses and rubbed her eyes. Sometimes she thought of retiring, considering she could now use her time more profitably than sitting in judgment on an old man who was probably a lot more capable of safe driving than many a youngster. "Let's be off, then," she said.

"All rise," said the court official, and Mrs. T-J entered, followed by her companion JPs. The first thing she noticed was a wasp. It was careering round the courtroom, bashing into windows that were set high in the wall to prevent observation either in or out. There were few things that frightened Mrs. T-J, but wasps were at the top of a short list.

"Before we start," she said magisterially to the court usher, "may we expel the wasp?"

The usher frowned. Was she serious? He knew the dear old thing was getting on, but she always seemed in full possession of her marbles. Very sharp, in fact, and she knew that persistent offenders dreaded coming up before Mrs. Tollervey-Jones.

It was several minutes before the wasp was firmly squashed and the business of the court commenced. The magistrate sitting on Mrs. T-J's left leaned towards her to say that he thought the first case was a nonstarter, and saw that she was gazing up at the ceiling.

"It's gone. Squashed. It is an ex-wasp," he whispered. He had great respect for the chairman of the bench, but she really was behaving oddly.

"I know," she said firmly. "I was thinking. Something on my mind. Settled now, though. Let's get on, shall we?"

Ever since Mrs. T-J had encountered that unpleasant character with the van who had accosted her on her own driveway, she had repeatedly seen his face in her mind and knew that she had seen it before. So many faces of that sort—closed up, belligerent—had passed in front of her in her time spent in courtrooms. Was it one of them? And now she had remembered. He had been involved in that dreadful case of a young lad dying of an overdose in a house frequented by addicts on the edge of town. And now there had been another death there, a girl found by police curled up on a filthy mattress and clutching a moth-eaten teddy bear. House all boarded up now, of course, but too late for two young people.

FIFTY-FIVE

❧

THE ENTIRE VILLAGE WAS NOW TAKEN OVER BY TOMORROW'S soap box grand prix. There had been last minute objections from the police on safety grounds, but somehow Mrs. T-J had managed to smooth things over.

"She ain't goin' to be cheated out of the ride of her life in *Jam & Jerusalem*!" Tony said to Irene, as he pushed her up the street at teatime to have a look at the impressive ramp erected by John Thornbull and helpers. A crowd stood around as bolts were tightened and trial runs made sure that the edifice was safe. A streamlined vehicle, shaped like a rocket and labelled *Silver Streak II*, was repeatedly pushed up the ramp backwards and then released to check that all was well.

"You'll wear it out, boy!" Tony said to its driver.

"Don't you worry, Tony Dibson, we've got *Silver Streak II* ready for tomorrow!"

Tony and Irene wandered on, turning down to the playing fields and home. As they reached their cottage gate, and Tony turned the wheelchair, Irene said, "Aren't we going round the field? It'll be a good opportunity before the crowds get here tomorrow."

"It'll be a bumpy ride for you," Tony said.

"Never mind about that! You'll want to see everything." Irene smiled. "I reckon my ride down the field will be nothing compared with them soap boxes. They'll career down the High Street and try to avoid all the potholes the council hasn't mended."

The big marquee had been erected a couple of days previously, and now all the craft and sundry stalls were set out. There were few exhibits, most stallholders having decided it was risky to leave them overnight, and planned to turn up early tomorrow morning. The first race was at one o'clock, and the organisers had reckoned that most of the business on the field would be done during the morning.

Gavin Adstone was watching a couple of men setting up the bucking bronco, and his small daughter, sitting on his shoulders, chortled and pointed at the horse, shouting "Me! Me go on horse!"

"Hi, Irene! Listen to this silly child! As if we'd let her anywhere near a bucking bronco!"

"There will be Shetland pony rides for the little ones tomorrow," Irene said, blowing a kiss to Cecilia. "Is Kate taking photos? I'm sure there'll be some for the album."

"Time for the meeting soon," Tony said. "Are you coming back our way, Gavin?"

Gavin looked at his watch. "Good heavens, is that the time? Yep, we'll come back with you. Here, Cecilia can sit on Irene's lap, and I'll push the chair. It's hard going in the field. The meeting's in the pub, isn't it? Derek said half an hour at the most. All of us have jobs to do around the village, so it'll just be for emergency matters."

"Of which I hope there'll be none!" John Thornbull said, coming up behind them.

They walked slowly back past the village hall, and on

towards the High Street, leaving Tony and Irene to go back home. Gavin lifted a protesting Cecilia from Irene's lap, and turned into his house next door, emerging again to attend the meeting.

Straw bales were being set out to form a crash barrier down both sides of the street, and a bunch of young boys scratched about in them like chickens, until shooed away by Sam Stratford on his tractor. Outside the shop, Josie and Lois stood talking to Paula Hickson, Frankie and the twins.

"Where's Jack Jr.?" Gran said, walking up to join them.

"Down with the Youth Club lot," Paula said. "He's been there all hours after work at the farm for most of this week. Thank God for the soap box grand prix, I say. They're going to let him drive, and he's finally cheered up. My only trouble with him now is persuading him to come back home to eat occasionally. Mind you," she added hastily, "I know where he is this time, of course. And next week he's back at school. I'm crossing fingers and toes that he'll settle in again."

"Oh, look, here comes Mrs. T-J with her son. He's opening the whole shebang, isn't he?" Josie said.

"Not exactly. He's escorting the soap box queen. Hey, look what she's got him doing! He has to earn his moment of celebrity." Lois pointed down towards the church, where a forklift truck hoisted Mrs. T-J's son high to fix rows of bunting, crisscrossing the street, while she directed operations from the ground.

"The old girl's a wonder," Derek said, as he joined them. "She's really come up trumps. Wouldn't it be good if she won her race?"

"She will," said Gran, tight-lipped. "Never been known to be beaten at anything, that one."

"Ah, but don't forget the surprise entry in the women's race," Derek said, glancing at Lois. She put her finger to her lips.

"Surprise entry?" said Gran innocently.

"All will be revealed tomorrow," Lois said. "Well, I must be getting home. Lots to do before the morning. See you all first thing."

In the back room of the pub, the soap box committee met for the last time before the great event, and there was an air of apprehension and excitement mixed with the smell of stale beer. "Are we all here?" Derek said, looking round.

"All except John," Gavin said. "He's coming as soon as they've roped off the ramp so the kids can't play on it. He's thought of everything, our John." And I devoutly hope that I have, too, he added to himself. However hard he tried, he could not banish thoughts of Tim Froot and his designs on Kate. Supposing he showed up tomorrow, while Kate and Cecilia were unprotected? But he'd thought of that. He'd asked Irene if she would like Kate to be with her all day, allowing Tony to be off with the blokes around the course. It would be all hands to the plough tomorrow. Cecilia could toddle beside the chair and Kate could push. She could still stop every now and then to do some filming. That would fix any attempts Froot might make to corner her into threatening conversation.

Dry throats were taken care of by the landlord, and the meeting commenced. "We won't have the formality tonight, Hazel," Derek said. "Each one of us can bring up any last minute concerns, and then we'll get back to our jobs around the village."

"I'll make notes, anyway," said Hazel. "Might be important. You never know, do you?"

DOWN BY THE CANAL, DEEP INSIDE THE CRUMBLING WAREHOUSE, a huddle of sad characters grouped around Ross. He'd questioned them one by one to see if any knew the whereabouts of Jack Hickson, but most were too befuddled with sour beer and meth to be of any use. He made a bed for himself out of old car seats dumped in a corner, and stretched out. He'd wait until the best one of them was sober, and then by offering him something to put him back into nirvana, he would tease out any information there might have been going the rounds regarding Hickson.

He had picked up the evening paper, and opened it to the news page. A large photograph of a scarlet soap box occupied a quarter of the page, and the accompanying story advertised the grand prix taking place tomorrow in Long Farnden, first race at one o'clock. Right! Ross stood up and waved the paper in the air. "He'll be there, for sure!" he said to an unresponsive audience. "His whole family out on the street, and the kid probably involved in the racing. How can he keep away?"

JACK HICKSON HAD SEEN THE SAME STORY IN THE PAPER, HIGH UP in his eyrie above the street and out of sight of the shoppers in town. He had been out among the crowds earlier, this time shielded by an old panama straw hat he found dumped in a bin in the park. Pulled down over his eyes, he had slouched along in a raincoat that came down to his shoes, and was grateful that he had a day free of the hot, prickly beard. He was now adept at changing his identity in small ways, and was confident that sooner or later he would find Ross. And when he did, he had planned down to the last detail what he would do.

But now, tomorrow was the soap box grand prix in Farnden, and his family would be certain to be out with the visitors on the streets. By now he was expert at slipping between groups of people, becoming invisible when cops or sniffing dogs loomed. He would go and observe. At least he could take a look at little Frankie and the twins, and above all at his firstborn, Jack, who was certain to be there amongst the vehicles. He remembered taking him to a race meeting at

Silverstone, and even though he was only six, he had been fascinated by the cars and the noise and the smell of high octane fuel.

And, of course, Paula would be there.

FIFTY-SIX

FATHER RODNEY WAS ON HIS KNEES IN THE CHURCH, PRAYING for fine weather and a successful day. It was cool and quiet, and the powerful scent of flower arrangements set in place for the visitors filled his head and gave him a strange otherworldly sensation. Perhaps this was what heaven would be like? He pulled his thoughts back to the matter in hand. "Above all," he prayed aloud, "keep us all safe on this important day. Amen."

"Hear, hear, vicar," said a voice from the back of the church. It was Mrs. T-J, and she walked briskly down the aisle towards him. "Just thought I'd pop in for a quick word with the Almighty," she said.

"Not for help in the ladies race, I hope," joked Father Rodney. "Fair play for all must be our watchword."

"Don't be ridiculous," said Mrs. T-J. "I shall win without divine help No, my prayers would echo yours, more or less." She knelt down in the front pew, and bowed her head. All was silent for a few minutes, and Father Rodney did not quite know what to do. Obviously Mrs. T-J had a hotline, and did not need his assistance. When she stood up, he smiled and said he would no doubt see her around the village. He wished her luck in her race, and she nodded confidently. "Make sure you're watching," she said. "It will be something to remember when *Jam & Jerusalem* crosses the line."

Although the dew was still on the grass in Lois's front garden, there were plenty of people walking to and fro past her gate. Most of them waved cheerily and commented on the sunny morning. "Hope it lasts!" Lois shouted back a dozen times. She picked a bunch of flowers to put in a vase, which, as Gran said, would sweeten the ladies' toilets at the back of the village hall.

Derek had been up at dawn, and Lois had not set eyes on him since. He had said he would see her this evening, if not before, but they could keep in touch on their mobiles. She had agreed with Gran that one of them would take a flask of coffee and a sandwich and force him to down them, wherever he was and however busy. "He'll want to be in good shape for the dance this evening," Gran said, as Lois stuffed the flowers in a glass vase. "And here, let me do that. I don't know where I went wrong, Lois Meade, but you can't knit or sew, nor arrange flowers. I don't know what your grandmother would say."

"Thank goodness she's not here to say it, then," Lois said. "And anyway, I got better things to do than learn how to turn the heel of a knitted sock that nobody would ever wear these days."

In this mood of amiable disagreement, they set off down the High Street, first to put the flowers in the portaloo, and then splitting up, Lois to help Josie in the shop, and Gran to the village hall to join the team working on WI refreshments.

"Morning, Mum!" Josie said from the shop doorway.

"Isn't it exciting? There's so much activity, and I've had more people in here by nine o'clock than would come shopping in the entire normal day. I can certainly do with another pair of hands. Come on in and get your pinny on!"

Lois was so busy for the next hour that she had no time to look at what was going on outside in the street. Then she heard the unmistakeable sound of the Tresham Silver Band approaching, and knew the soap box queen procession had started.

"Come on, Josie, let's take a look!" she said, and they both stood at the shop doorway with the crowd that had gathered all along the street. The Silver Band led the way, and behind them came the queen, a ten-year-old ash-blonde beauty, smiling and waving her sceptre from her seat of honor in the gleaming carriage that had served generations of Tollervey-Joneses. This was drawn by Mrs. T-J's trustworthy black mare, now old and safe. By the queen's side sat Robert Tollervey-Jones, a mild-faced charmer, taking care of the queen with gentlemanly grace.

"The Tollervey-Jones Show, then," said Josie.

"Of course," Lois replied. "But he does look nice, and he's making sure the queen gets all the attention."

"Is he married?" Josie said speculatively.

"Yes, and happily," Lois said. "And, by the way, is Matthew Vickers on duty here today?"

"Naturally," Josie said. "And did Dad ever tell you subtlety is not your strong point?"

"He wouldn't know subtlety if it jumped up and bit him on the nose," Lois said. "Come on, we'd better get back and do some more selling."

IN THE FIELD NEXT TO THE RAMP, AT THE TOP END OF THE VIL-lage, the stars of the grand prix were lined up for inspection. *Silver Streak II*, the allotment holders' entry, stood next to the local estate agents' vehicle, which was designed with great imagination in the shape of a cottage with roses round the door. Several soap boxes had been pared down to a skeletal essential of frame, wheels and brakes, and a finely honed steering mechanism. Others had been made to a heavy-as-possible design, based on the sound scientific principle that the heavier they are the quicker they go. And then there was the scarlet wonder, *Jam & Jerusalem*, sparkling and confident, with a neat little flag bearing the WI badge tucked behind the driver's seat.

"I trust there will be a guard present to make sure there's no attempt at nobbling," Mrs. T-J had said to Derek. He had assured her that he himself would be at the starting point and with his team on duty there would be no chance of hanky-panky of any sort.

The soap boxes were being carefully inspected by the owner of the local garage, and his chief concerns were sound brakes and efficient steering. As he bent down to examine the Youth Club entry, challengingly labeled *Rebellion*, he scratched his head. "I suppose it's okay," he said. "That steering wheel has a bit more play than I'd have liked to see. Still, there's certainly no danger there. You'd better get a message to John Thornbull to tighten it up a bit."

The morning passed quickly, and as crowds flocked round the playing field, the bucking bronco and the tug-of-war events were by far the most popular. Derek stayed for the tug-of-war result, and cheered heartily when the oldies won. "Never thought I'd be on the oldie end of the rope!" John said.

"Experience before enthusiasm," Derek said, as he and John walked back up to the ramp.

Jack Jr. stood on guard beside *Rebellion*, and said that he was sure all was fine. "Nothing to be done to this wonder" he said, patting the silver, rocket-shaped box.

"Right, back to work," said John, and disappeared into the crowd.

*   *   *

JACK HICKSON SR. WAS, OF COURSE, ALREADY IN THE VILLAGE, today disguised as a woman, in a dowdy brown wig and somber grey coat. He clutched a tatty old bag he'd found in a charity shop for twenty pence, and concealed his hands in his pockets as much as possible. He felt sure nobody would recognize him, and moved freely through the crowds. At one o'clock, he joined the lines of people waiting noisily for the first race. The church clock struck, and with a fanfare from Tresham Silver Band, the soap boxes lined up on the ramp were off, gathering speed as they went down the slope of the High Street, urged on by a huge wave of excitement from their supporters.

In this first race, Lois with Josie at the top of the shop steps, watched with sympathetic shouts as the streamlined *Silver Streak II* coasted to a gentle halt a hundred yards from the start, much to the fury and embarrassment of its driver. Race marshals Gavin Adstone and Douglas Meade moved smoothly on to the track to clear away the offending soap box and attention turned to the winner, a delighted young man in suit, collar and tie, every inch the estate agent, driving the cottage with roses round the door.

"I'll give you twenty pounds for it!" yelled a wag outside the pub.

Behind the cheering supporters stood Ross, pressed into a corner by the pub door, glass in hand and eyes constantly on the move, scanning the crowds as they passed in front of him.

FIFTY-SEVEN

～

THERE WERE ONLY TWO CONTESTANTS FOR THE LADIES CHAL-
lenge, the race that all were waiting eagerly to see. They
were both sitting in their vehicles, prepared for the signal to
be off. Only those clustered round the start had seen who
they were, as they had emerged quickly from the bungalow
behind the ramp and had quickly pulled down their helmet
visors.

"This'll be a good 'un," said Irene to Kate Adstone. "I
really don't know who I'd put my money on."

"I wish I'd entered now," Kate said. "It's difficult to tell
which is which of those two. I reckon their soap boxes were
made by the same team!"

The two vehicles were sensible plain wooden boxes with
seats, set up on small wheels that looked as if they had seen
better days. The steering was exactly as the kids had had in
those years that Tony Dibson remembered, a wooden bar
with a loop of rope, and there were brakes in accordance with

the rules. Tony appeared, ruffled Cecilia's curls, and asked Irene how she was enjoying the day.

"It's great! But you watch this, Tony. This is going to be the best race of the day."

Derek had disappeared, and Gavin Adstone had taken over the starting signal.

"They're off!" said the commentator, and the two soap boxes rolled sluggishly down the ramp and began to gather speed as they hit the road.

Gavin left the ramp and came over to where Kate stood. "Seen anybody we'd rather not see?" he said. She shook her head. "I wish we could be down at the finish," she said.

"If they get there," Gavin said. "Why don't you run down to the pub, Kate," Gavin added, forgetting for a moment that he had planned to keep her under scrutiny all day. "Tony and I will look after Irene and Cecilia."

"It'll be finished by the time I get there," Kate said.

"I doubt it," Gavin said. "You'll more than likely pass them halfway there."

GAVIN WAS WRONG. THE TWO ANONYMOUS DRIVERS WERE crouched over their steering ropes as if their lives depended on it. Every so often one would turn to look at the other and nod, whether a friendly gesture or one designed to discountenance, it was impossible to tell.

Derek, waiting with Josie down by the finishing line, grabbed his daughter's hand. "This could be the end of a beautiful relationship," he said.

Josie shook her head dumbly. She was too tense to speak, and squeezed his hand.

Then the two boxes appeared round the corner and headed down the final straight stretch to the pub.

"Neck and neck!" choked Derek. "Ye gods, Josie, this is terrible!"

"Buck up, Dad," Josie squeaked. "You've got to present the prize to the winner, don't forget."

Derek groaned, and then suddenly let go of Josie's hand. "Hey, look! There's Jamie! He made it, after all, bless the lad. Oh, oh, no . . . she's seen him . . . and lost it . . ."

One of the drivers had turned and spotted the new arrival, taken her hand off the rope to wave and steered straight into a straw bale. The other soap box, now at snail's pace, coasted slowly on.

"Go, go, go!" roared the crowd.

At last the vehicle crept over the finishing line, with the driver's arms held high in the air in triumph. The applause was deafening, and when the defeated box had been ignominiously pushed along to the finish, the taller of the two women got out of her seat and removed her crash helmet.

"Well done, Mum," said Lois, helping Gran out of her vehicle and giving her a huge hug. "The best girl won! But did you see Jamie over there? He made it! Come on, let's go and find him."

"In a minute," said Gran with a stately wave to her cheering admirers. "There's a small matter of a prize. I think you should stay and watch, Lois. It'll look like you're a bad sport if you don't." She patted her hair back into shape and walked towards Derek, who was clutching a vast bouquet of roses. "Thanks very much," she said. "You all right, Derek? You look really pale."

Derek mutely shook his head. All he could do was give her a peck on the cheek, and hand her over to her newly arrived grandson, Jamie.

GRAN THE DEMON DRIVER, WITH JAMIE, JOSIE AND LOIS, made their way back to the shop steps to watch the last races of the grand prix.

"Who's in the final, then?" Jamie asked. He had had a

nightmare journey from the airport, his plane having arrived three hours late. But now he was here, and quickly joined the family euphoria at the obvious success of the day.

"Well, thank God, *Jam & Jerusalem* is still in the running!" Lois said. "That's the WI entry, driven by her up at the hall. Then there's the estate agents' cottage and the pub lot. Who else, Josie?"

"The Youth Club's great little vehicle, *Rebellion*, driven by young Jack Hickson," she said to Jamie. "The Hicksons are new to the village. Dad reckoned he clocked up the fastest time so far in its heat. It would be nice if Jack could win. He's had a rough time one way and another lately, but we'll fill you in on that later."

JACK HICKSON SR. PUSHED THROUGH TO THE FRONT OF THE crowds at the finishing line, taking no notice of the angry looks from people who had been there first. He had overheard conversations about his son being the youngest driver, and having seen other vehicles crash spectacularly into the straw barriers, he was anxious. Nobody had been hurt, so far as he could tell, but even so. . . . He knew that if something happened to the boy, he would rush to the rescue, no matter what were the consequences. He wished they would start, and then it would all be over and young Jack would be safe.

Only a few feet away from him, on a bench by the wall of the pub, sat Ross, yet another glass of beer in his hand. His eyelids threatened to close, and he forced himself awake. He had come here with a purpose, and although he had seen nothing of Jack Hickson, he must not let himself give up. He shook his head to clear it, and then he saw him. The bugger had got a woman's wig on! But his profile was unmistakeable. That nose could not belong to anyone else, and certainly not to a woman.

Now wide awake, Ross felt in his pocket. The knife was

safely there, and he slid it out of its sheath with trembling fingers, keeping it concealed. He stood up. His plan was working out, and he slowly slipped through the crush of people, towards the front row of watchers, where his quarry stood. He knew exactly what he would do. As the soap boxes neared the finishing line, there would be the usual roaring of voices, and this would give him cover whilst he worked his way to stand next to Jack. He wanted his enemy to know who was about to settle the score, and then, before Jack could move in the dense crowd, he would ram the knife home. In the melee sure to follow, he would scarper as only he knew how.

"They're off," shouted the voice on the loud-hailer, and all eyes turned to the track, waiting for the finalists to appear.

FIFTY-EIGHT

✣

DEREK STOOD BY THE FINISHING LINE, WATCHING CAREFULLY to make sure the track was clear. Several of the straw bales had been knocked out of place by the swelling crowds, but were not a serious obstruction. In any case, it was too late now to do anything about it. The cheering was coming down from the start like a tidal wave. Then they were in sight, and Derek frowned. There were only two boxes on the track. The others must have failed soon after the start. So now it was just *Jam & Jerusalem* desperately trying to edge past *Rebellion*.

"Age versus youth," said Kate Adstone at his elbow, and Derek smiled. "Come on, Jack!" he yelled, and then remembered he was supposed to be impartial. Ah, well, in this tumult nobody would have heard him.

When the two were halfway to the finish, Derek saw out of the corner of his eye a movement in the front row of watchers. Several turned angrily to see who was causing a disturbance, and a straw bale was pushed at an angle, leaving a gap between spectators and advancing soap boxes.

"Straighten that bale!" he shouted at the top of his voice, but nobody heard. The soap boxes were close now, both losing speed as the slope flattened out to the finish.

JACK JR. WAS HOLDING HIS BREATH. NEARLY THERE! HE HAD never felt so powerful, so elated. This'll show 'em!

Then, as his soap box, still in the lead, slowed down to a gentle roll, he saw a face in the crowd that changed everything. It was his enemy, and in a split second Jack saw him rip off a wig from the person next to him, and then he knew them both. It was the man who was his enemy, and the one now without the wig he knew at once was his father.

And all in that split second he saw a knife flash and he turned his wonderful, winning soap box through the gap in the bales into the crowd, straight at his enemy, and scored a direct hit with the sharp nose cone of *Rebellion*.

FIFTY-NINE

⌘

Mᴿˢ. T-J ᴄʀᴜɪsᴇᴅ ᴛᴏ ᴛʜᴇ ꜰɪɴɪsʜ, ᴀᴡᴀʀᴇ ᴛʜᴀᴛ ꜰᴏʀ sᴏᴍᴇ extraordinary reason, *Rebellion* had crashed into the barrier. She stepped out of *Jam & Jerusalem* and accepted Derek's congratulations, then turned immediately to where she had seen Jack Jr. leave the track. As she walked over, she realised there was no applause, nor was the WI theme tune playing, and nobody sang. In fact, it was eerily quiet.

"What's going on here?" she said authoritatively, but John Thornbull raised his arms sideways, banning her approach. "Best stay where you are, Mrs. Tollervey-Jones," he said. "We're trying to clear a space."

Then two policemen emerged from the crowd, and in no time had moved curious onlookers out of the way. An ambulance, already on duty in the village in case of need, came screaming down the track, and Mrs. T-J saw to her horror that three blanket-wrapped figures were then loaded on to stretchers and lifted quickly inside. The silence continued until the ambulance had left the village, and then a different kind of noise began. This time it was full of anxious voices and crying children. Some adults were crying unashamedly, too.

"Attention, please," said a voice over the loudspeakers. "There has unfortunately been an accident on the track, but those involved have been taken to hospital, not thought to be seriously hurt. We are therefore happy to announce that the champion driver of the first Long Farnden grand prix is Mrs. Tollervey-Jones, well-known charity worker and magistrate!"

Somebody tentatively clapped, and slowly others joined in, until a decent reception was given to the worried-looking champion. She made an effort, waved and smiled, and accepted the silver cup, which she had given for the occasion, from her grinning son Robert.

"Well done, Ma," he said, and kissed her cheek. As he did so, he whispered in her ear that in his opinion the casualties were more than seriously hurt. She nodded, and said that as soon as possible she would be in touch with the hospital to discover the truth.

As soon as Lois could make her way from the shop to the place where she last saw Paula Hickson, little Frankie in her arms, she saw that she had gone. "Did Mrs. Hickson go with the ambulance?" she asked a stranger.

"Wouldn't know," he said. "There was a woman holding a baby, and she screamed and ran when that box went off the course. I think she went down to where it happened."

Lois retraced her steps, and found Derek with his arms around Paula, and Josie holding the baby. "Douglas has gone to find a policeman to take her in to Tresham," Derek said. "Only a police car could get through this crush."

"I can take her," Lois said. "I left my van outside the village, parked down by Gypsies' Thicket. Come on, Paula, and you, Josie. It'll be quicker than waiting for the police."

"What about the twins?" Paula said.

Lois saw then that the two were standing behind their mother, looking terrified.

"They can come home with me," said Gran. "Come on, loves, we'll go and find some ice cream. Everywhere's sold out, but I've got a secret horde in my freezer. We'll see you later, Lois."

The twins looked doubtfully at their mother, but she nodded and said they were to go along with Gran. "I'll soon be back," she said. Lois shepherded Paula and Josie, still holding Frankie, through the lingering crowds and down to where her van was parked.

PAULA HAD RALLIED A LITTLE, AND SAID WOULD IT BE POSSIBLE TO call the hospital on a mobile and find out if they were all . . . She dried up here, and Josie looked at her mother. "What d'you think?" she said.

"Probably best to wait, Paula," Lois said. "Not far now, and you know what mobiles are. The signal will probably fail, and then we'll get a muddled message, and it could be a really bad thing to do."

"Okay," Paula said, and took Frankie from Josie. "He should be in his safety seat," she added, "but I expect if we get stopped I can say it's an emergency."

"We won't be stopped," said Lois. "I know a back way to the hospital. Only about five minutes and we'll be there. Hold on, Paula."

JACK HICKSON SR., BANDAGED UP LIKE THE INVISIBLE MAN, KNEW that Paula would be coming. He knew this absolutely, and had insisted on waiting in reception so that he could be with her from the moment she arrived.

"Are you all right, Mr. Hickson?" The young nurse looked at him anxiously. She had been told to not let him out of her sight, as he could easily be suffering from confusion with delayed concussion.

"As well as can be expected," he said, patting her hand with a swathe of bandages wound round his arm and wrist.

"Let's sit down, then," she said. "You'll still be able to spot your wife when she arrives."

SIXTY

❧

AH, THERE YOU ARE, MRS. HICKSON," THE YOUNG NURSE SAID. Paula had half run into the reception area of the hospital, followed a little way behind by Lois and Josie once more holding Frankie. He began to laugh as he was joggled up and down by Josie as they made for the entrance, and Josie kissed him and held him tight.

As Paula approached, she suddenly saw a bandaged figure stand up from a chair behind the nurse. "Paula," he said, and held out his hand.

"Jack! Are you all right? What on earth happened? Where is our Jack and is he all right?" And then she burst into tears, as her wounded husband did his best to put an arm round her.

"Would you come with me, please?" the young nurse said. "Perhaps you would like to wait here?" she said to Lois and Josie. "Whose baby is it?"

"Mine," said Paula, holding out her arms to Frankie.

"Ours," Jack answered, and kissed him lightly. "I'm his father. Let's go, please."

Frankie began to bellow as this strange man touched him, prohibiting further conversation until they met a senior nurse waiting at the entrance to the children's ward. "Into my office, please," she said kindly. "Do sit down," she added. "We need to have a talk before we go to see young Jack."

"Oh, my God," said Paula, in tears again, "is he all right?"

"Of course he's all right, Mrs. Hickson," the nurse said, raising her eyebrows. "Very much so, if you don't mind my saying so. We're having difficulty keeping him quiet. Now, you must understand that he was quite seriously bruised and concussed in the accident. I can't think how the organisers got away with racing those dreadful soap boxes. No safety belts, apparently! And then we have to pick up the pieces. . . ."

"Funny way of putting it, nurse," Jack Sr. said. "Just how much treatment does our son need? And when can he come home?"

The nurse explained that the bruises would go away in time, although the boy would be sore in quite a lot of places, mainly where *Rebellion* had slammed into his chest as he hit the crowd. He had been thrown back, and hit his head on the raised seat frame behind him.

"Was anyone else hurt?" Paula said. "I wasn't down at the finish. I couldn't bear to look in case he came in last. By the time I got down there it had happened. But people said there were three stretchers put in the ambulance?"

The nurse paused and looked at Jack. "Well, obviously your husband was badly cut and bruised. I believe there was a knife."

"Who had a knife, Jack?" Paula said urgently. "What the hell was somebody doing with a knife?"

Jack shook his head. "Don't know," he said. "It all happened so quickly. I didn't see. Just felt the sharp pain in my arm and hand." He looked away from her, thinking that it hadn't taken long for him to break his resolution to tell her only the truth from now on. But now was not the time for long explanations. They needed to see Jack, and get him home as soon as possible.

When young Jack saw his mother and little Frankie, and then his father, being led down the ward by the nurse, he stopped shouting and trying to climb out of the bed with raised sides where he'd been put for his own safety. He stared from one to another, and then back to his father.

Frankie began to struggle when he saw his big brother, and Paula smiled unsteadily. "What you been getting up to now, then?" she said. "And here's your dad come to see you. You nearly killed him from the look of him."

"Hi, Dad," Jack said. "I wasn't aiming at you, y' know," he added in a strangled voice.

"Yeah, I know, lad. An' I'm not that badly hurt. Women always exaggerate," he added.

"Too right," said the boy, and nodded wisely. "I suppose the old battle-axe won?"

"'Fraid so. But you were not the loser, son, not by a long chalk."

By the time Paula and Jack Sr. emerged back into the reception area, Lois and Josie were desperate for news. When they heard that Jack would be fine, they relaxed.

"This is his father, Mrs. M," Paula said.

"We've met," said Lois caustically. "In the rain," she added, and stopped there. There was little point in going over old dramas. God knows what will happen to him, she thought. But it looks as though there's been a get-together here, for the moment at least.

"I'm Mum's daughter," Josie said, feeling left out. "Shall I take Frankie for you, Paula? I just love giving him a cuddle, and he seems to like me."

"Could I have a quiet word, Mr. Hickson?" Lois said, as the others went across to the café for drinks.

"You want to know about the other bloke, I suppose," he said, a spasm of pain crossing his face.

"I know a bit already. If you could just tell me if it was your workmate at Parks and Gardens? The one you had a fight with?"

Jack nodded. "It was him," he said. "I think he had been following me, and right at the last minute he appeared from nowhere. I knew at once it was him." He said nothing about his own long and fruitless attempt to find Ross. "He said something," he continued, "but I couldn't hear because of the cheering. Then I saw the knife and tried to get away, but I was hemmed in by the crowd. It was then that young Jack's soap box came straight towards us. The knife caught my arm as the fool went down."

"And?"

"He was killed instantly," Jack said slowly. "Hit his head on a stone bollard on the pavement. The knife fell to the ground, and a cop picked it up."

"What are you two talking so seriously about?" Josie said, as they returned with a tray of coffees. "We should be celebrating that things weren't any worse!"

Lois said nothing, and nor did Jack Sr. Frankie amused them all with his attempts at drinking apple juice through a straw, and the third stretcher was not mentioned again.

Sixty-One

❧

GAVIN, KATE AND CECILIA AMBLED HOME WITH TONY AND Irene Dibson. They didn't talk much, except to say that it had been a wonderful day. Until the last minute, that is.

"Took the shine off it," Tony said. He struggled to get the wheelchair over a rough patch on the pavement, and Gavin insisted on taking over.

"I saw it all," Kate said in a small voice. "I was so excited, and so was Derek. He was standing at the finishing line and we'd just had a word when they came down the track. He was rooting for young Jack, like most other people. Then it happened. I couldn't believe my eyes. *Rebellion* seemed to be going so well."

"Well, actually," began Gavin hesitantly, "there might have been a bit of a problem with the steering. The garage man was checking the vehicles at the start, and he said something about too much play on the wheel. But Derek was going to have a word with John Thornbull to tighten it up."

"Oh, Lord!" said Kate. "D'you think that's what happened? Why it went off course?"

"They'll find out," said Irene. "There's bound to be an investigation. Three people were hurt, weren't they? I do hope they're all okay."

"Don't you worry, missus," Tony said, taking over the chair and pushing up his garden path. "Derek will see to it."

DEREK WAS WAITING ANXIOUSLY FOR HIS MOBILE TO RING WITH news from the hospital. He had been busy trying to clear people away from the accident so that the ambulance could get near, and he did not really know the details of who was hurt—or worse. He had seen three stretchers taken, and that was all.

He was keeping busy, helping out wherever it was needed, dismantling the straw bale barrier, taking down the ramp, collecting up notices and so on. "Heard anything yet?" John Thornbull shouted to him from his forklift truck. Derek shook his head. "I'll let you know, boy," he said.

Preying on his mind was the obvious question. Had the steering failed on *Rebellion*? He could not now remember whether or not he had asked John to check it. So much had been going on, and he had been required everywhere at once. The sensible thing to do would be to ask John right now, when he was there in front of him.

"John!" he shouted. "Can you come down here a minute?"

They stood by the half-dismantled ramp and John thought hard. "I couldn't swear to it," he said, "but I don't think you asked me. I know I didn't look at it, and I think I would've if you'd asked. But honestly, Derek, there were people firing questions at me from all sides and I really can't remember. Do you think that's why the box went into the crowd?"

Derek frowned. "I'm not sure, of course," he said, "but it

was just at the time there was a scuffle on the edge of the track and a straw bale went crooked, leaving a gap. Seems a bit of a coincidence. We shall know a bit more when Lois rings, I hope."

A man Derek recognized as a local journalist approached. "Can I have a word, Mr. Meade?" he said. "Just a few details to add to my paper's big feature about the grand prix."

Oh God, thought Derek. I know exactly what he wants to ask. "What can I tell you?" he said as pleasantly as he could. No point in antagonising the press.

"It was the accident that occurred in the final. Do you know who got hurt? A young boy driving, I believe? And two other men? Do you have their names?"

Derek shook his head. "Sorry, no, I don't. I am waiting for a call from my wife. She took the mother of the boy to hospital."

At this point, Derek's mobile rang. "Excuse me," he said, and walked away, up the garden path and into the bungalow. The old lady who lived there beckoned him in, and shut the door firmly in the journalist's face.

"Lois? Thank God you've rung. What's the news?" He dare not phrase the question he wanted to ask. Is Jack Jr. dead? But then he didn't have to, because Lois told him the good news that he was hurt but alive, and so was his father, who had been in the crowd, disguised as a woman!

"And the other bloke?"

There was a pause, and then Lois cleared her throat. "Didn't make it, I'm afraid. He hit his head when he fell. But there was something dodgy about him. It seems he had a knife and had gone for Jack's father. Lucky that *Rebellion* went into the crowd just at that moment and stopped him. I gather he'd intended to kill."

"Blimey! Looks like it's more complicated than we thought."

"I'm just leaving now. Jack's dad has to stay in overnight, so I'm bringing Paula and Frankie, and Josie, back home."

"And young Jack?"

"He has to stay for a while until they're sure he's okay to release."

"Sounds like prison," Derek said, without thinking.

Again a pause from Lois. "That might happen," she said, and rang off.

CECILIA WAS SAFELY ASLEEP IN BED, AND GAVIN AND KATE SAT with a drink in hand watching the local news.

"Here we go," said Kate, as the announcer said that a successful day in Long Farnden had been marred by an accident resulting in three people being taken to hospital. Luckily, they had some good shots of the soap boxes in action before the final race, and a great one of Mrs. Tollervey-Jones spurring on *Jam & Jerusalem* as she careered round the corner by the green. Then there was a shot of *Rebellion* turning off course and screams and shouts as the crowd tried to escape.

"Pity we can't see exactly what happened," Gavin said, leaning forwards to look more closely. "Mrs. T-J is in the way."

"It still looks grim," Kate said. "Perhaps they'll tell us who was hurt, and how badly."

But the item ended there, with no further details of names or the condition of the people involved.

The phone rang, and Kate went to answer it. "Josie? Are you back home?"

Josie explained she had just got in, and was ringing to say she'd picked up an evening paper in the hospital and had some news that might interest them.

"How's the boy?"

"Ah, it's not about the accident. But young Jack is okay, and so is his father."

"His *father*?"

Josie gave her a brief account of their meeting in the hospital, and then said again that she had something else to tell them. She knew Paula Hickson had talked to Lois about things that had happened in the past, and this had something to do with where she worked once as a catering assistant.

Kate's heart stopped. The construction development company and Tim Froot. She had forgotten all about him for one whole day.

"It's about that building business in Tresham. You know that Dutch one? I think you said Gavin used to work there?"

"Me, too," said Kate. "What's the story?"

"Gone bust," said Josie. "The boss is up for fraud and embezzlement, trafficking and God knows what else. They arrested him yesterday. Kate? Are you still there?"

SIXTY-TWO

ᘐ

J ACK JR. HAD PLENTY OF TIME TO THINK WHAT HE WOULD SAY
when the police asked him questions. It had been agreed
that in view of the trauma he must have suffered, they would
try to keep him resting and quiet over Sunday, and begin
their questioning on Monday. He went along with this, sure
that they would want his account of what had happened. He
had no intention of telling them the truth, which was that
he had steered straight at his and his father's enemy, with the
intention of seriously harming him. He knew he had succeeded, although when he asked the nurses they just flaffed
about, not telling him.

Now, bright and early on Monday morning, he was ready
for them. He had remembered that stuff about the steering not being right. The man from the garage had said so
to Derek Meade, and he'd said John Thornbull would take a
look at it. But had he? Jack had hardly left *Rebellion*'s side all
day, until the final race had ended. He could not remember
anybody looking closely at the steering, or anything else on

the box, for that matter. If anybody had asked him about the steering, he would have denied that there was anything wrong with it. He knew it was perfect.

He helped himself to an apple from a bowl of fruit the nurses had brought him, and continued to think. He thought of possible answers to questions that were certain to be asked. It might be a good thing to blame the steering, and get Mr. Meade and John Thornbull to support him. Yes, that would be best.

To the nurse who had just come on duty, he smiled sweetly. He was determined now to get out of this place as soon as possible. He was fed up with the parents of screaming kids who looked across at him, all alone and without visitors, and came over to be nice to him. Little did they know, he thought, that he had ordered his mother to stay away and look after the others, and his father was still having tests somewhere else in this great rabbit warren of a hospital.

He needed to plan. With any luck he would be allowed home today or tomorrow, and then there would be a while before they would expect him back at school.

"Now then," the nurse said. "How are we feeling today?"

"I don't know about you," said Jack Jr., "but I'm feeling fine. I hope the doctor will say I can go home today."

"Ah, well, we shall just have to wait and see. Now, do you want anything?"

"To go home," said Jack Jr., on the principle that if you said something often enough it was bound to happen.

The nurse had read his notes, where he was described as a mixed-up, feisty youngster, who needed firm handling. "Patience is a virtue," she recited gently, "possess it if you can, seldom in a woman, never in a man."

"If I'm a man," retorted Jack Jr., "why am I in a sodding children's ward?"

"No beds free in the men's ward. One of them occupied by your father, I believe? Would you like a visit from him? I know he's walking about."

Jack Jr. considered this, and said he thought his dad would be coming down later to see him anyway. He needed some more thinking time before he rehearsed what he would say to the police. His dad would know at once if he was lying, but now he had no need to lie. The steering had not been checked, and the garage man had said it was loose. That was all he needed to say to anyone who asked.

"OF COURSE YOU MUST GO IN TO SEE HIM," LOIS SAID FIRMLY TO Paula, who had called her to say would it be all right if she got Floss to fill in for her at the hall this afternoon.

"And don't worry about asking Floss. I'll do your hours myself. I'd quite like a chat with Mrs. T-J. I bet she's impossible now she's the soap box champion. Still, she did do well, the dear old thing. She's put Farnden WI on the map! Several calls have come through from newspapers and telly people, and not *all* wanting to know about the accident. *Jam & Jerusalem* is a star!"

"Thanks, Mrs. M," Paula said. "The kids are taken care of, and I can take in my two Jacks in one fell swoop!"

"Oh, right," said Lois. She wondered whether she could sound out Paula on the husband and wife situation, and decided against it. None of her business, Derek would say. She wished Paula well, and said to give her regards to young Jack. "He's in the news at the moment," she added, "but he'll soon drop out of it again, so don't let him get too bigheaded."

Paula said that now she would have Jack's father to help control him, she reckoned her wayward son was going to be a lot easier to handle in the future. So there's my answer, thought Lois.

Gran came in with coffee, and asked who had been on the phone. Lois was tempted to tell her it was a business call, but then relented and gave her a brief account of Paula's call.

"Oh, that's great," said Gran, "and not before time. A boy

needs his father, especially at young Jack's age. I'm off now," she added. "Triumphant meeting of the WI *Jam & Jerusalem* committee."

"But you weren't on it," Lois objected.

"I'm deputizing for you," said Gran. "I told them you'd be too busy this morning, but I knew you'd want to spend some time with Jamie before he goes back."

Old bag, that was meant to be a subtle reminder, said Lois to herself, but she smiled. Still, she's right. But first, a call to my friendly neighbourhood policeman.

"Morning, Lois," said Cowgill. "How are you, and how's your clever husband? A great day yesterday. Must have raised a mint for the village hall refurbishment?"

"Not counted up yet. Anyway, that's not what I'm ringing about. What's more, you know it's not."

"Right. So what exactly did happen in the last race? Chris is going in to see the Hickson boy this afternoon, and anything you can tell us would be a great help."

"Before we get on to that," Lois said, "Derek says it's possible *Rebellion*'s steering was faulty. He was supposed to have got John Thornbull to check it, but thinks he may have forgot. Now let's talk about the man who was killed. You've checked, I expect?"

"He had no identification on him, but you know who he was, don't you, Lois. Come on, light of my life, save me some valuable police time."

"Hunter Cowgill," said Lois, "don't push me too far. Think back. Jack Hickson Sr. had a major bust up at Parks and Gardens, and injured a man who'd quarrelled with him. So, if you remember that Jack Hickson Sr. was standing next to the man who died, and a knife had been drawn a couple of seconds before *Rebellion* crashed into them, doesn't that make you wonder?"

"What are you saying, Lois? Do you mean young Jack's father killed him?"

"No, not that way round, stupid! The man flashing the knife was after Jack Sr., aiming to settle a score. It was when he fell backwards and hit his head on the bollard that he bought it. Got it? I don't know his name, but I'll probably find out. Just tell Chris to go easy on young Jack. What happens next will probably affect the rest of his life. Let me know how it goes. Please."

Cowgill heard her end the call and remained staring at the receiver. Then he called for his assistant, Chris, saying that on no account was she to go to the hospital without talking to him first. Then he asked her to get him John Thornbull on the phone straightaway.

THE SHOP HAD BEEN MUCH BUSIER THAN WAS USUAL ON A MONday morning, but now there was a lull, and Josie sat down on her stool behind the counter and looked through the morning paper. She wondered if the Dutch company story was in the business section. It was, with many distressing details. The door opened and she looked up. It was Matthew Vickers, in uniform and with a broad grin on his face. "Love you," he said, by way of a greeting. "Will you marry me? If not, I shall be forced to take you down to the station, and warn you that anything you do say may be given in evidence."

Josie stared at him. "Have you been drinking?" she said. "And in uniform, too? I shall be forced to report you to your superior. And, since you asked me so romantically, the answer is . . ." She hesitated dramatically, and then said in a very small voice, "Yes, please."

Sixty-Three

❧

LOIS AND JAMIE WANDERED ROUND THE MARKETPLACE IN Tresham, looking idly at a number of stalls set out under a big banner advertising a charity event. Twenty charities were represented, selling a variety of handmade and commercially produced goods. Each had its display and piles of leaflets explaining who they were and why they needed money.

"There she is!" Lois said suddenly.

"Who?"

"Dot," said Lois. "I knew she'd be here. Come on, let's go over and speak to her."

Jamie frowned. So this is why his mother had mysteriously suggested they might go into town to do some shopping this afternoon. It was not exactly what he would have chosen to do in his brief time at home, but she had been insistent. Now he remembered who Dot was. She was a Nimmo, and he'd been at school with one of the latest generation. That one had been an engaging character, certainly, and no fool. But he did as little work as possible, and could not wait to leave school and join his father's gang of small-time crooks.

Mum was after information, and Dot would be the source.

They approached the Alzheimer's Society stall, and Dot beamed. "This is your Jamie, then?" she said, stretching out her hand. Jamie shook it firmly and smiled back. These Nimmos were irresistible.

"Pleased to meet you," continued Dot. "I'm sorry to ask you the minute we've met, but would you be an angel and get me a bottle of lager from the pub over there? I'm dying of thirst. Here, here's the money."

So, she wants a private word with Mum, he thought, as he crossed the busy square to the King's Arms.

"Tell me quick," said Lois.

"His name is Ross, well, sometimes Ross, and his sister lives down by the canal. He's no good, never has been. Mixed up with drugs and more than likely responsible for the death of that addict girl what was in the paper recently. In trouble for lurking outside school gates. Here, I've written down the rest. Addresses and so on. Go on, put it in yer bag. Jamie's coming back."

"Thanks, Dot," Lois said, and then turned around to Jamie. "This is a good cause, son," she said. "It won't be long before me and your dad will need its help."

All three laughed politely, and then Dot was nobbled by a friend from Sebastopol Street.

"Come on, Mum," Jamie said. "Let's get a coffee and a huge, creamy chocolate éclair. Do they still have them over in the Royal Café?

"Why else would I bring you to market?" Lois said, with a sideways glance at him.

"Huh," he said, and took her arm. "There's no answer to that, Mrs. M," he added fondly.

*   *   *

CHRIS SAT IN A WARD SIDE ROOM TALKING GENTLY TO JACK JR. He had been allowed out of bed, and told everyone who passed how completely better he was. "Nothing wrong with me now," he shouted to the doctor who was doing his rounds.

"Hush, Jack," Chris said. "You still need to be careful. Nothing worse than a relapse."

"I thought that was something old women get?" he said, with an innocent expression. Chris was about to correct him, and then realised that he knew anyway. A tricky one, this.

"Before we talk about Saturday," she said, "I think you might like to know the likely cause of the death of the man Ross."

"Never heard of him," Jack said.

"The one you crashed into. I expect you know he sadly died, but maybe you don't know what killed him?"

Jack's heart began to pound. Here it came, and he crossed his fingers behind his back and hoped he could get his story right. "No. What did?"

"There was a scuffle and as your soap box went into the crowd, they parted and he fell backwards, hit his head on a stone bollard and died instantly. According to witnesses standing close by, they had tried to stop him before he fell, but it all happened too quickly for anyone to grab him."

With an unerring instinct for self-preservtion, Jack Jr. said nothing.

Chris looked closely at him, but his expression was bland. "It seems there had been a fault on the steering," she continued, "so you couldn't have done anything to stop it." And may God forgive you, Inspector Cowgill, she added to herself.

Jack Sr. appeared at the door, and young Jack went towards him. "Hi, Dad," he said.

"Seems they're letting us out tomorrow," his father said. "We can go home together."

*   *   *

COWGILL WATCHED THE SHOPPERS FROM HIS OFFICE WINDOW, turning over in his mind the last few days' events. He had been assured by Chris that she had used his exact words when visiting Jack Jr. in hospital, but he had not heard from Lois.

Now Chris stood behind him, wondering whether to break the silence or to wait until he spoke. She was beginning to sense when she should keep quiet and when to offer suggestions. But she was taken by surprise by what happened next. He suddenly turned from the window and shot across the room, flung open the door and disappeared down the corridor. She heard his footsteps clattering down the stone steps and prayed that he would not slip. After all, he was getting on.

By the time he reached the ground floor, he was gasping for breath. All eyes followed him in astonishment as he sped across the reception area and vanished through the heavy double doors of the police station.

Lois and Jamie were just turning into the lane that led to the car park, when they both heard a shout. "Lois! Wait!"

Now all eyes were on the man who pushed his way through the crowds. "Police!" he was saying. "Make way for police!"

Lois and Jamie stopped and turned around. "What the hell?" Jamie said. "Doesn't look like a policeman to me."

"Oh, yes," Lois said, "he's a policeman all right. Here take the car key and wait for me. Shan't be long."

She stood waiting until Cowgill caught up with her, and then took his arm. "You really shouldn't run," she said, "not at your age. Here, let's go and sit down on the bench over there."

The wooden seat had been placed in a small paved garden in memory of a former mayor of the town, and was a haven of peace just off the busy market square. Cowgill sat down, insisting that he was fit as a fiddle, and age had nothing to do with it. Lois sat close to him and put her hand on his arm.

"What's the latest on the Hicksons?" she said.

He had got his breath back, and turned to look at her. "They'll be all right," he said. "The father still has some questions to answer, but it will be sorted out without too much damage to the family. As for young Hickson, I am not at all sure about him, Lois. You can twist me round your little finger, unfortunately, and I instructed Chris how to talk to him, how to tell him what happened to Ross without mentioning that there will have to be further enquiries. It may well be that I have perverted the course of justice for you, young lady, but we shall see. The boy is young, and has had a rough deal so far. If those idiot parents of his keep an eagle eye on him, he may decide on the right course. Anyway, time will tell."

Lois was quiet for a moment, then she leaned towards him and gave him a lightning kiss on the cheek. "Thanks," she said. Then she stood up. "Happy ending, then?" she said, smiling at him.

"Maybe," said Cowgill, rising to his feet and towering over her in policeman mode. He returned her smile and said, "But there was one other thing."

"My car license has expired? Caught speeding through Farnden?"

He shook his head. "No, nothing like that. I ran after you because I am so excited about Josie and Matthew! You know what it means, Lois!"

"Um, yes. They are engaged, and will be getting married?"

"*And*," he said with emphasis, "it means we shall be related!"